The Love

We

Left

Behind

Katherine Slee

LAKE UNION
PUBLISHING

Published by Lake Union Publishing, Seattle

www.apub.com

Amazon, the Amazon logo, and Lake Union Publishing are trademarks of Amazon.com, Inc., or its affiliates.

ISBN-13: 9781542027946
ISBN-10: 1542027942

Cover design by Heike Schüssler

Cover illustration by Jelly London

Printed in the United States of America

For Dylan & Scarlett

Anam Cara (n. Gaelic)
*A person with whom you can share your deepest
thoughts, feelings and dreams*

PROLOGUE

Oxford, 1996

The sky was slick with rain, the promise of more to come hanging in gunmetal clouds. Thousands of droplets fell, striking the alabaster stone of Queen's College clock tower under which a girl, just shy of twenty-one, stood waiting.

Her hair was tied at the nape of her neck, a handful of strands escaping from underneath the hood of her rain jacket. At her feet was a large backpack, military in style with the straps drawn tight, and she bent down to tuck something into the front pocket.

Every so often she drew back her sleeve and turned her wrist to check the time on her watch, absently running her finger around the silver face and fiddling with the dial, as if she didn't quite trust what the two thin hands were telling her.

On the other side of the road, a couple of students were hurrying against the rain, one with a book held over his head, laughing as they went. The girl followed them with her eyes and saw them duck inside the doorway of a café that was due to close when the clock struck six.

Tilting her head back, the girl stared up at the ancient bell that hung directly above and wondered what would happen if it were to fall. If there was no chime of the approaching hour would that somehow suspend time and give her a few more minutes to decide?

A soft boom on the horizon pulled her line of sight down and across, towards the river.

Brontide, she thought to herself. A sound like distant thunder. It was a word she first read whilst hidden away in the corner of her local library, a place she used in order to shelter from her real life. She never forgot its meaning, simply filed it away with all the others that were tucked neatly inside her brilliant mind.

But even a mind as brilliant as hers couldn't control another's will. It was a mistake to put all her trust, her faith, into one person. Because everyone gave up on her eventually, and she was stupid to think he might have been any different.

As she glanced once more at her watch, the bell began to call out how late the day had become. She shook her head, rubbing at the corner of her eye as she shouldered her rucksack and stepped towards the kerb, holding out her arm and waiting for the approaching coach to stop. She didn't look back as she climbed on board and paid her fare. Nor did she allow herself to cry as she sat down at a window seat and watched the familiar streets pass by in a blur.

If anyone had been able to search inside that mind, they might have heard it whispering a million words to her all at once: of sorrow, of regret, of the knowledge that she wasn't enough. But not a single one of those words was powerful enough to describe how it felt when her heart fractured into a thousand shards of pain; shards that she would carry within her soul every day and every night to come.

NIAMH

Mizpah (n.) – a deep, emotional bond between people

Oxford, 1995

It was an inconsequential type of day. At least, that's how it appeared to be at first sight. There was nothing unusual about the low-hung cloud that was suffocating the autumn sunshine, nor was it strange to see so many students whizzing along on their bikes.

Term had begun just shy of a week ago. Freshers' week had been and gone, a new collection of undergraduates arriving at their respective colleges with trunks and suitcases and pockets full of nerves. Introductions had been made, procedures and rules explained, ceremonies involving swearing in Latin about never bringing a naked flame into the Bodleian Library completed, and now it was Friday afternoon at the end of the first week.

In the middle of the city, on the south side of the High Street, stood the oldest college of them all. Founded in 1249, it was built with golden stone and thick oak doors, and currently home to several hundred students and professors. In a room up high, with slanted ceilings and leaded windows guarded from the outside by gargoyles, two girls sat cross-legged on the floor. One was smoking a hand-rolled cigarette, blowing out thin lines of smoke through the open window to the world below. The other was leaning forward to paint her friend's face with rouge and kohl, tilting her head to one side as she worked.

In the far corner sat an ancient wingback chair strewn with books, scarves and a burgundy fedora. Next to it was a bookcase filled with legends and tales of old, along with silver photo frames, stacks of CDs and all manner of knick-knacks collected over the years.

On every other conceivable surface, from the desk to the windowsill and even by the door, there were vases and jugs and a couple of empty bottles, each and every one filled with blood-red roses.

'*Prosit*,' the taller of the two girls said as her friend sneezed twice in a row. 'I didn't know you were allergic?'

'I'm not,' Niamh replied, rubbing the tip of her nose and looking around the room at the dozens and dozens of flowers. 'But there're so many of them.'

'There's more in Duncan's room,' Erika said as she rummaged through her make-up bag. 'Peter sent them this morning.'

'I thought you told him to stop.' Niamh took a last drag of her cigarette then stubbed it out on the window ledge.

'I want to make him think he might earn my forgiveness for just a little bit longer,' Erika said with a grin as she unscrewed a tube of lip gloss and held it out to Niamh.

'No thanks,' Niamh replied as she stood and went over to the mirror to appraise Erika's handiwork. 'It always sticks to my hair.'

'You could wear it up?' Erika came up behind Niamh and twisted all those curls into a knot at the back of her head, then let them go and wrapped her arms around her friend's waist. 'I am sorry about Peter.'

'Why? I'm not the one he cheated on.'

'But you are the one who I abandoned because I was stupid enough to fall in love with a total *kuk*.'

4

'He wasn't that bad.' Niamh looked around at the roses, a stream of non-verbal apologies that didn't really mean anything at all. Peter was the sort of person who was used to getting what he wanted, including Erika. What he hadn't bargained for was her strict moral compass; she was highly unlikely to ever forgive him, no matter how much money and sentiment was thrown her way.

'You tried to warn me and I refused to listen to all that wisdom inside your beautiful skull.' Erika rested her chin on Niamh's shoulder, her bottom lip sticking out in its own version of an apology.

'You can't help who you fall in love with,' Niamh said, looking at their reflection. If someone had told her a year ago that the two of them would end up being so close, she would have laughed or snorted, or done something to convey how completely ridiculous such an idea was. Not only was Erika gorgeous and popular and annoyingly confident, she was also disgustingly rich and privileged in a way Niamh couldn't begin to imagine. Girls like Erika simply didn't make friends with girls like her and, for what must have been the millionth time since they'd met, Niamh wondered if it was all too good to be true.

'I disagree.' Erika stepped away, going over to her wardrobe and proceeding to empty most of its contents on to the bed.

Niamh watched her in the mirror, noticing as she wiped at the corner of one eye, the pink of which she hadn't been able to disguise with concealer.

'Are you OK?' she asked, perching on the end of the chair and rolling another cigarette.

'I'm fine,' Erika replied with an exaggerated smile, which only made Niamh think she was the complete opposite.

Erika pulled off her sweatshirt and tossed it on to the floor, then picked up a leopard-print dress and turned to her.

'Too obvious?' she asked.

5

'Not for you,' Niamh said with a shake of her head. 'You could wear a bin liner and still look like a supermodel. Explain why you disagree about falling in love.'

'Do you remember that party?' Erika asked as she picked up another dress, bright pink and short enough to make anyone's mother blanch.

'You're going to have to be more specific.'

'The one in that converted church when Duncan spent most of the night arguing with the barman?'

'And then ended up snogging him in the loos. Yes, I remember.'

'Peter insisted on coming with me to meet you and Duncan. But I didn't want him to.'

'Why?'

'Because I knew I was falling for him, which meant I was afraid you would tell me he wasn't good enough.'

He wasn't. Niamh could still remember the very moment she first laid eyes on him. All tanned skin and sun-kissed hair with a smile that was more predatory than genuine. But when Erika had introduced them, she'd looked at her so expectantly that Niamh knew she had to be supportive of her friend's choice, no matter what.

Perhaps if she understood a little better what love actually felt like, she could have helped Erika see sooner that Peter was never going to be her knight in shining armour. Niamh's own love life had never amounted to more than a few stolen kisses or disappointing fumbles after too many drinks. Nobody had ever made her feel special or loved, despite how hard she'd wished for it.

Which was why it had hurt so very deeply when Erika had poured all of that vibrancy and attention on to someone Niamh knew wasn't deserving of it.

'Who are you dressing up for?' Niamh asked as Erika slipped her legs into a pair of micro leather shorts, then stood on tiptoe and turned around to peer at her backside in the mirror.

'You, my *älskling*,' she replied with a wink. 'Always you. Now, what are you planning to put on?'

'Who said I'm even going?'

'But you must.' Erika tugged on a pair of thigh-length boots and glared at Niamh in the mirror. 'Duncan is on one of his missions and I refuse to leave you behind with nothing but a pile of books for company.'

Spending an evening alone wasn't anything new for Niamh. She was more than accustomed to her own company, but ever since she had come to Oxford and become friends with an over-enthusiastic Swedish goddess, her social skills had slowly improved to being something close to normal. Besides, the inherent shyness she had battled with for years had absolutely no sway with someone who seemed to possess neither fear nor shame.

'I have no desire to watch you and Duncan stalk out some new prey.'

'Then join in,' Erika said as she began to apply gloss to her own lips. 'Let the three of us make a night that we will still talk about when we are too old to dance, let alone anything else.'

Niamh considered her options, knowing all too well that if she said no, Erika would only wait for Duncan to get back and then there would be no point at all in trying to resist.

'Fine. But I'm not staying all night.'

'Of course not. Wouldn't want you turning into a pumpkin. Here,' she said, reaching across to take something off a shelf and holding it out to Niamh. 'Take him with you.'

'What for?' Niamh asked as she looked down at the tiny plastic troll with mad spikey hair and a lopsided smile.

'For *lycka*.' Erika bent down to give Niamh a kiss on the cheek. 'I brought him back from Stockholm because he reminds me of . . .' She glanced at the photo frame on her bedside table, inside of which two girls were hanging upside down from the branch of a tree. Their smiles were wide, their knees scuffed with dirt and they were holding tight to one another's hands. Erika gave a small shake of her head, then turned back to Niamh with a smile. 'He reminds me of you, my beautiful, crazy little troll.'

Niamh looked across at the bookcase, at all the weird and wonderful things Erika kept as reminders of moments in her life she didn't want to forget. The sentimentality of it had surprised her at first, given how pragmatic Erika could be. When she had got to know her a little better, witnessed the tears shed whilst watching romantic comedies, and once having to stop her from punching someone who dared call Duncan a fag, the keepsakes didn't seem quite so strange. But it wasn't until last December that Niamh discovered why the collection existed at all.

She had gone into Erika's room and found her slumped in the corner clutching a photograph, a near-empty bottle of vodka at her feet. Through drunken tears Erika explained how it was supposed to be the birthday of her best friend, Astrid, but she had died two summers before from a brain aneurism. A here one minute, gone the next freak accident that leaves behind all kinds of damage. Not least because Erika and Astrid had argued the day before she'd died. A stupid, nonsensical argument about borrowing a dress for a party. But it was an argument that Erika could neither forgive herself for, nor forget.

It was the first time Niamh had met someone who understood the true meaning of loss. It was also the first time she ever told anyone the whole truth about her own childhood, not just the filtered-down version. Erika had hugged her tight, said they were bound together through grief, and Niamh finally began to experience the intoxicating pull of friendship.

'You think I look like a troll?' She took the strange plastic creature from Erika and twisted its hair into a peak. Glancing over at the photograph, Niamh noticed, as always, how similar she and

Astrid looked; they could even have passed for sisters. It should have been weird, given how quickly she and Erika became first close, then inseparable. But the joy of having a best friend was in such stark contrast to all the years before they'd met that Niamh refused to let herself worry about the ghost of someone she would never know.

'If you're going to be ungrateful,' Erika said, 'I shall simply pilchard him back.'

'Pilfer,' Niamh said with a smile as she tucked the little troll into her pocket and went out on to the landing, turning left in the direction of her room. 'Pilchard is a type of fish,' she called over her shoulder. 'Bit like herring, only smaller.'

'Pilfer,' Erika repeated to herself, following Niamh along the corridor and watching from the doorway as Niamh opened her own wardrobe and tried to figure out what to wear. 'Pilfer, pilfer, pilfer. It sounds silly when you say it over and over.'

'Then write it down.' Niamh tossed Erika a notebook bound in navy fabric and embroidered with tiny flowers. 'Write it all down so you never forget.'

'Tell me another one. One of your funny little words.' Erika went across and sat down on a small green sofa by the window and eased apart the pages, then brought the notebook to her face and inhaled deeply. It was a peculiar habit the two friends shared, one of several that had bound them ever tighter over the past year. A bond that occurred through happenstance – two souls in the same place at the same time for whatever reason, but who had stayed together out of love. Because they did love one another, though in a completely different way to how Erika had once told Niamh she felt whenever she kissed Peter.

'Mizpah,' Niamh said as she ran her fingers through her mane of hair, deciding that there wasn't much point in trying to tame it. 'It means a deep, emotional bond between two people.'

'Miz-pah,' Erika repeated, writing down the word and its meaning in looping script. 'I think I shall call you this from now on. Especially in public.'

'Please, don't,' Niamh said as she came out of the bedroom and gave a little twirl. 'What do you think?'

'I think' – Erika put down the notebook and came over to Niamh, unbuttoning the velvet waistcoat she had chosen and tossing it aside – 'that you should wear this instead.' Reaching into the wardrobe, she handed Niamh a thin black cape interwoven with stars, then walked over to a record player sitting on a table. 'And before you open that little mouth of yours to object, try it on. You will see that I am right. Now we should dance. And drink vodka. And find us each a handsome boy to kiss. But before that,' she said, whirling around as the first notes of a song closed the space between them, 'we should make a promise.'

'A promise?' Niamh asked as Erika took hold of her hands and they began to spin.

'Yes. That we will never again let anyone, especially a boy, come between us. Hoes before bros and all that.'

Niamh smiled at the mixed-up words, thinking of all the weird and wonderful things she loved about the girl with a gap-toothed smile and hugely optimistic view of the world. Being bound to her was just about the most amazingly sentimental thing that had ever happened in Niamh's life and the knowledge of it settled inside her like a golden nugget of hope.

'I promise,' Niamh said as she held out her little finger and waited for Erika to link it with her own. 'Hoes before bros, no matter what.'

ERIKA

ROSES

London, 2012

The scent of damp lingers in the early morning air. I can feel the soft splat of dew against my bare calves as I run across the lawns of Kensington Gardens. As always, I stop by the statue of Peter Pan and stretch my arms up high before bending forward, enjoying the gentle pull along my hamstrings.

My eye falls upon a fellow jogger, his breath heavy and laboured, his run more of a shuffle than a sprint. He gives me a small nod as he passes and I look away to the river, where a pair of coots is swimming side by side. Two lines of rippled water follow behind, muddling the reflection of the sky above into a swirl of blue and palest grey. It makes me turn around, seeking out whatever it is that seems to be missing.

There's something about the day that doesn't quite fit. The feeling was there when I woke, followed me as I shut the front door and tucked my key under the pot of begonias still in bloom. A sort of niggling sensation that stayed with me as I ran all the way along Portobello Road, swishing past me through rails of clothes that the stallholders were setting out for the day's market. It whispered to me as I turned the corner on to the High Street, which was already busy with traffic.

Perhaps it's due to the dog who trotted over as I entered the park, looking up at me in a way that suggested we'd met before. Or could it have been the song I heard playing on the radio of a car that was waiting at the lights as I crossed the road? It was a song that seemingly played on a loop throughout that long, hot summer when so much of my life suddenly changed.

I'm being ridiculous. It's nothing more than memories getting me a little spooked because so much is about to change all over again. No doubt it's just my subconscious, reminding me that in only a few short weeks I will be running through a different part of London, with a different person waiting for me back home. No more the pink mews house tucked away behind Portobello Road that has become a kind of sanctuary for Layla and me over the years. Every morning I run through the dawn, twice around the park and back again before standing in a claw-footed tub, praying there's hot water in the tank.

Soon enough my routine will have to change. I won't be coming back to the sound of a creaking floorboard as I cross the hallway into the bathroom, nor will there be the scent of coffee and spun sugar that seeps under the door from my favourite café only one street away. And no more shared bottles of chilled wine on a summer evening, the windows open to the night as Layla bustles around the kitchen throwing herbs into pots and trying not to burn everything in sight.

My life is about to become exposed brick and oversized windows in a converted warehouse all the way across town. There will be no silk scarves bought on a beach in India draped over the back of chairs, no Metallica played at full volume to welcome me home. Instead it will be the scent of beeswax and cologne, along with Miles Davis and the tapping of fingers on a keyboard.

The wedding is so close, so very real, but it sometimes feels as if it's happening to somebody else. Like I'm watching it from behind a curtain, peeping through the crack. Only yesterday I was standing in front of a mirror whilst a stick-thin sales assistant tightened the corset of my gown. (I'm convinced it was the same one who did Layla's fittings. A girl with a sharp, sour face who told Layla that all brides lose at least a couple of pounds before their big day.) I remember staring at my reflection and thinking that I didn't recognise the woman I'd become. A woman who was willing to stand up in church and declare my love, my fidelity, to a man who can swear like a trooper in four different languages, make the best scrambled eggs I've ever tasted, and who calls his mother every Sunday without fail.

Not that there's anything wrong with being close to your mother, it's just not something I can really relate to. Layla is my family, has been ever since we first worked together behind the bar of our local pub, and soon Hector will be too.

My feet have brought me back to the same spot where I always finish my run, even though my mind is clearly somewhere else. Going up on tiptoes, I look both ways across the street, almost as if I'm waiting for something to happen, something to appear that wasn't there a second ago.

Stepping off the pavement, I cross over and join the queue that's already snaking out of the door of my favourite artisan café.

Whilst I wait, I scroll through my phone, mentally mapping out the upcoming week and firing off a couple of replies to emails that came in overnight. There's a deal I've been working on ever since the start of the year, one that could prove to me that stepping away from the corporate world was actually a good idea. My salary may have been drastically slashed when I joined the non-profit sector, but my work-life balance, my mental health – all the crap you're told is actually the key to happiness – is literally bubbling over. I need this to work, but more importantly, I *want* this to work for all sorts of reasons that I never considered when my career consisted of doing nothing more than making rich people richer. I seem to have finally figured out where I want to be and who I want to share it all with.

Which is awfully clichéd, I know, this whole sense of self-worth, of finding your purpose and all that, and sometimes I have to laugh at how long it's taken me to realise that money really isn't the answer. So much of that is because of Hector and his everlasting patience with me. He's taking me out this evening to a new Catalan restaurant that's owned by someone he met on his last book tour. Before, I would worry about having nothing in common with his friends, the people he spends his time with – because, let's face it, finance is exceedingly dull to anyone who doesn't work in the industry. Now I feel included, part of the conversation, someone who actually has something worthwhile to say. It's liberating and I wish I'd had the guts to make the leap a long time ago.

Looking up, I scan the never-ending queue and the packed tables inside, my weight shifting from foot to foot like it does when I'm waiting at the lights, poised and ready to run.

'Drapetomania,' I mutter to myself. It's a word I collected during my undergraduate years from a fellow student who was writing a paper on racism during the American Civil War. But I have no need to flee, do I?

In the café I wait, listening to the sound of milk being frothed, spoons being stirred and music spilling from the radio that rests on a high shelf behind the polished wooden counter.

It's from this radio that a familiar song begins to play, the same song I heard as I crossed the street in front of a dark green sports car. Once again, it pulls my thoughts back to a summer years before when I was just a girl with a heart full of hope.

I move forward to collect my order, and that's when I see him.

14

Leo.

Shit. What am I supposed to do?

Of all the people in all the places, why him, why now?

Another second goes by, during which my heart squeezes so tight it makes me gasp, then I spin on my heels and push my way back out of the café.

But it can't be Leo, not after all this time. There is simply no way he could be there, in *my* café, just sitting by the window, sipping his coffee as if it were the most natural thing in the world.

My laughter soon turns to tears and I rub them away, my shaking hand blocking my line of sight so that I trip over a bucket full of roses and land with a cry and a thud of knee against concrete.

I hate roses.

'You all right, love?' the florist asks as he pokes his head out from behind an enormous bunch of lilies, watching as I scramble to my feet, righting the bucket and muttering an apology before sprinting away.

'Layla?' I call out as I slam the front door behind me and run straight upstairs.

A creak of floorboard makes me turn my head towards the door at the other end of the landing, underneath which a shadow passes, along with the sound of someone opening and closing a drawer, turning on a tap and brushing their teeth with an electric toothbrush. I picture the room beyond, with black-tiled floor, roll-top bath and a hanging pot of ivy that trails almost to the ground.

'Everything will be OK,' I say to myself with a slow inhale as I wait for my world to fall back into place. Then the bathroom door opens and Layla steps out wrapped in a bright-pink towel.

'Jesus,' she shrieks, leaning against the doorframe. 'You scared the crap out of me.'

'Sorry,' I reply, staring at her face, at the full lips, tanned skin and eyes as blue as the Caribbean Sea.

'Everything all right?' Layla says, running her fingers through damp curls.

'Yes. I mean, I think so.' Because there are so many memories rushing around inside my head. All those neat little boxes I carefully and meticulously filed away that are now open and fighting for my attention.

'What happened to your leg?' Layla steps towards me and I back away.

I look down to see a trail of dried blood running down my shin. I turn and go to my room, sitting down on the edge of the bed to peel off my running shorts.

Layla is hovering on the landing, tiny droplets of water falling from her hair to the carpet.

'Did someone hurt you?'

'No,' I say, but my heart would seem to disagree because its rhythm is off. Two slow beats followed by one that skips and falters, making my whole body feel on edge.

'Let me get dressed. Then you can tell me what happened.'

'I'm fine.' I peer at my knee. The cut isn't deep, not much more than a graze, but there's a pulling sensation when I press against the skin.

I stand up and walk across to the wall of wardrobes and slide one open to reveal row upon row of designer clothes, each item carefully organised into colours, styles and seasons. I rub the hem of a black silk blouse between finger and thumb, then pull down a skirt from the very last hanger and shut the door, only to open it again and tilt my head to look up.

At the top is a shelf, bare of anything other than dust if you only look the once. With one hand on the shelf and a foot on an open drawer, I pull myself up to the top of the wardrobe and stretch my arm back into the dark space. My fingers creep over cobwebs, and no doubt a couple of dead spiders, before they find what I'm searching for.

I sink down on to the bed. In my lap is a tapestry bag with a drawstring neck, embroidered with brightly coloured bumblebees and butterflies.

One by one I take out all the contents and line them up on the windowsill, neat and ordered like soldiers, winking back at me in the morning sunshine. The feeling they arouse in me is a bit like finding a long-lost earring stuffed down the side of the sofa. Something you haven't thought of in ages, but recognise nonetheless.

Picking up a miniature porcelain boot, I slip it on to my thumb then put it back down. Next to it is a thimble made out of emerald glass with a golden rim that always makes me think of a wishing well, toasted chestnuts and a bitter caramel sweet I once broke my tooth on. A tooth I seek out with my tongue, feeling the chip worn smooth, and I try not to go back to the day it happened, because she was with me.

Going back to the wardrobes, I open them each in turn, tossing aside t-shirts and pyjamas, pulling open drawers and peering inside boxes. Then I move across to the dressing table, glancing at a tube of hand cream as I open the top drawer where a notebook and a small velvet box are waiting.

There is no need for me to open the notebook to know all the words hidden inside. Instead I reach for the box to find a pear-drop diamond ring as large as my thumbnail, which I slip on to my finger, turning my hand towards the light. It's comforting and makes it easier to shut the notebook away.

'Is that new?' Layla asks as she comes back, holding two steaming mugs of coffee and nodding her head at my skirt.

'What's wrong with it?' I say, smoothing my hands over the layers of lace, just as the memory of another day and a visit to a second-hand clothes shop appears in my mind.

'Nothing.' Layla passes me one of the mugs. 'I like it. It's just not very you.'

Maybe it is, I think to myself. Maybe what I saw, *who* I saw, in the café was precisely what I needed to make me finally own up to what is missing from my so-called perfect life.

Layla's at my side, watching me in that inquisitive (some would say downright nosey) way of hers and I can smell eucalyptus, a branch of which always hangs from the shower head and permeates her skin with its scent.

'Whatever it is, you can tell me.'

Opening my palm, I let go of the small emerald thimble that I picked out of the line on the mantelpiece. It falls to the floor, rolling across to bump against the wall.

'Is that a thimble?' Layla asks, crouching down to retrieve it, then holding it to the light, turning it round so that thin lines of green glance over her hand.

'It reminds me of someone I used to know.' I clear my throat and pick up my mug. The bitter scent fills my nose and I'm transported back to a small café in Oxford that sold sugary pastries and coffee so thick you could stand a teaspoon in it.

'Do you ever get the feeling,' I say, 'that you've woken up in someone else's life? That you're not quite where you're supposed to be?'

'What's going on?' Layla puts the thimble down and perches on the end of my bed.

I let out a sigh, trying not to think of the reason I started collecting all these random things in the first place.

'I can't do it,' I say as I take a long sip of coffee and stare at my reflection. Suddenly I'm struck with the strangest sense of time slowing down, then spinning around and flinging me back in time – back to an attic room in Oxford where two girls were getting ready to go out, completely unaware of what was about to happen.

'Do what?'

'Marry Hector.'

'Not this again,' she says. 'Yes, you could get hurt, but you could also end up living happily ever after.'

'There're no such things as fairy tales.'

'Nor is there such a thing as perfect, but for some strange reason, nobody is ever good enough for you.' There is a distinct undertone of disapproval in her voice, one that I know has more to do with her past relationships than me and Hector.

'Surely it's better to walk away now?' I ask, taking another sip of my coffee and wincing as the heat hits the back of my throat.

'If you do, it will destroy him.'

Walking away is so much easier than admitting life hasn't quite worked out the way I thought it would. On the surface all the boxes are ticked – rewarding job, financially secure, gorgeous fiancé with an adoring, stable family. But it's still not enough.

'Layla,' I say as I put my mug down and turn to face her, 'there's something I need to tell you.' Something I should have told her years ago, perhaps back when we first met. But secrets are so easy to keep when you think they're protecting you from harm. And for a while they did, but now I need to be honest about the real reason I left Oxford, and everyone in it, behind.

'I think you need to talk to Hector, not me.'

Except I don't want to talk to Hector. Because if I do then I would have to tell him everything, not just the bits about my life I've filtered and polished to look their very best.

I go across to the window, looking at my collection one by one before putting the thimble back in place.

Layla comes to stand next to me, no doubt trying to figure out how the line of unfamiliar objects is relevant to me announcing that I no longer want to get married.

'All of these things are linked to a specific moment in my life that made me stop and think.'

'What's this really about, Erika?' Layla asks as she picks up a tiny silver key, then puts it down next to a hand-painted turtle.

'There were three of us back then.' I reach into the tapestry bag, take out a crumpled Polaroid and hand it to her.

Layla peers at the faces, bright with youth and possibility, only one of which she knows. She looks at me, then back at the photograph, reading aloud the names written on the strip of white at the bottom.

'Erika, Duncan and Niamh,' she says, her eyes travelling back and forth between us. 'Oxford, 1996.'

'They were like my family,' I say, looking at the people I find so impossible to forget. 'We used to be so close.'

'What happened?' Layla asks as she gives the photo back, and I can imagine her noticing both the similarities and subtle differences between the woman standing before her and the one smiling back from the past. 'Why haven't you ever told me about them?'

'Because of Leo.'

'Who's Leo?'

'For fifteen years I've wondered if I should have chosen differently,' I say with a glance at the watch wrapped around my wrist. It feels like time is running away from me, too quick to catch on to. As if stumbling across Leo was only the beginning of something more.

'If it weren't for him, everything would have stayed exactly the way it was supposed to.'

NIAMH

Quatervois (n.) – *a crossroads; a critical decision or turning point in one's life*

Oxford, 1995

At the corner of Turl Street and Broad Street a second-year law student cycled past, freewheeling as he took the turn. He had to swerve to avoid a tourist who stepped off the kerb in order to take a photograph of Oxford's gleaming spires. When he glanced back he saw the photographer was completely ignorant of what had nearly happened, and it made him think, momentarily, of how a fraction of time has such a compounding effect on the world.

Pushing down on the pedals, he barely slowed as he reached the crossroads, speeding past the King's Arms and catching both the sound of music and the scent of stale beer.

As he mounted the pavement he kicked one leg over the saddle in a practised dismount and wheeled his bike through the lodge of New College, heading in the direction of the student bar.

The temperature went up by about ten degrees as soon as he stepped inside the dank, misty space that was filled with a combination of cigarette smoke and sweat. At one end of the room were a couple of strobe lights, constantly flicking through the colours of the rainbow as they landed on the bare skin of the gathered masses. The majority of them were bouncing around to the sound of Pulp's 'Disco 2000' that was blasting from a speaker balanced precariously on one of the tables.

The first college bop of term (otherwise known in all other parts of the world as a disco), had a traffic-light theme. The idea was that if you were single you wore something green, yellow if you weren't quite sure and red if you didn't want anyone to come within spitting distance of you, let alone try to stick their tongue down your throat.

The learning curve was sharp, and not just for the academic side of college life. Living in such close proximity to one another meant everyone knew who you were, what you were studying, where you went to school and therefore which social circle you belonged to.

Near the bar, wearing DM boots, skinny black jeans and chain-smoking Marlboro Reds were a group of boys who never washed their hair and listened to The Cure on repeat. Next to them stood a gaggle of grunge girls with ankle-length skirts and oversized jumpers. The sort of girls who still fantasised about Kurt Cobain, were strict vegetarians and refused to shave their legs.

In the centre of it all, gathered around the table football, was a group of boys wearing crested shirts, blue jeans, loafers and signet rings on the little finger of their left hand. They were drinking pints of beer from plastic cups and tossing insults around like a rugby ball.

'Your round, Leo,' one of them hollered across to the second-year law student. In return, he raised two fingers and sauntered across in the direction of the bar.

As he did so, he noticed another, smaller, group of misfits: three people who either didn't know, or had chosen to ignore, the dress code. They were deep in conversation, heads bent close together, ensuring that no one else was invited to join in.

The boy was long and lean, legs stretching out under the wooden table to reveal polished black brogues. He was wearing a pin-striped suit, complete with a cravat that hung loose around his paler-than-pale neck. He had a down-turned mouth, at least two days' worth of stubble and a mop of messy black hair. If you only glanced at him through the fog of hormones and beer, you could be mistaken for thinking he was, in fact, Jarvis Cocker.

One of the girls sitting next to him had legs that went all the way up to her elbows, highlighted by tiny leather hot pants and over-the-knee boots. She was also wearing a bright-pink leotard emblazoned with the word *Flashdance*, and her hair was tied on top of her head in a lopsided bun.

But it was the third member of the group, the one the other two were leaning forward in order to hear, who had caught his attention.

She was wearing black jeans and a white vest top underneath a fringed cape embellished with tiny silver stars. One side of the cape had fallen off her shoulder to reveal the edge of a tattoo, but he was too far away to see it clearly. Her hair was like a lion's mane – dark blonde and wild – framing her face, and she was smoking a hand-rolled cigarette that she gesticulated with as she spoke.

Perhaps she felt him watching, or perhaps he had sent her some kind of subliminal message, because first she paused, then she turned her head to see. Her eyes skimmed over his face, resting on the Italian flag on his dark-blue rugby top, then down to his feet. Her mouth curled up in a half-smile as she stood and walked over to the bar, squeezing herself in between two lads wearing Oasis t-shirts who seemed unable to decide what to do with their hands.

Tom, a small blonde boy who made up for his lack of height with a double helping of arrogance, sidled up to the girl at the bar, slipping his finger under the collar of her cape and lifting it back on to her shoulder.

'Are you tired?' Leo heard Tom ask as she tilted her head back to see who had touched her.

'No,' she replied and the sound of that single word seemed to fill Leo's head, blocking out all the other noise and chaos around him.

'You should be,' Tom said with a languid smile, angling his torso towards her as he spoke. 'You've been running around my mind all night.'

Her mouth twitched and she blinked rapidly as she handed over a five-pound note to the barman in exchange for three drinks. The movement made all the bands of gold around her wrists jingle and jangle in secret mirth. He heard the absence of an 'h' as she said thank you for her change, and he watched transfixed as she pushed past Tom and headed back towards her friends without so much as a backward glance, let alone a verbal retort.

'Cock-tease,' Tom shouted, then lit a Marlboro Light and turned to Leo. 'Or a lesbo. I mean, look at them. Imagine the taller one's legs wrapped around you whilst the other one watched.'

Leo didn't bother to reply. His attention was all on her, like a scene from a film where everything apart from the lead actress was soft and out of focus.

'Remind me again why we're here?' Niamh asked, setting down the drinks on the table and sluicing a little froth on to the painted wood.

'You're my wingman,' the gangly boy replied, crossing one of his lengthy limbs over the other and pouting as he inhaled on his own cigarette.

'I don't think he's gay, Duncan,' Erika said as she reached forward for her drink and took two quick swallows.

All three of them looked in the direction of the table football where a couple of boys were having a drinking race. The slighter of the two was left gasping as his opponent finished first then dumped his empty glass upside down on his head and demanded that the other boy remove his trousers in forfeit.

'You said the same thing about Quentin.' Duncan took another drag of his cigarette, using his thumb and forefinger to remove a sliver of tobacco from his tongue. All the while he kept watching as the defeated lad shuffled around the table football with his trousers around his ankles.

'You stole him from me,' Erika said with a yawn.

'Darling, it's not possible to steal something that never belonged to you in the first place.' Duncan propped his feet up on a spare chair, laced his fingers together and cupped them behind his head.

'Perhaps I shall go and steal your new little pet.' Erika pointed at the lad standing at one end of the table football with arms raised and a deep flush on his cheeks. She laughed as someone went up behind him and promptly pulled down his boxers. 'Perhaps I shall keep you up all the night with the sound of my headboard banging against the wall.'

'As scintillating as this all is' – Niamh stood and shouldered her bag, inside of which were several battered hardbacks and a notepad stuffed with loose sheets of paper – 'I really need to go back and make a start on this essay.'

'Don't be such a bore.' Erika grabbed her hand, leaning across the table and staring up at her. 'You can't leave me here with Duncan. He'll find someone to take advantage of and then I'll be all alone.'

'Let her go.' Duncan extracted a plastic wallet of tobacco from his inside pocket and began to roll another cigarette. This one was laced with a couple of buds from an altogether different kind of plant than tobacco and had become something of a nightly ritual, along with too much coffee and not enough food. 'She needs to pretend that historians actually do some work every once in a while.'

'Says the person who sits up all night watching rats and claims it's research.' Erika drained her glass, shivering as the double shot of vodka coated the back of her throat.

'The rats are my friends.' Duncan placed his hands on his chest for emphasis then twisted the end of his joint and tapped it on the table. 'They are far more loyal than you two bitches.'

'Speaking of bitches,' Erika said with a nod towards the door.

Niamh looked over, groaning as she realised who it was. Octavia, Cleo and Juliette – three girls from their year who went everywhere together, with matching Gucci loafers and cashmere jumpers over pink polo shirts with the collar turned up. Whenever Niamh came across them they would look her up and down, then whisper something to one another and laugh, a sound bitterly reminiscent of the mockery Niamh had had to endure through school.

'No doubt they're here hunting for a husband,' Duncan said, tucking the joint behind one ear.

'Well, you would know.' Erika nudged Duncan with her foot.

'She accosted me,' Duncan said with a shiver. 'I can still feel her slug-like tongue trying to force its way into my mouth.'

'I'm sure you've had far worse things than Octavia in your mouth.'

'Pot. Kettle. Black,' Duncan said, punctuating each word with a poke of Erika's arm.

Niamh checked her watch, trying not to think of how much of the evening she'd spent listening to her friends swapping notes on their love lives. 'Don't wake me up when you get back,' she said, raising one hand in farewell as she walked towards the exit, tucking her cape around her neck in response to the evening chill that greeted her at the top of the staircase.

At the same time, Leo looked up, then across to the corner where moments before three people had been sitting, but now there were only two. Without stopping to think he left his half-finished pint on the side of the table football and ran up the stairs two at a time.

It had begun to rain, just a little but enough to make him wish he'd stopped to collect his sweater. He rubbed at the back of his neck, a nervous habit left over from childhood, as he scanned the quad, then set off at a pace as he spotted her pushing wide the door that led out to New College Lane.

The heavy oak door swung shut behind him, a resounding thud that bounced off the walls of the narrow lane.

'Are you following me?'

She was leaning against the wall, one foot tucked behind the other and arms folded across her chest as she watched him approach. He caught the lilt in her voice that told him where she was from and the knowledge made him smile, because up until that point she had thrown him completely off balance.

'No,' he said, shoving his hands in his pockets and fiddling with his keys. 'Well, yes. But not in that way.'

'What way is that?'

'I don't know.' He shrugged, scuffed the ground with his foot and noticed that the sole of his shoe had come loose. 'A weird stalker kind of way?'

'Then what?'

'What?' He was aware of the words coming out of his mouth, but seemed to have lost the capacity to make any sense.

'Why are you following me?' She spoke slowly and with care, no doubt thinking him either stupid or drunk, or probably both.

'I wanted to apologise for Tom.' This was partly true. But another part of him was grateful for Tom's callous nature, because it had given him an excuse to follow her out into the night.

'Who's Tom?' She was clearly losing interest because she glanced at her watch and then along the lane away from him.

'The idiot at the bar.'

She flicked her hand in dismissal and pushed herself away from the wall as she spoke.

'I've had enough run-ins with public schoolboy twats to last me a lifetime.' It was a line Erika had used only the other day when the two of them had been discussing her break-up with Peter. The words felt strange on her tongue, as if she should know better than try to be more like her best friend, and she ducked her head, hoping the stranger wouldn't notice the blush on her skin.

'Bit harsh.'

At this she hesitated, and seemed to notice him properly for the first time.

'How so?'

'You don't know anything about me.'

Niamh looked at him then, noticing the floppy dark hair that kept falling across his face, the deeply tanned skin, which suggested a summer spent somewhere exotic, and the designer watch around his wrist. A rich kid, part of a tribe that was so unwelcoming to outsiders, to commoners, like her. But there was something more: an unusual feeling of curiosity that he had aroused in her, which was both intriguing and unsettling.

'Which one were you?' Niamh pointed at the flag on his shirt, three stripes of red, white and green.

He pinched the fabric of his shirt as he looked down, then nodded as he realised she thought he'd chosen it in recognition of the bop's traffic-light theme. 'None of the above,' he said with a grin. 'I came straight from the library. What about you?'

'What do you think?' She responded by twirling on her heels and sending the back of her cape spiralling through the air.

Everything about her was about twenty years out of date, and yet all he could think was that she was absolutely perfect.

'I'm Leo,' he said as she stopped spinning and fixed him with a look.

'That's nice,' she said as she began to walk away.

'Aren't you going to tell me your name?' he called after her, watching as she turned the corner in the direction of the High Street.

'Not yet,' she called back, and he willed her to stop, to turn around and come back. Yet part of him was afraid of what would happen if she did.

In that moment, both of them were overcome by the sense that whatever had just happened, whatever it was that put them in the same place at the same time, was only the very beginning.

ERIKA

PEAR-DROP DIAMOND RING

London, 2011

'Hector,' I call out as I kick the front door to. 'Are you home?' It always feels a bit strange letting myself in to his flat, but ever since he signed the deeds to this place he has been insistent that I can come and go as I please. Lately, I've been spending more time here than at home with Layla, and I am very aware of her partially disguised annoyance about being left without a housemate. My feelings for Hector have returned without any kind of warning, so that suddenly I have found myself in a very serious and grown-up relationship. It feels different than before, almost as if I might actually be learning how to let go, to allow myself to be happy with him.

Why then does the sense of dread seem to linger in the back of my mind, somewhere close to all those feelings of doubt I keep telling myself are no longer important?

Slipping off my heels, I let out a small sigh of relief. Work is definitely more low than high at the moment, which means I need wine. With one quick glance at my phone, I decide to ignore the pull of the endless stream of emails and make my way to the kitchen. For the most part, Hector's flat is open-plan, one vast space intended to be divided into sections by rugs, bookcases or strategically placed furniture. At present, everything apart from one ancient leather sofa and his beloved plasma TV is all huddled together in the centre of the space and covered with old dust sheets.

Most of the kitchen worktops are currently taken over by discarded pots, chopping boards and food packaging, the results of which are simmering in a cast-iron casserole dish on the hob. I can't resist a peek and a taste, murmuring in appreciation as my mouth is rewarded with a mix of cumin and just the right amount of chilli. What Hector lacks in tidiness, he more than makes up for with his culinary skills.

Opening the fridge, I discover a half-finished bottle of Sancerre and pour myself a more than generous measure. The sweet hit at the back of my throat is enough to take the sting out of my mood and I refill my glass, noticing a sieve full of mussels draining in the sink. Which means Hector has something to tell me, because whenever he does, he always makes a sharing pot of *moules-à-la-crème*, with mountains of garlic and coriander.

'Hector?' I call out again as I walk across the polished concrete floor to where a cast-iron spiral staircase leads up to the master bedroom.

Whilst the rest of the flat is being decorated (slowly, and with the sort of deliberate care that I should embrace, but actually find ridiculously annoying), Hector has moved his writing desk into the bedroom. Most evenings I come back to find him scribbling furiously, with headphones on and a haphazard pile of research books and abandoned sheets of paper at his feet.

He isn't here, but evidence of his day is strewn all over – biscuit crumbs and empty coffee mugs on the desk, a dark-blue sweatshirt draped over the reclaimed Victorian radiator and damp towels on the end of the bed. This last one is a particular bone of contention between us, but whenever I try to pull him up on his slovenly ways, he simply kisses me long and slow and tells me not to fuss about the unimportant things in life.

Draining my glass, I pick up the towel, take it into the en suite and dutifully hang it up on the rail by the sink, resisting the urge to wipe away the evidence of his morning shave that clings to the marble. I am, however, unable to ignore the tube of toothpaste that's missing its cap.

Swapping my work clothes for one of Hector's shirts, I pad barefoot back downstairs and into the kitchen area. Behind the floor-to-ceiling cabinets is a smaller space intended to be Hector's study. So far, he has painted two walls the palest shade of green, but wants the one directly opposite the window to be more of a 'feature', whatever that means. He claims it's so when he's staring into the distance, searching his mind for a perfectly constructed sentence, he has something more inspiring to look at than over-priced paint.

I start by clearing the floor in front of the wall, stacking books and magazines to one side, taking extra care with his comics because I know he loves them. Next, I pick up his boxes of records, one by one, and move them nearer to the window, because God forbid any of his precious collection be tainted with either paste or paint. As I turn around, my eye falls on the record player waiting patiently in the corner for someone to turn it on.

Flicking through the boxes, I make a mental note to actually organise his collection once the shelves are in place and the speakers mounted on the wall. By decade, perhaps, or even genre. Anything to ensure that I don't stumble across an album that I long to play but would do nothing more than send me hurtling down a path paved with nostalgia.

But the reminders are everywhere, and not just on the cover of an album that I used to hear being played through the paper-thin walls between our rooms. There was always music and coffee, and mountains of biscuits that I would eat whilst trying to make sense of all those books we were expected to read. There is something so transcendent about music and its ability to transport you back to a single moment in time, to flood your brain with images of a day or person you really don't want to think about.

I miss him. I miss Duncan and his love of all things British. I miss his kindness and even the smell of weed that seemed to permeate all the walls of our little hideaway at the very top of an ivory tower. Most of all I miss who I was when I was with him, with both of them, and I hate myself for never being able to stop caring.

Choice made, I crouch down and ease the disc from its cardboard cocoon, turning it over to inspect for both dust and scratches, although the likelihood of either is pretty slim. Hector is meticulous about two things in his life: his records and the very best coffee money can buy. Lifting the stylus from its perch, I sit back on my heels, close my eyes and wait for the sound of Ella Fitzgerald singing about summertime to fill the gaps in my heart.

For the next hour, I immerse myself in the laborious process of hanging wallpaper, balancing on top of a ladder and stretching a brush up to the ceiling. If I remember not to look down, I should be fine. The music is turned up loud, the windows are open to the night and for a moment I can simply be a girl relishing in the sweetness of domesticity and pretending that this is precisely where I'm supposed to have ended up.

'Erika?'

I scream at the sound of my name, one leg sticking out behind me as I place both palms flat against the wall and try not to topple to the floor.

'Shit, sorry,' Hector says as he rushes across to hold the ladder steady.

I look down at him, all ruffled hair and tanned skin. He's wearing overalls and has paint spatters on his bare arms. I watch as he looks the full length of me, from my feet, all the way up and under the hem of the shirt I've borrowed, and back again.

'Are you coming down?' he asks.

I shake my head as I sit on the small metal square at the top of the ladder. 'Where were you?'

'I had to go out and get something,' he replies, stepping away from the ladder to peer at my handiwork.

'What?'

'Just something.' He runs his fingers back and forth across the wall. He's searching for the join, which I know won't be easy to find, and this little slice of victory makes me smile.

'How was work?' he says, stepping into the middle of the room and looking from corner to corner at the same time as reaching into the pocket of his overalls.

'Tatiana was late, again,' I say, but he's not really listening to me. I can tell by the slow nod of his head, the way he's chewing the inside of his cheek and the absent look in his eye. Normally I would put this down to him being lost in his imagination, something he's either seen or heard that's suddenly filled in a piece of the puzzle he's trying to pull together into a book. But if that were the case, he would have looked about in search of a pen, or blurted out a random piece of information and asked me to remind him about it later.

The music stops; only the soft crackle of needle over plastic is now whispering from the speakers. Hector spins around and goes into the kitchen where I can hear him banging pots together and opening and closing the fridge.

'Hector?' I call out to him as I descend the ladder, pausing at the player to stop the record from spinning.

He's at the sink, rinsing the mussels over and over, even though I'm sure they were clean enough already. Next to him is a bunch of cabbage roses wrapped in brown paper, their fat, perfumed heads looking across at me in accusation, although I don't quite know what it is I've done. If he went out to buy them, then I don't understand this sudden change of mood. He's annoyed at me about something; I can tell by the way he shuts off the tap in one angry motion, then turns to face me, arms folded and water dripping from his fingertips on to the floor.

'Michelle's pregnant,' he says, reaching forward into the fruit bowl for an apple. He turns it over in his hand before taking a large bite, wiping away a dribble of juice from his chin. 'I spoke to her just now. She's due at Christmas.'

'Wow, that's . . .' I don't know what it is. Incredible? Amazing? More like a very risky move given that Hector's sister already has twin boys to contend with.

'Rather wonderful, I know.'

He's looking at me in that way of his that both terrifies and excites. It's the very same way he first looked at me across a firepit all those years ago. For a moment, I think he's going to say something, then he thinks better of it and reaches back into the fruit bowl, hunting underneath the apples for a clementine that he rolls across the work-surface to me.

'Penny for them?' he says as I pierce the skin with my thumbnail. A fine spray of citrus mist shoots into the air and lands on my wrist.

The problem is, there are too many thoughts to share and I have no idea where I would even begin. Of course, that's assuming I've got any intention of actually telling him the real reason why I am not clamouring to be impregnated, unlike so many of my friends.

Take Michelle. Once upon a time she was the very definition of a party animal. She even married a DJ with his own residency in Ibiza. OK, so the fact he is a Viking god may have had something to do with it, but my point is, the second she fell pregnant (which was rather close to the wedding, but let's not dwell on specifics; they are so clearly soulmates), she changed. Even Layla commented on it and she is the most domesticated, maternal person I have ever met.

Gone were the nights spent downing shots and being the last person to leave the dance floor, replaced by conversations about whether it was best to let a baby cry it out or allow them to sleep in the bed next to you. Not to mention baby-led weaning, cracked nipples and the omnipresent topic of education.

Don't get me wrong, I adore her two boys, even with the temper tantrums and smears of dirt and god knows what else all over both their faces. Not to mention the previously pristine Ibizan villa that sits on a hillside within walking distance of the beach and which, back in the day, was host to the wildest of parties. But children change everything, and there's no returns policy attached to a baby.

If only Hector thought the same way.

Jesus, my heart is racing and I have to scrunch my hands into fists, hoping that Hector can't sense just how close I am to crying. If ever I was going to tell him, now would be that time. But what if it makes him look at me differently, once he finds out what I did? What if by telling Hector the truth about Leo, I end up losing him all over again?

'Erika?' he says, resting his forehead on mine and I breathe in the scent of turpentine and garlic, with a layer that is unique to him hidden within. It would be so easy to kiss him, to drag him to bed and lose myself in his embrace. But I keep running away from the question that I know he is always so very close to asking.

'Are you hungry?' I ask, stepping away and searching in a cupboard for some clean plates.

'Always,' he says with a sigh and I try not to hear the sadness in his voice.

'I saw one of those dogs on my way home tonight,' I say, watching as he goes across to the fridge and opens the door, staring at something inside – or perhaps he's only pretending. He doesn't reply, instead taking out a bottle of beer and popping the lid before downing half the contents in one.

'You know,' I prattle on regardless, 'the ones that the Buddhist monks used to guard their monasteries. What are they called again?'

The casserole is starting to catch but he makes no move to turn it off, despite the acrid scent of burnt meat that's swimming in the space between us.

'Shar Pei,' he says, taking another long sip, his eyes never leaving my own.

'Yes, all wrinkly and adorable. This one was grey and made me think of a baby hippo. It was trotting alongside a cyclist who had a cello strapped to his back.' I'd stopped to watch them cycle past, allowing myself to wonder where he was headed. Then, just before I was about to cross the road, I caught sight of a woman with light-brown hair and wearing a long gypsy skirt walking across from the other side. She smiled at me with painted lips, then disappeared around the corner, leaving me with nothing more than the image of a girl I used to know.

The memory of Niamh, along with all her otherness, follows me like an unwanted ghost of Christmas past who appears at the most unexpected of moments. Always standing out from the crowd, a bright dot of colour in an otherwise grey and mundane world.

'Would you stop going on about a dog, Erika,' Hector says as he drains his beer and looks at me. 'I'm trying to ask you something.'

And then he's in front of me, down on one knee and producing a small black box from the pocket of his overalls, saying words that are going into my ears but for some reason I don't seem able to hear.

It's so not the way I imagined he might propose, which I'm guessing is precisely why he's done it this way. Although looking around the flat I now realise that perhaps the clues were there all along. The flowers, the bottle of vintage champagne chilling in the fridge, as well as a makeshift table out on the balcony, covered with a bedsheet and an unlit candle stuck inside an empty wine bottle.

I should say something. Something poetic or romantic, or just anything at all would be better than standing here open-mouthed, staring down at a pear-drop diamond ring. It's a little much, if I'm honest, but he chose it for me. He went into a shop, no doubt spent an absolute age trying to decide between all the array of sparkles on offer, and he did it because he loves me.

'Erika?' he says, and I can almost taste the fear behind his words.

'Ask me,' I say as I kneel down in front of him, wiping away a rogue tear and trying not to think about another boy from so long ago. 'Ask me again.'

'Erika Lindberg,' he says and I notice there are tears collecting at the corners of those beautiful eyes. One blue, one green, but both of them trained on me. 'Will you marry me?'

My response is lost inside his kiss as he picks me up and spins me around in a move that I'm sure would look like so much of a cliché if we had somehow managed to capture it on film.

There's a word for this, for this overwhelming sense that I'm about to embark on a different kind of future, but I can't remember what it is. You always think it's the big moments that change your life. In fact, it's the little ones, the ones that sneak up on you, hidden beneath dirty overalls and burnt casserole, that really matter.

If only I could bottle this, trap it inside a box so that I might open it up over and over in order to remember how much I am feeling right now. I wish more than anything that I won't forget. I also wish that I don't somehow fuck it up all over again, because he deserves better than that, this incredible, wonderful man who is asking me to be his.

NIAMH

Sillage (n.) – *the scent left behind when someone leaves*

Oxford, 1995

'So what, he followed you out of the bar to apologise for his friend being a *kuk*?' Erika shook salt on to her chicken pasta salad, then reached across the table for a bottle of mayonnaise, which she proceeded to squirt all over the mixture of leaves and meat.

'Apparently so.' Niamh inspected her own meal, removing every slice of red onion from her bowl and passing it across to her friend.

They were sitting at a table in the corner, as tradition dictated, in their preferred café within the Covered Market. It was a small, cluttered space but the food was good and the prices not too high.

The market itself was comprised of a series of indoor streets, either side of which stood brightly painted shops that sold everything from cards to cookies and even vinyl LPs. Niamh had been to the music shop earlier, flicking through the endless rows of records and chatting with the owner before deciding on her purchase. The bag containing her choice was tucked between her feet, along with a couple of oranges from the grocer's stall.

'What else did he say?' Erika was attacking her salad with the same vigour she did everything else in life. Huge forkfuls of food were shovelled into her mouth and her glossy lips smacked in appreciation with every bite.

'Not much.' Niamh pushed her own food around the bowl, her appetite lost amongst all the thoughts and feelings that were swimming through her mind.

'Are you going to see him again?' Erika nodded her head at Niamh's food, waiting for permission before pulling it towards her and upending the contents into her own bowl.

'Why would I?'

'Because you told me about him.'

'And?'

'And' – Erika waved her fork at her friend – 'you never tell me about any of the boys you like.'

'As if.' There was a reason why she so rarely talked to Erika about boys. Namely how insecure her friend, with all her beauty, made Niamh feel.

Niamh rubbed at the corner of one eye, inspecting the residual black of eyeliner that came away along with a particle of sleep. She had been awake long after the Queen's College clock struck twelve last night, trying to make sense of all the periodicals and essays her tutor wanted her to read. She had heard her friends stumbling back to their rooms, ignoring them when they knocked on her door and turned the handle, only to find they were locked out.

But it wasn't just the historical arguments about politics and prejudice that had kept her awake. Nor was it the endless stream of sirens and drunken students outside her thin, leaded windows on the High Street below. No, it was that boy, Leo, with his awkwardness and unsettling smile, who had kept interfering with her thoughts and worming his way into her dreams.

'Seriously?' Erika gave Niamh a gentle kick under the table, pulling her attention back to the café. 'I was there last night with my boobs fully on display. Ready and willing to lie on my back for someone's entertainment. Yet it's you he flocked to, like a bird to the honeypot.'

'Bee.'

'Birds like honey too,' Erika said with a shrug. 'And you love all my little indiscretions.'

'Idiosyncrasies.' Niamh finished her mug of tea but thought better of ordering another as her nerves were already fizzing and she hadn't eaten anything since the previous day.

'Whatever,' Erika said as she slurped her double espresso, then added another cube of sugar to her cup. 'You are avoiding the subject.'

'Because there's nothing to tell.'

'And yet you still told me.'

'Told you what?' Duncan slipped into the empty seat and reached over to steal a slice of chicken from Erika's bowl. She stabbed the back of his hand with her fork and he responded by going in for another piece.

'Someone followed Niamh out of the bar last night.'

'You jammy bitch,' he said, darting a look at Niamh. 'Was he any good?'

'Jesus.' Niamh rolled her eyes, but accepted the cigarette Duncan was offering and leant forward for a light. 'Nothing happened.'

'So why did he follow you?'

'Because she is some kind of elfin *gudinna*.' Erika waved the cloud of smoke away then rummaged in her bag to pull out a credit card. She shook her head as Niamh went to place a crumpled fiver on the table.

'What did you buy?' Duncan asked, bending down to rifle through her purchases. He took the cardboard square out and turned it over to reveal the portrait of a woman slumped over a bar, cigarette in hand and a look of either boredom or despair on her painted face.

'Joni Mitchell?' he said as he exhaled a long line of smoke. 'I thought we'd agreed you were going to be moving forward with your musical education, not burying yourself deeper in the past?'

Niamh held out her hand, waiting for him to return the record. 'Why, so I can join in the debate as to whether Blur or Oasis are the reigning kings of Britpop?'

'God no, but at the very least would you consider listening to Suede?'

'I do,' Niamh said as she put the record inside her crumpled black leather bag, which was covered with pin badges and had a leopard-print scarf tied around the handle. 'Every night, because you insist on playing "Animal Nitrate" on repeat.'

When she sat back up, she caught sight of someone walking through the market in the direction of the café. Before he could notice her, she turned her back to the window and inadvertently scraped her chair on the orange and yellow tiled floor.

It had only taken a second or two, but her movements were rigid and false, making Duncan crane his neck to see.

'Is that him?' He leapt up, sending his own chair clattering to the floor as he left the café to stand in the middle of the street watching Leo walk away.

Niamh came outside, holding her bag by the strap and using her free hand to tug at Duncan's arm.

'Look at that arse,' he said with a low whistle. 'If you don't follow him, I will. Although' – he took one last drag of his cigarette and dropped it to the floor – 'he looks more like Erika's type than mine.'

'Isn't everyone her type?'

'Oh no,' Duncan said, glancing at Niamh and then over his shoulder to where Erika was still sitting inside the café. 'She's always been rather partial to a bit of posh.'

Niamh followed Leo with her eyes, watching him turn right at the butcher's and tried not to think about what the chances were of him walking past the café at the exact same moment she was sitting inside by the window in full view.

But then perhaps he had done so before on any one of the other Saturdays the three of them had sat in that café having brunch. Perhaps they had passed one another but never noticed, never really paid attention to who had been there all along.

'He could be useful.' Duncan was still standing in the middle of the street, not bothering to move as people tutted and muttered about him being in the way. He looked down at Niamh, who had to look up, despite her platform soles. 'You know, finally be the one to rid you of your innocence.'

'Leave it, Duncan.' The last thing she needed was the two of them discussing whether Leo was a suitable candidate to pop her cherry, deflower her, actually go further than second base with. It had never been an issue back home, mainly because it had never been an option. But since arriving in Oxford it became apparent that one of the most popular extra-curricular activities was having sex – lots and lots of sex with as many beautiful strangers as you could squeeze in around lectures.

'I have an essay to finish,' she said as she shrugged on her coat and waved goodbye to Erika, who was busy devouring an enormous portion of apple crumble with lashings of cream.

'I'm making pasta for dinner.' Duncan kissed her on both cheeks. 'And there's a housewarming in Cowley later, so don't forget to buy some booze.'

Pasta. Of course it would be something Italian. Just one more reminder of that boy and his smile. And by booze, Duncan invariably meant wine, red and full-bodied and nothing less than a tenner would suffice. Her friends meant well, their hearts and intentions were always in the right place, but the security and freedom that came with money meant that sometimes they failed to understand she couldn't afford what they took for granted.

Exiting the market, Niamh turned right, side-stepping a couple of cyclists. The pavements were filled with a mixture of students and tourists alike, all jostling for space and intent on where they needed to be.

Coming out on to Broad Street, she looked up as a drop of wet fell on her cheek. The sky was filled with cloud, a patchwork of grey and white completely covering the blue. It made her think of Leo, of the way the drizzle had settled on his curls like a dusting of icing sugar. Her own hair would never behave so well, and so she pulled a band from around her wrist, using it to secure a knot on top of her head.

As she walked through the rain, retracing her steps from the previous evening, she couldn't help but think that fate was playing her for a fool. But she didn't know if where she was headed was even his college, Leo's college. Just because he'd been in the bar last night didn't mean he lived there.

Still, she needed a specific book in order to complete her essay, which, according to the library system, had been taken out by Robin Mackenzie-Forbes, a second-year history student at New College.

Checking the code on the piece of paper she had been given by the college porter, she pressed down firmly on the silver square keypad affixed to the ancient stone wall. Two floors up and Niamh read the nameplate next to the dark wooden door before knocking, twice.

'It's open,' someone called from within. Niamh nudged the door with her foot and stepped inside.

The room was large with a leaded bay window overlooking Holywell Street, in front of which sat a grand piano. There was a three-seater sofa that dipped in the middle, a battered leather armchair and an enormous TV on a stand in the corner with piles of video cassettes stacked against it. Two doors led off either side of the room, one of which was open to reveal a small, rectangular bedroom with a single bed, the floor barely visible under a pile of dirty laundry and books.

In the centre of the room was a desk, pushed up against the wall. It was there that a boy sat, wearing a rugby shirt over a white t-shirt, dark-blue jogging bottoms and nothing on his feet. He looked up, staring at Niamh from behind a pair of glasses, which made him seem younger and more approachable somehow.

'Hi,' Leo said as he stood, knocking over his chair and sending a few sheets of paper zig-zagging to the carpet.

'You're not Robin,' Niamh replied, peering back round the door to reread the nameplate attached to the wall and smoothing her hair from her face. She wasn't prepared for this, wasn't wearing the sort of outfit that was required when coming face to face with a boy who made her heart stammer and shake.

'He's my room-mate.'

'I gathered that. Is he here?'

'Nope.'

'Bollocks.'

'Can I help?'

'He's got a book I need for my tutorial. Well, for my essay that's for my tutorial. Which is on Monday.'

She was there, in his room, talking to him with that soft, lyrical voice about a book.

He was there. Again. Staring at her in that way of his that made her nervous and tumble out her words without thinking.

'I could look in his room, if you like?' If he looked, it meant she wouldn't leave and he didn't want her to leave, perhaps not ever.

'It's a diary. About the abolition of slavery.' She shrugged off her fur coat and draped it over one arm as she nodded her agreement. Underneath she was wearing a thin-strapped vest top and around her neck were several silver chains, the ends of which disappeared between her breasts. Leo felt himself stir as he realised she wasn't wearing a bra.

Ducking into the bedroom, he was aware of her moving around the main room as he nudged at a pile of dirty laundry with his big toe. He looked inside his room-mate's trunk only to find some *Hustler* magazines and a packet of Durex, the seal still intact.

'I can't see anything.' He stood in the doorway, watching as she peered at the contents of his desk. The hem of her red suede skirt was wet and the backs of her legs were spattered with tiny flecks of dirt. Her hair was piled on top of her head, but sections of it had escaped and were sticking out at odd angles.

'Are you English?' She tossed the question over her shoulder.

'I'm from London,' he replied, looking over at Robin's desk and realising he'd never be able to find anything of use amongst all the random bits of paper and cups he always used instead of an ashtray. 'But my great-grandfather was Italian.'

She gave a small laugh. 'I meant are you studying English?'

He looked across to see her pointing at the stack of books next to his desk. The top one was open to reveal a print of William Blake's *The Ancient of Days*, a poster of which hung in his own bedroom, next to the window.

'Law, actually. I just like reading.'

'Huh.' It wasn't a reply as such, more an acknowledgement that he had somehow surprised her.

Loads of people had books on Blake, Niamh thought to herself. It was nothing more than a coincidence. Just because she had been reading *The Little Black Boy* only last night, deciding whether or not to reference it in her essay, it didn't mean anything.

Niamh ran through the scenario in terms of probability. There weren't that many history students in Oxford. Roughly six hundred per year split across twenty-nine colleges. She was the only one in her college studying the American Civil War that term, so did that mean the chance of someone from a different college choosing the same subject was higher or lower? And in turn, what were the chances of that person being the room-mate of a boy who seemed to be appearing every time she turned around?

Leo was trying to find something better to talk about than a history book, but every time a thought popped into his mind, it was smothered by the sight of her with raindrops caught in her hair and tiny goosebumps all the way up her arms.

'I should go,' Niamh said, rocking back and forth on her heels and staring over at the piano.

'Do you play?' He took one step closer, registering the rise and fall of her chest as he did so.

'I thought only music scholars got these rooms?' She moved towards the piano and traced the tips of her fingers over the ebony and ivory keys.

'We were lucky,' he said, going over to stand at the other end.

'Seems like more than luck to me.' Niamh could almost smell it, the scent of money and privilege. She didn't need to ask in order to understand that for some people, luck came more from heritage than anything else.

'When you see Robin' – she glanced out of the window, then up at the brightening sky – 'can you let him know I really need that diary.'

As she spoke, she stepped behind the piano, away from him, and he reached out a hand, but left it hanging in the air above her arm.

'I could drop it round later.'

She lifted her eyes to his and he noticed a tiny particle of sleep caught in one corner.

'There's no need.'

'I don't mind. I just need to know . . .?' He left the question unfinished and she seemed to be considering whether or not to reply. It felt to him as if there were so many questions he should be asking, but he was afraid she might not tell him anything at all if he did.

Part of her wanted to stay, to examine each and every part of the room, every clue. But she was also terrified of him, of the way he looked at her.

'Niamh. Univ.'

'University College?'

Niamh nodded as she swung her coat around her shoulders and headed for the door. 'On the High Street, opposite Queen's. You can leave it at the lodge, if you like.'

Leo stood, just as he had done the night before, watching her go and doing absolutely nothing to make her stay. He felt like an idiot, but the way his heart was dancing about inside his chest prevented him from moving. He was quite simply incapable of anything more than breathing in the faint scent of tobacco and oranges that Niamh had left behind.

ERIKA

MINIATURE STORYBOOK

London, 2010

The church clock strikes ten as we walk arm in arm through the back streets of London heading for our regular Sunday hang-out. Spitalfields Market is in full swing, bustling with locals and tourists alike, all vying to grab a piece of the artisan scene that is rapidly taking over East London. When Hector first brought me to his part of the city, he told me a little of its origins, of how the market was named after the ancient priory and hospital of St Mary's Spital and once stood in a field. But mostly I think he likes living in an area that is considered to be cool, populated by artists and creative thinkers alike.

I've found that I like nothing more than spending Sunday mornings sitting at a table by the window of our favourite café, chosen because of its rustic food that I told Hector reminds me of home (and he wholeheartedly approves of their particular brand of coffee). In fact, it reminds me more of a certain café back in Oxford, but that's not a part of my life I ever really talk about.

Today, I am in desperate need of both carbs and caffeine to help me make up my mind about two very different yet similar situations involving charismatic, but slightly overbearing, men. The first is whether or not I should tell my boss that I really don't think it's appropriate to use my connection to the Browne family and their vast resources in order to set up an investment meeting. Layla is nervous enough as it is about stepping into the fray, especially as Oscar, her younger but oh-so determined brother, is now the company CEO. The second dilemma is about where I will be living in the not-too-distant future.

Hector gave me a key a little over a week ago, telling me that it was an invitation to spend more time with him, rather than asking me to actually move in. He's in the process of buying somewhere, even asking my opinion on whether to stick to Shoreditch or edge closer to Clerkenwell. Not that there seems to be a huge difference between any of the places he's put on his shortlist. They're all open-plan, refurbished warehouses that are achingly cool and way overpriced, but Hector can pretty much afford to buy anything he wants, thanks to both the bank of Mum and Dad and several bestselling novels.

I know what he really wants is for me to leave my pink mews house behind in favour of his rainwater showerhead and walk-in wardrobe, but as is so typical of Hector, he also understands that it at least needs to appear as if I'm the one making the decision.

It's not the decision I'm worried about, more about what happens next. Because moving in would only be the first in many pre-determined steps towards the happily ever after that Hector has talked about pretty much since the day we met. Most girls would give up a kidney for such obvious declarations of love. My issue is what happens if those declarations turn out to be untrue, just like before.

'Oh,' I say as we exit the south end of the market and cross the road to find that our preferred spot is closed due to a flash flooding. 'What do we do now?'

'It's fine,' Hector replies, looping his arm around my waist and steering me in the direction of Brick Lane. 'Spontaneity won't kill you.'

But it nearly did once. Or at least threatened to shatter my entire existence so completely that I swore never to leave anything to chance ever again.

'What do you fancy?' Hector has stopped in front of a brightly painted café with tables spilling on to the pavement. Sitting at one is a man with a baby strapped to his chest. He is currently using one hand to shovel forkfuls of smoked salmon and scrambled egg into his mouth and the other to scroll through his phone.

'Somewhere quiet,' I reply, slipping free of his touch and walking away. I need time to think, but there's always so much to think about, to calibrate and digest, that it's beginning to feel as if I'm no longer capable of deciding on anything at all. And that man with the baby, who he wasn't paying the slightest bit of attention to, has most definitely darkened my mood. Part of me wants to turn around and go over to him, snatch his phone away and toss it into the street. Doesn't he realise that the perfect little human he has created is worth so much more than checking the football scores?

It's not him or the phone, or even the sight of that adorable little baby that's got me so worked up. Something has been brewing for weeks now, only I'm slightly afraid of letting the truth out into the open. I have no idea how Hector will respond to what it is I think I need to do, nor do I really know if it's the right choice.

As I turn the corner I spy a shop that looks a little out of place amongst all the gastropubs and independent boutiques.

Inside it's like someone has simply dumped the entire literary works of fiction into one small space with no thought to any kind of order. Bookshelves line every wall from floor to ceiling, with countless more positioned on tables of every shape and size – there's even a rolltop bathtub filled to the brim.

'Looks like the books are holding up the walls,' Hector says as he ducks his head to pass under a worm-eaten beam. 'Smells a bit weird too. Like bonfires and mouldy oranges.'

'I like it,' I reply as I pass through a narrow archway to find myself in a much larger space, which is just as disorganised as the shopfront. At the back is a staircase covered in a red velvet carpet, worn thin along the centre. As I climb, I can smell something else behind the smoke and citrus – the familiar scent of old paper and ink, which transports me back to all those hours spent locked away in the Bodleian, along with so many of my fellow students. As always, I try not to think of one student in particular.

Is that what attracts me to Hector? Have I simply swapped one genius for another, or is there something more, something deeper that binds me so tightly to him?

The sound of a mantel clock pulls my attention around and back to the front of the shop, where a table is adorned with a townscape in miniature, complete with houses, a frozen pond and villagers wrapped up in woollen scarves. It looks as if it's been left over from Christmas, with fake snow hidden under a thick layer of dust, reminding me of the markets back in Stockholm with their sweet treats and lights that blinked through the winter's gloom.

Hector comes up next to me and peers inside one of the dolls' houses, picking up a porcelain figurine then putting it back down again and wiping his fingers on the back of his jeans.

'Look,' I say, tugging at his sleeve as I point to the last house on the table, which seems to be fashioned into a school. One of the rooms has been laid out like a library, complete with tiny, hand-folded books and I reach inside, stealing one away.

I know why I chose it, this particular book, and not just because of all the scents that are hidden around the shop. Books and sweetened coffee were just two of the multitude of things we had in common, along with oranges secretly eaten in libraries, and hand-rolled cigarettes. We also had just as many things that made us so very different to one another, not least the ability to keep a promise.

Hector's looking at me, no doubt noticing that I'm chewing the inside of my lip, which we both know means I'm keeping something from him.

'*Little Women*,' Hector reads over my shoulder. 'Isn't that the one about a family of four impoverished sisters, but one of them dies?'

I had an argument about it once, in a pub by the river where an albino peacock strutted around looking for scraps or, more likely, an ankle to peck. She claimed that Meg was the epitome of sadness because she gets the life she always thought she wanted, only to discover that the idea of something is so often better than the reality.

Ever since, it has struck me as profoundly unfair that the most authentic, hopeful version of myself was back when I had very little understanding of what it really means to be free, to have nobody else to blame for all the choices you make. How sad it is to think that I peaked before I knew it was happening, that the happiest moments of my life will forever be tainted by the mistakes I made because I dared to believe everything would be OK.

'Can we go?' Hector asks with a yawn and a pointed glance at his watch.

'Give me a minute,' I say as the sound of another clock chimes through the air. I turn, seeking out the culprit and catch sight of myself in a full-length mirror propped up against the wall. The glass is mottled and half-covered by an oil painting that looks like a bad copy of a Rembrandt, but the woman staring back at me seems a little lost, almost afraid. The pristine white t-shirt tucked into skinny grey jeans, military-style jacket and ballet flats aren't exactly the Barbours and pearls I once envisaged. In all fairness, my fashion sense has evolved into something far less adventurous than the way any of us used to dress.

'Who are you?' I whisper to my reflection, tucking a strand of hair behind one ear to allow a diamond stud to wink back. The watch around my wrist is designer, along with the tote bag hooked over my elbow. My hair is highlighted every six weeks without fail and I run every morning before breakfast to ensure I stay a covetable size eight. In short, every single part of my life is controlled, each possible outcome considered before deciding which way to turn. Yet it wasn't that long ago I didn't even wear a watch, let alone worry about what message I was giving to the world through my choice of clothes.

Peering over the bannister, I watch as Hector walks around the bathtub, looking inside but not sure as to whether or not he should touch. He is kind, he is quietly ambitious and he never pulls me up on how badly I've hurt him before. But is that reason enough to move in with someone? He tilts his head, catches me watching and sends up a smile at the same time that I slip the miniature book into the pocket of my jeans.

It gives me a small thrill, the knowledge that it is there. A bit like a secret I have no need to keep.

'What about this one?' Hector holds up a book, the cover barely clinging to the spine. 'Doesn't Layla have a poster of this at home?'

I would recognise that painting anywhere. It's by Blake, one of Layla's favourite artists and someone she used as inspiration for her final degree exhibition. It's also a poster that seemed to hang from every wall of every student bedroom back in Oxford. Because we are but sheep, all too afraid to be different. Apart from her. Apart from the girl I used to know who made a point of standing out, of refusing to bow to convention.

'I'm pretty sure she already has it,' I say as I make my way downstairs, pausing on the other side of the bathtub and reaching for a collection of *Grimms' Fairy Tales*. It is the exact same one I used to have as a child, complete with a green and gold cover. I would hide under the duvet, reading by torchlight long after I was supposed to go to sleep. There was something so very gruesome about those stories, yet they didn't scare me at all. Monsters and demons and all the things that go bump in the night have never been the problem. It's always the other voices, the ones that tell me I don't deserve what I've got, that give me nightmares.

'I used to read those as a kid,' Hector says as he tosses his book back on the pile. 'Gave me the creeps, especially the weird little people who fixed things. What are they called, dwarves?'

'Elves,' I say, remembering the story about an elderly cobbler who was helped by magical elves. I can picture Hector in his childhood home, with snow falling outside the window and a shaggy black dog asleep on the floor. It makes me think of Sweden, of the darkness that lingers throughout the winter, stealing all the colour from the sky.

'I'm thinking of quitting.' The words are out before I've had a chance to consider them and I open the book for something to do, listening to the creak of the spine and reading the inscription written on the inside cover.

To Darcy, it reads. *May your dreams be filled with all the wonders hidden inside this book. Love from Granny K xxx*

There's no date, but a quick flick through the first few pages tells me this particular edition was published in 1915. Perhaps Darcy loved the stories of Cinderella and Rapunzel, grew up to watch them portrayed on the big screen in glorious Technicolor. Or maybe she hid the book away, terrified of the witch who wanted to cut out a girl's heart simply because she was beautiful. Either way, this is more than just a book; it's a story of someone who I will never know, which I find morbidly curious, but also incredibly sad.

'Quitting what?' Hector says as he reaches across the bathtub for my hand, dipping his head and trying to meet my eye.

'Work.'

'I thought you wanted to give it a year.' He drops my hand and shoves his own into his pockets.

'I know, but . . .'

'But what?'

It was Hector's idea to reconnect with some of my old work colleagues after I returned from travelling, to put out some feelers to see if anyone was hiring. I was hesitant at first, but also had no desire to sit around the house watching daytime TV and feeling sorry for myself. The decision to come back to London was mine, just as I chose to leave in the first place. But now? Now it feels like I've once again become a cog in a machine, forever making money but not actually doing anything worthwhile. I thought Hector understood this better than most. I thought he was on my side.

'I don't know,' I say as I close the book and lay it gently on top of the pile. 'Perhaps because I thought I'd left that world behind. I hated who it turned me into, which was why I went travelling in the first place.'

'But that kind of nomadic life was never going to be sustainable.'

'Why not?' I walk past him and out of the shop, squinting as my eyes adjust to the bright. 'It felt like I was on the cusp of something when we found each other again. We talked about it. You said I should follow my heart for once, instead of my head. But coming back here, all my energy, all my dreams, have been swallowed up by the constant pressure fuelled by envy and desire.'

'Then do something different.'

'It's not that simple.'

'It's also not that complicated.'

56

I watch as a black taxi trundles past, an advert for Calvin Klein's new unisex perfume plastered all over the doors. We seem to be plagued by advertisers who tap into our insecurities, telling us that if we buy more stuff we will be fulfilled. But in order to buy said stuff we need more money, which means we need to work harder and longer and subsequently never have the time or energy to enjoy all our wonderful belongings. It's suffocating but incredibly addictive and I know I am just as guilty as anyone else of believing the myth that happiness can be bought.

'Is it something I've done?' Hector falls into step alongside me.

'No, Hector, it's about me.' About the person I used to be, who woke each morning with no expectations or plans. A person who swam in the sea and carried all her belongings in one bag, only ever buying something new when it was necessary, and never bothering to dry, let alone style, her hair. I thought I'd finally become someone *he* might have been proud of, if only we'd had the chance.

'Let me look after you.' Hector takes my arm, asking me to stop. 'Stop being so stubborn. Take your time, figure out what it is you want to do. All you have to do in return is say yes.'

We're standing outside a newsagent and I glance inside. Partly because it means I don't have to look him in the eye, but also because I'm craving a cigarette, which is weird as it's been years since I've smoked. But then I seem to be craving a lot of things lately that have more to do with the past than the present.

'Let's not argue,' Hector says as he pulls me close and kisses me on my forehead like a father placating a child and I resist the urge to stamp my foot in frustration. 'Why don't we plan a trip away somewhere, just for the weekend? Perhaps even Stockholm, so I can meet the rest of your family.'

'We've talked about this.' Or rather, Hector has talked about it. Mainly because he comes from such a close-knit, liberal-minded, all-round amazing family and so has absolutely no understanding of what it feels like to no longer be welcome at home.

'Your uncle is great and all, but at some point I'd love to see where you grew up.'

'Maybe,' I say, which we both know is really a no.

'Or Oxford?' Hector counters. 'You could give me the grand tour of all those hallowed halls. Go punting, get drunk on Pimm's and have sex in the library.'

'They wouldn't let you in,' I say, biting back a smile because the idea of doing all those things with Hector is so very tempting, if only it weren't for all the memories of that particular city.

'How long is it since you left?'

'Fourteen years,' I reply, even though he knows this part of the story already.

'And you've never been back?'

'Why are you asking questions you already know the answer to?'

'There's a new guy at the publishing house. Would have been at Oxford about the same time as you.'

I don't reply as I head inside the newsagent, breathing in the cloying scent of sugar and antiseptic.

'His name's Ben.'

'Well that narrows it down nicely.' I walk along the aisle, stopping to pick up a packet of fig rolls. Duncan always claimed it was a biscuit, but really it's more like a cake. Lucozade and fig rolls, the hangover cure all three of us used throughout that year, along with shrimp salad and hotdogs (a Swedish staple I sort of miss, along with *surströmming* and pickles).

'Went to Teddy Hall. Studied English.'

I nod, but don't say anything, because there's a lump lodged at the base of my throat. Even though I'm pretty sure I never met

Ben from Teddy Hall, that doesn't mean he didn't know one of the others, which in turn means he might know the truth about me.

'Anyway,' Hector says, picking up a packet of Hobnobs and putting them back down again. 'He's going back next weekend for a reunion dinner. Made me wonder why you've never done the same?'

'I don't get invited because I never graduated,' I say, taking another packet of fig rolls along with some small, circular waffles wrapped in cellophane. They won't be as good as the *frasvåfflor* bought from the Christmas market in Stockholm, but the combination of cinnamon and sugar might help lighten my mood.

'But still. What about your friends? Is there really no one from Oxford you stayed in contact with?'

'*För guds skull,*' I say, stamping my foot. 'Leave it alone, Hector. I don't want to go back. To Oxford or Sweden. So just stop asking me, please.'

Heading back to the counter I look up at the rows of cigarettes, then higher to a line of bottles on a shelf. Vodka is best drunk ice-cold and neat in order to avoid a hangover, but I want to get drunk, blind drunk, so that I might forget, just for a little while.

Because the people closest to you shape your life, even if it's inadvertent, even if you haven't seen or spoken to them for years. You carry them and their opinions with you, listen to their voices telling you which way to go. Nothing is ever just down to you, but rather all the people you meet along the way.

'Why can't I forget about them?' I whisper to myself, feeling inside my pocket for the tiny book.

'They made you,' Hector says. 'Which means they can't be all bad, surely?'

He thinks I'm talking about my family. The people he has never met. But there are other people, three to be precise, who had so much more influence on my life, and on the present, than he could ever understand.

Turning my wrist over, I check the time, but I'm not really sure why it feels important. It always seems to be following me, the counting down of hours to some momentous event I haven't been invited to.

At some point I need to forgive myself for all the mistakes. One day I have to accept that everything I said or did had consequences, not only for me, but everyone I hurt in the process.

One day, I hope I can tell Hector, and he will love me all the same.

NIAMH

Cingulomania (n.) – *a strong desire to hold someone in your arms*

Oxford, 1995

The house party was a bad idea. About fifty over-enthusiastic students were crammed into a three-bed semi just off the Cowley Road, all of whom were either looking for someone to shag, or looking for a place to shag their lucky conquest.

Niamh had made her way through the living room, where a throng of skinny skater kids wearing Adidas trainers, jeans and tighter-than-tight t-shirts were jumping around to The Stone Roses, making the walls shake. Someone in the downstairs loo was throwing up what looked like blood but was in fact snakebite and black. Her friend was sitting behind her, slowly rubbing her back whilst simultaneously snogging a boy who looked like Evan Dando from the Lemonheads.

Upstairs was a mass of bodies in darkened rooms. Some were smoking skunk and staring at a lava lamp; others were fumbling under duvets and trying to remember the name of whoever it was they were feeling up.

In the kitchen were a bunch of trust-fund girls near-identical to Octavia, with sleek ponytails and the collars of their polo shirts turned up. They were smoking Marlboro Menthol and drinking Chardonnay whilst talking through their noses about the size of their parents' country pads.

Niamh decided to hide in the garden, where Duncan was arguing with a Liverpudlian lad called Chris about which was the better nightclub – Cream or the Astoria. She watched with envy the flirtatious back and forth, the way in which Duncan made a point of touching Chris's arm when he spoke, laughing at things that weren't even funny.

She caught sight of Erika in the kitchen, talking animatedly with the Chelsea set and making them all laugh. It made Niamh a little jealous, and not for the first time, of how easily Erika slotted into every single situation she found herself in.

'Why are you hiding out here?' Erika asked as she came outside, clutching a bottle of vodka in one hand and pulling down the skirt of her micro dress with the other.

'I'm not hiding.'

'Yes, you are. And you are all nervous and itchy whenever the doorbell rings. I have been watching.'

'Twitchy.'

'That too. Are you expecting someone?'

She wasn't. But then again she was, or at least hoping he might show. Even though that was ridiculous because what were the chances of Leo knowing anyone at the party? Probably about the same as him being the room-mate of the person who had the book she still needed.

'Drink this,' Erika said, holding the bottle out to her, swaying a little. 'It will give you courage.'

'For what?' Niamh coughed as the alcohol hit the back of her throat. She glanced over to see Duncan and Chris disappearing into the shadowy depths of the garden. In the half-light, it was hard to tell if they were still arguing, or whether their mouths were busy with something altogether more personal.

She envied Duncan's ease with himself, Erika too. Both of them had such a way with people, with strangers, that seemed so impossible for her to master. Were they given lessons in popularity, or was it passed down through the generations like DNA? Or perhaps it was simply that their gilded existence meant it was so much easier to be happy.

'For life,' Erika replied, spreading her arms wide and tilting her head back to the stars. *'Den som lever får se.'*

Niamh frowned as she figured out the translation in her head. 'That doesn't make any sense.'

'Yes it does. It means *Time will tell*. Although the Norwegian version is *He who lives gets to see*, which Astrid always liked better.'

Niamh took a long swallow of vodka, waiting for something more, because Erika only ever spoke about her dead friend when she was drunk. If she ever asked about Astrid, Erika would simply shrug and say she was perfect and then promptly change the subject. Which did nothing more than fuel the curiosity Niamh had about her predecessor.

'She was such a shy little mouse,' Erika said with a sigh. 'But always filled with clever ideas, just like you.' The last three words were punctuated with a gentle prod against Niamh's collarbone, then Erika took hold of Niamh's hand and turned it over, tracing over the lines that gypsies liked to read.

'Her fingers were super long and she liked to paint each of her nails a different colour. I think I loved her because she was like nobody else I had ever met.'

Niamh thought about how Erika was like nobody she had ever met, but, as ever, it was tainted by the idea that perhaps if she didn't look so much like Astrid, Erika would never have chosen her in the first place.

'You miss her,' Niamh said, taking her hand away.

'Every day.' Erika sniffed, then cupped her hands around Niamh's face. 'But now I have you, so the hurt is not always so terrible.'

'What would you say to her if she was here?' The question came out before Niamh could decide whether or not it was a good one to ask.

'I have no idea,' Erika replied, taking the bottle from Niamh and swirling the clear liquid around and around. 'What would you say to your mother?'

'I'd tell her I hate her for what she did.'

'Love and hate always sleep next to one another,' Erika said as she took two swallows from the bottle, wiping the back of her hand across her mouth when she was done. 'Now, are you going to hide out here, or come and find someone to take your mind off that boy from the bar?' Erika took Niamh by the hand and led her back to the party.

The last thing Niamh could remember was falling off her bike as she stopped at the traffic lights next to Merton Street. It wasn't even a spectacular crash, more a slow lean to the left, which resulted in her sprawled over the kerb with her arse on display. Not for the first time, she was left thinking that Erika was either some kind of Olympian athlete or an alien. All those years growing up in Sweden had no doubt made her constitution impenetrable to the perils of booze as well as the cold – even in the depths of winter she never wore more than one layer under her coat and always slept with the windows open.

Niamh was not so lucky, and had spent most of Sunday morning either with her head down the toilet or curled up under the duvet promising herself that she was never going to drink again. Turns out that half a bottle of vodka was not the best idea when you were only just scraping five foot five and weighed less than eight stone.

Duncan had been wonderfully kind all morning, if a little too attentive, asking if she wanted a strip wash, given that she was incapable of dragging her cute little backside down to the showers and she was beginning to pong a bit. He had cooked her bacon sandwiches smothered in HP sauce and even run down to the shop to procure both Nurofen and a giant bottle of Lucozade.

All that kindness was wrapped up in a parcel of gossip about everything that Niamh had been too drunk to notice at the party. He had perched on the end of her bed, eating all the sandwiches she couldn't stomach, telling her about how Erika had set her sights on some poor lad called Callum whose father owned half of Yorkshire. He had promptly fallen deeply under her spell and Erika announced that they were going to run away to live in the Highlands, at which point Niamh had pulled the duvet back from her face to ask if Erika was aware that the Highlands were in Scotland, not Yorkshire?

Niamh had spent the rest of the day thinking about how easy it was for Erika to move from one adoration to the next. Clearly Peter was no longer of any concern, which of course made her question if at some point Erika – beautiful, dazzling Erika – would decide she no longer had any use for her shy little Irish friend?

All of which meant that she had not, as intended, written a blindingly brilliant closing argument about how the American Civil War was fuelled by slavery, not greed. Instead she had limped her way through a rather banal and decidedly unoriginal script that she had handed across to her tutor just over an hour before with an apologetic smile.

The tutorial itself had been less traumatic than she feared. Dr Olsson had a reputation for being a tad misogynistic, but when Niamh greeted him in Swedish he had smiled, nodded curtly and offered her a cup of coffee. When her tutorial partner arrived in a bluster of noise and dropped belongings, she was sitting by the window telling Dr Olsson all about her larger-than-life friend whose family produced vast quantities of timber from a forest outside of Östersund.

She had known who he was even before he stretched out his hand in greeting, his short, thick fingers squeezing hers a little too tight. Robin looked like a country bumpkin, with shirt untucked and buttoned the wrong way, holes in the sleeves of his cardigan and red corduroys that were at least two inches too short. But he spoke with conviction through plummy vowels, one knee bouncing up and down as he filled the room with his arrogance.

It was no longer raining when Niamh left her tutor's building and stepped on to the pavement, but the wind had changed direction, making her think of Mary Poppins and her annoying habit of bursting into song at any given moment. A bit like Duncan, really, only he was decidedly less tuneful.

'I'm sorry about the diary.' Robin came trotting up alongside Niamh and looked down at her from behind a pair of aviator shades that didn't match the rest of his dishevelled appearance.

'No, you're not,' Niamh replied.

'You're right,' he said with a grin. 'Without that diary, my essay would have been rather shit.'

He put his hand in the small of her back, guiding her across Broad Street, and she gritted her teeth at the impertinence. He may have thought he was being gentlemanly, but in fact all it did was re-enforce her earlier opinion that he believed himself superior to her in every way.

'Do you always have to win?' Niamh asked, thinking yet again that so many people at Oxford seemed to turn everything into a competition. She would have given him the diary without even stopping to consider if by doing so it put her at a disadvantage. But then again, maybe her naivety was part of the reason she was still, more than a year into her degree, trying to figure out her place in that peculiar melting pot of money and brilliance.

Niamh turned to face him to find him standing with arms folded over his chest and legs deliberately wide apart so that she only had to tilt her face a little in order to look up at him.

Robin sniffed. 'Your reference to that Blake poem was rather clever, if a little short-sighted given it was written nearly a century before the point in history we were supposed to be discussing.'

'Dr Olsson didn't seem to think so.'

His eyes swept over her from head to toe and back again, the scrutiny making her uncomfortable. 'You're not at all what I imagined.'

'Oh?'

'From the way Leo described you I was expecting someone more . . .' He twirled one hand through the air, as if this action would somehow conjure the word he couldn't seem to find. 'More Leo.'

'More Leo?'

'You know,' he said with a smirk. 'Chelsea not Cork. Chanel not charity shop. I *tink* you get my meaning?' The word was said with deliberate emphasis on the missing 'h', making Niamh clench her jaw at the all-too-familiar dig. It was infuriating, and not only because Erika was never teased for her accent or insulted for her language mistakes. Niamh knew she wasn't being targeted because she was Irish; she was being targeted because she was poor.

'I don't have time for this.' Niamh shook her head as she strode in the completely wrong direction because she needed to get away.

Away from such a blatant insult that was based on the assumption that she wasn't the right kind of girl for a boy like Leo simply because she didn't have a trust fund or parents who bred racehorses like so many of the others she'd been to school with. It was so ridiculously narrow-minded it made her want to punch something, preferably Robin's annoying, smug face.

She was still irritated as she stomped her way across the cobbled streets, muttering to herself about entitled rich boys who felt the constant need to bully and patronise girls like her. But there was another voice in her head, the one that always picked at her insecurities, telling her that Robin was right; why would a boy like Leo be interested in a poor little mouse like her?

Niamh was still fuming as she stepped inside University College Lodge, not bothering to check her post as she walked alongside the Main Quad. At the end of the covered passageway, she tapped in the entry code next to where a stone memorial of Shelley lay behind iron railings. The sound of her footsteps echoed around the stone stairwell as she climbed to the first floor, but she didn't stop at the sound of Duncan singing from behind the doors that housed the communal showers. Instead she went up another floor and headed for the corner, where a tight spiral staircase took her into the eaves of the building.

Even before she pushed open the fire door at the top of the stairs, she knew. Even before she let her eyes settle on the sight of someone sitting in the corridor, back to the wall and legs stretched out in front of him, she had sensed it. As he lifted his head to see her approach and put down the book he was reading, she felt the smallest part of her heart give way.

'You're here,' Niamh said, finding that her feet were refusing to move and so she stood half in the corridor and half at the top of the stairs. 'Why?'

'I brought you this.' He stood up and stepped forward, holding out the diary she had needed for her tutorial, but was now less than useless to her. She went towards him so that he might not be the one to bridge the gap.

It felt important somehow, the need to meet him halfway. She wanted to show him that she too was a part of the decision, and not just responding to whatever he said or did.

'Thank you.' She took the diary and opened the door to her room, holding it with one foot as he stepped inside.

Looking around, he was overcome by the mixture of chaos and order all tumbled in together. There was a desk straight ahead, its surface invisible underneath stacks of papers and books as well as an open packet of fig rolls and a near-empty bottle of Lucozade. To the right was a bay window with padded seats, the leaded panes overlooking both the High Street and one of the college gardens. On the opposite side was an adjacent bedroom, the frame missing its door, and a single bed, underneath which a bundle of shoes and boots had been shoved.

She was watching him, seeing the way he moved about her private space as she pretended to busy herself with unpacking her bag, taking off her jacket and hanging it back in the cupboard. He turned as she did so and she didn't mind him looking at her, because he did it in a completely different way to that of his roommate only minutes before.

'Would you like a cup of tea?' she asked, picking up the kettle in search of something to do and filling it from the sink in her tiny bedroom. She stared at her reflection in the mirror that also acted as a splashback, aware of the high colour not only on her cheeks but all the way down her neck. She was sweating, the beat of her heart felt strange and she couldn't stop her hands from shaking.

He was there. In her room. Making her feel all sorts of things that were causing her head to spin. He'd gone out of his way to find her, so perhaps Robin was wrong? Perhaps Leo was more than just another entitled snob?

He moved aside the same fur coat she had been wearing when she came to his room and sat down on the narrow green sofa next to the window, watching as she put the kettle on to boil, then went back into her bedroom to rinse out a couple of mugs.

She was dressed in a tight, black waistcoat over red velvet leggings and boots that looked like they belonged to Oliver Twist. Her hair was twisted back into a bun and there was a pencil stuck through its centre. He wanted nothing more than to pull it free, to breathe in the scent of her that seemed to be clinging to every surface of the room. Just as before, he could smell tobacco and oranges, but now there was a trace of something else underneath.

'Milk?' she asked as she climbed on to her bed and opened the window to retrieve a bottle from the ledge outside.

'Please.'

There was the clink of spoon against china as she stirred, head bent and eyes down, concentrating on the task in hand.

Say something, he thought to himself, sitting with hands clasped together and resting on his knees.

Say something, she told herself, but all the words she carried around so effortlessly from day to day had turned into a kaleidoscope of nonsense.

He half stood, half squatted as she set the book down next to him and the mug on the carpet by his feet.

'I can't use it,' Niamh said. 'I've just come from my tutorial, so it's too late.' She turned away and ran her fingers along the shelf of records next to her desk, her nails catching on the spine of each one. She stopped at the far end and took out the penultimate sleeve, tipping out the vinyl and placing it on a nearby turntable. The movement calmed her, as it always did, and she waited for the first crackle to spill from the speakers, seconds before the sound of a bass drum and plucked guitar took over.

Leo saw the slant of her shoulders change as the song began. He noticed the way her body was beginning to unfurl, almost as if the notes were sneaking inside her, gluing her to the melody.

He was aware of how the energy in the room was building, and not just because of the hypnotic vocals of a man and a woman singing about broken love. He recognised the song as one his mother used to play, but he couldn't remember who it was by.

Niamh felt him come up behind her but she didn't dare turn around. The knowledge that what she did in that precise moment would change it all was so exquisitely painful that she didn't want it to end.

He understood that what he did in those next seconds would send him down one of two paths. The conscious acceptance that this was a decision he would remember for the rest of his life terrified but also excited him.

The song came to an end and she turned and lifted her head to his, lips parted and eyes sweeping over every pore, every line, as if committing them to memory. She was afraid, but she didn't know if it was of what would happen if he kissed her, or what would happen if he didn't.

'Niamh.' He said her name slowly and she felt the sound of it land on her skin. A moment more and everything would be altered, changed, and then recounted in years to come.

His hands came up to her face, the weight of her held in his palms like an antique bowl too delicate to touch. He could feel the pulse at her neck and gently pressed his thumb to it, hearing her intake of breath as he did so.

It was as if he had inserted a thin, sharp needle into her spine, causing every single one of her nerve endings to scream in a way they never had before. All thoughts of probability, of likelihoods and fate slipped from her mind as she leant into him and allowed herself to wonder how he might taste.

The door reverberated against its frame as someone kicked at it from the other side, followed by a long call of 'Helloooooooo', the last vowel elongated like a yodel.

'Niamh, are you in there?' Erika called out, even though the question was redundant given the music that was still spilling from the speakers.

Niamh went over to the door, opened it a fraction and peered out.

'What are you doing?' Erika stepped forward then realised Niamh wasn't letting her in. 'Why are you hiding, or,' she said with a Cheshire Cat grin, trying to peer over Niamh's head, '*who* are you hiding? Is it him? The boy from the bar?'

'Go away,' Niamh hissed.

'Suit yourself,' Erika replied with a huff. 'But we made a promise, remember?'

'I remember,' Niamh said. But at that point all she could think about, all her brain would allow her to focus on, was the way that boy, that stranger, was making her feel.

ERIKA

GOLDEN MONKEY

Cambodia, 2009

The sun is barely visible above the horizon, but already the sky is made up of a tumble of colours, with the ancient temples of Angkor Wat jutting out from the landscape ahead.

On the seat next to me is an empty cage with a few feathers stuck to the bars, and there's a plastic string of flowers wound around the pole that's holding up the roof of the tuk-tuk that's transporting me to the sacred site. It's my third day in a row at the temples, but the sight of those stone towers is just as breathtaking as the first time I caught sight of the hundreds of apsaras carved into the walls.

Of all the places I have visited, Cambodia is by far my favourite, and the sacred temples, with their sheer scale and symbolism, are simply stunning. Just like the ancient pyramids of Egypt, the stone from which Angkor Wat is built was quarried elsewhere and floated down the river on rafts, with the help of over six thousand elephants to move everything into place.

'How much?' I smile at a young boy who is sitting leaning against a pillar riddled with age. At his feet are various carved animals and representations of Buddha, most made from wood, but also painted metal.

'Two dollars,' he says, holding out an elephant carved from the blackest of woods. I consider it, but shake my head and point to a pair of golden monkeys at the back of the collection. One is sitting with his palms pressed together and head bent; the other is holding on to a knobbly nut.

'I'll take them, please,' I say as I search through my bag for a crumpled five-dollar note.

The boy looks up at me with a frown. 'You no want Buddha?' He points to a rather jolly little carving with a garland of fresh marigolds hanging around its neck.

'I like the monkeys,' I say, handing over my money and he holds it up to the sky before nodding his agreement and tucking it away inside an old ice-cream pot. Duncan liked monkeys. He was due to come here that summer as part of a conservation pro-gramme, which included working in a monkey sanctuary. I remem-ber him saying he wanted to bring one home, call him Cyril and have him ride in his basket every morning as he cycled into town.

But I have no idea if he even came here, let alone whether he managed to smuggle a new friend all the way back home. It's stupid, but part of me hoped he might still be here, hiding in the temples, waiting to jump out at me and somehow close the gap of time so that we might forget about that fateful night when all our secrets were spilt, and be friends once more.

As I walk, I can feel the statues jutting against my hip. Gone are the designer totes and leather suitcases, replaced by a hand-woven shoulder bag and a rucksack I bought from a military store in Vietnam. When I first left London nearly a year ago, I holed up in the same five-star hotel in Goa where I'd been for a detox yoga retreat with Layla and Michelle. But after the initial panic wore off (because, let's face it, I'd walked away from everything with no plan, no checklist, nothing but my passport and a suitcase full of clothes), I found myself aching for a different kind of experience.

My decision to leave the safety net of luxury was made whilst standing in the Arabian Sea, staring up at a sky overwhelmed by stars. I knew that leaving London had to mean something, that I needed to prove to myself I was capable of keeping the promise I'd made years before. A promise I'd made to him, just before I ran.

Don't be ordinary, I said to myself, listening to the beat of the sea as the tide pulled against my calves. *Don't let the past define you.*

Ever since that night, I have travelled through Asia with little more than sunscreen and an old Discman that seems to have arthritis because it never works during a rainstorm. My clothes are bought from local markets, I have slept in beach bungalows and backpacker hotels, eaten the spiciest street food known to man (including frog stuffed with *kroeung* paste which was surprisingly delicious), and cut off all my hair in an attempt to survive the oppressive heat.

Not only that, but I decided to sell my phone in Bangkok and I only ever check my emails when I stumble upon an internet café. It is liberating being alone; I adore the total freedom of having nobody know where I am after so many years of being glued to my BlackBerry, of constantly being at someone else's beck and call. Slowly but surely, I have grown accustomed to having no expectations for my day.

Moving through the temples, every so often I catch sight of one of the Buddhist monks, the bright orange of their robes like dots of fire against the stone and trees. One is standing in a doorway watching me approach and I press my palms together, bowing my head in greeting. He simply mimics my movement, then walks away.

Layla would love it here, having embraced Buddhism whole-heartedly whilst researching religion for her degree show. I wish she were here so that we could argue about whether death is the force that propels us ever onwards, or simply get wasted on cheap beer and flirt with the gangs of tanned, athletic gap-year boys that seem to multiply the closer to the beach you get. We try to swap emails every week, but I haven't actually spoken to her since leaving Bangkok and it feels strange somehow, as if my universe is a little off-kilter because of her absence.

You chose this, the voice in my head says. A voice that I thought was finally, finally, leaving me alone; but no, it's always there, lurking and waiting for the perfect moment to make me realise that there's nobody else to blame.

You chose to run, again.

It's true. Was I naive to think putting oceans and mountains between us would make any difference to how much I miss him? How much I miss all of them?

Get a grip. This is my voice now, like a slap to the face that's forcing me back to the present, to the memories and escapism and more bloody culture than you can shake a monkey at. *Pay attention, for goodness' sake, because one day soon you have to go home; you have to make a decision about what happens next.*

I come to a standstill before a pond that is almost luminescent with green algae. All around me, people are taking photographs, posing next to the statues or trying to entice some of the local monkeys down from the trees. I take off my sandals and dip my toes into the wet, thinking of days spent on the river, drinking Pimm's and believing we would be friends forever. And another day, when a boy took a girl out for a punt, bringing with him bottles of Guinness (because she was Irish, so clearly that's the only thing she ever drank) and the promise of something more.

We used to tell one another everything, even though one look at her face gave away how she felt about that boy. When did it stop? At what point did we ease apart?

I've lost count of the number of times I've started to Google them, then changed my mind. Not knowing is somehow easier, less painful than the imaginary lives I have conjured for them. But still, every time I catch sight of a boy with dark curls, or hear a voice with that oh-so familiar lilt, my heart skips a beat and for a split second I'm torn between wanting it to be them and *not* wanting it to be them. It's more than that, though; it's the fear they wouldn't want to see me, even after all this time.

Looking down into the water, I'm overcome with the sense that there is someone else, another version of me, hovering below the surface.

'I don't think you should throw that in.'

I turn to find someone watching, then glance down at my hand, surprised to discover that I'm holding one of the golden monkeys.

'I wasn't going to,' I reply, yet I have no memory of taking the statue out of my bag in the first place.

'They're supposed to be good luck.' Hector points at the statue then to the treetops above. 'I guess that's why they're allowed to live here.'

If he is surprised at seeing me, he isn't showing it. He looks good, with hair cropped short and darkly tanned skin that make the two different colours of his eyes all the more obvious.

Layla would say it was the universe playing tricks on us or, more likely, shouting as loudly as possible that there has to be a reason we keep finding one another.

'I was going to leave it at one of the shrines.' I drop my hand to my side as I look around, waiting for my heart to return to a more normal rhythm. The nearness of him is unsettling, but I can't quite decide if it's because I want him there or not. 'What are you doing here, Hector?'

'I could claim it's just a coincidence.'

'Or you could just tell me.'

He smiles, which pretty much ends all my resolve to try and pretend that I haven't missed him, or thought about him during the loneliest of nights.

'Are you with the tour?' he asks, and I shake my head to avoid the necessity of forming words with a mouth that wants nothing more than to kiss him. 'Didn't think so, you don't look quite so out of place.'

I look from him to the rest of the group, with their pristine trainers, sunburnt cheeks and every single one of them holding a phone aloft.

'Shameless, isn't it,' he says as he points at a sea of faces, all smiling towards a rectangular screen. 'No doubt the ancestors are turning in their graves at how ridiculous we've become.'

The sound of a ringtone emerges from the pocket of his cargo shorts and he has the decency to look embarrassed.

'Sorry,' he says as he checks the screen. 'Escaping from the daily grind is easier said than done.'

'It's fine,' I say as he turns to look at me and I let him take his time so that I too can re-examine every detail of his face. It's the same face, the same look, as the very first time we met and it is just as disconcerting now as every single time he has looked at me. Because I've only ever seen that look between two people once before – in a turreted room guarded by gargoyles, with the sound of Stevie Nicks accompanying the kiss that almost was.

Is that what I've been searching for? But Hector isn't Leo, so what is it that I'm still so bloody terrified of?

It feels like the world has stopped, just for a second, to allow us to consider and appreciate what has happened. Which as yet is nothing more than two old lovers making banal conversation at a holy site. But it seems as if more is about to happen, or at least could happen, if either one of us would dare to step up to the plate.

'Layla posted a photo of you,' he says, his eyes never leaving my own. 'On Facebook.'

'How sweet of her to not tell me.' And it is sweet, because she has somehow reached through the continuum of time and space and pulled together the two strands that are Hector and me. I love him, I've always loved him, but have never had the guts to believe it could last.

'She's posted quite a few,' he says, which makes my heart sing, just a little, because it means he's been checking up on me. 'I think it's her way of staying connected to you.'

'This still doesn't explain what you're doing here.'

'Research trip. For the next book.'

Now I'm not so much of a technological outcast that I haven't been keeping tabs on him. Which means I know all about his bestseller, a book about love, loss and bucket-loads of despair. I'd like to say I provided some of the inspiration, gave him at least some sort of recompense for breaking his heart (again) by inadvertently rewarding him with literary acclaim.

'And you just so happened to be visiting the temples at the same time as me?'

'Not exactly. Layla might have mentioned something in her last post.'

Two days ago I emailed her, giving all the details of the cockroach-infested hostel where I was staying, as well as wishing I could luxuriate in a bubble bath instead of standing under a shower that dribbled rather than flowed. I'd also said it didn't matter, that it was worth it due to the incredible temples – ones that I'd bought a three-day pass to because once was never enough. Still, the chances of him being close enough to come and find me were pretty much slim to none.

'Are you stalking me?'

'In the nicest possible way.' He grins at me, mopping at the back of his neck with a scrap of material. As he does so, I catch a glimpse of the Celtic tattoo that snakes its way up and around his bicep and my insides do a little dance of delight.

A week later and I'm still living in his hotel room, which is in a much more exclusive part of Siem Reap than my dodgy hostel. Twice he's cancelled his flight, claiming food poisoning when his agent kept calling to ask if inspiration had finally struck. He's also refusing to even consider going home unless I promise to go with him. But I don't know if I'm ready to make any big decisions, especially when my heart is urging me to let him in.

He's been writing all morning. When I woke, he was sitting out by the pool with a silver coffee pot and two cups laid on the table and his glasses pushed back on to his head. I kiss his back, but he is engrossed in the story, completely overtaken by his inner muse.

'How's it going?' I ask as I sit down next to him. 'Did you figure out the issue with perspective?'

He nods and murmurs his response, then grabs my hand, using the other to point across the pool.

'Over there.' He grins back at me like a schoolboy, turning his head to watch as a monkey with a baby clinging to its back emerges from the undergrowth. She trots across the tiles, pausing only to give us a suspicious look before climbing on to a table and helping herself to a leftover sandwich.

'I'm scared, Hector.'

'Of the monkey?'

'No, you idiot, of going home.'

'Why would you be scared?'

'I left for a reason.' There's always a reason, but I'm starting to realise that they are all linked.

'So? You are allowed to try something different.'

'Like what? I've never done anything other than banking.' I can't remember ever considering a different career, because banking meant money, which meant independence. It's why I went to that recruitment fair, met with the right people, sat through countless interviews and spent two months training in a foreign city. I thought I knew what I was doing. Now I'm not so sure.

'Take a leap of faith, just this once. I'll always be there to catch you.'

'I won't take money from you.' Not that I've got a huge amount to spare. Most of it is tied up in the house or investments, and I lost a chunk of shares when I quit my job and ran away to Goa without giving my boss any notice. He was livid, so much so that he refused to even consider giving me what I was owed. I never pushed him on it, despite Layla telling me I needed to stand up to the misogynistic pig, because I was so determined to cut all ties, to start again without anything hanging over me.

Now, however, that extra cash would actually be useful. A cushion of sorts to allow me to return home and take my time figuring out what to do. My lifestyle over the past year hasn't exactly been frivolous, but the piggy bank is most definitely no longer full.

'Who says I'd give you any?' His tone is light, but we both know there's an undercurrent of frustration, because money has always been such a touchy subject between us.

'But maybe this time,' Hector says as he runs a hand up and down my leg, 'you could let me take care of you.'

'I can take care of myself.'

'I know.' He places a kiss on my shoulder, then behind my ear, sending ripples of desire all over my skin. 'But won't you at least consider it?'

'It's weak.' I let out a sigh as he turns his attention to the sweet spot where my neck meets collarbone. Trying to have an argument is impossible when he's distracting me in such a delicious way.

'It's not weak to compromise.'

Layla compromised once. She gave up everything for the man she completely and utterly adored, only to have him take her love for granted. I'm amazed at how she's managed to stay so positive, so hopeful for the future, rather than turn into a bitter, twisted mess of a person who never trusts anyone enough to let them in.

'Women are always compromising for men,' I say, pushing him away as a waiter walks past, holding aloft a tray of chattering glasses. 'But men so very rarely do the same in return.'

Hector looks at me and I can almost hear the words inside his head telling me to stop being so bloody stubborn. Not to mention the fact I'm sure he would change his entire world for me, if only I actually asked him to.

'I have a surprise for you,' he says, reaching down to take something out of a paper bag. 'I saw it in the gift shop.'

It's a bowl. A small, porcelain bowl with blue crackled glaze and a silver rim. There's a jagged line filled with speckled gold on one side, an imperfection made good.

'Wabi-sabi,' I say as I pick it up and turn it upside down, noticing how the repair goes all the way through.

It's a Buddhist way of looking at the world centred around the acceptance that beauty is both transient and imperfect. I first saw it during a tea ceremony in Japan when I was poured a stream of matcha tea from a pot that had subtle fractures in the glaze. The host told me that Japanese artists left them there on purpose as a reminder of the wabi-sabi nature of life.

'There's a certain beauty in imperfection, don't you think?'

He's teasing me, making it abundantly clear that I am the one who has to change, to stop chasing the impossible idea of perfection.

NIAMH

Cathect (v.) – *to invest emotion or feeling in an idea, object or person*

Oxford, 1995

The note must have been slipped under her door at some point during the afternoon. It wasn't there when she left for the library, but when she returned, a corner of white was peeping out at her.

Niamh bent down to pick it up before unlocking the door, turning the single piece of folded, lined paper over in her hand as she dropped her bag on to the sofa. Perching on the end, she eased the edges apart and skimmed over the few lines that were written in messy script.

Fancy going for a punt? it read, and she had to look twice to check whether the 'u' was in fact an 'i'.

If so, meet me tomorrow at noon by The Folly. The location still didn't make clear whether he was asking her to go for a drink or a trip down the river, and the idea of both made the pit of her stomach draw tight.

If it's a no, the note went on, *let me down gently via Pigeon Post. A packet of biscuits (preferably chocolate Hobnobs) should help heal my bruised ego.*

Niamh smiled to herself, enjoying the melting sensation inside her. For hours beforehand she had walked around with an annoying knot in her belly. It had appeared the very moment Erika interrupted her and Leo and whatever it was they were about to do. The knot had persisted as Niamh mumbled some kind of excuse about Leo needing to leave, checking the corridor for signs of Erika before shoving him out the door.

The knot had wriggled and complained when only minutes later Erika reappeared and proceeded to ask all manner of questions about Leo. She kept giving off little puffs of annoyance whenever Niamh admitted to not knowing the answer.

'I don't trust him,' she announced when Niamh said that his room-mate was a bit of a twat.

'Clearly,' Niamh replied, picking up Leo's mug of tea and tipping the contents down the sink.

'He has chosen to share a room with somebody who you have just said is repressive.'

'Repugnant.'

'I agree, but you get my point.'

'Stop acting like my mother.'

'Don't be ridiculous,' Erika said as she helped herself to a couple of fig rolls and flicked the switch on the kettle. 'I care about you so much more than she does.'

Niamh didn't reply, instead emptying the contents of her bag on to the floor and replacing them with a sheaf of papers from her desk. Picking up her coat and keys, she glanced around the room, not really aware of what she was looking for, then headed to the stairs.

'All I'm saying is be careful.' Erika licked her fingers clean as she followed, her voice echoing off the thick stone walls. 'Boys like the chase more than anything, and I worry for your innocent little heart.'

'I'll probably never see him again,' Niamh called out as she traipsed down two more flights of stairs. She could still remember the absolute terror she felt in the moment before he was about to kiss her. She could still remember what it might have felt like, what could have happened next, if Erika hadn't inadvertently scared him away.

'Why are you so against him?' Niamh asked as she walked across Main Quad and out to the High Street. She turned back to face Erika and was struck by an irritating sense of déjà vu. Because it had happened before, only last term. Niamh had started a flirtation of sorts with a boy who sat in the same seat in the Bodleian Library every day, next to the window and diagonally opposite Niamh's preferred spot. For about a week there had been nothing more than sideways glances or half a smile, until Niamh had, quite literally, bumped into him coming around one of the book stacks and an awkward but highly charged conversation had followed.

'I don't even know him,' Erika said, seemingly oblivious to the fact she was standing barefoot on the pavement.

'You didn't know Sam, either.'

'That was different.' Erika looked away and down, which told Niamh that it probably wasn't so different at all.

'Different how?'

Erika lifted her gaze, studying Niamh's face for a moment before speaking. 'Because he came on to me.'

'Of course he did.' Niamh bit down on her back teeth, trying to rid herself of the knowledge that the one time she'd thought she might have a chance at a relationship it had, unintentionally, been destroyed by her beautiful friend.

'He simply wasn't good enough,' Erika said.

'For you?'

'No, for you, my *älskling*.' Erika reached out her hand towards Niamh's face, but she swatted her away.

'Are you OK?'

'I'm grand,' Niamh replied, holding aloft a sheet of paper adorned with typed lines of black. 'Need to crack on.'

'Let's go out later,' Erika said as she bent to place a kiss on Niamh's cheek. 'We can forget about boys and get absolutely bubbled.'

Niamh didn't bother to correct her, instead offering up a half-hearted smile and setting off in the direction of the Bodleian. At the pedestrian crossing she glanced back along the road, making sure that Erika was no longer there, then turned down a narrow alleyway. At the end, she hopped across the road, through a cast-iron gate and down a path towards Christ Church Meadows.

The expanse of green stretched out before her, flanked on all sides by row upon row of trees. She walked at a pace, taking in great lungfuls of air and telling herself to stop being so ridiculous; he was just a boy. She kept going until she reached the river, the far bank of which was lined with houseboats; the water was calm and long since empty of any early-morning rowers.

It was there that she stopped, peeling off her boots and socks then dipping her toes into the water. She blanched as the chill shot up her legs and made her whole body shiver, but the shock was exactly what she needed to try to reset her mind.

'He's just a boy,' she repeated to herself as she moved her feet through the current and watched the rippling reflection of the clouds overhead.

The problem was, he wasn't just a boy. He had so easily opened up a piece of her heart and whispered all the possibilities that had yet to occur. She had never been in love, choosing long ago not to believe that one person could have such an effect on her. But how else could she explain what was happening, what had already happened, as a result of pretty much nothing at all?

He hadn't done anything; they had barely said more than a few words to one another and yet she couldn't quite put aside the idea that it was meant to be.

Searching through her bag, she took out her beloved Walkman and opened it to check the label on the mix-tape inside. Pressing down on the well-worn play button, she allowed her thoughts to be covered by the sound of someone singing about a gold dust woman and persuading her heart that all would be OK in the end.

Pulling her boots back on, Niamh stood and headed towards town. She fully intended to spend the afternoon hidden in amongst the Bodleian bookcases, hoping that fate wouldn't deal her any more sucker punches, at least for now.

But that was exactly what it had done, smacking her right between the eyes when she opened Leo's note. Although there was no way of knowing if it was even from him, given that he hadn't signed his name.

What if it was from Robin?

The thought snuck its way into her mind, rewarding her with another jolt to the stomach. The only way he could have known where she lived would be if Leo had told him. Which, of course, he could have, given that she asked him to tell Robin about her need for the diary. But then why bring it to her himself, and only after it was too late to be of any use?

She wouldn't go. It was a disaster waiting to happen. No doubt she would turn up only to discover that it was, disappointingly, an invitation from Robin-the-repugnant. Or maybe Leo only wanted to meet in order to let her down gently? He would explain to her why he had nearly kissed her but actually never meant to, it was a heat-of-the-moment kind of thing and could they possibly pretend it had never happened?

She definitely would not go.

Why, then, had she returned to her room and was already searching through her wardrobe looking for the right outfit, one that could accommodate both a pint and a punt?

'What are you so pleased about?'

Niamh's head whipped round at the sound of Duncan's voice and she saw first his head peering round the doorframe, then the rest of him as he slunk into her bedroom.

'Nothing,' she said, but the smile in her voice was all too apparent. He stared at her, lips pursed, before touching one forefinger to his nose and pointing the other straight at her.

'The boy with the amazing arse,' he gasped. 'Erika told me he'd paid you a visit. Does this mean what I think it means?' He looked over at the pile of discarded clothes on her bed.

'I'm not going.'

'Why not?'

'It's a bad idea.'

'You, my darling, deserve a little bit of excitement more than anyone.' Duncan pushed her out of the way and began to rifle through her drawers. 'Which is why we're going to find you something that screams gorgeous, with just the right amount of sass.'

'I figured it out,' Leo said as he lifted the long wooden quant out of the river, allowing it to drift through the water then slip between his fingers until the prong found the muddy bed below.

'Figured what out?' Niamh was sitting on a faux leather seat by the till, facing towards him. She had taken off her boots and was trailing one hand through the water.

'The song,' Leo replied, easing the quant out to the left and sending the punt round a sharp corner. He had to duck out of the way of a willow tree then manoeuvre the quant round to the other side of the punt. This gave Niamh another opportunity to stare at him without being caught.

He was standing barefoot at the back of the boat (apparently only Cambridge students punted from the platform behind where she was sitting – who knew punting was such a particular type of boating experience?). Both his trousers and the sleeves of his jumper were rolled up. He was clean-shaven, his hair was carefully coiffed away from his face and she could just make out a thin, golden chain around his neck.

But it was something else that caught her eye – the second toe on each of his feet was longer than the big one. It would have been an inconsequential kind of thing if it weren't for the fact Erika shared the same physical trait. She had taken great delight in telling Niamh that all Rubenesque paintings depicted gods and angels with longer second toes, which clearly meant that she, in turn, was from heaven itself. Niamh smiled as she wondered what Erika would think about the idea of Leo being carved from the same stone.

'I had to call my mum and ask her.' Leo darted a look at Niamh, then back to the river ahead. 'But I remember it now. It's the one from Formula One.'

What he didn't admit was that he'd called his mum and announced he'd met the girl he was going to marry. Nor did he tell Niamh of the way his mother's voice had gone up by at least an octave as she began to barrage him with questions, most of which he had been unable to answer. The one thing he could tell her was that she looked just like the female singer from the band his mum was always listening to.

'Debbie Harry?' she had asked.

'No, Mum, the one who dressed like a cross between a hippy and a witch.'

'Stevie Nicks!' His mum had practically shouted the name, making Leo laugh. There had followed a slight swerve in the conversation as she regaled him with details of the one time she had seen Fleetwood Mac in concert. The call ended with him having to promise that yes, he would introduce them the next time his parents were in town.

Of course, that depended on him not screwing up this date, which was entirely possible given how completely inadequate Niamh always made him feel.

'You told your mum about me?'

Leo stumbled a little as Niamh brought him back to the here and now. He leant back on the quant and tried to style it out as he met her gaze.

'Is that a problem?'

'No,' she said, but the frown on her face told him otherwise.

'Does your mum listen to Fleetwood Mac too?'

She looked at him, then took off her hat and ruffled her hair.

'How come you're studying law?' The change of subject was sudden and deliberate, and Leo mentally punched himself for having annoyed her so early on.

'My dad's a lawyer.' He looked away from her and cleared his throat. Family history wasn't supposed to be on the list of first-date questions, but somehow he'd stumbled down a path from which there seemed to be no return.

'So?'

It was an innocent enough response, but he could tell she understood more than she was letting on. After all, how was he supposed to explain that his dad wasn't exactly the sort of person it was possible to say no to? Did he really want to tell her all about growing up as the youngest in a family of over-achievers?

She had touched a nerve, that much was obvious. It made her both sad and a little triumphant, because he had pressed down on a part of her past that she had no desire to share. Or did she? There was a certain vulnerability to him that she hadn't expected, and it was clear that he got on better with his mum than his dad. She wanted to know why, but was also afraid of how much she would have to reveal about herself in return for an honest answer.

'I wanted to go to film school, but he said it was a waste of time.'

Niamh thought back to the towers of VHS cassettes in Leo's room, the film posters on the wall that she had glanced at but not really seen, along with a pile of *Empire* magazines.

'Bit of a leap from film school to Oxford.'

'Everyone else in my family came here.'

'Define "everyone".'

'Well, apart from my eldest sister. She went to UCL and is now a top-notch surgeon at King's.' He caught the element of sarcasm in his voice, as was his tendency whenever he spoke about his perfect sibling and all her judgements about him.

'How many sisters do you have?'

'Two. And three brothers.'

'Jesus, there are six of you?' She laughed, and he grinned at her in return.

'You say that like it's a bad thing?' Which at times it was. The chaos of a large family, the lack of privacy, the pressure of being the youngest and living up to all those different levels of expectation could be suffocating.

He wanted to tell her; more than that, he wanted to take her back, show her what it was like to be him growing up. In turn, he wished he could go back in time with her, see her as a small child and ask her how she had experienced the world. All those years when they were strangers seemed a waste. The whole thing was ridiculous, but he couldn't shake the idea that everything he had been through, each and every tiny moment of his life, had brought him to her.

'I didn't mean it like that,' Niamh said, lifting her hand clear of the water and watching as droplets fell from her fingertips and back into the river. 'I'm just surprised, is all.'

And jealous, supremely jealous of the fact he had such a large family. No doubt they lived in a mansion high up on a hill somewhere, the rooms always filled with music and laughter and the sound of all those memories clicking together to create the picture-perfect life.

'What about you?'

'What about me?'

She answered too quickly and he should have known better than to pry, but he couldn't help it. He wanted to ask so much more, but was equally afraid of pushing her away before anything had even begun.

'Brothers or sisters?'

'Not that I know of.' It was a stupid reply, laced with so much suggestion that she wished she could take it back.

She could tell he wasn't prying though, even if she didn't like all the questions he kept asking. He was being nice, more than nice, so why was she acting like such a miserable cow? He'd told his mum about her, for God's sake; surely that meant he liked her?

'Here's a question,' he said, the tip of his tongue grasped between his lips as he steered them away from another punt coming towards them, then came to a stop next to the riverbank.

'Go on.'

'Book or film?' He took hold of both the tow rope and a small canvas rucksack, then leapt ashore. Niamh, meanwhile, got to her feet then promptly sat back down again as the punt pitched her from side to side.

'Depends on the book.' She shook her head as he offered his hand, then stood up slowly with both arms outstretched.

He watched as she shuffled along the punt, pausing every so often when her balance threatened to tip her overboard. He had to stop himself from laughing at the look of total annoyance on her face, but secretly hoped she might fall in, just so he could wade in to rescue her.

'Give me one example of a book that's better than the film.'

'Easy' – Niamh placed one foot on the bank, wobbled, then pitched forward to land on all fours – 'Little Women.'

'Little Women is your favourite book?'

She brushed off the grass cuttings from her jeans, breathing in the scent of it, along with mud, mossy water and every now and then something clean and sharp and coming straight from him. It was disturbing her thoughts and making it so very difficult to concentrate on anything other than the memory of how she had felt when he almost kissed her.

'I never said that.'

'Didn't have to,' he said with a grin and she punched him lightly on the arm.

'Lolita,' she countered, ignoring the way he was still looking at her.

'No way. That was Kubrick's defining moment.'

'But the film wouldn't exist unless Nabokov had written the story.'

'True,' he said, setting down the rucksack and undoing the straps. 'But how can you argue that what's on the page is more powerful than on the screen?'

'Easy.' She saw him take out two bottles of Guinness, some plastic glasses and a packet of chocolate Hobnobs. 'You create your own film inside your head. Silence of the Lambs was way more terrifying when I was imagining it for myself than when I finally saw it on video.'

'Bollocks. Hannibal Lecter is one of the most iconic film characters of all time.'

'And yet first he was simply a character in a book.'

He went as if to say something, then narrowed his eyes at her and passed over one of the bottles. He waited for her to take a sip, watching how her lips curled around the rim, and then the sight of her tongue darting out to lick the corner of her mouth.

She saw him shift his weight, noticed the way he tried to surreptitiously adjust the waistband of his jeans and it made her want to reach out and slip her fingers underneath, to feel the warmth of his skin. But there was this irritating voice inside her head, one that sounded decidedly like Erika, warning her to be careful, that if she rolled over too quickly then all that would happen was the boy in question would lose interest and move on to his next target.

'*One Flew Over the Cuckoo's Nest.*' Leo raised his own bottle as he spoke.

'Never seen it.'

'Tell me you're joking.'

'Nope.'

'Fine. Tomorrow night. My place.'

'I can't.'

'Why not?' He felt the Guinness catch in his throat and tried not to gag on it.

'I've an essay due first thing Thursday.'

'But you had a tutorial on Monday.'

'I did. And I have another on Thursday.'

'Right.' What an idiot to think that she was interested.

He was aware of her leaning forward and the very edge of her arm brushed his when she reached for another biscuit.

So many emotions were running through her, tossing her resolve all over the place and she wished she could peer inside his mind, find out exactly what it was he was thinking and whether it was anywhere close to being the same as her. Another voice, this one belonging to Duncan, whispered in her mind about taking a chance, and so she decided to do something that normally she'd never have the courage for.

'I could meet you afterwards though.' It was just a few words, but so heavy with the possibility of both happiness and regret. She held her breath, waiting for his response.

His head shot up and she saw the way his face folded into a completely different shape from how it had been only a moment before.

'You could?'

'I could.' Jesus, it was terrifying being so close to him and there it was again, that feeling of being out of control. The knowledge that she would remember this moment for the rest of her life, look back on it as the barometer for everything that was still to come, like the ultimate test for which she had no way to prepare.

Leo was overcome by the sense of the inevitable. Was this then all that life contained? A series of fractured moments that individually meant nothing at all, but when you looked back made perfect sense?

He put down his bottle then hesitated, but only for a fraction of time. He wanted to take a picture of that very second, to never forget the way she looked in the instant before he kissed her. So that he might bring it out again whenever he wanted and remember.

He was so close that she could see her own reflection in his eyes. She could feel his pulse through the thin cotton of her t-shirt as he reached under her jacket and around her waist, her own pulse quickening as soon as he touched her.

The kiss was slow, hesitant and gentle. But the force with which her body responded was at complete odds to anything she had ever felt before. It was like a million tiny ants were running up and down her spine, along her legs, in through her belly button and then swirling around inside her.

As his mouth met hers, all other thoughts, all of his fears, were replaced by a deep sense of longing. It began on his lips, darted over his tongue and all the way down to his groin, then it shot back up to vibrate inside his brain.

It felt like the most perfect part of his life that had ever been, and perhaps ever would be, and all he could think about was that she was the only thing in the entire world that mattered.

ERIKA

Small Glass Perfume Bottle

London, 2007

The restaurant is crowded, filled to the rafters with pre-Christmas revellers caught up in the festive spirit. The décor is supposed to be French bistro, but all the twinkling lights, fake snow and cheesy Christmas tunes are making it feel brash and clichéd.

The seats are made of red faux suede, the leg of the nearest table is propped up with a folded piece of paper and the lighting is courtesy of candles stuck into empty wine bottles. All of which is making me feel decidedly overdressed in my belted white dress and Chanel handbag.

As I raise my glass, all the bracelets around my wrist jangle in annoyance. Just the one, I tell myself as I scan the menu in search of something that's not laden with calories or carbs. It's only a couple of weeks until I'm supposed to be lying on a beach in the Caribbean and I don't have the time to run off any extra pounds.

Everything needs to be tied up before I leave on Boxing Day, but the Finnish deal is proving troublesome, not least due to the CFO who seems to be fashioning himself on the Grinch. As is so often the case when I'm met with such a ridiculous example of an alpha male, I can't help but suspect that it's all for show, because I'm a woman. I hoped that by this stage in my career the misogyny would stop. If anything, it seems to be getting worse. Even back when we pitched for the deal, one of the first questions the CFO asked me was whether or not I was married. I mean, seriously, would it offer him reassurances if I had a husband at home to keep me in check?

'Erika?'

I look up to see one of the juniors staring at me, eyebrows raised and holding a bottle of champagne aloft.

'Can I tempt you?'

'I'm good, thanks.' I take another sip of wine and decide that I am going to need more than one glass to get me through the evening.

'Sure?' he says, reaching across the bar for my hand and rubbing his thumb over my knuckles as he gazes adoringly into my eyes.

I really don't have time to do the whole dating thing right now, especially not with someone who is so fresh out of university that he probably still eats Pot Noodle and has an Xbox in his bedroom. I extricate my hand from his, sighing with relief as my phone begins to vibrate. I peer at the screen, then grab my coat from the back of my chair because she hardly ever calls me this late.

'Back in a sec.' I toss the words over my shoulder, weaving through the tables and out to the street. It's raining, which is just perfect because my coat's going to get ruined, but the call is from the one person I promised never to ignore.

'Layla?' I can hear her crying on the other end of the line. 'What's wrong?'

'I've left him.' Her response comes out in between muffled sobs, as if she's been upset for some time.

'What do you mean, you've left him?' Not that I'm distraught to hear this; part of me has wanted her to dump Christophe ever since I first met him.

'He's been having an affair.'

'Fuck,' I say as the door swings open behind me and the sound of Rihanna singing about an umbrella tumbles into the night. It's a song that seems to have played on repeat since the beginning of a long, very wet, summer. I offer up half a smile to the woman who has come outside for a smoke. 'Where are you? You keep cutting out.'

'On the Eurostar. We're about to go through the tunnel so I should be at King's Cross in an hour.'

She really has left him. I don't know whether to feel sad or relieved because, in my humble opinion, Christophe is an arsehole of the highest order. Not that I've ever said as much to Layla, but I still can't quite believe that she is coming home.

'I'll come meet you,' I say. I need to be there to hug her and tell her that everything will be OK. I also need her to be there for me, to fill in the gaps of my life that don't make sense without her.

'Are you sure?'

'Anything for you.' Layla saved me when I first moved to London, even though I never told her how or why. Now it's my turn to help build her back up to the girl she used to be before a boy came along and ruined everything.

Making my way along the damp, dark streets, a sharp, icy breeze swarms around my ankles, lifting the hem of my dress and making me shiver. Breathing in, I catch hold of a scent that makes me turn and retrace my steps until I come to a shop that looks about one hundred years out of date.

Opening the door, I'm overwhelmed with a myriad of perfumes, all fighting for my attention. There are glass cabinets on the walls, each filled with clear-glass bottles that would have looked at home in a Victorian apothecary. There's a sales assistant in the window, adding the finishing touches to a festive display.

'Feel free to look around.' She smiles over her shoulder, looking at me from head to toe as she does so.

It's here somewhere, the scent that teased itself through the night and into my memories. A reminder of a time before I understood what it meant to have your heart broken.

Walking around the shop I breathe in long and deep, searching out my target like a demented bloodhound. Bottle after bottle I sniff then discard for being too flowery or too sharp. I should go and meet Layla; there's nothing here for me. I never should have come inside. What's the point in searching for something that should remain in the past?

Because they never came after you. And there's the rub, the horrible shard of reality that's stuck inside my gut and refuses to ever go away. I thought they loved me; I thought at least one of them might want to hear my side of the story, give me a chance to explain.

Is this why I keep chasing them, or at least the memory of what happened between us? It's masochism at its best, which is a particularly annoying habit of mine. The constant push and pull between me wanting to move on, to live my life without regret, and never actually being able to.

Just as I'm about to give up and head to King's Cross, I catch a fragment of it, soft but pure. Turning my head, I notice a candle resting on a console table by the till. The wax around the wick is still liquid, which suggests that I inadvertently extinguished the flame when I came into the shop. But the scent is distinct and strong enough to make me feel a little sick.

'That's one of our original fragrances,' the sales assistant says as she notices me pick up the candle. 'It was discontinued, but we've decided to do a limited edition just for Christmas.'

'Do you have it as an eau de toilette?' I ask, watching as the sales assistant reaches into one of the glass cabinets and takes down a small glass bottle with a ribbon tied around its neck.

'You'll never guess what his mother said to me,' Layla says as I shut the front door behind us and we make our way through to the kitchen.

'I dread to think.' Christophe's mother is achingly beautiful, with cheekbones you could cut cheese on. Not that she would ever let such a tasty morsel pass those pursed lips. Much better to be skinny and judgemental than do anything that even closely resembles fun – she even wore black to her own son's wedding, which pretty much sums her up.

Layla hovers in the doorway, no doubt noticing both what has and hasn't changed since she left. For the most part, the kitchen is the same, other than the sofa because the old one was ruined by the people I rented the house out to when neither of us were living in London.

Still, must be a bit strange to come back here. Familiar, but strange. I know it felt odd to me. The first night after I arrived back from New York, it took me ages to get to sleep, listening to the same old sounds that accompany a home, sounds you don't ever think about. The soft gurgle of water running through pipes, or the low hum of the fridge. Added to which the sense of disappointment that comes with realising you're no better off than before you left. I hate to think what it must be like for her.

I open the fridge in search of something to drink, but it's empty apart from a few cartons of chicken soup and some milk. Instead I reach inside the freezer and take out a bottle of vodka, setting it down on the work surface and hunting in the cupboard for some glasses.

'She said I should be grateful.' Layla fingers the bottle, running them down the icy glass and drawing the outline of a cartoon shark, complete with lopsided grin.

'For discovering your husband has been cheating?' I say as I slide a glass over to her, watching as she fills it halfway, then downs the contents in one.

'Yup,' she says, wiping her mouth with the back of her hand then refilling her glass. 'Said it was far better to have everything out in the open. That I should simply accept the fact men have different needs than women.'

'Are all French women that psycho, or is it just the mothers?' I steal the bottle away, because even though she is perfectly within her rights to get absolutely plastered, dealing with a hangover on top of a broken heart is more than she deserves right now.

'God, I wish I'd never found out.' She drops her forehead onto the work surface and lets out a long, deep groan.

'You don't mean that.'

'Don't I?' Layla's head comes up and she meets my gaze. 'We were happy, Erika. We were so bloody happy, and—'

'And nothing, Layla. He cheated on you. Which means he would have done it again.' I don't add that chances are this isn't the first time he has strayed from the marital bed.

Granted, he is the epitome of tall, dark and handsome. Someone who makes you look twice whenever he enters a room. But there has always been something about him that makes me uncomfortable. He's never said or done anything outright, but he has the extraordinary ability to wind me up with nothing more than a look. He's always reminded me of Peter, the boy who thought that hundreds of flowers could cover up the fact he was an utter *kuk*.

102

Proves that I should always listen to my gut, especially when it comes to men.

Layla begins opening and closing cupboards, clearly in search of something to eat. But I can't remember the last time I sat down and ate a meal here, much less cooked. I have been so very good at either eating at my desk or meeting people straight from work. Anything to avoid coming back to an empty house.

Layla opens a packet of biscuits that I'm sure are well past their sell-by date, but I figure are a better option than more vodka. She takes them all out one by one, then starts to stack them into the shape of a pyramid, scattering crumbs and chocolate all over the floor in the process.

'I blame Facebook,' she says, shoving half a biscuit in her mouth then immediately spitting it out into the sink.

Turns out that social media is responsible for revealing the extent of Christophe's deception. Layla was absently flicking through a mutual friend's photos and came across one posted a week earlier. Christophe standing between two women, both blonde, both skinny and polished in the way only Parisian women can be. That in itself wasn't a problem, but the hand that was resting on one of the women's waists wasn't wearing a wedding ring. Added to which, the photograph had been taken on a night when he claimed to be in Berlin on business, but the tag told Layla her husband had in fact been drinking vintage champagne in a club only minutes from the marital home.

'Did he even apologise to you?' My dislike of Christophe isn't something I have ever voiced. Layla seemed genuinely happy, if a little homesick, since her move across the sea, and I never wanted to get in the way of their relationship. Been there, done that and look at what it's cost me.

'Sort of.' Which means no, but probably best not to push her just yet. 'Why don't you have anything to eat, Erika? I'm bloody starving.'

'We can order takeaway.' I rummage in the cutlery drawer for an old menu. 'Chinese or Indian?'

'Curry. Definitely a curry. And make sure you order some extra poppadoms because you always steal mine.'

I dial the number of our local curry house, acutely aware that I am so very pleased she is home. It's totally selfish, I know, and I've done my best to hide it, to pretend it isn't the case. Which is all kinds of ridiculous, given that I left for New York pretty much as soon as we graduated. But she had Christophe. If she missed me, I doubt it was to the same extent I did her.

'Can I ask you something?' she says when I hang up the phone.

'You can ask . . .'

'You never really got on with Christophe.'

It's a statement rather than a question, but something that has remained unspoken between us, almost as if we have both always been afraid of what my answer might be.

'I don't think we ever gave one another a chance.' Christophe came out of nowhere. One minute Layla and I were a team, our friendship brilliant and intense, making me feel in some way justified for leaving Oxford. The next minute there was silence as Layla fell completely and utterly in love with a man who did so little to hide his contempt for me. It was all so painfully familiar, which might have had something to do with why I never trusted him.

'My family's a bit mad, a bit loud,' Layla says with a yawn, stretching her arms above her head and showing me just how thin heartache can make you.

'Your family is amazing.'

'Exactly.' She reaches out and gives my hand a squeeze. 'You love them and they love you. But Christophe never quite fitted in.'

'That's his fault, not yours.' Or maybe it has more to do with the fact I need Layla's family, but Christophe has his own waiting for him back in Paris. I managed to make a life for myself after

Oxford, but so much of that was dependent on Layla and, by extension, her family. I spent so much time in her parents' home. So many meals shared in the Browne family kitchen, which to this day is always filled with the scent of her mum's baking and the endless stream of conversation that comes from a house that is never empty.

'Why didn't you tell me?' Layla asks, peering into the bag from the perfumery and taking out the bottle still wrapped in red tissue paper. 'That you didn't like him?'

I let her open the bottle, bring it to her nose and inhale the spicy perfume. I don't really know why I bought it, given it's not something I'll ever wear.

'It didn't seem fair,' I say, watching as she dabs her wrists with the stopper, then once more behind each ear. The smell is overwhelming but wrong, because it doesn't belong on her skin. I didn't say anything, even though I know that beautiful men have a bad habit of making girls cry. At the time, I told myself that Layla was old enough to make her own decisions, but now I think it was more to do with me being afraid of that same mistake happening all over again.

'On you, or me?'

I close my eyes for a moment, pinching my nose shut because the perfume is making me think about someone, and I don't want to think about her, not now, not when I should be concentrating on the one true friend I still have. If I'd told Layla how I really felt about Christophe, I doubt our friendship would have survived.

'Christophe always hated having to share me with you. He was so jealous that I loved someone other than him.'

It's like she knows, but she can't possibly know, because I have never told anyone from this part of my life about the people who were so dominant in another part. Perhaps we are all guilty of the same repeated patterns when it comes to love. It's always the same old shit, just in a different city.

NIAMH

Monachopsis (n.) – *the distinct feeling of being out of place*

Oxford, 1995

'I can't believe you dragged me here,' Niamh said as she handed over her coat to the girl behind the desk at the hotel cloakroom.

'I can't believe you're complaining about the free booze,' Erika replied as she lifted two glasses from the tray of a passing waiter and handed one to her friend.

'But it's all so false.' Niamh took a long sip as she followed Erika along the corridor to where a throng of people were entering the ballroom at the far end. 'Even you're pretending to be someone you're not.'

Erika stopped at the double doors, in front of which was a huge easel with a poster attached, detailing all the firms who were gathered in the hallowed halls of the Randolph Hotel for the annual Milk Round. Every year, the best and the brightest that Oxford had to offer were lured to various locations around the city by law firms, investment banks and FTSE 100 companies. All of them were promising roads paved with gold if only you would sign away your life after graduation to the corporate machine.

Niamh had no intention of being sucked into their false promises of a so-called better life, but Erika had other ideas and managed to convince her that anything was better than another night in the student bar.

'You deserve to be so much more than ordinary, Niamh. But at some point, you have to learn to play the game.' Erika looked her up and down, then gestured to the room in front of them. Pretty much every person was dressed either in a suit or a pencil skirt and blouse. Erika herself was wearing cropped black trousers, a cream silk blouse and a pale grey jacket. Her hair was freshly blow-dried and her face was carefully made-up.

In comparison, Niamh was still wearing the same clothes she had pulled on that morning – a red, tiered gypsy skirt, a plain white t-shirt and an ancient pair of cowboy boots.

'If you don't at least try to fit in, you'll end up like your mother.' Erika drained her glass, then swapped it for a fresh one as another waiter went by.

'If you're going to be a bitch, I'm leaving.'

'No, don't.' Erika slipped her arm around Niamh's waist. 'I'm sorry. You know I didn't mean it. But what is the point of coming to Oxford if you're not going to do something with it?'

Whatever happened to figuring it out as you went along? At what point did Niamh wake up in a world where everyone around her had a ten-year plan? And why did absolutely every part of success seem to revolve around money? She may have had absolutely no idea what she wanted to do with her life, but Niamh was determined that it would be based more on actually living rather than feeding back into the narcissistic ways of the Western world.

'Right,' Erika said. 'Time to mangle.'

'Mingle.' Niamh looked past Erika to a long, rectangular room with windows on two sides. There was a round table set up in the centre and a row of red velvet chairs along one wall. But nobody was sitting on them; instead they were clustered in small groups, diligently paying attention to the person at its helm.

'Bunch of wanker bankers,' she muttered to herself as she picked up a leaflet, on the front of which was a group of young people, bright and sparky graduates no doubt, standing in the foyer of an enormous glass building. It was supposed to inspire her, make her want to join the ranks of the chosen few, but all it did was make her feel sorry for anyone who did nothing but make rich people richer.

It also made her think of Leo, as most things tended to. Because he was part of that world, that gilded existence that came from being born into money. It was a world Niamh had no idea how to navigate, let alone be comfortable in.

'Come on.' Erika gave Niamh's ankle a not-so-subtle prod with the tip of her stiletto. 'We're here to make something brilliant of our futures.'

'You sound like one of these ridiculous leaflets.'

Niamh drained her glass, then looked around for somewhere to put it. It seemed a little rude to dump it on the tables that were adorned with yet more leaflets about the challenges and rewards that life as an investment banker would yield.

'I have absolutely no desire to work for any of these soulless institutions.' She set her glass down, but when she turned around, Erika had inserted herself into a neighbouring group and she was left looking up into the face of a stranger.

'Not even for a thirty-six grand starting salary?' he asked, taking a sip of his own drink.

'Hello.' Erika reappeared like a rabbit out of a hat, extending her hand and flashing both her teeth and her cleavage. 'And who might you be?'

'Charlie.' He shook Erika's hand, glancing at her briefly, then returned his attention to Niamh. He was looking at her with a strange expression on his face, and she couldn't quite work out whether he was silently laughing at her or was just a bit pissed.

'I'm Erika and this is my friend Niamh. She's an absolute genius and in need of some ideas about what to do after graduation.'

'Isn't everyone at Oxford supposed to be a genius?' He smiled at Niamh and she figured out what it was that was different about him. His top lip was decorated with a thin, silver scar, which was only apparent when he smiled. She allowed herself to inspect the rest of him – fitted navy suit with a waistcoat underneath, silver cufflinks and a Windsor knot in his tie. It made her think of country gents, of hunting and horses and copious amounts of tweed.

But there was a soft burr to his voice that suggested Ireland via an English boarding school. He also had the smallest of holes in one earlobe, which made Niamh think that perhaps he didn't have a rod up his arse like everyone else in that room.

'Sorry,' she said. 'Did you say thirty-six grand?'

'I did.'

Niamh turned the leaflet over, looking at yet another photograph of a sparkly, shiny skyscraper stretching into a cloudless sky.

'I'm not really sure it's my cup of tea.' She handed the leaflet back and turned to walk away.

'What are you studying?' Charlie asked as he stepped to the side, blocking her exit.

Niamh fiddled with one of the chains around her neck, rubbing the metal between finger and thumb as she weighed up the pros and cons of answering. He had an agenda, that much was clear, and it felt a little as if he were performing a sales pitch in order to earn his commission. But he had a kind sort of face, and was one of the only people in the room who wasn't looking at her as if she didn't belong.

'History.'

'Then there's always research instead of trading.' He nodded as he spoke. 'You don't have to be a maths graduate to join.'

'Oh, she's an absolute whizz with numbers.' Erika rested her hand on Charlie's shoulder, using the other one to pull Niamh further into the conversation.

'Would you stop?' Niamh pushed Erika's hand away.

'I assume you did maths as part of your Highers?'

'We had to.' But if he was asking, then he probably already knew all about the Irish education system. It seemed as if it was his job to find out everything he could about her, to determine whether she was the sort of person his superiors would approve of.

'What did you get?' He was still blocking the exit and Niamh tried to look past him. 'If you don't mind me asking.'

'A one.' If she answered his questions, he would let her go.

'In maths?'

'In everything.'

'Seriously?' The tone of his voice made Niamh snap her head back to him. She was expecting to find disbelief or amusement on his face, but instead there was only admiration.

'Seriously. I was a bit of a nerd. Spent more time in the library than down the pub.'

'In that case you should seriously – I can't believe I just said that – consider applying for our summer intern programme.' He reached into his jacket pocket and took out a business card. 'It's a great way to get a feel for all the different areas within the bank.'

Niamh looked at the small, white card embossed with a corporate logo and the contact details of a stranger, then tried to hand it back.

'Thanks, Charlie. But it's really not for me.'

Charlie curled his hands over hers. 'How about I buy you a drink? We can reminisce about the Emerald Isle and I'll try to get you to change your mind?'

'Where are you from?' Niamh asked as she withdrew her hand.

'Dublin.'

'Then it's definitely a no,' Niamh said with a laugh.

'Cork?' Charlie said with one raised brow.

'By way of Galway.'

'That explains the accent. I always get the piss taken out of me whenever I go home. Get told I've spent too much time on the wrong side of the sea.'

Niamh thought of Robin, and all the others she'd met who found it amusing to make fun of her accent. It was just one of many things that made her stand out in this ostentatious world she found herself in, and not in a good way.

'Stop flirting with her, she's taken,' Erika said as she steered Niamh away from Charlie and towards the exit. 'But you can come find me later.'

'I might just do that,' Charlie said, draining his own glass and watching them go.

'Are we done?' Niamh leant into Erika's side as they walked away, overcome with the need to sit down.

'Not yet.' Erika paused to peer into each of the rooms as they passed. 'I want to go and schmooze with the lawyers.'

'Why? You've always said you wanted to be a banker.' Niamh glanced at her watch, wondering if Leo was in the room where Erika wanted to go. She also wondered whether she wanted Erika to bump into him there without her.

'Look, you know as well as I do that money makes a difference to what kind of life you can live.' Erika picked up two more glasses and passed one to Niamh. 'I have every intention of making as much of it as I possibly can so that I no longer have to listen to my mother's god-awful advice about finding some lord or duke or whatever to marry.'

'I thought you made it a point never to listen to your mother?'

'I do, but I need her to realise I'm nothing like her.'

'I thought she was rather grand.'

'Of course you did. Because she is an expert at making people fall in love with her.'

Sounds a bit like you, Niamh thought to herself, but knew better than to make any kind of comparison between Erika and her mother. Apparently all the freedoms and privileges that Erika had grown up with came with the assumption that she would follow the path laid out for her by her parents. Having met Leo, Niamh now wondered if controlling parents was a curse bestowed on all the uber-rich students she seemed to be surrounded by. It also made her wonder whether coming from nothing was in fact better, because the expectations were so much lower.

'The point is,' Erika said as she stared across the room at a thirty-something man who was watching her watching him. 'Once I've climbed the corporate ladder to the very top, I shall be in need of a husband.'

'You just said you didn't want to get married.'

'No, I said I had no desire to be dependent on someone else for money. But it would be nice to have someone to share it all with, don't you think?' She may have been talking to Niamh, but all her attention, all her subtle adjustments to her posture and the way she licked the side of her mouth, were very much directed at the man across the room.

'I think I'm going to leave you to it.'

Erika gave a little tut as she looked down at her friend. 'Niamh, *älskling*, you can't put the future off forever.'

'I'm not.'

'Don't sulk. It doesn't suit you.'

'I wish Duncan were here. He'd back me up.'

'That's because you are his favourite.' She reached out and tapped the end of Niamh's nose. It was an annoying habit of hers that only ever came out when she was drunk or in need of a favour. 'Mine too, which is why you are coming back home with me for Christmas.'

So it was a favour, but for Niamh not Erika. One that was not-so-cleverly disguised as yet another invitation to spend the holidays with her. Erika understood all too well that the only thing waiting for Niamh back in Cork was the prospect of a couple of shifts at the local pub and a Boxing Day visit to her adoptive grandfather, whose home smelt of wet dog and mould.

It was this quiet understanding between them, one they never needed to actively speak of, that made Niamh feel so connected to her friend. Like an invisible cord that would gently tug whenever the other was in need.

'I'm going to get a drink,' she said, looking around in search of the bar.

'You have a drink.'

'Not this shite.' Niamh abandoned her glass filled with pale-yellow bubbles and nodded back towards reception. 'I mean a real drink. I'll see you in the bar.'

The floor was polished walnut, the walls were painted a deep shade of burgundy and the bar stools were made from the softest brown leather. A row of clear-glass spherical lights hung over the bar and there was a double-height bay window at the far end that looked out on to Magdalen Street. Just as in the rest of the hotel, everyone there was dressed to impress, including someone standing in the window, wearing a pale-grey suit.

Leo.

Niamh hesitated, unsure whether she should go up to him or turn around and go back to her college, hide up in her attic room and pretend that the whole situation didn't make her feel ridiculously uncomfortable.

But it was too late; Leo had spotted her and was walking over with that irritatingly perfect smile of his.

'Hey,' he said as he bent down to kiss her and she hated the way her stomach flipped in response. Just like it always did whenever he touched her or looked at her or stood in the same room as her. In fact, it happened even when she thought about him, and the knowledge he could affect her in such a way, no matter whether it was intentional or not, was terrifying.

'What are you doing here?'

'Giving Erika moral support.'

'From what you've told me, I would have thought that's the last thing she needs.' He tucked a strand of hair behind her ear.

'Don't be mean.' She fiddled with the knot of his tie, staring at a small shaving nick on his throat. 'She's only got my best interests at heart.'

'So do I.' He bent down to kiss her again and whispered against her mouth. 'I missed you last night.'

She kissed him back, registering the taste of whiskey on his lips. 'I rather liked having a whole single bed to myself.' It may have been less than a fortnight since their date on the river, but time seemed to condense itself in that city, so that two weeks became more like two months, or even longer.

After that first kiss she had given in, allowed herself to fall completely and utterly under his spell, and when all their heated fumbles turned into actual, full-blown, mind-bendingly delicious sex, it made Niamh silently grateful that she hadn't given herself to anyone before. They had spent every night since in each other's beds, only leaving one another to attend tutorials or shower, and each morning when Niamh woke she had to mentally pinch herself that he was really there, with her.

Duncan had teased her about it, told her she was already flushed with love. Erika had been less enthusiastic, asking why

Niamh was hiding Leo away if he was really that fabulous? Niamh had smiled, said something innocuous about it being too soon to tell, but really she was nervous that once Leo met her friends, something of the magic between them would be lost.

It was like nothing she had ever felt before: that need, that desire to be with someone all the time. To touch them and have them touch you in return. To tell them every tiny thought that popped into your head, no matter how ridiculous, because it all seemed so important, as if every second she spent with him mattered.

'Stay there,' he said, holding up his empty glass and kissing the end of her nose. 'I'll be back in a sec.'

She watched him go to the bar and lean across to order more drinks. A minute more and someone came up alongside him – an older gentleman, who placed one hand on Leo's shoulder and gave it a squeeze. He too was wearing a suit, but had removed his jacket and tie. But it wasn't his clothes that made Niamh draw breath, rather the curl of hair at his temple, dark brown and speckled with grey. Most of all, it was the slight upward tilt to his nose and the way his smile stretched clean across his face, a face that was so very similar to the person whose shoulder he had just squeezed.

'Holy Mary, mother of God,' Niamh muttered to herself. 'It's his bloody father.' She glanced down at her clothes, tugging at the hem of her top and wishing she'd thought to wash her hair that morning.

'What did you come dressed as?'

Niamh looked back up to see Robin approaching, wearing a double-breasted suit complete with buttonhole and bow tie. His cheeks were flushed and there was what looked like a piece of flaky pastry stuck to the side of his mouth.

'Fuck off, Robin.' Niamh had absolutely no desire to speak to him, not least because he seemed to be doing his best to embarrass her in their tutorials, mimicking her accent and even asking her if she believed in leprechauns when they were supposed to be discussing the Salem witch trials.

'Leo, mate,' Robin called over his shoulder to where Leo was still standing at the bar and Niamh flinched as she saw his dad glance in her direction. 'You need to tell your girlfriend to calm down.'

'Jesus, what is it with boys like you?' Niamh moved a little to the side so Robin was standing directly between her and the bar. She could feel her emotions beginning to swirl, and wished she had time to figure out what to do with them. But with Leo's father in such close proximity, she was finding it difficult to stay calm.

Leo had spoken to her about his father, about the expectations he was supposed to live up to. But he had also told Niamh about summers spent learning how to sail, or playing cricket on the beach being taught how to bowl a googly. Niamh could hear the love Leo had for his family. She had listened to every single one of his stories with a mixture of jealousy and awe, but the idea of actually meeting his father, of having him judge her, was enough to make her want to run and hide.

'Sweetheart.' Robin leered at her and she backed away from the staleness of his breath. 'I promise you I am most definitely not a boy.'

'No, you're an entitled little gobshite.' It was too much, it was all too much for her to simply stand there and be insulted again and again. So what if she didn't act the part – or play the game as Erika put it? Even if she did, even if she put on a dress, painted her face and smiled sweetly at all those sycophantic fools, they'd never truly accept her because she didn't come from the right stock. Like a horse to be sold at market, except to them she was nothing more than a mule.

'Niamh.' Leo came up alongside her, a warning note in his voice.

'Stay out of this, Leo. You wouldn't understand.'

'No,' he said, taking hold of her arm and trying to steer her further from the bar. 'But I do understand that this really isn't the best place for it.'

'Why?' She tugged herself free of him and deliberately raised her voice. 'In case I embarrass you in front of Robin? Well, guess what? I couldn't give a toss about how much money all your mammies and daddies have. It doesn't make you better than me.'

Robin chortled to himself as he lit a cigarette. 'No, but it does allow us to buy some decent clothes.'

The noise that escaped Niamh's lips was halfway between a roar and a sob. Without stopping to think about what she was doing, or contemplating the fact she was doing it within plain sight of Leo's father, she snatched the drink from Leo's hand and threw it in Robin's face.

She didn't bother to wait for either Robin or Leo's response as she stormed from the bar. Nor did she collect her coat from the cloakroom or tell Erika that she was leaving, although no doubt Erika would have congratulated her for finally sticking up for herself. All she knew was she had to get moving, get away from that place before she did something she would really regret.

God, Leo thought to himself as he watched her leave, *she is infuriating*. Seconds later he followed her out of the hotel. She was infuriating and gorgeous and brilliant, and nothing like any other girl he had ever met. Which is precisely why he had been about to introduce her to his father, but then things had spiralled out of control, although he wasn't exactly sure why.

'Niamh!' he called out as he saw her dart across Magdalen Street in front of a speeding cyclist, who only just managed to avoid her.

'Niamh!' he called again as he waited for a city bus to pass, then sprinted across the road to catch her up.

'Leave me alone, Leo.' She tossed the words over her shoulder as she heard him calling out her name. She was half walking, half jogging along Broad Street with her arms wrapped around her middle in an effort to stop shivering. The season was on its hinge, just about ready to creak all the way open to winter and she cursed herself for leaving her fur coat behind.

'What happened in there?' he asked as he came up alongside her.

'You wouldn't understand.'

'Try me.'

She stopped walking, breathed out a cloud of chilled breath and stamped her feet on the ground. 'It's all so very easy for you, isn't it?' She glanced over at him, then started walking away. 'Private school, normal parents, loads of siblings to show you the ways of this messed-up world. I've been alone my entire life.'

'OK, firstly, private school can be just as shit as anywhere else.' His own teeth began to chatter as they waited at the kerbside for a trio of cyclists to pass. Instinctively, he reached out his hand as they crossed the road, allowing himself a small smile when she didn't pull away.

'I suspect you were rather good at being a teenager,' Niamh said as he drew her close and wrapped his arm around her. She leant into him, breathing in his warmth. 'Captain of the rugby team, good grades, popular. All the girls falling at your feet.'

'I wasn't actually captain.'

Niamh banged her hip against him. 'But you did play for the firsts.'

'I did.'

'And you were popular.'

'I had friends.'

'And you got your first shag off the hottest girl in school.'

At this he couldn't help but laugh. 'Well . . .'

'See,' she said as they walked past the King's Arms and she longed to duck inside and lose herself at the bottom of a bottle. 'Your version of being a teenager is so very different to mine.'

'Then tell me.'

She didn't reply. Instead, she turned her face into his jacket and allowed him to steer her into the college lodge, around the quad and then up to his room. It was only once she had pulled on one of his jumpers and cocooned herself under a blanket on the sofa that she began to talk.

'I was adopted.'

'Shit.' Leo handed her a tumbler of whiskey.

'Not until I was ten,' she said, taking a long sip and shaking her head as the booze hit her stomach. 'Before which I grew up in a convent.'

He had no idea how to respond, so of course he said the first idiotic thing that popped into his head, and instantly regretted it.

'What happened to your real mum?'

If she was irritated, she didn't show it as she rummaged in her bag for a cigarette.

'Then I got a scholarship to the school where Brian, my adoptive father, taught.'

'You went to private school?'

'Yup,' Niamh said as she inhaled deeply on her cigarette. 'Longest seven years of my life. Fucking awful place.'

'Why?'

'Oh God, Leo, you haven't got a clue.' Niamh let out an elongated sigh and scratched at her scalp. 'Imagine being the only one in your class whose car is a battered old Volvo. Or someone who spent their holidays in a caravan park on the Galway coast instead of the Caribbean. Imagine what it would be like buying your clothes from jumble sales and turning up on mufti day only for everyone else to be wearing brand-new Nikes and leather jackets.'

'I guess.' Leo perched on one arm of the sofa and sipped his own drink, completely at a loss as to what he should say.

'It's not money I object to,' Niamh said after a while. 'It's the people who have it I can't stand.'

'Does this mean you can't stand me?'

'You're different.' She looked at him then, properly, for the first time since leaving the hotel.

'I am?'

'You don't wear your wealth like a badge of honour. Or ask what someone's doing in the holidays just so you can try and top them by announcing you're going to your parents' ski chalet by private jet.'

He slipped in next to her. 'For the record, my parents have neither a chalet nor a jet.'

Niamh smiled and he resisted the urge to kiss her.

'But you've always had someone there for you. On your side, no matter what.'

She thought of the moment during her first term when she'd finally understood what it meant for someone to truly have your back. There was a student newsletter, artfully entitled *Pranks, Wanks & Armitage Shanks* that was pinned up every week in all the college toilets. It was supposed to be light-hearted gossip, but the Christmas edition claimed that Niamh had borrowed several essays from a fellow history student and passed off his work as her own.

When Erika read the newsletter, she took down every single copy and set fire to them in the middle of the Fellows' Garden. As a crowd gathered, she took great delight in informing them that in fact it was the other way round; *he* had borrowed Niamh's notes because he (once again) couldn't be arsed to do the work himself. What he didn't know was that Niamh had deliberately put in false information in one of her essays about a rare book known as *The Golden Turnip*, which supposedly disproved all previous theories about the disappearance of the Princes in the Tower.

The student included this piece of evidence in his next essay, narrowly avoiding any punishment because his professor saw the funny side of his mistake. But he and his girlfriend (who just so happened to be the editor of *Pranks, Wanks & Armitage Shanks*), weren't so forgiving. Luckily for Niamh, neither was Erika and it made Niamh adore her all the more.

'Why did you grow up in a convent?' The question was out before he'd thought it through, and she shifted her weight away from him before replying.

'Because according to the Catholic Church, it's a mortal sin to have a child out of wedlock.'

'Surely you don't believe that?' Leo put down his glass, aware of how the whiskey was loosening his mind and spewing out words before he'd considered the repercussions of what he said.

'It doesn't matter what I believe,' Niamh said as she reached forward to pick up Leo's glass. 'The whole system is screwed because it's a sin to have sex unless you're married.' She drained the glass of its contents, then sat staring out at nothing at all. 'It's most definitely a sin to have a baby unless you're married, but it's illegal to either take birth control or have an abortion.'

'Wait, what?'

'Which means that if an unmarried girl, or woman, of any age discovers she's pregnant' – there was a tremor to her voice and he noticed the gathering of tears at the corners of her eyes – 'more often than not she's shipped off to a convent until the baby's born. After which she goes home, back to her old life. But the baby stays with the nuns either until some poor sod takes pity on them, or they turn eighteen and can supposedly fend for themselves.'

Apart from Erika and Duncan, he was the only person she'd ever admitted this to. It was shameful, where she came from, to be an illegitimate child, and for years she'd pretended to ignore the whispers of 'bad blood' that followed her along the school corridors.

Niamh extinguished her cigarette, then tucked her feet up underneath her and leant against his shoulder. For a moment they simply sat, listening to the sound of one another's breathing, neither of them quite sure what to do next.

'Didn't you want to find out about your real mother?' He hated the idea of her as a little girl, locked away in an institution with nobody to love her.

'Of course I bloody did.' She was crying now, and it hurt him, physically hurt him, to watch. 'But it was never an option.'

'Why?'

Niamh lit another cigarette, then changed her mind and stubbed it out before standing up and going over to the piano. She sat down at the keys and began to run her fingers up and down the octaves. The sound was calming, something else for her to focus on other than the raw fury that she carried with her always.

'All documentation is sealed. It's illegal for either the mother or child to try and find out about the other.'

'Fuck.' There was no other word to summarise all the feelings he was trying to process. 'That's awful.'

'It could have been worse,' she replied with a shrug.

'How? How could it possibly be any worse?'

'Pass me that, would you?' Niamh said as she nodded at where her bag lay discarded on the floor. He picked it up and came across the room to her, holding the bag at arm's length because he still couldn't figure out if she would let him touch her.

Reaching inside, Niamh took out a small leather notebook. It was one she always kept with her, but there was something tucked away in the back cover that she'd never shown anyone at all.

'She left me this,' she said, handing Leo a sheet of folded paper that was worn thin by fingers and time. 'Sister Ingrid gave it to me, though I don't think she was supposed to. It means I wasn't a mistake. It means she loved me, if only for a little while.'

Leo read the words written down over two decades before. Words from a woman to her unborn child, telling her she would have kept her, if only it were possible. It also explained so much about Niamh that Leo had never questioned before, but was now starting to make sense.

'I don't know what to say.' Leo handed the letter back, watching as Niamh folded it in half, then half again and tucked it back in her notebook.

'I wish I could talk to her. Find out what she's like.' Niamh stared out of the window, then at Leo as he sat down next to her. 'Do I look like her? Does she hate cheese as much as I do?'

'You hate cheese?' he asked, tapping out the beginnings of a tune on the piano.

'And mushrooms.'

'Everyone hates mushrooms. That doesn't count.'

She took a long, slow breath, hating the way it caught around her heart. 'Sometimes it hurts so much,' she said, wiping at her eyes and trying to ignore how her hands were shaking. 'It's like I've got this knot of wire trapped in my stomach and every time I think of her it presses tighter.'

'Do you ever think of looking for her?'

Niamh let out a short laugh of exasperation. 'All the time. But where would I even start?'

'What about the nun?' He cocked his head to the side and looked at her. Even through her tears she was the most beautiful girl he'd ever seen. Even more so because of the vulnerability he hadn't before thought was there.

'Sister Ingrid?'

'Yes. She could help.'

'And end up being excommunicated from the Church? I don't think so.'

'If you don't ask, you'll never know.'

Niamh picked at a hangnail on her little finger as she spoke. 'Tell you what, in my next letter to her I'll say you're on your way to shake up the establishment with your pie-in-the-sky idealism.'

'Now you're just taking the piss.' He reached out a hand to poke her in the side and she tried to swat his hand away, but he grabbed hold of it and pulled her along the piano stool to him. 'Your mum would be proud of you,' he said as she dropped her head to his shoulder and he held her close.

'You think?' The words came out barely more than a whisper, but just to hear someone say that, even if it wasn't her, meant more than Leo could ever understand.

'For sure.'

Just like that, a little piece of the wire in her belly wriggled loose. It allowed her, for the first time since forever, to hope that something more, something better, was still to come.

ERIKA
PAINTED TURTLE FIGURINE

London, 2005

The Browne house in the run-up to Christmas is so very similar to the family home back in Stockholm, filled with people and presents and copious amounts of champagne. It is one of my favourite places in the entire world (closely followed by Grandma Nelle's house in the Bahamas), and I probably spend way more time here than would normally be polite. Luckily for me, Layla's family are nothing short of welcoming, always happy to set an extra place at the table and keep your glass topped up to the brim.

At present, there are all manner of people dotted around the kitchen, peeling potatoes, shelling peas and coating an enormous fish in rock salt. My job is to unwrap all the decorations from their tissue-paper cocoons and hang them on the tree by the back window. From here I can eavesdrop on the conversations being passed around like a basket of bread, with the soft timbre of Grandma Nelle's voice acting as a reminder that the family origins are so very far from London.

'It needs more spice,' Nelle says, smacking her lips together and stirring the iced tea with a long silver spoon.

'You mean it needs more rum,' Layla's mum replies with a laugh, touching my arm as she goes to the fridge to take out a handful of herbs. At first glance you wouldn't have thought she and Layla were related, given her porcelain skin and light-blonde hair, but look closer and you can see the same slant to the eyes, the same full lips and wide, open smile.

'You found yourself a fella yet?' Nelle calls out to me and I see Layla give her a gentle whack. 'It's about time you found someone to keep you warm at night.'

'I'll keep you warm,' Layla's brother, Oscar, whispers in my ear and I swat him away because I am more than wise to the dangers of such devilishly handsome men.

'Did I ever tell you about my Swedish godfather?' I say, reaching into the box and taking out a glass bauble dusted with stars. 'He lived up near a lake with nothing but a mad old goat for company. Drunk as a skunk on his homemade *grogg* most of the time, which meant he didn't feel the cold even when it was the arse-end of winter. But he was kind and taught me how to throw the perfect uppercut if ever a boy got too frisky.'

'Has Layla told you about our plans for Paris?' Oscar winks at me before helping himself to a handful of peas. 'I want to open a private members' club within spitting distance of the Palais du Luxembourg.'

'I've already told you,' Layla says. 'It's not really the sort of thing the French would go for.'

'Might be a way for you to ingratiate yourself with the locals,' Oscar replies. 'Plus it would mean you'd finally be earning your keep.'

'You're so annoying.' Layla picks up a piece of bread and chucks it at her brother, who dodges the roll with a grin. 'Erika, hit him with something, would you? Preferably something hard and sharp that will leave a mark.'

126

'I need to go and fetch another box,' I say, picking up the now empty one and heading for the hall. As I do so, I catch the tail-end of a conversation and turn my head to see Christophe at the top of the stairs, leaning against the bannister with his phone clamped to his ear. My French isn't good enough to understand every word, but his tone suggests that the person he is speaking to isn't, as he claimed when he left the kitchen, his boss back in Paris.

'Erika?' he says with a smile as he comes down the stairs, phone still in hand. 'Are you spying on me?'

'Not at all,' I reply, biting back the urge to slap that arrogant look off his face. 'I was just on my way to the garage.'

'Taking out the trash?' He makes no effort to disguise the way his eyes sweep the full length of me.

'Why are you here, Christophe?' I ask as I make my way to the other side of the house, all too aware that he is following. 'It seems like there's somewhere else you'd rather be.'

'What, pass up the chance to help stuff a turkey and listen to Grandma Nelle fart her way through dinner?' he says, spreading his arms wide. 'I'm surprised you're not back in Sweden with your own family. Oh wait,' he says with a smirk. 'I forgot.'

I push open the door to the garage and dump the empty box on top of an old chest freezer, trying to ignore the desire to lock him inside of it.

'You should be more grateful,' Christophe says as he peers through the window of Layla's father's beloved E-Type. 'Without Layla, you'd have nowhere else to go.'

I hate that he knows about my family situation. I also hate the fact he is the reason I barely see my best friend any more.

'There you are.'

We both turn to see Layla approach, a little unsteady on her feet as she's been sampling the rum Grandma Nelle brought with her from the Bahamas. Her hair is like a halo of curls all around her face and her cheeks are flushed a deep pink. She's beautiful and creative and one of the kindest people I've ever known, but I've always feared that wasn't enough for her husband.

'*Ma chère femme*,' Christophe says as he pulls Layla close and kisses her full on the lips, but not before darting a look at me.

'I think I'll leave you to it,' I say as I leave, pausing in the hallway before deciding not to go back to the kitchen. Instead I go into the main living room, which has a vaulted ceiling, deep cream sofas and fresh flowers adorning every surface. There's another, smaller room set behind sliding, panelled doors, which I open to find a reclining chair by the window and a wall of books.

I make my way around the room, stopping to peer at some of the titles and taking down a copy of *Colette*, just like the one I had at university but never got around to reading. Where has all the time gone? What have I actually done during the intervening years, and how did life become so hectic that I never seem to have the time to breathe, let alone 'find a fella' as Grandma Nelle seems to think I should? Except I did find someone, only to push him away.

Putting the book back on the shelf, my eye falls on a stack of CDs. Running my finger along the plastic edges, I stop when I spy one that is all too familiar. Glancing around, I open a cupboard to reveal a sleek, black music system that seems out of keeping with the rest of the décor.

There is no crackle, no gentle hiss before the music begins, which sort of spoils the anticipation. But the music is as rich and powerful as ever, transporting me back to an attic room that was always filled with the sound of a bass guitar and a woman singing about all kinds of love.

'Stevie Nicks,' Layla's mother says as she enters the room and I nod my head in reply. 'Such a beautiful voice.'

'I haven't heard this for years,' I say, turning the CD over and staring at the face of a stranger, but one who reminds me of someone I used to know.

'Is everything OK?' Layla's mother asks, and I suspect she's noticed the tears collecting in my eyes, or the way I can't stop biting down on the inside of my cheek.

'Fine,' I say with a smile, putting the CD back on the shelf. 'Work's pretty full-on at the moment.'

'I do worry about you.'

'There's no need; I'm fine.'

'But still. This time of year can't be easy.'

I wait, listening to the end of the song because I'm already sure of what's coming next.

'Do you not think it might be time to reach out?' she asks, one hand resting on my arm. 'Speak to your mother?'

'I can't.' I can't because I have no idea what I would say, or even if she would listen, if any of them would listen to my side of the story. How long has it been since we were all together back in Sweden? Ten years? It all seemed so perfect, at least for a moment, because looking back on it now, I think that's when everything started to unravel.

Layla's mother tucks a strand of hair behind my ear and the sentiment, the kindness, is just one more reminder that Christophe is right: without Layla I really have nowhere else to be. 'You say that, but families forgive one another eventually.'

I laugh, a bitter note of disappointment and regret. 'That depends on your definition of family. Besides, it's not as if they've ever extended the olive branch to me.' Nobody ever came looking or tried to listen to my side of the story, which tells me exactly how little they all care. I think part of me knew it would happen, that they'd abandon me when they found out what I'd done. But that never stopped me from hoping I might be wrong.

'Perhaps if you told me what happened, I could help? Speak to them on your behalf?'

'That's very kind, but . . .' Before I can finish, Layla bursts into the room, grabs me by the hand and drags me into the garden.

'Layla, stop,' I say as I stumble on the path.

'He's leaving.' Layla is holding on to a bottle of white rum with one hand and swiping at a nearby bush with the other.

'Who? Christophe?' I wrap my cardigan around me and tuck my hands into my armpits. It's freezing out here, but Layla seems oblivious. I watch as she unscrews the bottle and takes three long swallows.

'Says he has to go back to Paris.'

'Why?' I take the bottle from her and sniff at its contents before taking a swig. It's not quite as punchy as some of the other rums Layla's grandparents produce, but it's enough to make every single one of my hairs stand on end.

'Work, of course. He says it's too important to let any of the juniors handle it. I hate being married to a lawyer.'

I think back to the conversation overheard only minutes before. Christophe said something about a promise, or was it a secret? Either way, I can't be sure and so probably best not to say anything to Layla; she's clearly feeling bad enough as it is.

'When's he going?' I hand the bottle back, wincing a little as Layla takes two more swallows.

'Tonight.'

'Tonight? But it's only three days until Christmas.'

'No rest for the wicked. Come on.' Layla heads in the direction of the pool house, brandishing the bottle over her head like some kind of drunken tour guide.

The day is turning, the sky slowly melting from blue to almost black and the path across the lawn is lit by a string of tiny lanterns hanging from overhead branches and swaying in the evening breeze. We pass by the swimming pool, drained and covered for winter but host to all manner of decadent parties when the sun is high in the sky.

At the pool house Layla stops and plops down on to a wooden chair now devoid of any cushions.

'I thought it would be more romantic.'

'What would?' I ask, thinking that baking fish and peeling potatoes isn't exactly the ideal scenario for romance.

'Paris.' Layla slumps forward and I sit down next to her, easing the bottle from her grip and screwing the lid back on. It has been nearly three years since Layla left London to set up home in an *appartement* in Paris, complete with a view of the Eiffel Tower from its balcony. On paper it should have been perfect; in theory she should have been blissfully happy. But Paris, for all its beauty and wonder, has failed to become a real home.

'I thought you found a new studio?' We walked the streets of Montmartre together only a few months ago, searching for a space in which Layla could paint.

'I did.' Layla sits back up and draws her knees into her chest. 'I mean, I have.'

'But it's not working?'

'Nope. Seems that whatever filled Monet and Van Gogh and all those other geniuses with furious inspiration seems to have passed me by.'

I think back to Layla's graduation show, to all those colours that seemed to melt together and create different pictures depending on which angle you looked at the canvas from. I know pretty much nothing about art, but even I could tell how incredible Layla's work is. Or rather, was, because ever since moving to Paris she seems to have become clouded by disappointment and hasn't been able to paint anything she's willing to exhibit.

I blame Christophe. But I can't tell her I think it's her husband who's draining her creativity, who's turning her into someone she doesn't want to be.

'I think you'll find their inspiration came from copious amounts of opioids,' I say as I shuffle close and wrap my arm around her too-skinny frame. 'And absinthe. And probably a load more booze.'

'Not much fun getting shit-faced by myself.' She rests her head on my shoulder and I breathe in the scent of her coconut shampoo.

'I'm sorry.' I'm so sorry I can't be there for her. I'm also sorry that she can't be here, for me.

'Can't you move to Paris?' She tilts her head up to look at me.

'Tempting as that is . . .' I say with a sigh, because the idea of living in Paris with her is like something out of a film. I can picture the two of us walking along the Seine, eating croissants (although I think it's against the law to eat carbs if you're a French woman), drinking vintage champagne and being charmed by all manner of inappropriate men. The reality is, I don't belong in Paris; but then I don't seem to belong anywhere at the moment.

'Promise me you'll come visit again soon?'

'I'll try.'

We sit together a moment, the sound of Bonnie Tyler being played at full blast sneaking out of the house and across to us. It's all so easy, so familiar, being here with Layla and her family, but I know it can't last. I know that the bubble of Christmas will burst in only a few short days and then she will head back to Paris and I will be here, alone.

'What are you doing for New Year?' Layla asks.

'I thought you were going to be in Paris?'

'I've got this sudden urge to do something else. Be someone else.'

'I know the feeling.'

'Then let's do it,' she says, looking up at me like an expectant child. 'You and me. Fly off somewhere without telling anyone. New York, maybe? Or even Sweden? Didn't you used to go skiing in the mountains over New Year?'

'I'd rather be on a beach than freezing my arse off. Speaking of, can we go back inside? I can barely feel my toes.'

'Fine,' she says, not bothering to hide the petulance in her voice. 'One of Oscar's friends is having a house party out near Henley. We can go there instead.'

'Do we have to?' I say as I stand, then help her to her feet. Any friend of Oscar's is bound to be debauched, ostentatious and arrogant beyond belief.

'He went to Oxford, I think. Or was it Cambridge? You might know him.'

Over the years I have learnt people assume that if you went to Oxford, it means you know everyone who ever went there, right back to the thirteenth century when the university was first created. It's a bit like discovering someone comes from Manchester and asking them if they know your friend Kate.

'Insanely gorgeous, judging by his Facebook page. Looks Italian, even though he grew up in London.'

It's like all the air has been sucked from the sky, replaced by a sudden heaviness inside me.

'What's his name?' The chances of it being him, being Leo, are surely close to nothing. But then again, fate and I don't have the best track record when it comes to men.

'Not sure,' she says as we stumble over the lawn and back to the house. 'Something beginning with S maybe? I'll ask Oscar.'

'No. Don't. We can do better than a house party.'

'If you say so.' Layla stops by the back door, turning around and leaning against the wall, her head turned up to the starless sky. 'What if I've made a mistake?'

'About what?' Although I can guess. Or I can at least hope, but that's just me being selfish because I miss her; I miss having her in my life for more than a few days at a time. I miss our Sunday trips to the market, followed by a long, lazy brunch and then an afternoon spent on the sofa watching cheesy films and eating too much cake. Most of all, I miss having someone to take care of, to worry about another life other than my own.

'Do you think Christophe would have moved here for me?'

No, I don't. Because in my experience men are so rarely willing to sacrifice any part of their lives unless it benefits them directly. I blame all the fairy tales that condition young girls to grow up believing they can only achieve a happy ending if a Prince Charming is part of the deal. In contrast, boys grow up reading stories about adventures and generally having fun.

The only person I have ever met who was willing to give up anything of himself for the sake of love is Hector. He used to joke that I wore the trousers in our relationship, that he was the damsel who needed rescuing. Perhaps that's why it didn't work out: because I simply didn't have the courage to try for his version of happily ever after.

'You are allowed to change your mind,' I say, although I doubt Layla would ever leave him. 'Come home?'

'This is one thing I don't think even you can fix,' she says with a drawn-out sigh, then clamps her hand to her mouth before bending over and vomiting into the bushes.

'Come on,' I say, rubbing her back and waiting for her to empty her stomach of all that rum. 'Let's get you to bed.'

Upstairs I help her get undressed, pull a clean t-shirt over her head and wipe a cool flannel over her face. I think she falls asleep even before her head hits the pillow, mouth agape and arms flung out either side. I wonder how many nights have ended this way for her recently, if she's been covering up her sadness with too much wine, and my heart aches for the distance between us, but also because of the person who has taken her so far away from me.

There's a small turtle figurine on her bedside table. I pick it up and trace the thin lines of paint with my finger. I have a near identical one at home. We bought them from a market in the Bahamas the first time I went to visit. The fact it's here makes me wonder if Layla brought it with her from Paris, or whether it's just one more thing she left behind when she moved across the sea.

Duncan and I once had a conversation about inevitability, about how at some point you make a conscious decision to push your life in a certain direction. The three of us sat up late, attempting to be philosophical, but given how much vodka we used to drink, I doubt much of what we said made sense. But ever since, every time I think about what has happened, I can't help but wonder what my life would be like now if I'd chosen differently.

Looking down at Layla, lost in a drunken slumber, I wish she had chosen differently too. It feels like it's happening all over again. That I'm losing all the people I love, one after the other, and there's nothing I can do to stop it.

NIAMH

Gorgonise (v.) – *to have a paralysing effect on someone*

Stockholm, 1995

The three of them were sitting in a room that could only be described as a library. Floor-to-ceiling shelves lined two of the walls, with a huge fireplace and double-height windows on the others. There was a trio of dove-grey sofas set out in a U-shape in front of the fire, with pillows and throws aplenty to keep them warm.

The past week had been spent exploring Stockholm and visiting Christmas markets to buy traditional woven reindeer, and glass baubles to hang on the tree. Niamh had spent most of her waking hours either eating or helping to prepare more food that would be eaten at a later hour. As a result, she was stuffed and well rested, but also feeling a little guilty about being so content.

Erika's parents lived in an enormous red-brick house on the outskirts of Stockholm. All week, there had been a constant stream of visitors, some of whom stayed overnight, but most simply popped in for a glass of champagne and a sliver of gravadlax on thinly sliced rye bread. Niamh liked to sit in the kitchen and lose herself in the unfamiliar scents of a Swedish Christmas. She would help herself from the omnipresent *smörgåsbord* (including cheese, which she ignored, cured meats and pickled herring, which surprisingly she had developed a taste for). There was always somebody on hand to top up her steaming mug of *glögg* and she would amble quite happily through the rest of the house, either in search of a quiet corner in which to read, or simply listening to all the conversations that danced around her.

'What does *smyga* mean?' Niamh asked as she reached forward for another treat from the platter on the coffee table. It was late on Christmas Eve and the house was subdued after hours of eating, drinking and swapping presents from under the tree.

'Hmm?' Erika turned her head, half her face disappearing into a cushion as she did so. They were attempting to watch *Return of the Jedi* because Erika liked the 'little bear people' and Duncan thought it was hilarious that she couldn't actually pronounce the word 'Ewok'.

'*Smyga*,' Niamh repeated, biting down on a star-shaped biscuit and glancing over to where Duncan was barely visible under a furry blanket. His mouth was hanging open and the sound of his snoring was mixing with the swoosh of a lightsabre from the television.

'Why do you ask?'

'You said it earlier. Upstairs in your room when you were getting ready and arguing with your mum.'

'Did I?'

Niamh nodded and licked the salty juices from her fingertips. 'You were talking about the summer. You said, *Jag försöker bara att vara hjälpsam.* And then your mum replied, *Du kan vara så smyga ibland.* I thought it might be "smug", but that doesn't quite make sense because then you said you'd learnt it from her.'

'Since when do you speak Swedish?' Duncan asked with a yawn as he rolled on to his side and reached out an arm for his mug of *glögg*.

'I don't. But Sister Ingrid was Swedish.' Niamh stood up and stretched her arms above her head, feeling the pull of skin at her stomach and wondering if she could possibly fit in another biscuit. 'She used to read me fairy tales and I still remember some of them.'

Duncan and Erika shared a look. So seldom did Niamh talk about her life back home, let alone her life at the convent before she was adopted, that they weren't really sure how to react.

'Plus I did German as part of my Highers, so I can kind of get the gist of what you're all saying.'

'I shall have to be more careful about what I say around you and your enormous brain,' Erika said as she kicked off the rug under which she was cocooned, peeled off her socks and stood up. 'It means sneaky.'

'Why did your mum accuse you of being sneaky?' Duncan drained his mug and lay back down.

Erika clicked her tongue against the roof of her mouth, which the other two both understood to mean that she was irritated at being caught out.

'Because I was trying to do something nice,' she said, picking up the empty mugs and looping her finger through the handles. 'And she thinks I should have asked you first.'

'Asked me what?' Duncan said.

'Not you.' Erika pointed the mugs in Niamh's direction. 'Her.'

'Me?' Either she'd had too much *glögg* or it was far too warm in that room because she was starting to lose track of the conversation.

'Apparently I should have asked whether you wanted to apply for a summer internship.'

'You didn't.' Duncan sat bolt upright, looking between the two girls with a mixture of excitement and fear. 'Did she get in?'

'She has an interview. As do I, but I am sure it is a boot-in.'

'Shoo-in,' Niamh replied as she slowly sat back and tried to process what it was her so-called friend had done. Without her permission. Without even asking what she wanted to do with her time off in the summer. Which was so bloody typical of Erika, so she shouldn't have been that surprised. But this was extreme, even for her.

'It means we can spend the first part of the summer in London and then go inter-railing through Europe.' Erika looked over at Niamh with raised brows, shifting her weight from foot to foot as if she were a small child who needed the loo.

Niamh didn't reply because she was thinking back to when Erika told her about the gap year she had planned with Astrid. A year that would have been spent travelling across Europe, working in bars by the beach and falling in love with unsuitable men. It was a year that never happened, and Niamh couldn't shake the feeling she was being used to fill in the memories Erika thought she would get to make with someone else.

'What am *I* supposed to do?' Duncan slapped Erika on the backside and she pushed him away with her bare foot.

'You already told me you're going on some weird monkey expedition to Cambodia.'

'Am I not even invited?'

'You can't just decide what I'm going to do all summer.' Niamh stood up, then sat back down again. She needed to move, to put her energy into something other than the desire to hit her friend over the head with a cushion, hard and repeatedly.

'What were you planning on doing instead?'

'I don't know, because it's months away. But that's not the point.'

'Then what is the point?' Erika said with a distinct smirk and Niamh picked up the nearest cushion and hurled it in her direction, where it fell to the floor with barely a sound.

'Not only are you *smyga*, you are also *irriterande* and *kontrollerande*.'

'Even I understood what that meant,' Duncan said as Erika went over to sit by Niamh.

'You can stay with me. My parents have an investment flat they sometimes use in Chelsea, so you won't even have to pay any rent.'

Niamh didn't reply, because on the one hand she knew that part of what Erika had done was not due to malice, but rather an irritating desire to fix things. She just wished it wasn't always her that Erika was trying to fix. Was she really so sad and desperate and incapable of figuring anything out for herself that she needed a recalcitrant fairy godmother?

'Look,' Erika said as she crossed one long limb over the other. 'If you really don't want to do it, then just call Charlie and tell him.'

'I will.' Except she no longer had Charlie's business card. Nor could she remember his last name. Neither of which she thought Erika was likely to provide her with, even if she did have the nerve to ask.

'And whilst I am living my best life, you will be sitting all gloomy in Cork. Alone and miserable and wishing you had listened to me.'

She was infuriating because she was right, although Niamh was loath to give her any kind of satisfaction by telling her so. And would it really be so bad, living rent-free in one of the best parts of London?

Leo lived in London. Not that he was part of the decision, or indeed a reason to spend the summer there. Still, Niamh allowed herself, just for a moment, to imagine what it might be like to get up every morning and go to work in an industry she'd never thought was within her reach. How it would feel to try on the cloak of privilege, to rub shoulders with the uber-rich and spend her evenings exploring the city with Leo as her guide.

Of course, she couldn't say any of this to Erika, who would no doubt have her own ideas as to who Niamh should be spending her free time with. Standing up for what felt like the umpteenth time, she went over to the nearest bookcase to pretend she was looking for something to read instead of thinking about a boy.

'Niamh?'

Niamh turned her head at the sound of someone calling her name and saw Erika's mother walking across from the kitchen with a parcel in her hand.

'I'm so sorry,' she said with a smile as she came into the room and cast her gaze over the empty mugs and half-finished platter. 'I put this aside earlier in the week and forgot to give it to you.'

'What is it?' Erika asked as she sprang to her feet and peered over Niamh's shoulder.

'It's not for you,' Erika's mother replied as she guided Niamh over to a desk positioned by the window. She opened a drawer and took out a long silver letter opener and placed it on the desk next to the parcel.

Niamh turned the parcel over. There was a London postmark and the address was written in a familiar hand. She could feel the warmth of him seeping through her, not realising until that moment quite how much she had been missing him.

Two weeks. It had been two weeks since she'd last seen him.

'How did he know where to send it?' she asked to no one in particular. She had told him she was spending the holidays with Erika's family, but nothing more. No details, no specifics of where exactly she was going to be.

'I told him,' Duncan said.

Erika glared at him. 'Why?'

'Why not?' Erika's mother asked and her daughter fell silent, because there was no real justification for her being so against Niamh's relationship with Leo.

'What is it that you so dislike about Leo?' Duncan said, no doubt fuelled by *glögg*, as he'd never normally push Erika so openly for an answer, one they both knew she wouldn't want to give.

'I don't dislike him.' Erika ran her fingertip along the length of the fireplace, inspecting it for dust that she knew wouldn't be there.

'Which means you are jealous,' her mother said with a small laugh. 'God forbid one of your friends should dare to fall in love with someone other than you.'

'*För guds skull,*' Erika said, kicking at the fireplace like a petulant child. 'I get it. Thank you for reminding me all over again what a terrible person I am.'

'Oh, *älskling.*' Erika's mother came across and laid her hand on her shoulder, only for Erika to shrug her off. 'At some point you have to forgive yourself for what happened and move on with your life. It's what Astrid would have wanted.' She tilted her head to try and catch her daughter's gaze, then sighed and turned to leave the room, calling over her shoulder to the others, 'There's more food and champagne in the kitchen. Do please help yourselves.'

'You see what I have to put up with?' Erika said once her mother was barely out of earshot. 'The woman's a monster.'

'She adores you,' Duncan said. 'And yet all you do is push her away.'

'A psychology degree doesn't make you Freud. Pass the *kanel-bullar*, would you?'

'How can you possibly eat another thing?'

'Years of practice. Come on,' she said as she pulled at Duncan's jumper and poked him in the ribs. 'We need to fatten you up a bit. Put some meat on those bones.'

'Get off.' Duncan squirmed and laughed as she continued to prod at him, trying unsuccessfully to push her off the sofa and on to the floor.

'Leave him alone,' Niamh said, not taking her eyes off the gift she had received. It was a hardback book, bound in white leather with silver stars embossed into the cover and along the spine.

'Show me.' Erika pushed herself away from Duncan and climbed over the back of the sofa. *'Little Women.'* She read the title of the book Niamh was staring at, watching as she opened the accompanying card, which had a simple picture of an angel on the front.

Merry Christmas to the one who has well and truly gorgonised me. Leo x

'Gorgonise?' Erika said, snatching the card from Niamh and reading it for herself.

'It means to have a paralysing effect on someone.' It was a word she had learnt years ago, when reading the legend of Medusa. The fact Leo thought he was using it in an affectionate way made her giggle.

'Seems someone's finally lost her cherry.'

'So?' Niamh asked, although the insinuation was clear. Why else would Leo buy her such a thoughtful, personal gift unless she'd given him the only thing he could possibly want from her? After all, Erika had warned her from the very beginning that boys in general are only after one thing.

'I can't believe we haven't even met him properly yet,' Duncan said. 'It's like you're ashamed of us or something.'

'It's not that,' Niamh said, darting a look at her friends.

'Then what?' Erika asked.

'I just . . .' Niamh hesitated, knowing that she couldn't tell Erika the real reason. That the idea of Leo meeting Erika was terrifying because she had this annoying habit of making boys fall in love with her. 'It's all so new to me. I promise you'll meet him when we head back to Oxford.'

Erika gave a non-committal sort of huff then announced she was going to get more drinks.

'It's hard for her, being back here.' Duncan went over to the back wall of shelves, picking up a photo frame and handing it to Niamh.

'Doesn't mean she's allowed to be such a bitch.' She looked at the photograph of Erika and Astrid. At a guess, she would have said they were about sixteen, which meant it couldn't have been taken long before Astrid died. In the photo, Erika was kissing Astrid on the cheek and she in turn was smiling, showing off her dimples.

'Why did her mum say she had to forgive herself for what happened? It's not Erika's fault Astrid had an aneurism.'

'Is that what she told you?' Duncan said with half a smile before peering over his shoulder and out into the hall. 'She drowned.'

'Drowned?'

'In the lake, up by their summer house.'

'But that still doesn't make it Erika's fault.'

Duncan hesitated, looking from Niamh to the photograph, out to the hall and back to Niamh. 'Look, I shouldn't be telling you this.'

'You can't not tell me now.'

'Fine.' Duncan let out an overly dramatic sigh as he flopped on to the nearest chair. 'So there was a boy.'

'Of course there was a boy.'

'Do you want me to tell you or not?' Duncan took a packet of tobacco out of his pocket and started rolling a cigarette. Niamh glanced out of the window, thinking it was somewhere between brave and stupid to even consider going out in the cold for a smoke, but she wasn't going to risk interrupting him again. Not when he was about to tell her something that Erika clearly didn't think Niamh should know. Which was a little hurtful, if Niamh was honest, as it suggested she wasn't as close to Erika as she thought.

'Erika's family used to spend every summer up at the lakes, and Astrid always went too.' He licked the edge of the cigarette paper before rolling it into a tight, slim cylinder. 'That year Erika fell hard for a boy called Patrik. Problem was, so did Astrid.'

'Let me guess,' Niamh said. 'He chose Astrid.'

'Bingo,' Duncan said, pointing the roll-up at her. 'But they decided not to tell Erika.'

'Ah.'

'Ah, indeed.'

'So how did Erika find out?'

Duncan ran the roll-up under his nose, then tucked it behind one ear. 'She invited Astrid to go for a swim, out to one of the islets that are dotted around the lakes. Astrid was nervous, but Erika persuaded her it would be fun. And once they were on the islet, Astrid told Erika about Patrik.'

'How do you know all this?'

Duncan shrugged, which meant that there were some parts of the story Niamh knew he'd never tell. 'It came out one night when neither of us could sleep. Anyway,' he went on, crossing one long limb over the other and stifling a yawn, 'they argued then Erika ran off and swam back to shore. Erika knew Astrid wasn't a strong swimmer. She should have waited to make sure she was OK.'

Niamh put the photo back on the shelf, next to dozens of others capturing so many moments of a friendship that spanned a whole lifetime. No wonder it was so difficult for Erika to come home. Everywhere she looked there were reminders of the person whose death she felt responsible for.

'She never told me.'

Duncan raised one eyebrow. 'Well, she wouldn't, would she? You know how intensely proud she can be.'

'Huh.'

'What?'

'That's exactly what Leo said about her.'

'Stop worrying,' Duncan said. 'Even if she did fancy him, Erika would never do that to you.'

'It's not her I'm worried about.'

'You really like him, don't you?' Duncan said as he watched Niamh flicking through the pages of *Little Women* with a distracted look on her face.

Niamh looked over at him as she perched on the edge of the desk, then peered through the glass and out to the never-ending darkness beyond.

'Part of me wishes I didn't.'

'Why would you say that?'

'Because what if he doesn't feel the same way?'

Duncan pointed over at the desk. 'If someone sends you a limited edition of your favourite book, all the way to Sweden, it means they like you.'

'I guess. But what if it all goes wrong?'

'Then it all goes wrong. Erika and I will be here for you, no matter what.'

Niamh rubbed her hands over her face, trying to get rid of the doubts that were bubbling away inside her mind.

'I can't imagine Erika would be too upset if it didn't work out.'

'If you were sad, she would be sad. Although if he ever hurt you, I would probably warn him to run as far away as possible.'

Niamh managed half a smile as she imagined Erika chasing Leo down the street, no doubt brandishing an axe and wearing a Viking helmet for added emphasis. The smile disappeared when she thought about how it might feel if Leo was no longer part of her life.

'Sometimes it feels like I can't breathe when I'm around him.'

'That's perfectly normal when you love someone. At least, so I've been told.'

Love. Such a simple yet complicated word. It could mean so many different things, like loving ice cream or your dog. But loving another person wasn't something Niamh had ever really come across before. OK, so she probably did love Duncan, and even Erika, despite her infuriating ways. But the way she felt about Leo was so much more in every conceivable way. She had a physical reaction every time she thought about him or lay under the covers at night, wishing he was there beside her.

One minute you're single, thinking only of yourself and whether you can track down a diary in order to finish the first essay of term. The next minute you're staying with your best friend's parents, being welcomed into their incredible life, but all you can think about is how much you wish he was there.

The vulnerability of her heart made her tremble, because just like he had opened it up, so too could he rip it apart so deeply that she might never recover from the pain.

'They're putting Musse Pigg on next door,' Erika said as she came back into the room carrying her youngest cousin, who was half asleep and sucking her thumb.

'Musty pig?' Duncan asked.

'It's a weird Swedish tradition of watching Mickey Mouse or Donald Duck. I have no idea where it comes from, but we are all in the living room if you want to join?' She looked over at Niamh with another question behind her eyes, one hand absently stroking her cousin's head.

It made Niamh think about how naturally Erika took on the maternal role, how much it seemed to suit her. She did it with her and Duncan all the time – fussing over them when they had a cold, making sure they were eating properly and always worrying about the future. It was suffocating, but in a way Niamh also quite liked it, because her adoptive parents had always been rather distant.

But there was another side to Erika, one Niamh had always done her best to ignore. That desire to always win, to always get what she wanted, no matter the consequences. She may not have been directly responsible for Astrid's death, but Erika still put her own feelings, her own pride, before her friend. If she'd done it before, Niamh knew she would probably do it again.

'I propose a toast,' Duncan said with a grin as he got, rather unsteadily, to his feet and raised his drink. 'May we never forget how completely and utterly perfect the three of us are and,' he went on with a deliberate wink at Niamh, 'may we never be afraid to fall in love.'

'He has to prove that he is good enough.' Erika nodded at the book before leaving the room.

'For me or you?'

'All three of us,' Erika called over her shoulder. 'We come as a parcel deal.'

'Package,' Niamh said with a barely stifled yawn. 'I think I'm going to call it a night.'

'OK,' Erika said, blowing Niamh a kiss goodnight. 'But remember we are going to visit my uncle tomorrow. You'll need an extra layer as it's always bloody freezing at his house.'

ERIKA

Miniature Silver Key

France, 2003

The chateau is perched at the edge of the Loire Valley, complete with hand-painted walls copied from Versailles, manicured gardens, opulent furnishings and marble statues around every corner.

The wedding party is most definitely in full swing, with several guests having headed out to the countryside at the beginning of the week in anticipation of all the revelry to come. Both families have thrown their full weight and bank balances behind the celebration, like an unspoken competition as to who could be the most generous, the most lavish with their affections.

The bride has been at the centre of it all, giddy with love and nerves as everyone she holds dear has come together to witness her big day. I didn't get here until Wednesday evening, jet-lagged and apologetic for being late, again. I found Layla and her brother playing tennis on the floodlit courts, batting insults back and forth with every shot. That in itself wasn't unusual, more the fact Layla was doing so whilst wearing nothing but a bikini and smoking a cigar.

Luckily the gown she has chosen for the day itself is less revealing, with a lace-panelled bustier and layer upon layer of froth under the skirt. It makes her look a little like the Sugarplum Fairy and reminds me of another dress discovered in a shop on the King's Road, but it is perfect for the hopeless romantic that my best friend will always be.

It's now the night before, and everyone has gathered for one last meal before supposedly getting a good night's rest. Trestle tables have been set up on the sprawling terrace, with a veritable feast laid out from which people can help themselves. The band is playing tunes of old and everywhere you look there are waiters carrying silver trays of champagne.

A warm breeze climbs up the terrace, bringing with it the cloying scent of roses from the dozens of plants that surround the chateau on three sides. I would like nothing more than to escape to the stillness of my room, but I know it would be rude for the chief bridesmaid to disappear so early on.

'Mademoiselle?' A waiter appears at my side, proffering a tray of drinks and I take one with a smile and a *merci*, noticing both the line of sweat at his brow and a shaving cut on his throat. It's the same waiter Layla was flirting with last night, during a rather raucous and drunken game of poker.

Something is going on between Layla and Christophe, but I haven't been able to find a moment alone with the bride-to-be in order to ask exactly what the issue is. I think she's avoiding me, and not just because I arrived two days late.

I sip my champagne, enjoying the cool crispness of the bubbles that always taste better in summer. Looking beyond the terrace, I see a couple disappearing behind one of the topiary bushes, one of whom looks suspiciously like Christophe, but I only caught the back of his head, so it could just be my subconscious showing me things that aren't really there. The woman's laughter hovers in the air even after she is out of sight. Everywhere I turn there are people, all of whom are far too busy enjoying themselves to notice that the groom is quite possibly playing away.

I need to find Layla. I need to talk to her, find out if she shares my suspicions. Last time I saw her she was heading upstairs to change, but that was ages ago and I can't see her anywhere out here. Which means she's either hiding, or passed out on the bed, as she has been known to do.

Inside the chateau all is calm and still, other than waiters gliding along the corridor with empty glasses. Something else too, a sound I'm not accustomed to hearing but recognise in an instant. The soft wail of a child, the call rising and falling like the beam of a lighthouse that disappears at the end of each turn.

I follow the sound, peering into rooms filled with furniture but empty of people. Moving along the corridor, I hesitate before stepping inside the next room. A young mother is lying on a mustard-yellow sofa, her head resting on the arm and her eyes closed. She's awake though, I can tell by the way her fingers are curling and uncurling into fists, along with the constant twitch of her feet, which are clad in silver stilettoes.

The noise culprit is lying between his mother's legs, eyes screwed up tight and both legs pumping in annoyance. His face is a deep shade of pink and the material of the sofa either side of his head is damp with tears.

'Excuse me?' I knock gently on the door, then a little louder as I don't think I can be heard above the baby's wails. 'Are you OK?'

'Not really.' The woman's voice comes out cracked and broken, along with a fat tear that she hastily wipes away. 'He won't stop crying.'

This is something of an understatement, but I know better than to attempt sarcasm with a sleep-deprived mother.

'How old is he?' I ask, edging closer and seeing how mother and child share the same dark, almost black, hair. Hers is like a sleek wave of ebony, tumbling over the back of the sofa, whilst his is sticking up in tufts all over his head.

'Six months,' she says through a heavy sigh, shifting her weight as she sits up. The baby decides this gives him permission to complain all over again, but he startles at the sight of me squatting down by his side. He stares at me, unsure how he's supposed to react to a stranger.

'What's his name?' I smile at him as he turns his head to the side with his mouth half open as if he can't decide whether he should still be crying.

'Leonardo. We call him Leo, for short.'

He is the first Leo I have come across since. It shouldn't really be so much of a surprise, but the shock is enough to make me draw breath.

Slowly, I reach out a finger, easing it towards Leo's little face, then slip it inside his palm. I smile as he grips it tight. A moment more and he brings his fist and my finger to his mouth, two wet lips sucking at skin.

'Is he hungry?' I frown at the mother, who is watching me with a mixture of curiosity and gratitude.

'All the bloody time,' she says with a painful laugh. 'But he won't eat, he just wants milk. Which isn't enough and so he cries. All night long. I'm so frickin' tired.'

'Sounds like you need a break,' I say, easing Leo into a sitting position and he twists his head to look at his mother, then back to me.

'He seems to like you,' Leo's mother says with a yawn.

'Why don't I look after him for a bit?' I have no idea why I've made such an offer, but his little wrists are so squidgy and gorgeous and I really don't want to say goodbye just yet.

'Why would you do that?'

Good question. One that I think I know the answer to, but it is far too convoluted to explain, especially to someone who I've only just met.

'Honestly, I don't mind. I could take him for a walk around the gardens. Fresh air might make him forget whatever it is he's so pissed off about.'

'Are you sure?' Leo's mother is already on her feet, peering in a nearby mirror and pushing back her eyelashes with the tips of her fingers. 'I mean, wouldn't you rather be enjoying the party?'

Actually, no. I would far rather be here, playing childhood games and singing nursery rhymes to the most adorable of creatures. It's a little peculiar, this desire for domesticity, not least because I have done my best to avoid it at all costs. But babies are such helpless, innocent things and this Leo knows nothing about me or my secrets, which means we should get along just fine.

'I think you need it more than I do,' I say with my most reassuring smile.

She hesitates a moment, no doubt grappling with the decision as to whether she should leave her child with a virtual stranger. Then she takes a long, deliberate breath, kisses her son goodbye and half walks, half runs from the room, the sound of her heels echoing all the way along the corridor and outside.

'Come on then,' I say as I strap a discarded Baby Björn around my waist and hoist Leo inside, making sure he's facing out. His little arms and legs begin to pump with excitement and I place a gentle kiss on his downy hair then whisper in his ear, 'Let's go for a walk, see if we can't find some fairies hiding in the trees.'

For a second I think of Layla and Christophe, and my original plan. But then Leo lets out a shout of annoyance and I figure that I should try to steer clear of any marital disputes.

Overhead the sky is clear, with a moon bright enough to show us the way. As we reach the edge of the gardens I notice the long beam of a car's headlights making its way up the drive. My hand curls around the iron frame of the gate as I wait to see if the approaching guest is who my heart wants it to be.

As the car door opens and the passenger gets out, I feel my gut tighten in reply. I knew he was coming. Layla had the decency to warn me, along with a not-so-subtle piece of information that both myself and Hector are currently single.

What I didn't know was how it would feel to see him again after so many years. I could hide, but it wouldn't be fair to subject Leo to a face full of twigs and leaves. Besides which, he would probably scream and let everyone know where I am. Or I could run, well, walk quickly, back to the chateau and hope he hasn't seen me,

But he has seen me. Even though I can't see his face clearly, I can tell because his hand is still holding on to the top of the taxi door and his body is turned towards me, lit up by the car's full beam and making Leo squirm in annoyance.

'You have a baby,' Hector says as he walks up to me, accompanied by the soft crunch of gravel.

'He's not mine,' I say as I take in the sight of him.

'I'm assuming you haven't stolen him?' He's smiling. It's a smile that stretches the full width of his face and Leo lets out a shout of delight.

I know, little one. He's rather scrumptious, and yet I was stupid enough to let him go. But it was for the best; it was to protect him, as well as me.

I let out a small laugh, because of all the situations I have turned over in my mind, coming face to face with Hector whilst carrying someone else's baby has not been one of them.

'I took pity on an exhausted mother.' I glance back in the direction of the chateau, from where the sound of music and laughter is echoing across to us.

'How's the party?' Hector says, tickling Leo under the chin and moving close enough for me to see the stubble on his cheek.

'Good.' It's all I can manage as I try to swallow away the lump in my throat, wishing I had another glass of champagne to hand.

'Sorry I'm late.' His gaze travels all over my face. 'I got a bit lost in Paris. Missed my train.'

I can't help but smile, because it is so very like Hector to get lost. I can imagine him wandering the streets around the Sacré-Coeur, or sitting in front of Monet's water lilies and forgetting to check the time. We were supposed to go there together, before I broke us apart.

'You look incredible,' he says, finally bending down to kiss me on the cheek. His lips hover close enough to mine that all I would have to do is move my head a fraction to the right.

'You look exactly the same.' I step back, wrapping my hands around Leo's middle and contemplating the man standing only inches away. His clothes are more fitted, his hair cropped a little shorter, and the watch around his wrist is new. But the way he's looking at me is the same as always.

'I should get back,' I say, setting off towards the chateau and not waiting to find out if he's following.

'Is this yours?' He falls into step beside me, a leather holdall in one hand and a tiny silver key resting in the palm of the other. 'It was back there, on the ground.'

'Nope.'

'What do you think it's for?' he asks, holding the key up to the sky as if the light of the moon might reveal its secrets.

'Who knows?' I point to my right where a series of outbuildings are clustered together. 'This place is crawling with cellars and secret passageways.'

'Bit small for a door though.'

'Unless you're Alice.'

I stop as we reach the steps leading up to the terrace, searching the party for Leo's mother. There she is, right in the centre of the dance floor, arms raised above her head. I feel bad for disturbing her moment of reckless abandonment, but Leo's head is resting against my chest and he keeps rubbing at his eyes.

'Probably just something left over from another wedding,' Hector says as he slips the key inside his pocket.

'Probably.'

'Or maybe it's the key to your heart.' He bumps his hip against mine and stares down at me with a lopsided grin.

'That's the corniest line I've heard in years.' I dutifully roll my eyes at his terrible pun, but I can't deny how the way he's looking at me has reignited something that's been missing for what feels like a lifetime.

'I've plenty more,' he says, leaning a little closer. 'If you're interested?'

The song that's playing begins to fade, swiftly replaced by the opening nine notes to a song that immediately takes me back to Oxford. Within seconds the dance floor's population has doubled in number, with dozens of bodies flailing about to Pulp's 'Disco 2000'.

Everyone always gets so giddy about nostalgia, thinking back to a time when life seemed so much better than it really was. Because the past is never what you believe it to be, and going back there would be a terrible idea, no matter how much I still care about Hector.

'I'm sorry to hear about you and Rachel,' I say, thinking of how excited Layla was to share that morsel of gossip via email.

'No, you're not,' he says with another grin.

'I heard she was rather sweet.'

'She was. Complete opposite to you, which was kind of the point.'

He's looking at me in that way of his, but I must not meet his eye, because I can already sense in which direction he's trying to steer the conversation. I never explained why I broke up with him. At least not properly, because I didn't know how to. One minute we were blissfully, irritatingly happy, the next he's trying to plan a future so perfect that it made me feel physically sick at the possibility it might all be taken away. So I destroyed it. Purposefully destroyed what we had before it could destroy me.

I owe him, I know that, and enough time has passed that he might actually have forgiven me. Question is, have I managed to forgive myself?

'I read your book,' I say, deliberately changing the subject as I raise a hand to wave at Leo's mother. She squints back in our direction, then drains her glass and looks around for somewhere to leave it.

'You did? Did you like it?'

It's a simple enough question, for a simple enough story. One that's been told a thousand times before. But he managed to wind through some of the whimsy and magic of fairy tales past, which I admit was a welcome surprise.

'Would it have been better if she died at the end?'

'She did in the original version. But my agent said the reader would want a happily ever after.' He helps me undo the straps of the Björn and lifts Leo out.

'Do they even exist?' To anyone who might be watching, we must look like the epitome of the perfect family. It's what Hector always said he wanted with me, but even now I don't know if I would have ever been capable of giving it to him.

'They could,' he says, watching as Leo snuggles under my chin and I instinctively begin to rock back and forth. 'If you gave one a chance.'

'You should head inside,' I say, climbing the steps and heading towards Leo's mother. 'Find someone to show you your room.'

'Where's your room?' he calls after me and I hesitate, knowing that he's given the choice to me.

I turn around, and the honesty of his gaze is enough to undo all of my resolve.

'First floor. End of the hall on the left.'

I have always loved watching him sleep. The way he looks so completely at peace, no matter how stressful his day might have been. I have witnessed him sleep through thunderstorms and police sirens, raucous neighbourhood parties and midnight fireworks. I, on the other hand, am a fitful, restless sleeper. As a child I would often wake to discover I was curled at the bottom of the bed, trapped beneath the sheets, dreaming of a serpent that was trying to devour me in a single bite.

Glancing at my watch, I see that it's a little after five a.m. I could get up, search the chateau for some strong, black coffee and check through all the emails that have been piling up ever since I left New York. Or I could try to go back to sleep, which wouldn't be a bad thing given that in only a few short hours I need to be bright and breezy and super excited about my best friend's wedding.

Shit. Layla. I never did go and find her. I hope she's not mad at me for leaving the party early. Although if she discovered the reason, there's a risk she might suggest we make today a double celebration.

She has always been such a huge fan of Hector. And so was I, which is precisely why this is a very big, very messy mistake.

It doesn't mean anything. I am categorically not going to fall for him all over again. But is it possible to fall *in* love if, technically,

158

you've never actually been out of it? What is it with weddings and how they make you behave in strange and unexpected ways? It's like they exist outside the realm of normality, and whatever happens as a result of all the happiness and champagne is nothing more than a page torn from a storybook.

But he is so very lovely. And ridiculously talented in bed. I'd forgotten just how talented, or maybe I'm kidding myself and knew all along, which is why nobody since has made it past the third date.

It's been a very long time with nobody to share my bed, let alone my life. But is going back the safe option, or the dangerous one? I've already been questioning how much longer I can stay in New York with nothing more than work to occupy my time. At the moment, it feels like I'm simply going through the motions of being happy, because on the surface, at least, I portray all the signs of being that way. But coming home to nothing other than the monotonous sound of an empty fridge is enough to make me wonder if I would be better off back in London.

I need to think, which is impossible when he's lying there, naked and so very tempting.

Hunting in my suitcase, I take out my iPod and trainers, then head to the bathroom to get changed. When I come back into the bedroom, Hector is half-awake and on his side, watching me.

'Are you seriously going for a run?'

'Can't sleep.' I hover in the doorway like a child caught doing something they shouldn't. He knows I run to clear my head, to set straight all the voices in my mind asking me to do something I don't want to.

'Come back to bed.'

I inch closer and sit on the very end of the bed, hands folded in my lap and doing my utmost not to stare at his torso, or the tattoo that curls around his bicep. Those arms were wrapped around me last night, holding me close and making me believe that giving in to him was the right thing to do.

'If I do that,' I say, making no effort to stop him as he pulls me back down and nuzzles my neck. 'I might never leave.'

'You say that like it's a bad thing.' His hands are under my top, teasing my skin and muddling my thoughts.

'Hector,' I say, moving his hands away.

His head drops, along with my heart because at this precise moment I think I might hate myself even more than he does.

'I live in New York.'

'So?'

'And I can't give you what you want.'

'How do you even know what that is, Erika?'

'You want the happily ever after.'

'I think you do, too. You're just too scared to admit it.'

Up until that point, I was beginning to think it might be different. I even allowed myself to imagine what it might be like to have Hector in my life, fully in my life. It was so easy to fall back into bed with him, but reality always hits hardest when the morning shows itself in all its glory.

'I saw how you were with Leo.'

'What?' My head snaps round, because I'm certain I've never said anything to him. And yet that name is enough to make me scan through all the conversations we've ever had, all the moments when I might have inadvertently let something slip.

'Motherhood would suit you. It would suit us.'

He's talking about the baby, which in a way only makes things worse.

'I can't have kids, Hector.'

'With anyone, or is it just me you're so against the idea of having a future with?'

He is angry with me, really angry, and it's completely fair because I willingly opened myself up to him, only to snap back shut at the first sign of commitment.

I need to stop. I need to find a way out of this whole sorry mess, but there's a knot inside my heart that's swelling and pinching and making my eyes leak.

'Shit.' Hector jumps out of bed and crouches down in front of me. 'Oh Christ, Erika, please don't cry. You never cry.'

'What if I gave it all up for nothing?' Now I've started, I don't seem able to stop. It's like the knot in my heart has been waiting for one small gap to push through and out, spilling all my secrets and fears like milk from a bottle.

'Are we still talking about us?'

I can't give him the answer he deserves. It's too late for us, even though he's as close to perfect as anyone is ever going to get. Except for one small, absolutely crucial detail that I seem incapable of forgetting.

'I have to go,' I say, pushing him away and heading for the door.

NIAMH

Mamihlapinatapai (n.) – *a look between two people that suggests an unspoken, shared desire*

Oxford, 1996

Niamh had woken early that morning, peeling back the curtains to stare at a silver sky struggling towards spring. Leo was curled up next to her, one arm trapping her between him and the wall so that she was unable to move without disturbing him. The only problem was, she really needed to pee. A few minutes more and it was no good, so she wriggled out from underneath his arm, then scooted all the way to the end of the bed and on to the floor. She looked around in the half-light, picking up one of Leo's hoodies and tiptoeing from the room.

As she descended a flight of stone steps down to the bathroom, she brought the cuff of the hoody up to her face and inhaled deeply. It smelt of him: not just his aftershave, but that unique scent everyone has. Which was why she had been borrowing something of his every morning when she left for the library, so that she might have him with her always. It was sickening, the fact she'd turned into one of those soppy, lovelorn creatures who would gaze out of the window whilst doodling hearts and flowers all over her notes.

Only yesterday, when she was supposed to be reading up on the French Revolution, she found herself distracted by the idea of Leo riding through the countryside like some ridiculous hero from an Austen novel.

What had happened to her? She perched on the freezing loo seat and stared up at a mass of cobwebs overhead. There was no spider to be seen and it made her nervous, because they could be sneaky little buggers and she pulled the collar of the hoody a little tighter round her neck.

The morning air swirled around her legs as she washed her hands then climbed back up the stairs. At the top she paused, taking a moment to breathe in the quiet. There was no one else about; Saturday mornings were a precious chance for a lie-in, with no lectures or tutorials. It was only the hard-nosed rowers who made an appearance much before noon, when the quads would thrum to life, everyone making plans as to how the afternoon should be filled before piling into the beer cellar come opening time at six.

It made her think of her childhood, the one before she was moved across the country to live in a cul-de-sac with two well-meaning but distinctly aloof strangers. Back in the convent, they would be woken each morning at dawn, with prayers before breakfast and then a walk around the grounds or down to the beach. It was freezing in winter, not much warmer in summer, but those morning walks always managed to push aside the nightmares that found her every night.

Ever since, she had been a morning person. Years of the same routine set her body clock to always wake by six, no matter what time she went to sleep. Sometimes the idea of all the freedom she now had was overwhelming. The ability to make her own decisions and not be reliant on anybody else at all was something she had dreamt of for so long. But now she had it, she was afraid of making a mistake. Nor could she shake the idea that everything she was doing was setting her on a course which she could neither predict nor control.

How much of that fear was to do with Leo, she couldn't quite tell. But she knew he was playing his part, albeit inadvertently. Because nobody sets out to have such a profound impact on another's life, do they?

Back in his room, she perched on the end of the bed, staring at his face that looked so much younger when he slept, despite the stubble dotted across his jaw. She peeled the duvet back a little, tracing her fingers down his spine and circling the mole on his right shoulder blade before bending to kiss it.

'Morning, sleepyhead,' she whispered against his neck, sneaking her hand around his waist and down. He rolled on to his back and blinked up at her as she straddled him.

'I got you something.' She pushed his hand away from her arse and reached under the bed for her overnight bag (which was fast becoming something of a permanent feature). Heaving it on to the duvet, she took out a present wrapped in a bright-red bow.

'What is it?' Leo asked as he sat up and Niamh shuffled out of the way. He turned the present over, giving it a little shake.

'No, don't.' Niamh put her hand out to stop him from shaking the present again.

'So it's breakable?' Leo bent his head and took a long sniff.

'Would you just open it?' It was infuriating, his need to try to guess what was inside.

'Patience, patience,' Leo said with a grin, knowing full well that she had so very little of it. If the roles were reversed, she would have torn into the wrapping paper the moment he handed it over.

Slowly and with deliberate care, he undid the bow then peeled off each piece of Sellotape in turn. Whenever she reached out a hand to try to speed up the process, he would stick his toes into her thigh or hold the present above his head. Before long, it turned into a wrestling match and Niamh found herself flat on her back with both arms pinned above her head.

The sight of her all flustered and annoyed was enough to make Leo completely forget about the unexpected present that was lying on the floor. She was addictively intense, or was it intensely addictive? Either way, he was suddenly overcome by the understanding that this was another of those moments he would remember for the rest of his life. It came out of nowhere, smacking him clean between the eyes, and the words spilt out before he had a chance to consider whether it was the right time.

'I love you,' he said as he sat back on his heels.

'You do?' Niamh pushed herself up on her elbows, not quite sure how to respond to the sight of him, stark-bollock naked and with a strange look of disbelief on his face.

'I do.' He was certain, even more so than the night he'd first laid eyes on her. It was a feeling bigger than anything else, even sex, which with her had become almost transcendent. The feeling of never quite being able to get close enough to someone was terrifying in its enormity, and he knew that by telling her how he felt, he was risking the best thing he'd ever had.

Did he mean it? Niamh thought to herself. The doubt was there, front and centre, forbidding her from actually drinking in his admission of love. Did she love him back? Surely she must, because how else to describe the raw need she had for him? How else to understand the way in which her body came alive whenever he kissed her?

She had spent so much time as a child either asking for forgiveness or worrying about all the ways in which it was possible for a person to commit a sin. It made her nervous and shy, unsure of the world around her. So she would hide in her room, lose herself in a book or music and block out all the reasons why she wasn't enough. It became her way to forget, if only for an hour or two, that she had been so easily given up by the one person who was supposed to love her the most.

The end result, even after she had been adopted, was that she believed herself incapable of love, of being loved. Nobody had ever said those three words to her before, and so she had no idea what to do with them.

She wasn't saying anything, just lying there with an unfamiliar expression on her face. He could almost see the cogs of her mind turning over all the possible things she could say.

What if she didn't love him in return?

The idea that she had the power to take it all away, leave him empty and without purpose, made him wipe his hand over his face, then fall back down and kiss away her chance to reply.

'It's your turn.'

'Hmm?' Niamh said as her eyes came back to focus on her friend.

'What's with you today?' Erika asked, leaning against the end of the pool table and peering at Niamh. 'You're being a total space cadet.'

Niamh smiled, not just at Erika's use of a term she herself had introduced her to, but because of the reason she had been incapable of concentrating on anything at all since that morning. The memory of those words, not just the sound of Leo's voice or the way he had looked at her when he'd said them, but the way in which they'd snuck inside her, almost like osmosis, feeding her soul and opening up another part of her that she didn't even know existed. It was exhilarating, but also more than a little terrifying because Niamh had no idea whether she should have said them back straight away. She loved him. It wasn't a conscious decision, or even something she had given much consideration to, but rather an understanding that was there as soon as she looked for it.

But it changed everything. Love as a concept, as an idea, was so unfathomable to her, but to have it take root in her body as well as her mind meant she had no idea what was supposed to happen next.

'Nothing,' she said, bending forward to take aim and then depositing the eight ball in the far corner pocket. 'As you can see, I'm still perfectly capable of kicking your sweet little ass.'

'Nice shot,' Erika said, although Niamh knew she was annoyed at losing. 'Another game?'

'I guess,' Niamh said, glancing at her watch.

'Am I boring you?' Erika asked. 'Because if there's somewhere else you'd rather be . . .?' She left the question open, although really it was more of an accusation because Niamh had been spending so little time in her own bed, or with her friends, since meeting Leo. It stung, given how Erika had practically lived with Peter when they first got together, but Niamh had no desire to pick a fight with her best friend, least of all over a boy.

'What? No. Just hungry,' Niamh replied, looking over at the bar just as the pub door opened and a gaggle of glossy girls came in, teetering on heels and tossing their hair like thoroughbreds at a racecourse. 'Can we go?'

'You don't have to be scared of them,' Erika said as she grabbed Niamh's hand and headed for the bar.

'I'm not. It's just . . .' Niamh wasn't sure what it was, other than the way girls like that made her feel inadequate.

The group that had just come in were no different to Octavia and her lackeys, all wearing skinny black jeans and tighter-than-tight t-shirts, the bags over their arms and the watches on their wrists all designer.

It reminded Niamh of what Erika had said to her at the careers fair, about learning to play the game in order to fit in, and once more Niamh couldn't help but feel that she would always be left on the outside looking in.

How did you learn to be a certain way, and how much of it was simply a result of what you were born into? Was it absorbed by fashion symbiosis, or was it taught by a mother who never had a crease or stain on her clothes, let alone a chipped nail or lipstick on her teeth? It made Niamh want to go back and experience something of Leo's childhood to see if he was the sort of boy who was ever allowed to get mud on his shorts or leaves stuck in his hair.

The thought of him made her relax a little, so when the door opened again and he walked through, bringing with him a scattering of rain, she visibly flinched at the surprise.

'What's he doing here?' Niamh said as they approached the bar.

'Who?' Erika replied, standing on tiptoe and scanning the room. Niamh did the same, searching for an escape route rather than a person. Glancing at Erika, then back to the door, she wondered what the likelihood was of her being able to get out of the pub without being seen by Leo, and also coming up with a valid reason that Erika would actually believe for so doing.

At some point, she was going to have to introduce them. Find the courage to actually do it, like ripping off a plaster and hoping the wound was healed. She just wished that she wasn't best friends with the sort of girl everyone fell in love with.

'Leo.' Niamh pointed to the door. Both she and Erika watched as he cast his eye around the pub, not settling on them but instead on the girls who'd arrived moments before and were now sitting at a table by the window.

'Oh, so he's *that* Leo,' Erika said, watching as he folded himself into the group, high-fiving a lad wearing a monogrammed shirt and kissing each of the girls on both cheeks.

'What do you mean?' Niamh asked, aware of how pinched the words felt in her throat. There was also a faint ringing in her ears and a certain sickness in her stomach as she saw how at ease Leo was with all those people she did not know, people he hadn't mentioned he was meeting that evening.

It didn't mean anything. Just because she told him every part of her day there was no need for him to do the same. And just because the only people she ever spent time with, other than her professors, were Erika and Duncan, it was silly for her to assume that he wouldn't have a larger group of friends, friends he'd never introduced her to.

'That one there,' Erika said, leaning around the bar and pointing at the girl whose hand was resting on Leo's shoulder. 'Isabella Godfrey. I was unfortunate enough to be at school with her. Total airhead and world-class snob, but she always got what she wanted. Including your Leo.'

'He's not *my* Leo.' Except he was. Or at least she thought he was. 'When were they together?' She didn't want to know. She didn't want to know anything about a girl who looked like she belonged in an ad campaign. She had no desire to know when she was a part of Leo's life, especially as she seemed to suit it so much better than her.

'Last year. I bumped into her at the PW Ball.'

'The PW Ball?' Niamh remembered seeing an invitation to this year's event propped up on the mantelpiece in Leo's room. It was printed on thick, white card with Leo's name handwritten at the top. It was the sort of night that people talked about, mainly because unless you went to the right school, or moved in the right social circles, you didn't stand a hope in hell of getting an invite. When she'd asked Leo if he was going, he'd simply shrugged and said he hadn't decided. Niamh told herself it didn't matter, that he was under no obligation to ask her to go with him, but part of her couldn't help wondering if he hadn't asked because he knew she wouldn't fit in with everyone else.

'You remember,' Erika said as she signalled to the barman for two more drinks. 'Duncan came with me because you said you had no desire for people to ask what you were doing over Easter, just so they could then better it.'

'Right. Of course,' Niamh replied as she closed her eyes and fought back the urge to cry. If she'd gone to the ball last year, would she have even met Leo? What did it matter, given he was there with someone else? It still hurt, though, because he'd taken Isabella but hadn't thought to ask if Niamh wanted to go with him this time around.

'Isabella took great delight in telling me how she'd landed a Bonfiglio,' Erika said as she handed Niamh a drink, watching as she took several large swallows, put the glass down, then picked it up and took a couple more. 'You OK?'

'Great. Never better. What's the big deal about Leo being a Bonfiglio?'

'You don't know? Of course you don't know.'

'Don't patronise me.' Niamh clenched her jaw as she saw Isabella toss back her glossy mane, laughing at something Leo had said.

'I'm not. I mean, why would you know?'

'Enlighten me.'

'They're like the rock stars of Oxford. Ridiculously good-looking with the pedigree to match. All the boys went to Harrow then came here, seducing everyone in sight before heading back to London to work for the family firm.'

'Leo doesn't want to be a lawyer.' Niamh said the words, but she was no longer convinced by them. Leo had told her that the last thing he wanted was to spend another summer interning for his father. Instead, he'd told her all about an idea he had for a film, one that he wanted to make whilst travelling through Europe that summer.

'Peter went to school with Leo,' Erika said, crunching down on a piece of ice. 'I met him once, last year.'

'And?' Niamh swallowed away the bile that was building at the base of her throat. Because of course Erika had a connection to Leo. Of course they moved in the same social circle, one which had a stricter entry policy than a private members' club in London. What didn't make sense though, was why Leo had never said anything. Erika was there the night Niamh had met him, they were sitting at the same table, so was it even possible that Leo hadn't noticed? Why else wouldn't he have told her he already knew her best friend?

Erika clicked her tongue against her teeth, clearly deciding what best to say. 'I hear he's very popular.'

'So what you're saying is how on earth did I manage to convince Leo to go out with someone like me?'

She could see the way Isabella was looking at him, like he was something delicious she couldn't wait to eat. It made her feel jealous and confused, and also a little bit sick, because the idea of Leo kissing her, kissing anyone, made the whole room start to spin.

'No, *älskling*,' Erika replied with a slow, sympathetic smile. 'I'm saying that you should be careful.'

'Why?'

'In my experience, boys that beautiful rarely stay faithful for long.' She turned to whistle across at Leo's table.

'Erika, don't,' Niamh said, ducking behind her, then peering round to see Leo rise from the table and head in their direction.

'Why not?' Erika turned to look down at Niamh. 'Why are you hiding? I thought you really liked him.'

'That's the point.' Was she just another in a long line of conquests? Did Leo tell all the girls he slept with that he loved them?

Because there were bound to be more ex-girlfriends hiding in the wings, all just as perfect as Isabella.

Leo nodded at Erika as he approached, then made as if to give Niamh a kiss, but she turned her head away. 'I didn't know you were going to be here.'

'It's a pub, Leo. Erika and I are allowed to be here.'

'That's not what I meant,' he said, glancing at Erika then back at Niamh. 'I just assumed you'd be in the Univ beer cellar.'

'Well, you assumed wrong.'

'What's the matter?' he asked, taking hold of her elbow and stepping closer. He saw her open her mouth, a mouth he so desperately wanted to kiss, but whatever it was she was about to say was interrupted by her friend.

'I was just telling Niamh about Isabella,' Erika said, slurping through her straw and watching Leo for his reaction. 'Because I'm assuming you haven't.'

'Isabella?' Leo said as his head whipped round to look back at the group of friends he'd come here to meet. 'How do you know Isabella?'

'We were at school together.' Erika was smiling, but it didn't quite reach her eyes. They were level to one another, Erika's heels putting her at the exact same height as him, which might have been unsettling for Leo but more than satisfactory for her.

'But Niamh said you're from Sweden.' He shoved his hands in his pockets and darted a look at Niamh. She was leaning against the bar, picking at the label on her bottle of beer and looking anywhere but at him.

'She boarded at Marlborough for sixth form,' Niamh said, although neither Leo nor Erika seemed to be listening to her.

'You have something of a reputation,' Erika said to Leo, raising her own drink in toast and inclining her head back towards Isabella.

'So do you,' Leo countered, looking Erika up and down. 'Seen Peter recently?'

Niamh wished she could become invisible, or that there was something other than beer in her bottle and she could shrink like Alice and disappear through a tiny door that led to another world. She wanted to be anywhere but in that pub watching as Erika and Leo squared up to one another, staking their claim on her. But there was more to it than that, because it's impossible for humans to ignore beauty. She'd read somewhere about tests carried out with babies where they got them to look at photographs of strangers and monitored how long their gaze rested on each one. Unsurprisingly, the beautiful people got more attention, which is exactly what always happened whenever she was with Erika.

It wasn't just the beauty, though; it was the confidence that came with it. The way Erika wasn't afraid of anything or anyone. If it had been her, she would have gone straight up to Leo's father and introduced herself, then proceeded to dazzle him with both her pedigree and her brilliance. She would never have been teased by the likes of Robin and Octavia, and she certainly wouldn't have been too scared to introduce Leo to her friends.

Niamh tugged at the cuff of her sleeve, wishing she had chosen to wear something other than a bottle-green velvet dress with batwing sleeves. She was like the veritable sore thumb next to a group of coordinated sophistication and it made her fingers come up to fiddle with one of the gold hoops that hung from her ear.

'Can we go?' Niamh said, looking up at Erika.

'Niamh, please,' Leo said, stepping in front of her and blocking the way. 'What's going on?' What had happened between this morning and now? How was it possible to go from telling someone you love them to have them virtually ignore you only hours later?

'I'm not like them,' Niamh said, waving in the general direction of Leo's friends. Then she looked back at Leo and Erika standing next to one another and looking like the picture-perfect couple. 'I'm not like you, either.'

He opened his mouth, and she could tell he was doing his best to hold something back. His cheeks were flushed and he was blinking rapidly. It wasn't a million miles away from how he'd looked when he finally got around to opening his present. It was a cine camera that had taken her an absolute age to find. In the end, she'd taken a bus out to a small village near Banbury and spent over an hour talking to an ex-film technician who once worked at Pinewood.

'Did I get it wrong?' she had asked, chewing the nail of her little finger and trying to make sense of what was going on with his face. If she'd got it wrong, if she'd completely misunderstood the depth of his passion for film after so many nights spent listening to him explain the merits of camera angles and scores, then clearly she didn't know him at all.

'God, you're just perfect,' he had finally replied, and Niamh had swallowed down the lump that was making its way up her throat, wishing upon wishing that nothing could ever take him away from her.

'Why do you think you need to be like anyone other than you?' he said, drawing her close and smoothing a strand of hair from her forehead.

'That's what I keep telling her,' Erika said, then backed away with hands raised when Niamh shot her a look. 'I will wait for you outside. But don't be long because my stomach is rumbling like a thunderstorm.'

'Is it true?' Niamh whispered, breathing him in and feeling her heart give way.

'About Isabella?' he asked and she nodded. 'We dated, for about a term.'

'And you're still friends with her?'

'Not really. We just know a lot of the same people.'

Niamh didn't reply, because he didn't get it. He'd probably never get it, just like Erika and Duncan. She was so very different from them all, purely because of what she had been born into and, for what felt like the millionth time, she wondered what her life would have been like if she'd had a family, a real family, from the very beginning.

He could sense her anger and part of him wanted her to let it go, to say all the things she seemed to be so afraid of confessing. The other part of him was wishing they could go back to that morning, wrap themselves around one another and block out the entire world. Because everything made sense when he was with her, in a way it never had before.

She looked at him and wished she could peek inside his mind, figure out if the version of her that he saw was the one she wanted to be. He might think she didn't need to change, but it was easy to say that when you fitted perfectly into the world around you. Maybe she needed to be more like Erika, live in the moment and not give a fuck what anyone else thought about her. Confidence is key, fake it until you make it and all that bollocks.

Niamh reached out a hand and placed it against his chest. She could feel the heat of him through his shirt and it comforted her, grounded her in the moment so that everything else fell away. Even if it didn't last, even if this was all she would ever get with him, then perhaps it was enough. When she was with him, nothing else mattered and she no longer cared what anyone thought about her, other than him.

'I love you too,' she said, standing on tiptoe to kiss him full on the mouth. 'Always have, always will.'

ERIKA

FRESHWATER PEARL

London, 2002

'Are you sure she's coming?' Layla stands on tiptoes to try to peer over the heads of the crowds that are gathered outside London's most famous department store.

'She's always late,' I reply, not looking up from my BlackBerry as I fire off a couple of quick emails.

'This is why everyone should have a phone.' Layla checks hers for the millionth time, shoving it back in her bag then kicking me on the ankle. 'It's Saturday. Can't you ignore it?'

'Hmm?' I reply with a frown. 'Oh no, it's not work. It's the estate agent with an update on the house.'

'I still don't understand why you're buying somewhere over here when you live in New York.'

'London's a better market, and the rental yield will more than cover the mortgage. Besides,' I say with a gentle poke between her skinny ribs, 'it means I'll always have somewhere to come back to.'

'You can always stay with me and Christophe.'

'I have just about had my fill of your sickening displays of affection.' I have no desire to be within spitting distance of Layla's future husband, but it would have been rude of me to tell her that actually I'd rather spend a fortune on a hotel room than stay with them for the week. And even I can admit that being back here with her, even if it's only for a short time, has been blissful.

'Is this about Layla's inability to keep her knickers on?'

We both turn at the sound of a familiar voice, watching as someone with the bone structure of a supermodel and platinum-blonde hair snakes through the crowds. She gives us each a hug then grabs hold of Layla by the waist and steers her towards the store.

'You're late,' Layla says with a pout.

'I know,' Michelle says in return, giving the doorman a mock salute as he holds the door open for us. 'Which means you don't get to be mean.'

Together we walk around to the bottom of the escalators, tilting our heads back to stare up at the Egyptian carvings.

'You got laid,' I say and Michelle drops her head, a flush slowly creeping its way over her face.

'How do you do that?' Layla calls down from a few steps up, leaning around Michelle to stare at me.

'Supreme powers of deduction.' I point at Michelle. 'Plus her skirt's on the wrong way round and she smells most distinctly of Lynx deodorant instead of the Body Shop White Musk she's been wearing ever since she was a spotty teenager.'

'I was never spotty,' Michelle says as we reach the top of the escalator.

'All that horse manure you used to roll around in must be good for the skin,' I say and dodge out of the way as she tries to whack me.

'I hate that my brother told you all my secrets,' she says as we walk past row upon row of designer clothes and she pauses momentarily beside the shoe display.

'Did you know, there are around one hundred thousand pairs of shoes in this building?' I pick up a pair of satin Manolos with a kitten heel.

'Life's short,' Michelle says as she picks up another pair of shoes and visibly blanches at the price. 'Buy the damn shoes, Erika. Lord knows you can afford them.'

'Can't,' I say as I put the dainty shoe back with a sigh. 'I'm soon to be as poor as a church mouse.'

'A mouse who is about to become a property mogul on both sides of the Atlantic.' Layla grabs Michelle's hand and pulls her away from the shoe department.

'Wait, what?' Michelle looks back at me.

'She's had an offer accepted on a gorgeous mews house within spitting distance of the Portobello Road.'

'Are you moving back? Does Hector know?'

I trot after them because Layla is belting through the store like a greyhound chasing a rabbit.

'No.' Layla shoots me an evil look as we arrive at the entrance to the bridal boutique and she gives her name to a snotty sales assistant who checks her clipboard like a bouncer allowing us access to an exclusive club. 'She's too busy climbing the corporate ladder to think about her heart.'

I roll my eyes in spite of myself because we've had this fight already. She met me at Heathrow, literally bubbling over with excitement due to all the plans she'd made for my visit back home. Then I had to tell her I'd arranged to meet with an estate agent and so couldn't spend the following day at the spa with her. At which point she looked like she was having a fit, swiftly jumping from excitement to disappointment to rage when she realised that I wasn't actually going to live in the house I wanted to buy.

'Why buy somewhere in London if you've no intention of coming back?' Michelle asks.

'That's precisely what I said.' Layla folds her arms over her chest and fixes me with another scathing look. 'I reckon she's homesick. Desperate, in fact, but her pride won't let her admit it.'

'She's definitely desperate,' Michelle says with a snort, followed by a long yawn. 'And there was I, hoping perhaps you could spend at least some of the summer in Ibiza with little old me. I was even going to set you up with one of Torsten's friends. How long is it exactly since you've had a boyfriend?'

I'm starting to feel a little ganged up on, not least because Layla has already asked me at least a thousand times why I won't move back to London. Even when I pointed out that she was planning on moving to Paris, she smiled sweetly and said a single word in response – Eurostar.

The sales assistant looks us up and down, casting a critical eye over our faces and clothes, before pulling back the heavy velvet curtain and stepping aside.

The wall opposite us consists of four enormous windows with full-length mirrors hanging in between. To the left is a series of changing rooms with ivory curtains and discreet lighting. The other two walls are filled with every conceivable type of wedding dress, from simple and understated shifts, to full-on Cinderella with pink taffeta and millions of sequins.

'Who's Torsten?' Layla says as she walks along the near-side wall, stopping every so often to finger the fabrics.

'It's the DJ, isn't it?' I say. 'The one from that launch party for some street artist back in May.'

'On second thoughts,' Michelle says as she sticks her tongue out at me, revealing a diamanté stud stuck through its centre, 'I think you should stay in New York.'

'What DJ?' Layla is considering a lace gown with spaghetti straps and low neckline. 'What launch party? What are you two talking about?'

'You were in Paris.' I shake my head as Layla shows me the dress, then point across to a couple that are hanging near all the puffballs and bling. 'Being wined and dined and all the rest of it by Christophe.'

'I'm surprised you even remember,' Michelle says as she takes down a cream dress with intricate beading around the bodice. She holds it up against her torso, considering her reflection in the mirror, then passes it to me. 'You ran off the moment Hector arrived.'

'I wasn't sure he'd want to see me,' I say, turning the dress around and noticing the covered buttons that run all the way along where the spine would sit.

'My brother always wants to see you,' Michelle says as she takes down another dress, then heads in the direction of the changing rooms. 'That's the problem.'

I wanted to see him too; it's part of the reason why I went to the opening in the first place. Even though I was only in London for one more night, exhausted from back-to-back investor meetings all week and struggling through another bout of jet lag, I needed to see him.

'What do you think?' Layla asks as she hooks a gown over her head and presses the skirt to her hips.

'It's beautiful,' I reply. 'But is it you, or who you think you're supposed to be?'

'What do you mean?'

'You don't need anything extra.' I ease the dress over Layla's head, swapping it for a gown with a scalloped bodice made from hand-sewn lace and a chiffon skirt that would be perfect for dancing.

'Ta-da!' Michelle bursts out of the changing room, resplendent in a silver-sequined gown and holding her arms out wide as she skips across the room. It transports me straight back to a vintage store on the King's Road where we tried on the dresses we were wearing the night it all went horribly wrong.

Michelle forgave me for breaking her brother's heart. Despite everything, she has managed to stay loyal to both her family and friends and never once chosen a side. It hurts my head to think about how much the younger version of me could have done with some of her wisdom and kindness.

'I can see your nipples,' Layla says, barely stifling a laugh and then looking away as another sales assistant glares in our direction. 'Seriously, you have to take it off or we'll get thrown out. And it takes at least six months to get a dress made, so I can't afford to waste this appointment.'

'All right, Bridezilla,' Michelle says with a pout as she scuttles back to the changing room, Layla and me following close behind.

'Do you think you'll ever get back together with Hector?' Layla calls through the curtain to where I'm sitting, staring out the window and trying not to think about the last time I saw him, at the gallery opening back in May.

'Too late,' Michelle says as she comes out of the changing room, this time with her skirt on the right way. 'He's shacked up with a primary school teacher called Rachel.'

'What's wrong with her?' I can tell by the tone of her voice that Michelle does not approve of her brother's latest conquest. Looking along the street, I watch all those people going about their day with no idea that I'm up here spying on them. I could spy on Hector and Rachel too. No. Bad idea. Best not to find out, or even be tempted to look, because once you see, it's impossible to unsee how perfectly fine they are without you. *Remember the promise you made to yourself when you left Oxford – never look back, because regret is nothing more than a waste of time.*

'She dresses like a nineteen-fifties housewife and makes her own jam. Can you imagine what it would be like with her at Christmas?'

I can't help but laugh at the image I have been presented with. Michelle and Hector's parents live just outside Sheffield and spend most of their free time hiking through the Peak District with their beloved Alsatians. Parents and children alike are tall and annoyingly sporty, with opinions on absolutely everything. I only got to visit once, but I can still remember the argument about migrating butterflies that spread over the course of an entire week.

'It's your fault,' Michelle says as she punches me lightly on the arm. 'Instead of having you as a sister I'm going to be stuck with Little Miss Perfect.'

'Leave her alone,' Layla says as she comes out of the changing room and stands before us, hands on hips and a nervous smile across her face.

'Wow,' I say, eyes wide and filling with tears. 'You look incredible.'

'Really?' she asks, kicking her feet out from under the hem. 'It's so not what I thought I'd choose.'

'I bet you didn't think you'd end up marrying a Frenchie either.' Michelle goes to stand behind Layla and pulls the straps up higher.

'Although you did dream of getting married in a castle,' I say with a smile, because Layla once showed me a scrapbook she'd made years before, complete with a sketch of her and her future husband standing outside a castle fit for a princess.

'True,' Layla says, turning around and then peering into the mirror over her shoulder. 'It's just . . .'

'Just what?'

'Oh, I don't know,' she says. 'It feels weird. Being here without Sara.'

'Who's Sara?' Michelle asks.

'Former best friend,' I reply, watching as Layla's face folds itself into a frown and I know what she's thinking. I know what it means to lose the person closest to you. I find myself thinking about her, and about Duncan, during the moments you know you'll remember for years to come. And then it washes over me all over again, how much I have lost, not just from my past, but from my future too.

'What happened?'

'Nothing really,' Layla replies with a shrug. 'We just drifted apart after school. But now I have you two.' She plants a kiss on my cheek and I half-heartedly swat her away.

'Which makes you the luckiest girl in the world.' Michelle takes Layla's hands and together they begin to skip around the room. I watch them, their faces bright with love and the expectation of love, and I feel a little jealous at what they have.

'There's another dress hanging up in my cubicle,' Layla calls as she and Michelle skip over to the far side of the room and back, like a cross between *My Fair Lady* and a barn dance. 'I think you should try it on.'

I peek behind the curtain to discover a fountain of pale-blue crêpe-de-chine, with long, diaphanous sleeves and delicate pearlescent beading stitched into both the bodice and the hem. I allow the fabric to run through my fingers, so light it would be like wearing a summer breeze. It reminds me of a girl who would have worn it on any given day with platform boots and a chain of daisies in her hair.

I thought we would be best friends forever. I thought we would be doing this exact same thing one day. Trying on dresses and talking about our futures. I thought we would always be part of one another's lives, and it hurts every single time I imagine what could have been, if only I'd kept my promise to never let a boy come between us.

Moving my hand away, one of the beads comes loose, hanging by a single thread. I ease it free, glancing behind me as I slip it into the pocket of my shorts.

Michelle gives a low whistle as I step out of the changing room. 'Do not let my brother see you in that; he will have a heart attack.'

'You should let your hair grow out,' Layla says as she walks slowly around me.

'I seem to remember you telling me how shit it was when we first met.'

'Because it was. But if you had it longer,' she says, ruffling my hair so that it stands out at odd angles, 'it would be a bit more . . .'

'More what?' I immediately run my fingers through my hair and tuck it neatly behind my ears. Turning to the mirror, it strikes me that the person staring back seems to belong to a different era.

'You know,' Layla says. 'Like those girls back in the seventies, all miniskirts and thigh-length boots that would spread wide with one wink from Mick Jagger.'

'Yes,' Michelle exclaims. 'She would look awesome with big hair and leather trousers.'

'Now that would most definitely make Hector dump ridiculous Rachel and climb back into your bed.'

'Can we stop talking about Hector, please?' And stop talking about seventies groupies with mad hair, because it hurts too much to remember the girl with stars on her cape and music in her soul.

'Why?' Michelle says. 'Do you have someone hidden away back in New York you'd like to tell us about instead?'

'Nobody ever makes it past the third date,' Layla says as she turns around and indicates that I should unzip her, before heading back into the changing cubicle.

'I'm not sure this is really a bridesmaid's dress.' I look back at my reflection and wonder if perhaps I might buy the dress anyway. But would I ever wear it, or simply hang it in the back of my wardrobe to look at every now and then?

'Stop changing the subject.' Layla comes back out with the bridal gown looped over one arm. She glances at the counter, where a queue of other brides-to-be is gathered.

'I agree,' Michelle says. 'We need to know more details about your sex life, because surely you must be playing around with more than just numbers?'

'Not really.'

'Do you even like your job?'

'Why do you ask?' I take down a gown with a multi-layered skirt and vintage rose pattern. It's simple but delicate and would be perfect for a wedding at a French chateau. I show it to Layla, who turns it around and nods her approval before heading to the counter.

'You did classics, yes?' Michelle pulls off her t-shirt and dumps it on the floor, before taking the gown from me and slipping it over her head. 'At Oxford.'

'Yes.'

'But then you came here.' Reaching underneath the hem of the dress, she drops her skirt to the floor, completely oblivious to the looks we are now getting from both customers and staff alike.

'Your point is?' I know what her point is. I mean, who changes their mind after two years of studying at one of the most prestigious universities in the world? Someone who needed to leave what she'd done behind and find somewhere to start again, that's who. Somewhere nobody knew her, or her shame.

'From the moment I met you, you always had everything figured out,' she says, taking the dress off and holding it out to me. 'A five-year plan and the exact way you were going to get there. Meanwhile the rest of us were getting shit-faced on cheap student booze and shagging anything that moved.'

My student days at LSE were so very different to those at Oxford. At the time, I told myself it was because I lived off-campus

185

and was at least three years older than my classmates so had a been there, done that sort of mentality. Now I understand it's because I was too busy trying to convince myself I'd made the right choice.

'I used to think money meant independence,' I say. I also thought all that money would somehow make up for the fact I still miss him every single day.

'And now?'

'Now I'm terrified it's stopped me from doing anything worthwhile.'

'I always thought we'd have kids.' Layla comes back holding a thick, cream envelope. I feel bad for hijacking her moment, for inadvertently making it about me when we should be focusing on her.

'Surely you and Christophe have spoken about it?' I check my phone, registering the long list of emails that seem to multiply the more I try to ignore them.

'No, you and me.'

'I hate to break it to you, sweetheart, but I'm not that way inclined.'

'Oh shush your noise,' Layla says, slipping one arm through mine and the other through Michelle's. 'You know what I mean. Raising them at the same time, bonding over sleepless nights and people judging your every move. Summers spent somewhere warm, watching them grow, then wishing they'd stay young forever.'

I know exactly what she means because I used to think the same way, but about someone who, for all I know, could be knee-deep in babies already.

'You're such a hopeless romantic,' I say as we make our way back through the store.

'I like to call it optimism.'

'There's still time,' Michelle says, stepping on to the escalator and turning around to face us. Even two steps below she's the same height as Layla.

'I'm not really that keen.' I've always found these conversations difficult, not least because it's so awkward trying to explain my reasons to people who make no secret of their desire to raise a large family. Hector told me on our second date that he wanted five children and I assumed he was joking. But when I said as much to Layla, she told me I should be glad to have found someone who was willing to settle down and have kids as quickly as possible.

'Is that why you broke up with Hector?' Michelle peers round Layla to frown at me. 'Because money and a career are more important than a family?'

As we step back out into the day, I think about fate and how much emphasis people place on it when it comes to love. All the what ifs and maybes and countless tiny decisions that end up with two people being in the same place at the same time. If Michelle had decided not to attend the opening, would she have met Torsten nonetheless? Would fate or luck or serendipity herself have forced the two of them together because they were meant to be?

If the three of us hadn't gone to New College bar that night, would I have still ended up breaking us apart?

'It's not that simple.'

Michelle makes a sound halfway between a snort and a raspberry. 'It never is with you.'

NIAMH

Metanoia (n.) – *the journey of changing one's mind, heart, self or way of life*

London, 1996

Chelsea was like an alternate universe where even the dogs were well groomed and Niamh felt like she stuck out like the veritable sore thumb. Erika might have been wearing ripped jeans and Adidas trainers, but they were paired with a white silk blouse and one of her mother's hand-me-down Chanel handbags. Duncan was rocking his usual geek-meets-Savile Row attire, complete with braces, brogues and yellow-tinted sunglasses. In comparison, Niamh was wearing a paisley maxi-skirt with bells around the hem and a faded purple waistcoat that had one of its buttons missing.

For the past couple of hours, the three of them had been traipsing up and down the King's Road in search of the perfect outfit for the summer ball. Secretly, it was Erika's way of getting Niamh out of Oxford and away from Leo, if only for a weekend, but it had been sold as a shopping opportunity not to be missed. When Niamh had questioned why it was necessary to start looking for an outfit three months before an event, Erika and Duncan had shared one of their looks, then sighed in a way more suited to indulgent parents than best friends.

'It needs to be more . . .' Erika gesticulated with her hands in front of her body when Niamh held up a long, black dress split to the thigh.

'More boobs?' Niamh said with a laugh as she put the dress back. 'I don't really think that's an issue.'

'Outladdish.' Erika picked up a pair of silver stilettoes with rhinestone heels and waved them across at Duncan, who simply shook his head.

'Outlandish,' Niamh said with a yawn as she stretched her arms above her head.

'That's what I said. This is the perfect opportunity to wear whatever the hell we want.'

'Why can't we wear whatever the hell we want every day?' Niamh looked around the shop, thinking once again at how uniform all the so-called fashion was. Everyone dressing and thinking the same, afraid of standing out in any way and subsequently losing all that made them unique.

'She thinks that as soon as we graduate, her life will be nothing more than suits, pearls and Barbour jackets.' Duncan began to roll a cigarette, tucking it behind his ear and fumbling in his pocket for a light.

'That's so dull.'

'I agree, but Erika is determined to slot herself firmly into the status quo of the rich and even richer.'

'Stop talking about me as if I am not here.' Erika pulled out a black dress that was daringly short at the front, but with a frothy, layered train.

'Too drag queen,' Duncan said.

'Then perhaps you should wear it.'

'I wouldn't want to upstage you,' he replied. 'I'm going outside for a smoke. You coming?'

'No.' Erika reached out a hand to stop Niamh from following Duncan to the safety of the street. 'She is staying here and trying at least one more dress on.'

Niamh trailed her fingers over the sumptuous fabrics, surreptitiously turning the price tags over and dismissing everything outright.

'What's wrong with this one?' Erika asked, pointing to a floor-length beaded number with a low back and thin straps.

There was nothing wrong with it; it was exquisite and made Niamh think of actresses from the golden era of Hollywood. She and Leo had been going through a phase of only watching films that were at least thirty years old. Whilst she had fallen in love with the Hepburns, Leo had become obsessed with all things Hitchcock.

But no matter how beautiful the dress, and all the other dresses Erika had shown her, they each cost about the same as Niamh would spend on food during the course of an entire term.

'It wouldn't suit me,' Niamh said as she strolled around the shop, aware of how the assistant's eye had, just like in every other establishment they had been into, lingered on her a moment more than was either comfortable or polite.

Erika stood with hands on hips and a look on her face that told Niamh she was thinking very carefully about what to say. Which also told her that she was trying very hard not to say anything insulting. Things had been strained between them ever since they'd bumped into Leo in the pub and Niamh realised that he and Erika had known one another all along.

'Why don't we go for a drink?' she said, looping her arm through Niamh's and escorting her from the shop. 'Then perhaps I can persuade you to come back and let me buy the dress for you.'

'Erika . . .'

'And if you say no' – Erika placed one finger on Niamh's lips as she spoke – 'I shall be mortally offended and never speak to you again. Please, Niamh. If it's only about the money then let me help. I want to help.'

'You always want to help,' Niamh replied, because Erika would more often than not insist on paying for lunch or drinks or a pair of boots that Niamh couldn't quite afford. Not to mention when Niamh had been called in to see the college bursar because her accommodation fees for the summer term hadn't been paid. Before Niamh even had a chance to call her parents to ask for the money she knew they were so reluctant to give, Erika had marched back into the office and written out a cheque to cover the full amount.

'I'm not a bank,' she had said with a laugh when Niamh offered to repay her in instalments. 'It's a gift, not a loan.'

'At least let me buy the drinks,' Niamh said, trying not to think of just how much money she would owe Erika if she ever did ask for it back.

'Did somebody say drinks?' Duncan stepped between the two of them, draping his arm around each of their shoulders. 'Best idea I've heard all day.'

As they walked along the road, they came to the town hall where a small crowd was gathered at the bottom of a flight of steps. A moment later a bride and groom emerged from the building to a chorus of cheers and a stream of rainbow confetti that danced and swirled through the air. Niamh turned her head to look back, to see the couple kiss through their smiles, which rewarded them with another round of jubilant cheers.

She couldn't help but think of Leo, of what it might be like to spend the rest of her life with him. In turn, she was overcome by a sense of foreboding, as if that kind of happiness would never be hers.

'You're far too young to get married,' Erika said as she gave Niamh's arm a gentle tug.

'It's not that,' Niamh replied. Erika had been doing her best to avoid being in the same room as Leo for more than a few minutes at a time. Leo in turn would comment on the way Erika tried to manipulate Niamh, control her even. It was draining: the two of them so clearly on opposite sides of the table, with her in the middle trying to play referee. It felt as if she was in two relationships, always needing to appease someone's jealousy about how much time she spent with the other.

Niamh dropped behind as they navigated an elderly couple shuffling towards them and smiled to herself at how, if you fast-forwarded fifty years, it could have been her two friends. She imagined them in a retirement home somewhere, deaf and flatulent, still arguing over everything and nothing at all. It was something she had missed over the past few months. Not the arguing, because they would argue over whether the sun was shining given half the chance, but rather the simple ease of being with them.

As she passed by a dilapidated shop window, Niamh's eye was caught by the display. She stopped so abruptly that a man smacked into her from behind. He tossed an insult at her as he walked away, but Niamh was already going inside the shop.

'Niamh?' Erika called out as she came back to linger in the doorway, peering into the half-light and wrinkling her nose at the musty smell. 'What are you doing?'

'Give me a sec,' Niamh said as she ventured further, eyes wide and her head turning in all directions.

There were rails upon rails of clothing set up around the perimeter of the shop, with shelves climbing the walls above and rows of shoes underneath. Through the centre were chests of drawers, crates and even a dilapidated chaise longue, covered in hats and bags and trays of costume jewellery. Niamh stopped in front of a circular coffee table, around which several suitcases were stacked. Lifting the lid of one, she discovered dozens of shawls, and in another tiny silken purses with silver clasps. The whole place was chaotic, with no sense of order and absolutely stuffed to the rafters, but she loved it.

'There's more downstairs,' a wisp of a woman said as Niamh picked up a top hat with a bright yellow sash tied around the base. Niamh looked to where she was pointing and saw the beginnings of a staircase in the far corner.

'That's where we keep the good stuff.'

Niamh smiled her thanks and crossed over to the far side of the shop, breathing in the scent of time and memories that could only ever come from something old and pre-loved. The bannisters were barely visible under reams of scarves in every conceivable colour and there were bags and shoes on each stair.

'It's like Aladdin's cave,' Duncan said as he came down behind her, plucking a wig from a nearby head and walking across to a full-length mirror.

Niamh glanced over to see Erika taking down a blush-pink ballgown with an enormous bow around the middle. There were hundreds of dresses, all fighting for attention, some on rails and others hanging from the walls and up to the ceiling. Her eye fell upon a cream dress with long sleeves, covered buttons and an intricate floral pattern that wouldn't have looked out of place in the forties. Next to it was a flapper dress with a dropped waist and beside that was a peacock blue velvet suit with pearlescent beading along the lapels.

But it was a dress hanging at the top of a pillar, half-hidden behind a pair of angel wings, that made her stop and stare.

'Now that,' Duncan said as he saw what she was staring at, 'is what you might call a showstopper. You have to try it on.'

'Ta-da!' Erika exploded from a makeshift dressing room, sending the curtain rail crashing to the floor behind her. 'What do you think?' she asked as she strutted around the basement, her boobs bouncing up and down with every step.

'You look like the Sugarplum Fairy,' Duncan said as he climbed on to a nearby crate and passed down the dress to Niamh.

'I know, isn't it divine?'

'If you and Leo do get married, please make her wear that, and perm her hair so we can get the full eighties effect.'

'Can we talk about something else?' Niamh turned the dress round on the hanger and held it at arm's length.

'Yes, let's.' Erika unzipped her own dress and let it drop to the floor.

'Put some clothes on, you hussy,' Duncan said as he picked up the dress and hung it back on the rail.

'Don't be such a prude.' Erika went back into the dressing room and rummaged through her bag. 'It's not like you haven't seen it all before. Has anyone got any change?' She pulled out her pager and scrolled through the messages.

'Why?'

'I need to make a phone call.' She held one hand out to Duncan and used the other to pull up her jeans.

'What am I, your manservant?'

'If you were, I would have fired you years ago.'

'Here,' Niamh said as she handed over a fistful of coins. 'That's all I've got.'

'Thanks. There's a phone box over the road so I won't be long.' Erika slipped on her trainers and ran up the stairs two at a time, not bothering to tuck in her shirt or tie her laces.

'Come on then.' Duncan led Niamh to the changing cubicle and hooked the curtain rail back into place.

Standing before the mirror, Niamh tried to ignore the dark circles under her eyes and the grey pallor to her skin. She'd barely spent any time outside recently. Her days consisted of sitting in the library, trying to catch up with all the reading she was supposed to do, and at night she was tucked up next to, or underneath, Leo.

Part of her longed to be back in Ireland, to walk the coast and breathe in all that salty air. She needed the space to think, to process everything that had happened between her and Leo in such a short space of time. She wanted to be alone in her room with nothing more than a stack of records and well-leafed books for company. It was a startling thought, given how desperate she usually was to escape the oppressive quiet of home.

'How are the rats?' she called out to Duncan as she undid her waistcoat and shrugged off her skirt.

'Mr T escaped last week.' Duncan's voice sounded far away and Niamh could picture him rummaging through a box of trinkets, head down, feet in the air like something out of a cartoon.

'Mr T?'

'I named them based on their characters. Mr T is the biggest male and is always picking fights.'

'Am I supposed to know who Mr T is?'

'*The A-Team.*'

'Who?'

Duncan's head appeared from behind the curtain. He was wearing a filigree headband, a blue feather boa and enormous clip-on earrings. 'Jesus, Niamh. Did you spend your entire childhood in the library?'

'Pretty much,' Niamh replied as she stepped out of the changing cubicle and Duncan gave a slow whistle.

'We have to go,' Erika called down from the top of the stairs.

'Go where?' Niamh asked as she spied a pair of silver go-go boots on a high shelf.

'To meet Charlie.'

'Who's Charlie?' Duncan asked.

'Charlie is the man who has just offered both Niamh and my wonderful self a summer internship at Lehman's.' Her voice was high-pitched, like an excitable child, and she was clapping her hands as she looked over at Niamh expectantly.

'But I thought . . .' Duncan didn't finish his sentence, instead glancing at Niamh, who gave a very swift shake of her head. She had confided in Duncan that Leo had asked her to go travelling with him over the summer, after which Duncan had made Niamh promise to tell Erika sooner rather than later.

'Don't just stand there,' Erika said. 'We have to go and celebrate. Charlie's meeting us at six, which means we need to go get ready.'

'Well, if it's Charlie we're meeting then I guess that changes everything.' Duncan didn't try to hide the sarcasm in his voice, nor did he fail to notice the droop of Niamh's shoulders as she went back into the changing cubicle and slipped off the dress.

There's still time, Niamh thought to herself as she changed back into her own clothes. *There's always more time*, she repeated as she followed her friends out of the shop and headed in the direction of Erika's house.

Or at least that's what she'd been telling herself ever since she'd agreed to go to the interview that had resulted from Erika applying for a job on her behalf. It wasn't her dream to become part of the elite; that had always belonged to Erika and, Niamh suspected, Astrid too. Duncan had told Niamh to confess that she didn't want the job even before she went to the interview. But she hadn't been able to find the right time. Or rather she had decided there was no point in saying anything and upsetting Erika, because it was doubtful she'd get the job anyway.

Although there was a certain temptation to it, to seeing if she could be part of the elite, even if only for a few weeks. Perhaps it

196

might help her understand a little better about the world in which Leo lived, teach her how to act around his family if ever they were to be introduced. But it all felt so false, like trying on someone else's clothes, even though you know they won't fit. Erika wouldn't change who she was just to please a boy, but she didn't need to; she already had the perfect life.

'Is that what you're wearing?' Erika asked as she came into the bedroom where Niamh was getting changed.

Niamh looked down at the simple shift dress she'd chosen, paired with platform boots and a beaded jacket.

'I could always take it off,' Niamh replied as she slipped the jacket from her shoulders. 'Turn up stark-bollock naked and give them all something to talk about?'

'Leave the poor girl alone,' Duncan said as he hovered in the doorway. His hair was still wet from the shower and he'd changed into jeans and a white shirt. It would seem that even he thought it necessary to blend in sometimes, to not draw unwanted attention.

'I still think you should wear something else.' Erika tipped her head upside down and fluffed at her hair.

Niamh thought back to a conversation she'd had with Leo only days before. He'd woken in the middle of the night to find her sitting on the sofa surrounded by pages of notes and several empty cups of coffee. When he'd asked her why she was staying up all night to finish an essay that wasn't due until Monday, she'd confessed that Erika wanted her to spend the weekend in London.

'Do you always do everything she tells you?' he'd said and Niamh had opened her mouth to object, then shut it again, because she knew Leo was right.

'You know what.' Niamh sat on the edge of the bed and pulled off her boots. 'You go. Get drunk on champagne with a bunch of wanker bankers. Tell them how incredible you are and that you can't wait to join their little club.'

Erika flicked back her hair and stared at Niamh. 'You have to come.'

Niamh took a deep breath, imagining Leo was in the room with her, silently egging her on. 'No, I don't.'

'But I told Charlie you were coming.'

'Just like you told him I was accepting the job?'

'Well, yes. But . . .'

'But nothing. You should have asked, Erika.' Niamh unzipped her dress and chucked it in on the floor. 'You never bloody ask. You just bulldoze your way through life assuming that you are the only one who gets to make any of the decisions. But you are not my mother.'

'No,' Erika replied. 'Because I'd never abandon you.'

The silence was painful. Duncan's eyes darted between the two girls, waiting to see who would react first.

'Leo was right,' Niamh said. 'The two of you push me around, expect me to tag along without ever stopping to ask if I even want to.'

'You shouldn't listen to him just because he goes down on you.'

'What's wrong with you?' Niamh picked up one of her discarded boots and hurled it at Erika, who only just managed to duck out of the way.

'I'm sorry.'

'You're always bloody sorry.' She picked up the other boot and chucked that one at Duncan.

'What did *I* do?' he said as it flew past his head and landed with barely a sound on the deep-pile carpet.

'I can't keep doing this.' Niamh sank on to the bed and dropped her face into her hands. 'I'm not a child; I'm perfectly capable of making my own decisions.'

Erika came to sit next to her and Duncan knelt on the floor at her feet. Niamh didn't want to look because she knew that if she did, all her resolve, all her anger, would slip away.

'You don't need to decide right now,' Erika said as she tentatively placed a hand on Niamh's shoulder. 'But I always tell myself when facing two possible outcomes, to imagine they both go as well as can be, and then choose the one I want more. Simple.'

She was being asked to choose. Leo or Erika. The one thing Niamh had been trying to avoid all along.

'What happens if you fail?' Duncan asked.

'*Älskling*,' Erika said with a wink in his direction, 'I never fail. But if Niamh doesn't want the internship, that's fine. I can tell Charlie she's had a better offer.'

Niamh peered up at her through a curtain of hair, wiping her hand under her nose and sniffing loudly.

'Although I think it's a mistake to turn it down. You probably won't get another opportunity like this. Besides, Leo said he'll be in London too, so you'll still get to see him.'

Niamh sat up straight, blinking rapidly as she tried to remember when Leo might have lied to Erika about his summer whereabouts.

'Leo won't be in London.' She knew this because they had spoken about an altogether different kind of adventure, just the two of them, alone for all those days and nights. He'd shown her the outline for a script, told her all the places he wanted to visit, places he'd been to as a boy but wanted to experience anew. It gave her a certain thrill, to be the only person who he showed that side of himself to. But so far, Niamh hadn't said a word to Erika. She thought it would be far easier to break the news once Erika had secured an internship and Niamh had not.

'Yes, he will,' Erika said as she got to her feet and held out a hand to Niamh. 'He told me he would be working for his father's firm.'

'When?' It was the only word Niamh could come up with. Because everything else was cloaked by a heavy dollop of jealousy.

'The other week.'

'Where?' Except she already knew where. The Turf Tavern, where Leo had gone to meet a friend for a drink and she had stayed behind to catch up on all the reading he kept distracting her from. A night when he came back to her room bathed in the scent of whiskey, closely followed by the sound of Erika crashing along the landing to her own room. Neither of them had said anything about bumping into one another and she hated not knowing what else they might have chatted about over one too many drinks.

'Erika,' Duncan said as he swatted her on the leg. 'Let her make up her own mind about how she wants to spend the summer, and with whom.'

'Right. Not my decision. Got it,' she said as she glanced at her watch then back at Niamh. 'But at least say you'll come and get drunk with us? It won't cost you a penny . . .'

Niamh took a long, slow breath. Nothing happened, she told herself. It was just a coincidence. But had there been any other little secret meetings they had decided not to tell her about? She was being paranoid. They didn't even like one another. Why then was it impossible not to picture the two of them together, laughing and flirting and slowly edging closer? More importantly, why keep it from her unless they had something to hide? Niamh already knew how good Erika was at keeping secrets; now it seemed Leo was too.

'Tempting as that might be, I'm shattered. And there is an enormous bath next door that has my name written all over it.'

'Please?' Erika dropped to her knees and clasped her hands together in prayer.

'Go,' Niamh said with the smallest of smiles. 'Coerce all those rich bastards out of as many bottles of champagne as you can. I'll see you in the morning.'

'Sleep tight,' Erika said as she left the room. 'But no sneaking back to Oxford for some rumpy-pumpy. Promise?'

'I promise,' Niamh replied, thinking of how a bath and a whole night alone without having to watch all those men fawn over her beautiful friend was so very, very appealing.

ERIKA

MOONSTONE NECKLACE

London, 2000

The theme is Alice in Wonderland – because isn't that the theme of every bloody ball I've ever attended? There are gilded mirrors and chandeliers hanging in the entrance, where everyone is asked to pose for the obligatory photograph. There is a tunnel fashioned out of bamboo canes, from which oversized cards are hanging, and at the end is a wall of Prosecco, where we are allowed to help ourselves to the first of many. The floor of the main hall is covered in fake patchwork grass, with garlands of flowers suspended over each of the tables, all set with brightly coloured plates. At the far end is a stage, ready and waiting for the band to begin, with a space in front for us to dance.

Seven hundred students and guests, all gathered together in celebration of finishing our exams.

For this auspicious occasion, I have chosen to wear a strapless black dress with a blue crushed velvet coat and newly cropped, peroxide hair. My date for the evening is ensconced in a red satin gown with spaghetti straps, which highlights both the curve of her waist and the golden tones of her skin. Layla is skittish, like a child at Christmas, and changed both her shoes and hairstyle at least three times before we were allowed to leave.

'Something amazing is going to happen tonight,' she whispers to me as we arrive in the main hall, just as Britney Spears starts blasting from the sound system and everyone lets out a cheer.

'If you're going to start lecturing me on destiny, I'm finding another date.' I peer through the crowds in search of a familiar face.

'Don't be such a philistine,' Layla says with a gentle punch to my arm. 'Tell me there's never been a moment when you've just known something epic, something monumentally life changing, was going to happen?'

Luckily for me I don't have to reply, as bounding towards us is a girl wearing a gold-sequined dress that makes her look like a cross between an Oscar statuette and a mermaid.

'Isn't this awesome?' Michelle says. She is clutching a miniature bottle of Prosecco and drinking it through a straw so as not to ruin her perfectly applied pout.

'Do you know where we're sitting?' Layla asks, shouting over the music with an overenthusiastic grin on her face.

Michelle takes her by the hand, then Layla does the same to me, and together we weave through the crowd, acutely aware of the heads turning to watch us go.

It seems hard to believe that three years have disappeared before I've had a chance to blink. I never thought I'd be able to find another group of friends, let alone people who would accept me and enrich my life without me even realising. There have been study partners, jogging partners, friends and lovers all rolled into a bubble of denial. Because everyone will disperse after tonight, focus on their careers, meet someone, settle down. The circle is bound to shrink so that in time I will probably only be in touch with a handful of the people who I have become accustomed to seeing pretty much every day.

Hector isn't here, which is both a blessing and a curse because I do so want to see him before I leave for New York. Even though I know he won't want to see me. Breaking up is always so very hard to do, even more so when I couldn't give him the real reason why.

Michelle has been providing me with regular feedback as to his state of mind. At the last report Hector is still back home, drowning his sorrows, taking long walks with the dogs and pretending to write the next great love story. Apparently it's all about a Swedish girl who stole, then broke, his heart. Wonder who that's based on? I think she's telling me how miserable he is in the hope that I might change my mind. Hop on a train and run to him with open arms. What I can't tell her, just as I can't tell him or anyone, is why I don't deserve the happily ever after he was offering me.

Instead, I told him it wasn't the right time. That it was me, not him. All the usual clichés that did nothing to dispel the level of despair he showed me when I tried to give back the snow globe he bought me when we visited Edinburgh Castle. I've never seen a man cry before. Well, apart from Duncan, but he once cried at a bloody Oxo advert, so he doesn't count.

It's probably best that Hector's not here, even though I allowed myself to imagine this night with him all handsome and delicious in black tie, spinning me around the dance floor and kissing me without regret.

Everything about tonight is so different to how I imagined it would be. But then I also used to picture the three of us outside the examination halls, dressed in subfusc, each wearing a red carnation in our buttonhole and dodging out of the way as flour and champagne was ceremoniously dumped over all the finalists (although there was once an octopus, according to Duncan's legendary tale).

A waiter appears with our food, setting down a plate in front of Michelle. 'What's this?' she asks as she taps at the miniature pie with her fork.

'*Bouchées à la Reine*,' a boy with spiked hair and oversized glasses says. 'I'll have it if you don't want it.'

'Hands off, Piers,' Michelle says, flicking him with her finger and pulling her plate closer. 'I'm starving.'

I sat next to Piers on the morning of our first lecture because he was reading a copy of *A Room of One's Own*. In itself, this wasn't anything unusual, but considering we were both signed up to an economics degree, it made me curious, made me want to know more about the boy who still reminds me of someone I used to know.

It hits me then, the fact I will never again see him, or any of my friends, in the same context. From this very moment on everything about our lives, our friendships, is going to change and there is no way of stopping it, of going back and living it all over again.

'To the end of an era,' Piers says as he raises his glass and everyone around the table follows with a series of whoops and cheers.

'Are you nervous?' Michelle says through a mouthful of chicken vol-au-vent.

'Of what?' I reply, picking out the sweetcorn from her pie and adding it to my plate.

'New York.'

'She's not afraid of anything.' Layla drapes her arm around my shoulder, pouting for the digital camera that Piers is using to document the evening.

'Everyone's afraid of something,' he says, checking the screen then pointing the lens at Michelle.

'Snakes!' Michelle shouts as she points across the table at me. 'Oh no, wait, that's Hector. I had a pet snake when I was little. I fed it mice but Hector was terrified when I put it in the bath every week for a swim.'

'He's only taken showers ever since.' I smile at the memory of one night when Hector stayed over at mine and I said I wanted a

205

soak in the bath. He visibly blanched, then confessed his child-hood fear whilst pulling me into the shower and proceeding to rub bubbles into my skin.

'I still cannot believe you broke up with him.' Michelle reaches forward for a second bread roll. 'Surely the lure of having me as a sister-in-law is enough to make you stay?'

'I didn't realise you were such a hopeless romantic,' I say, push-ing all images of Hector away.

'I just want someone to share my life with. Isn't that what we all want, deep down?'

'Cats,' Piers says as he drains his glass.

'What about them?' I ask.

'I hate them. Evil creatures. And rabbits. They're way too cute and fluffy not to be dangerous.'

'That's just weird.' Layla is sitting next to me, but she's not really paying attention to the rather strange conversation that's developing. Instead she keeps curling a strand of hair around one finger and looking at someone on the other side of the room.

'Fish!' Michelle springs to her feet and runs around to give me a wet kiss on the cheek. 'You have a funny thing about fish.'

I can't help but shudder. 'It's their eyes, just staring back at you from the plate and whispering *murderer*.'

'You made Hector cut off the head when we were in that restaurant back home. Dad thought it was hilarious.'

And there it is. The subtle reminder that so much of what I took for granted no longer belongs to me. The family, the stories, the building of a life that will never be because I was too afraid to let Hector love me.

'Let's dance.' Michelle tugs at my arm but I shake my head.

'In a minute.'

'I'll go.' Layla gets to her feet, fidgeting with the fabric gathered at her hip. I look past her to where a group of boys are standing at the bar. A particularly striking one, all tall, dark and handsome, has just raised his glass in toast, or rather invitation, to my best friend.

It is all so very different to Oxford. Even though I knew it would be. I chose LSE in part because of how easy it is to get lost in London, but also because the university is sleek and modern and not suffocated by centuries of tradition.

In only a few weeks I'm leaving for training in New York. The beginning of a new chapter, one that I've been thinking about and planning for years, but now I'm afraid that this too won't work. Everything has left me feeling a little . . . I don't really know what I'm feeling. All I do know is that I was happy here at LSE. But this life is no longer mine; it's someone else's turn to slot into the system and now I have to grow up all over again.

I loop the beaded strap of my bag over my wrist and make my way back to the cloakroom. As I move round the tables, I look across to the dance floor, where Michelle and Layla are shimmying to the sound of All Saints singing about pure shores. Directly behind Layla is a boy who looks rather like Mr DiCaprio himself, and I send up a silent prayer that he won't end up breaking my friend's optimistic heart.

I should be with them. I should be dancing and drinking and celebrating the moment instead of sneaking out the back door. But it's all so reminiscent of another night, and the taste of regret is even worse than that sticky vol-au-vent.

The streets around Chalk Farm Tube are quiet, with only a few black cabs and the occasional cyclist daring to sprint through the city without any lights on. Heading over the bridge that leads back to Primrose Hill, I'm struck by the idea that I'm constantly moving in the same direction but never actually getting to where I need to be.

How impossible it was back in Oxford to imagine any life other than one that had all three of us in it together. Where are they now, and do they think of me the way I do them? Do they wonder if I'm happy or miss me so deeply it hurts to breathe when they picture my face? To know or not to know, it feels like a constant battle, and sometimes I find myself picking up the telephone even though I have no number to call. I miss their voices, their laughter, but most of all who I was when I was with them. And perhaps that's why I made a promise never to look, because what I did changed me, and I'm no longer the person they once knew.

Staring up at the moon, I let my feet guide me along the pavement, aware but not really paying attention to the people gathered outside the Queen's pub, or the person standing by the pillar box, shouting down his mobile at someone about a taxi. Nor do I notice the two men sitting on the pavement next to a couple of red phone boxes, iconic symbols that are dotted all over London, but slowly dying a death thanks to the likes of Samsung and Nokia.

'Careful, love,' one of them says as I stumble over his bag. That's when I look, and I see that he's wearing a hospital gown underneath a thin, patchwork coat.

'Sorry,' I say, looking at the other man, who is passed out, but still holding tight to a paper bag containing a lidless bottle. 'Is he OK?'

'He's grand,' the first man says with a crooked smile, drawing heavily on a cigarette and blowing rings into the night sky. 'He's me best pal. Smuggled me out so we could go to the pub, but they wouldn't let me in.' He gestures to his clothes with a low chuckle. 'Said I wasn't appropriately dressed.'

'Shouldn't you be in a hospital?' I say, looking around as if this will magically procure an ambulance, or at least someone who might know what to do.

'Here,' the man says, beckoning me closer. He reaches into the pocket of his coat and hands me something, clasping his fingers tightly around my own. A slow warmth spreads over my skin, creeping upwards along my arm as I gaze into his eyes, unable to look away from the flecks of amber and gold.

'Do you believe in God?' He lets go of my hand and I open it to reveal a rough rectangle of palest stone encased by gold wire and hanging on a thin chain.

'Not really.' I hold the necklace between finger and thumb, seeing how the stone isn't completely white but has shades of blue and green hidden inside.

'But you do believe in something?'

'I guess.'

'You have a purple aura,' he says. 'It means you should be careful what you wish for.'

I used to wish all the time. Stare up at the stars in the hope that I might one day catch a falling one, put it in my pocket and carry the magic with me always.

'That necklace once belonged to my fiancée,' he says, using the butt of his cigarette to light another. 'She said the stone was to help calm my mind, protect me when she wasn't around.'

He leans closer and I don't back away, or retreat from the lingering scent of antiseptic and alcohol that seems stitched into his skin. I don't flinch when he opens my palm and picks up the necklace, nor do I shudder when he loops it around my neck and places a gentle kiss on my brow.

'There's nothing more powerful or dangerous than love,' he says, sitting back and closing his eyes.

'I can't take this.' I finger the stone around my neck and imagine someone else once doing the same.

'I don't need it any more,' the man says with a wide yawn and pats his chest. 'They gave me a new heart in the hospital. When I woke up after the op it was gone.'

'What was?'

'The pain of losing her.' His words are hushed, his face a curious mixture of sorrow and relief. 'You carry that same pain. It's a burden not everyone understands.'

Don't cry. You must not cry in the middle of the street in front of a stranger. No matter that he seems to understand you in a way that nobody else has since . . . oh God, I can't even bring myself to think about it, so what hope is there of me ever being able to move on?

'Whatever you think you're running from will find you in the end.' His eyes are closed, his body still but there is a gentle rise and fall to his chest.

If only that were true. Because even though I was the one to leave, I still can't help but hope that one day he will come looking for me.

NIAMH

Kalopsia (n.) – *the delusion of things being more beautiful than they really are*

Oxford, 1996

It was one of those summer evenings that seemed too good to be true, as if someone had taken a brush to the sky and painted it the perfect shade of blue. Or thrown a rope around the moon and pulled it closer so that it cast an edifying glow over two hundred souls, all dressed in their finest for the New College summer ball.

'You look . . .' Leo couldn't say anything more as he watched Niamh walk towards him. His eyes trailed the full length of her, from the pile of hair on her head, laced through with diamanté flowers, all the way down to the silver sandals on her feet.

As she moved, the fabric of her dress rippled in the fading light, flecks of gold hidden amongst the pale-blue pleats. The front dropped to a low V with a band of fabric that looped around her waist and then up behind her neck.

'Hi,' she whispered as she approached, drinking in the sight of him in a well-fitting tuxedo and oversized bow tie.

'Goodness, aren't you two just the most picture-perfect couple.' Erika skipped over to them wearing the dress she'd tried on back in

London. It was now paired with a bright red petticoat that made the skirt lift up to reveal more of her legs, black stilettoes and a diamond choker.

It was Erika who had gone back to the shop and bought the dress for Niamh. She said she couldn't bear the idea of anyone other than her owning it. In return, Niamh told Erika she loved her, which made Erika look at her in a strange but happy sort of way.

'Hello, gorgeous,' Duncan said with a smile, looking from Leo to Niamh in turn. He was wearing a white morning suit with tails, a frilled, baby-blue shirt and carrying a cane. Niamh half expected him to start tap-dancing, but despite the flamboyance of his outfit, he still looked ridiculously suave.

'Come here.' Duncan held out an arm to Niamh, then waved to a passing waiter who was tasked with documenting the evening on film. 'Let's take a photo. I want to remember this night when I'm old and senile.'

'You're already old and senile.' Erika laughed, a little more shrill than was necessary, and Niamh looked up at her face, noting the dilated pupils and slightly manic smile.

Leo watched the three of them as they gathered together, posing for the camera. They were such an unlikely trio of misfits who had somehow managed to find one another and become the firmest of friends.

'This one's mine,' Duncan said as he held the end of the Polaroid photo, flapping it about and blowing on the film as the picture came to life. 'One day I can look at it and remember that you two used to be young and gorgeous.'

'I have no intention of ever getting old,' Erika said as she kissed Niamh on the cheek, leaving behind the shiny red outline of her lips.

'Better start saving for all that surgery.' Duncan kissed Niamh on the other cheek, then spun around and pointed his cane to the sky. 'Let's go explore,' he announced and Erika trotted after him, glancing back over her shoulder to see if Niamh would follow.

'Do you mind?' Niamh asked Leo, looking from him to her friends and back again.

'Go,' he replied with a slow, soft kiss. 'I'll come find you later.'

The college had been transformed into something of a wonderland, with a raised dance floor covering the Main Quad, complete with a ten-piece band at one end and a bar at the other. The Master's Garden had Chinese lanterns strung from every branch of every tree, acrobats cartwheeled around the lawn and there was even a fire-eater wearing nothing but a thong and blue body paint.

'Here,' Erika whispered in Niamh's ear as she opened her palm to reveal a tiny white pill. 'Take this.'

'It's perfectly safe,' Duncan said as he picked up on Niamh's hesitation. 'We've both had one already.'

Niamh thought of Leo somewhere in amongst all that excess, waiting for her. Would he mind? She had no idea what he thought about drugs; the most he ever seemed to partake in was too many pints and some whiskey chasers after a rugby match. He'd never said anything about the omnipresent aroma of weed that hung around Duncan's room. Nor did he ask how it was that both he and Erika found the energy to retain their status as scholars, despite their love of clubbing.

What she didn't know was how he would feel about finding her high as a kite and quite possibly hallucinating.

'Tell you what,' Duncan said, reaching into the breast pocket of his jacket and taking out a coin. 'Why don't we let fate decide?'

Niamh watched as he tossed it in the air, heard herself call out 'heads' and wondered what it might be like to leave everything up to chance. To not worry about tomorrow or the next day, but choose to live in the moment and never have any regrets.

'Tails,' Duncan said as the three friends peered down at the circle of silver on the floor at their feet. 'Well, that sucks.'

'Ah, sod it,' Niamh said, popping the Ecstasy tablet on her tongue and knocking it back with a glass of champagne that Erika thrust upon her. It was, after all, a night for excess and debauchery.

The main dining hall was not, as might be expected, set out for dinner, but rather transformed into a dimly lit casino, complete with bunny girls carrying trays of martini and champagne. Erika danced over to the craps table and proceeded to kiss the dice before each throw. It was a scene oddly reminiscent of every single Bond film Leo had forced Niamh to watch. Erika even threw her arms in the air every time she won (which was surprisingly often, given that Niamh wasn't sure if she had a clue how to play), at one point flashing her boobs to the entire room.

Niamh wandered back outside, lured by the sound of a bass guitar dancing over the roof of the chapel towards her. She weaved through the crowds, aware of how her heart was beginning to race and her mouth was insisting on smiling at everyone she passed.

The back quad was bathed in rainbow lights that spun up and over the grass. On a small, raised stage set up by the far wall, a DJ stood behind some decks next to two enormous speakers. A few people were attempting to dance, swaying their arms to the music, but all the while looking around at who else was there.

Buoyed not only by illegal substances, but also the presence of someone who understood her kind of music, Niamh went over to the stage. Standing on tiptoe, she whispered her request to the middle-aged man who was wearing a Ramones t-shirt and smoking a fat joint.

He smiled down at her, his eyes sweeping over her face and choice of outfit, then nodded slowly as he flicked through one of several boxes of vinyl at his feet.

As the first chords echoed through the night, Niamh kicked off her shoes and made her way to the centre of the quad. Eyes closed, she breathed the music deep into her soul, letting it take over all other feelings. As soon as the bass kicked in, she stretched her hands to the sky and began to turn. Over and over she spun, oblivious to all the people who were watching. Singing at the top of her lungs, letting go of all the fears and frustrations, she gave thanks to the band, to the woman who had saved her again and again.

Leo sipped his beer, waiting for the build-up he knew was about to come and which made him think back to that afternoon in her bedroom, when he had come so close to kissing her for the very first time.

'Isn't that the song from Formula One?'

Leo reluctantly turned his head to find Robin smoking a cigar and staring at Niamh.

'Something like that,' he said with a chuckle as he looked back to see Erika and Duncan sprinting across the lawn. A moment later all three of them were bouncing around, completely oblivious to everyone else.

The song finished, swiftly replaced by the Bee Gees telling everyone they should be dancing. One by one, people let themselves be taken over by the music. Soon the quad became a throng of bodies and limbs, with feet pounding on the ground and hands reaching to the sky.

Leo made his way over to her, replicating the huge smile she had on her face as she saw him approach. She flung her arms around his neck and threw back her head as he picked her up and turned her around.

'Aren't stars just the most sublimely beautiful things you've ever seen?' she said as she brought her gaze back down to him. 'I wish I could dance right through them, then land on the moon and see if it really is made of cheese.'

He could tell she was high on more than champagne and music, but he didn't care. It didn't matter because she was here with him. How or why it came about wasn't important. All that was still to come was lost as he kissed her to the sound of Blue Swede singing about being hooked on a feeling.

He didn't want to have to share her with anyone else ever again. It didn't seem possible that it was less than a year since they'd first met, since he'd phoned his mother and told her he'd met the woman he wanted to marry.

Nothing had changed; if anything his feelings for Niamh seemed to swell each time he saw her. So much so that his mother had somehow managed to persuade her husband to give Leo one last summer. To allow him the time to be young and in love before the corporate world took him prisoner. Despite a few grumbles about Leo already having had a gap year, Mr Bonfiglio had, as always, acquiesced to the better wisdom of his wife.

So it was that Leo and Niamh were going to spend the summer travelling across Europe and documenting all they discovered. The plan was to create a film about discovering who you are by loving someone else. A story that Leo hoped might be good enough to earn him a place at film school in New York after graduation.

'I can't wait to get to Kefalonia,' Leo said. 'To go diving in the caves and eat oysters fresh off the boat.' He also couldn't wait to put it all on film – everything from the way she chewed on the inside of her cheek when she was concentrating, to the nonsensical mutterings she made whilst sleeping.

'I want to go swimming with the mermaids,' Niamh replied in a sing-song voice, wondering if she was dreaming. She closed her eyes and pictured herself in a turquoise sea with the sun smiling down from above. She could taste salt on her tongue, feel the soft slap of wet against her skin and hear the sound of laughter from someone nearby.

Eyes open, she looked across the lawn to where Erika and Duncan were standing, Erika's head thrown back to expose the long line of her neck. Time was running out; in only a few days Niamh was supposed to be packing up and moving into Erika's place in Chelsea. But she was also supposed to be getting on a boat with Leo and heading for Europe with only a handful of clothes in an old army backpack.

Niamh had never been one for confrontation, least of all when it involved telling your best friend that you had, in fact, chosen a boy instead of her. Just like Astrid, and look at what happened to her. It felt as if the whole word was floating up and away, and the only thing stopping Niamh from spinning into space was Leo's arms around her waist.

Leo was still thinking about the concept of fate, of how one fraction of a moment can change a person's entire life. He knew the moment that had changed his, but wanted to know if Niamh was aware of how important, how significant even the tiniest of details could be.

'What made you come to the bar that night?'

'Erika.' Everything was always about Erika. And yet it was also so much more than her. Niamh could still remember standing in front of the mirror in her bedroom, contemplating what to wear. Then looking across at the pile of notes on her desk that she really should be concentrating on instead.

Leo too was thinking of that night. It had been his mother's birthday and he'd forgotten to call, so he'd stopped off at a phone box on the way back to college. Which in turn meant he took the corner faster than he should have and had nearly run into that tourist. He had been in a hurry, but at the time put it down to nothing more than looking forward to the first sip of a cold pint after a week spent buried in books.

'What was the real reason you came after me?' Niamh asked.

Leo was about to reply when he felt a tap on his shoulder and the waiter from earlier handed him another Polaroid. This one was taken as he'd kissed her on the dance floor under a sky filled with stars. He wanted to keep it, to show it to a gaggle of kids in years to come, telling them about the night he asked their grandmother to stay with him for the rest of their days.

'Niamh,' he said, drawing her close and loving the way she tucked so neatly under his chin. He also loved the fact she always had oranges in her bag and knots in her hair. Just as he loved how she believed in him as no one else ever had before. 'I need to ask you something.'

'You smell like rainbows and leprechauns,' she said with a giggle.

He couldn't ask her when she was high, no matter how incredible she looked. There was time. There had to be more time, because without her, nothing made sense any more.

'What's the matter?' she asked as she traced the line of his jaw with one finger.

Before he could offer up any kind of response, he saw her look beyond him, her features changing into a smile and then a frown at whoever was approaching.

'When were you going to tell me?'

Leo turned around to see Erika striding across the quad, closely followed by Duncan. At the same time, Niamh leant into him and he instinctively put a protective arm around her.

'What's going on?' Leo asked as he looked from Erika, all high colour and tight jaw, to Duncan, whose mouth was opening and closing like a goldfish, but no sound was coming out.

'As if you didn't know,' Erika spat back.

'No, I don't. Niamh?'

'Erika.' Niamh reached out a hand to her friend, then thought better of it.

'Don't you Erika me,' she said, poking Niamh in the shoulder over and over. 'We made a plan. We were going to spend the summer together, but now it turns out you'd rather go with him instead.' Erika glared at Leo, barely able to conceal her pain.

'You told her?' Niamh looked over at Duncan, whose only response was a vague grin.

'Of course he did,' Erika replied. 'Unlike you. Instead of doing the decent thing, you've hidden away in Leo's bed. I thought you were better than that.'

'This has nothing to do with Leo,' Niamh said as she shook her head and tried to bite back a little of her own anger.

'Bullshit.' Erika pushed Niamh and she stumbled backwards, hands outstretched in anticipation of a fall. 'It has everything to do with him.'

'Erika . . .' Duncan found his voice, but visibly withdrew when she shot him a scathing look.

'You barely know him,' Erika said, pointing at Leo.

'I know him well enough.' Niamh felt a blush creeping up her neck and over her face.

'Oh really?' Erika replied with a snort. 'At some point, he will find someone else. Boys like him can never stay faithful for long.' There were tears in her eyes now, thin lines of black falling down her face and making her look like a beautiful clown.

'Why can't you just be happy for me?'

'I am,' Erika said, reaching for Niamh's hand and turning it over to trace a finger over the lines on her palm. 'All I've ever wanted is for you to be happy.'

Niamh looked down at their hands, wondering how many times Erika had done the same thing, like some kind of hypnosis whenever she wanted Niamh to stop being mad at her.

'You know what,' Niamh said in a whisper as she took her hand away. 'I think you're jealous.'

'Of him?' Erika scoffed as she darted a look over at Leo. 'Oh, *älskling*, you and I both know I could do so much better.'

'And what about Astrid?' Niamh shot back. 'You couldn't be happy for her either.'

'You told her?' Erika said, staring at Duncan. Her voice was pitched and strange as she swiped at the tears that continued to fall. 'You promised you wouldn't tell.'

'Of course he told me,' Niamh said, her own voice laced through with sarcasm. 'I know all about what you did to your so-called best friend.'

'This has nothing to do with Astrid.'

'Bullshit, it has everything to do with Astrid. Would you have even spoken to me that day if I didn't remind you of her?'

Erika folded her arms across her chest and looked away. 'I don't know.'

'I think you do. I think this whole time you've been trying to replace her with me.'

'Niamh,' Leo said as he took her hand and tried to steer her away. 'I think maybe we should go.'

Niamh turned to look at him, at the open honesty of his beautiful face. He was the one person she'd never pretended with. Because no matter how much she adored Erika, a part of her always felt like she would never be enough.

'Please, Niamh,' Erika said, scrunching tight her eyes and dropping her head. 'Don't do this. You of all people know how much it hurts to lose someone.'

'Yes, I do. But not as much as you asking me to choose between us and him.'

Erika's face folded into a frown. 'I never asked you to choose.'

'Except you did.' Niamh was crying now too, fat tears of frustration that mixed in with all the sadness. 'Back in Sweden, when you said he had to be good enough for all three of us. But he never stood a chance, did he? Because nothing and nobody is ever good enough for you and your impossibly high standards.'

'It's such a fucking cliché,' Erika said with a snarl. 'You falling for the first guy you ever sleep with.'

'Shut up,' Niamh said, aware of both the blush creeping up her neck and the look of surprise Leo just gave her. 'For once in your life just shut up and stop trying to control me.'

'Control you? *Älskling*, all I have ever done is help you.'

'Well, maybe I don't want your help any more.'

'You can't just flick off a friendship like this.' Erika was practically screaming now, waving her arms about like a woman possessed. 'I have always been there for you, stuck up for you, paid for you. *För Guds skull*, Niamh, I even bailed you out when your parents refused to help.'

'I said I would pay you back.'

'How?' Erika said with a small, deliberate laugh. 'You turned down the one opportunity I gave you to actually make something of yourself. To finally fit in with the rest of us.'

'And there it is,' Niamh said, jabbing at the air between them with her finger. 'You think money makes you better than me? Well guess what, all it does is make you a controlling, self-righteous bitch.'

Erika's hand came out too quick for Niamh to duck out of the way, her palm landing sharp and hard on Niamh's cheek.

'You are nothing but a *förrädisk tik*. No wonder your mother didn't want you.'

The weight of Erika's words filtered into Niamh's heart like a jagged knife: so much worse than being hit. All of the high was gone in an instant. Everything that was so very wonderful about that night was wiped away as the truth finally spilled.

'How could you?' Niamh whispered, but her words were filled with loathing. She took two steps back, then ran as far away as she could from the pain she had been afraid of all along.

'Niamh, wait,' Erika called after her, but Leo held her back.

'I think you've both done enough.' Leo gave the briefest of nods to Duncan as he set off at a jog in order to catch up with the girl he seemed to spend so much of his time running after.

He could picture them together, him and Niamh, when they were old and grey. They would sit in two ancient armchairs, arguing about the price of milk or if there could ever be a better sequel than *The Empire Strikes Back*. Then she would throw down her knitting or whack him with her slipper and storm off in frustration.

'Niamh, wait,' he said, echoing Erika's own words as he saw Niamh passing through the door that led to Queen's Lane. He had such a distinct sense of déjà vu, spiralling him back to that night when he'd followed her out of the bar, intrigued by the girl with a quirky sense of style and a mouth he was desperate to kiss.

'What's the point, Leo?' She leant against the wall, looking back at him with tears running down her face. 'She's right.'

'No, she's not.' Leo cupped her face in his hands and lifted her chin so that she had to meet his eye. 'When are you going to realise that I love you, all of you, and it makes no fucking difference where you came from?'

'It matters to me.' Niamh tried to push him away, but she couldn't bring herself to put any effort into it. Because if she pushed him away, there was always the risk he might not come back.

'Why?'

'Because she gave me away.' The words came out in the middle of a sob and she clasped her hands over her mouth as if she could somehow put them back in again. For so long she had been cursed by the fact that she wasn't important enough or good enough for her mother to want to fight for her. Erika and Duncan had slowly managed to change that, made her believe that she too had the right to be happy.

But now it had been broken by the one person who claimed to be on her side, no matter what.

'She didn't have a choice.'

'You always have a choice.'

There was a certain bitterness hidden in her words, along with a huge dollop of sorrow and he didn't know how to make it go away. He wanted to make it all go away, to burn her pain, erase it, let her see how incredible she really was.

'Then let me make mine. I choose you, all of you, even the weirdly annoying bits.'

'I'm not annoying.'

'Even when you leave orange peel in the sink and squeeze the toothpaste from halfway down the tube?'

'You're the weird one for not liking oranges.'

He smiled as he wrapped her in his arms, inhaling her intoxicating scent and waiting for her to breathe, to let go.

'I don't care that you were a virgin.'

Niamh stilled against him, then gave a long, shaky sigh. 'I cared. I cared too much about so many stupid things.' Namely trying to change herself in order to fit in with people who, it turned out, didn't actually care about her at all.

'You should have told her.'

'I know.' But in turn, Leo should have told her about the night he bumped into Erika, when the two of them shared drinks and stories until late into the night.

'Erika will forgive you. She just needs some time to realise you're not going to leave her like Astrid did.'

Except Niamh couldn't rid herself of the idea that Astrid wasn't the only thing haunting her friend. Because she was fairly certain Astrid had never been a topic of conversation between her and Leo.

Which meant someone else must have told him. Someone who was intoxicatingly beautiful and so very used to getting her own way.

What did Erika tell him? The truth or the lie? It hurt Niamh to think she might have told him everything about Astrid, no doubt as a way to make him feel sorry for her. It hurt even more to know that Erika was so very good at keeping secrets from the people she claimed to love the most.

ERIKA

Cheesecake

London, 1999

'*Farbror?*' I call out as I enter the hall. '*De tar jag?*'

'Erika?' comes the reply as a scruffy little terrier bounds up from the back of the house, weaving in between my legs, his little tail going ten to the dozen in excitement. '*Är det du?*'

A moment later Alex Lindberg comes out of the kitchen, wiping his hands on a tea towel with spectacles balanced on top of his head. He is dressed in linen trousers, a white shirt and a deep-purple cravat, which for him is rather casual – he has been known on occasion to lecture in a three-piece suit, complete with ivory-topped cane and a bowler hat. He holds his arms out to me and I'm grateful for the hug, breathing in his familiar musky scent.

'Now, this is a surprise,' he says. 'I was starting to forget what you look like.'

'Ha, ha,' I say as I bend down to rub Paxman on his belly, making one of his back legs twitch in delight. I found him as I ran past the local newsagent one winter's morning when a hand-written advert caught my eye. Paxman was the runt of the litter, with scruffy grey hair and one ear that was always a little floppy.

But each morning without fail, a man and his dog now walk slowly around the park, watching the changing seasons and chatting to the people they meet along the way.

Buying him a puppy was a simple gesture, a small token of thanks for all he had done, but he deserves more than I've been giving.

'Is everything OK?' he asks as I hang my bag over the bannister, just as I have always done, and make my way to the kitchen.

'I'm not really sure,' I reply. Because ever since Hector made that comment about having a family of our own one day, I haven't been able to get my mind to behave.

'*Vad pagar?*' Alex asks again, watching as I busy myself with tidying away some dishes from the draining board. I'm certain that he sees how skittish I am, on edge and unable to keep my hands still.

'*Ingenting,*' I reply, picking up a wine glass and polishing it with a cloth, only for him to snatch it away and put it on a shelf up high.

'It's clearly not nothing.' He picks up the kettle and proceeds to fill it from the tap at the kitchen sink. 'Go sit outside,' he says with a nod of his head. 'I'll bring you out some tea and *ostkaka.*'

I do as I'm told, sitting on a curved wooden seat that's tucked into the corner of the garden underneath a trailing wisteria. It always catches the afternoon sun, which is just starting to peep around the house, snaking its way across my bare toes and warming my skin.

'Now,' Alex says as he sets down a tray on the cast-iron table by the fence that also doubles up as a potting bench. 'Tell me what's really going on.'

'I've met someone,' I say as I take his offering of Swedish cheesecake and home-made strawberry jam. 'And I think I need to tell him.'

Alex gives a slow nod of his head as he pours out two mugs of strong, black tea, adding milk to both and two cubes of sugar to his own. 'I always said the time would come.'

'I know.' I take a bite of cheesecake, letting the softness melt inside my mouth.

'If he's worth it, it won't matter what you did,' Alex says as he sits next to me.

'It will always matter.'

'To you, yes. But you had your reasons, and if he loves you, he will understand.'

'I guess.'

'But if you tell him what really happened with Leo,' Alex says as he relieves me of my empty plate, then cuts another slice, 'you also have to tell Layla.'

I shove another forkful of cheesecake into my mouth in an attempt to quash the rising panic that I can feel stirring in my stomach. Telling Hector is one thing; showing the truth to someone who has seen me virtually every day for the past few years is another.

'*Älskling*,' Alex says as he cuts himself a small sliver of cheesecake, along with a healthy dollop of jam. 'If you feel the need to divulge your secret, then who am I to stop you? But you may not be prepared for what happens next.'

That's what I'm afraid of. If I tell the truth, will it set me on a course back to where it all began? Layla is way too nosey not to want to know it all, every tiny little detail about each and every one of them. She'd probably want to meet them too, track them down, cultivate some kind of grand reunion. Because she is so wonderfully optimistic about the world, simply because she's never been broken.

'I wish I could go back.'

'Don't we all,' Alex says, resting his hand on my knee and giving it a pat. I lean into him, let him put his arm around my shoulder. It's a relief to share my burden, to have at least one person with whom I can talk about anything at all. For so long I've been watching every word, carefully considering the knock-on effect of what I say as well as what I do. It's exhausting, but I've always assumed it is better than the alternative.

'I'll always be on your side, Erika,' Alex says, kissing me gently on the forehead as he stands. 'And this will always be your home. But you need to be sure, because you made that choice for a reason.'

I know all this. It's why I haven't ever come close to telling anyone before.

NIAMH

Pistanthrophobia (n.) — *the fear of trusting people due to negative past experiences*

Oxford, 1996

It was one of those crisp autumnal mornings when the sky was clear and bright and the leaves were just beginning to turn. Niamh was up at Stavvers, the ugly seventies blocks that housed third-year students who chose not to go down the private rental route. Or, in her case, if you had nowhere else to go.

Her record collection was already set out neatly on the top shelf of her bookcase, but her other belongings were still waiting to be unpacked. The thought of one more year, one final year, had filled her with an acute sense of trepidation for weeks, even more so now that she was actually back.

The original plan had been to share a dark-blue terraced house with Erika and Duncan. Niamh's room was tucked into the eaves at the top of a narrow flight of stairs and had luminescent stars stuck to the ceiling. That plan had been ripped to pieces the moment Erika discovered that Niamh was going to spend the summer with Leo.

Instead of going to find Erika, instead of banging on the door and begging for forgiveness (which was exactly the kind of dramatic gesture Erika expected), Niamh had dug in her own heels and got on the Eurostar with Leo as planned. The entire journey had been spent penning a letter she knew she would never send. Every time she tried to explain what had happened, she would get angry with Erika for being complicit in creating the problem. After all, Niamh hadn't asked her to apply for an internship on her behalf. But then she also realised that by going along with it, she had made her friend believe it was what she wanted too.

Niamh had always known the summer was to be Erika's way of making up for lost time, a way to try to stitch herself back together after losing Astrid. If only she hadn't been so afraid of losing Erika, perhaps Niamh would have found the courage to tell her the truth. And now, because of her own insecurities, Niamh had lost her anyway.

The problem was, it wasn't ever really about an internship; it was about Leo and how Niamh had chosen him instead of Erika, just like Astrid had done too.

Three sheets of folded paper filled with words that made no real sense were still stuffed into the bottom of her rucksack in the hope that she might be able to forget about what she had lost. Because it wasn't just Erika she'd lost, but Duncan, and all the time she had spent with them, daring to believe that she'd found friends who would be there for her, no matter what.

Her brief return to Ireland, after a summer spent with Leo, was a veritable bolt to the brain. She and her parents had moved around one another with practised ease, barely exchanging a few words over breakfast before her father retreated to the safety of his shed. Niamh's mother paid more attention to the television than her, and so she had done what she always did and spent each day either in her room, or drinking endless cups of tea in her local café.

To be back in Oxford, standing in a room imprinted with memories of all who had been there before, made her want to run. There was Blu-Tack on the walls where once somebody's posters had been stuck, and there was a postcard from Budapest lying forgotten at the back of the desk drawer.

It all seemed to belong to someone else, someone who deserved to be there more than her. Because she no longer wanted to be there, but she had no idea where it was she would rather live. It made her wonder what her life would have been like had she chosen to study at any other university in the world. Or if she had been chosen by a different set of parents. Or, the one thing she turned over in her mind more than any other, if her mother had never given her away.

Leo would be there soon, and then everything would change. She knew that the day was one of those pivotal, life-changing events that people always talk about in retrospect. But what of the ones you instigate, the ones you choose to create? Because she still had a choice, she always had a choice, but until she saw him, she had no idea which path she would be forced to tread.

Niamh fingered the charm that always hung around her neck. She remembered Erika asking her about it the very first night they met. It was during the first term, when Niamh was spending most of her time either hiding in the library or her room. But she had been persuaded down to the bar one evening by someone on her course. As soon as she entered the dank, sweaty space, Niamh's attention was drawn to a girl by the pool table who was dressed in a tutu and army boots, deliberately leaning across the surface and revealing as much of those legs as possible to her opponent.

'My God, what is she wearing?'

Niamh had turned round to be rewarded with the sight of Octavia, lips pursed and eyes narrowed.

231

'I think she's a bit of a lash,' Niamh said, at the same time as Erika turned around and flashed her a smile so much more welcoming than any she had encountered since arriving in Oxford.

'I wasn't actually talking to you,' Octavia replied with a smirk, her eyes sweeping over Niamh in one dismissive movement. 'Not that I understood a word of what you just said.'

'That's because you are both *okunnig* and *bortskamd*,' Erika said as she came towards them, brandishing a cue. 'Perhaps I should shove this up your nose and have a poke about to see if there are any brains in that thick head of yours?'

Octavia rolled her eyes and walked away with a backward toss of 'bitch', but Erika either didn't hear or didn't care, instead draping one arm over Niamh's shoulder and steering her in the direction of the bar.

The conversation that followed was peppered with laughter as they tried to understand one another's accents, along with countless shots of vodka. It was the vodka which meant that when Erika pointed at Niamh's necklace and asked her where it was from, Niamh hadn't shied away from telling her it once belonged to her mother. She hadn't been able to tell her the whole story, not then, but the fact Erika hadn't pushed for more of an answer made Niamh think that perhaps one day she could.

Everything came back to that day – to a chance meeting between strangers who turned into friends, back when Niamh didn't think she would ever find anyone to share her life with. Now she was terrified of having made the wrong choice, because if Erika was right, if she and Leo didn't have a future, then she would be worse off than ever before.

'Hey,' he said as he opened the gate and walked around the perimeter of the kitchen garden. She was sitting on a wooden bench next to a wall covered in clematis. The leaves were a mixture of green and red with a thin autumn carpet at her feet. She was dressed in leggings and an oversized jumper with holes in the cuffs, through which she had poked her thumbs.

She attempted a smile as he bent down to kiss her, but then turned her head away.

'I got your message,' Leo said as he sat down beside her and saw that she had been crying. 'What's going on?'

What she chose to say next would resonate in her mind for years to come. She knew that the words held such significance, but she had no idea where to begin.

'It's OK.' Leo took hold of her hand. 'Whatever it is, you can tell me.'

The only problem was, 'whatever' was such an all-encompassing word, meaning he really didn't think he could cope with any of the scenarios that had been flashing through his mind ever since he picked up her voicemail less than half an hour ago.

'I'm pregnant.' She looked up at him, then pulled her hand from his.

'Oh.' Of all the things he had feared she might say, that one hadn't even crossed his mind. Which was both ridiculous and naive, because why wouldn't that be something she needed to tell him?

'That's all you have to say?'

'No. I mean, I don't know. What am I supposed to say?'

'Nothing, I guess.'

'I thought you were on the pill?' Besides which, they hadn't slept together since she had contracted food poisoning and couldn't bear to be touched. Then she had gone home to get ready for her final year of study. It was a year he had been looking forward to, just as he couldn't wait to get back to Oxford to see her again.

'I was,' Niamh said as she wrapped her arms around her knees, hugging them tight. 'But I guess being sick sort of nullified its effects. Plus, I forgot to take it for a few days. Anyway, makes no odds now.'

'Why didn't you say anything?' There had been endless conversations over the phone in the weeks when she was back in Cork. Along with letters and tokens of affection he kept sending her on a whim.

He had agreed to do some work for his father, a thank you of sorts for letting him have the rest of the summer off. The work was methodical and rather dull, and Leo had struggled to click with any of his co-workers. It wasn't just about being the boss's son, but rather his mind was distracted, because everything made him think of her. He'd taken to getting off the Tube early and walking up through Camden on his way home. It was in the market that he'd stumbled across an antiques shop, a veritable treasure trove of things that he knew Niamh would adore.

The next time he wrote to her, he sent her a music box that you had to wind with a silver key and had the twelve constellations painted on the underside of the lid. The time after that, it was a kaleidoscope made from a cat's eye marble, which cast beautiful lines of light as it was turned. In return, she had sent him mixtapes of all her favourite songs, and a packet of chocolate-covered honeycomb, because she knew how much of a sweet tooth he had.

She had ignored all the signs, because the idea of actually being pregnant was so ridiculously scary that she decided to treat it like a mosquito bite – if you resisted the urge to scratch it, it would eventually go away. Until it was obvious that it wasn't something she could push under the carpet and she had to figure out what to do next. Except walking into a pharmacy in Ireland and asking for a pregnancy test wasn't the easiest of tasks. And she had absolutely no desire to go to her family doctor, because then someone would know and have an opinion about her future.

Instead, she had waited until she got back to Oxford and simply popped into Boots on her way up to Stavvers. The sales assistant had barely looked at her as she handed it across the counter. Niamh had stuffed it into her bag and done her very best to ignore it as she walked up Woodstock Road. But it was there, one corner of the box poking out and taunting her with the truth it would reveal. Once she'd dumped her belongings in her room and unpacked her records, she knew there was no point in delaying the inevitable.

Peeing on a stick to decide your future was such a weird concept. There was a tiny collection of cells inside her that were already having such a significant impact on her life, even if there were no obvious outward signs. Apart from swollen boobs and an inability to stop crying, and that was even before she looked down and saw those two lines of blue.

'I didn't realise,' she said with an elongated sigh. 'Or rather, I pretended it was unlikely because we haven't actually had sex in a while.'

'Shit,' Leo said, staring out at nothing as the harshness of reality settled inside his mind.

'Shit, indeed.'

'Does anyone else know?'

'Not at the moment. I wanted to tell you first.'

'Right. I get that. But perhaps you should tell someone?'

'Why? So you don't have to make the decision for me?'

'I didn't mean that.' Or did he? Because he needed help, they both needed help, to try to figure out what the hell they were supposed to do next. Only he couldn't think of a single person he could tell who wouldn't either judge or try to steer them down a particular path.

'Besides, who the fuck am I supposed to tell?' She could feel the panic beginning to rise, just as it had ever since she had seen those two blue lines. It was a panic that was feeding off her fear, off her past and all the implications that had been running through her mind for weeks now.

'What about your mum?' Surely she could tell her mum? He would want to tell his mum, ask her advice and hopefully offload some of his own fear.

Niamh chewed on the inside of her cheek and rubbed the heel of her hand against her eyes.

'Did I ever tell you why they adopted me so late?'

'No.' And the way she said it meant he didn't want to know.

'She kept miscarrying. I think she lost nine babies in total, one of which was stillborn.' The words caught in her throat as she remembered her father explaining why her mum wouldn't get out of bed for three days straight. It had been the tenth anniversary of the day her son was born, and a week before Niamh was supposed to start at senior school. She was still a child herself, but had been forced to grow up so much that day, to understand more about the cruelties of life than she had been ready to know.

'When she turned forty-five, my dad convinced her to adopt, but I don't think her heart was ever really in it.'

'What do you mean?'

'As soon as I hit puberty she was constantly lecturing me about being responsible. She always said it was unfair that some women could have children, only to throw them away, when there were countless others who would love that little babby with all their hearts.'

'But it wasn't your fault.'

'Maybe not. But I was a constant reminder of what she wanted, the baby she couldn't have.'

Leo couldn't imagine what it must have been like for her, to go from a home where there were no parents, to one where the parents couldn't show her any affection. His own family were an endless source of irritation and interference, but he had never been short of love.

'Does this mean you don't want to keep it?'

The look she shot him was enough to make him flinch. 'Jesus, Leo, do you not remember what I told you about my mother? No matter how much it hurts that she abandoned me, she also let me live.'

'OK, OK. Forget I said anything.' He felt like a naughty schoolboy being reprimanded for breaking an unwritten rule.

For a while they just sat, both of them staring at the ground and trying to think of something to say. Niamh took out a cigarette and began to roll it between her fingers, then she brought it up to her nose and inhaled deeply.

'Don't look at me like that,' she said, putting it back in her pocket. 'I'm not actually going to smoke it.'

'Then what are you going to do?'

'*We*, Leo. What are *we* going to do?'

Leo scuffed his trainer on the ground over and over as if somehow the movement could help ease the mass of emotions swirling through him. He didn't want to be a father. At least, not yet. He had so many plans for the two of them, none of which involved even thinking about kids until they'd travelled the world, crafted blisteringly exciting careers and exhausted one another both physically and mentally. And now it was all going to have to change, long before he was even close to being ready for the responsibility of being a grown-up.

'We could get married?' He dared a look at her, but couldn't see her face behind that thick curtain of hair. He had wanted to ask her for months. He'd even gone so far as to buy an antique sapphire ring in Camden Market, which was currently in a drawer back in his student house, because he hadn't expected to need it that afternoon.

If only he'd asked her at some point over the summer, or at least come prepared, because now she would think that the only reason he was asking was because of the baby.

Niamh sat back, brushing her hair from her face then letting her hand rest on her middle. She'd thought he might ask her, dared to imagine it. But on a hilltop in Santorini when they shared a bowl of chips and a bottle of Guinness, not because he felt that he had to. Even if he had intended to all along, now it would forever feel forced, tainted instead of beautiful.

'I'd still be pregnant.'

'But it would be better, in the eyes of God and all that.'

Niamh got to her feet and strolled across to where a few roses were still clinging to the last remnants of summer. She didn't look back to see if Leo was following, but she felt the air shift behind her, and caught the faintest scent of basil that clung to his clothes.

'That's hardly the point,' she said, reaching out a hand towards the rosebush and wishing she could prick her finger on a thorn and fall into a dreamless sleep.

'Then what is?'

She turned around to look at him, searching his face for any sign of comprehension, but found nothing more than fear.

'Are all men this idiotic, or is it just you?'

'I honestly have no idea what you're talking about.'

'I am going to have a baby.'

'I know.'

'In roughly seven months' time.'

'I understand how pregnancy works, Niamh.'

'What else is supposed to happen in seven months' time, Leo?'

She waited. Watching as the cogs of his brain jumped forward to May and what it was that all final-year students would be completely immersed in at that time.

'Fuck.' This wasn't just about a baby. This was about the rest of their lives changing from that very second. One tiny sperm and one tiny egg coming together at a precise moment in time had flipped both their futures up and around and sent them crashing back to earth without giving them the space to breathe, let alone think. The odds of Niamh getting pregnant were too complicated for him to try and get his head around, but he knew they weren't as low as he'd stupidly thought.

'And after that? Even if I did manage to prepare for and then sit my finals without going into labour, who the hell is going to give me a job?'

She could contact Charlie. Ask him to give her a second chance, let her apply for another internship next summer. But would they consider hiring her with a baby on the way? Even if they did, who would look after it whilst she tried to clamber back on to the corporate ladder she had been so desperately trying to avoid?

'But you wouldn't have to go to work.' Why did he keep speaking without thinking? He was trying to help, to placate her somehow, even if he had no clue what they were actually going to do.

'That is so fucking misogynistic.'

'We can figure it out.' He had always been able to figure it out, but was it actually him, or the safety net that came with a stable family and money that meant his life had been pretty smooth sailing up to that point?

'How?' She was so angry at him for just assuming everything would be fine. Because he had no idea what it meant to fail, to screw up, to have anything ever go even the slightest bit wrong. The idea that perhaps he wouldn't be able to help after all terrified her. It made her think that telling him wasn't necessarily the best thing she could have done. She took a deep breath, steeling herself for the explanation, the truth, that she realised he needed to hear.

'Let's just say, for argument's sake, that we did get married. We finish our finals, move to London and you start working at your father's company. Do you really want to be the only twenty-something going home to nappies and puke?'

'But we won't be in London.' He had no desire to work for his father, or any other law firm. She knew this; they had spoken at length about what else he wanted to do with his life, so why was she now trying to steer him down a path neither of them had any intention of following?

She knew what he was thinking, but he needed to understand that his choices had been drastically reduced the moment he had impregnated her.

'We would need money, Leo. Babies are expensive and if I'm at home playing wifey, then you need to be at work, not chasing an impossible dream.'

'Hang on a sec, we're supposed to be moving to New York so I can enrol in film school. You were the one who said I should follow my dreams, not just do whatever my father wants me to do.'

'That's not the point, Leo.' She lashed out at the rose bush, sending petals cascading to the ground. 'Everything has changed, don't you see?'

'Of course I see, but shouting at me isn't going to help.'

'Maybe not. But it makes me feel better.'

She needed him, she needed all of him and not just the parts that were about love and sex. It was so enormously terrifying that she didn't think she could keep breathing unless she knew he would be there for her, no matter what.

'How are you feeling?' He took a step towards her, tentatively, as she was wound so tight he wasn't quite sure what she was going to say or do next.

'Awful,' she replied, sucking at a scratch on her hand. 'I want to vomit all the time, but can't actually be sick. I'm currently eating my body weight in cheese and ham sandwiches as they're the only thing that seem to help.'

'You hate cheese.' One step closer and she didn't flinch, so he reached out his hand and used it to draw her to him.

'Go figure,' Niamh mumbled as she tucked herself under his chin, feeling the beat of her heart settle as she did so. 'Babies clearly screw with your tastebuds as well as your mind.'

He breathed in the scent of her, so familiar and comforting that it made him even more aware of how much he needed her, all of her. The time spent in London without her had seemed to stretch and wane, every part of him itching to get back to Oxford so that he might hold her again. He would do anything to make her happy, but he wasn't certain that a baby would do anything other than fill her with regret.

'You . . . *we*, don't have to keep it.' He whispered the idea into her mind, allowing himself to think that perhaps there was a way out of the situation that wouldn't be too painful for her to cope with.

'Except we do.'

'What about—'

'No.'

He felt her stiffen against him and he moved her a little away so that he could look at her directly, get a better feel for what she was really thinking.

'You don't even know what I was going to say.'

'Give it up?' Niamh lifted her chin, biting down hard on her bottom lip to try to stop the tears from returning.

'It would be different.'

'How? How would it be different?' She was crying now; there was no point in trying to stop it, because once those tears began to fall there was nothing she could do other than give in to the emotions coursing through her body. 'One day that baby will become a child who thinks there must be something wrong with them. Because why else would their mother choose not to love them?'

'I'm just saying, we have options.'

'Such as?'

'I'm from a large family, remember? And Mum's been harassing my sisters for years about grandkids.'

He was smiling, but it hadn't quite reached his eyes, which told her he was finding it all just as overwhelming as she was. She'd had time to come to terms with it, even if it was nothing more than a niggling thought at the back of her mind. But he had been blindsided by the announcement that he was – surprise! – going to be a father.

'Have you told them about New York?' Niamh sniffed as she folded her arms over her chest, because she could guess his answer even before he gave it.

'Not yet.' He wanted to, but there had never been the right moment. He really wanted to do it when Niamh was there with him to back him up, because he knew that they would disapprove.

'Which means you're not sure they'd give us their blessing.'

It wasn't a question, because she understood him more than he wanted her to. Sometimes, actually most of the time, she figured out what was going on inside his head before he had a chance to do so himself.

'Have you told *your* parents?' It was a cheap shot and he knew it, but if neither of them had actually told anyone, kept it a secret from the world, was that not some kind of sign that perhaps it was all a bit too much too soon?

'That's different.' Niamh looked away. She hadn't told them because then there would be all kinds of questions.

'My family would look after us, Niamh. You don't have to worry.'

'They would look after *you*. But what would happen if they cut you off? Gave you an ultimatum about me? I don't want to be the reason why you no longer talk to your family.'

Because she knew that eventually he would come to resent her – and the baby – for it. Family was such a big part of his world; those people had shaped him into the man he had become and she knew he would be at a loss without them.

It was there, a split second before he could cover it up – the doubt on his face that told her more than she ever wanted to know. Because it's all well and good to say that money isn't important, up until the very point when it could all be taken away.

'We'll figure it out,' Leo said, pulling her back to him and trying not to picture his father's face when he found out he was going to be a grandfather.

'How?'

'I don't know.' He had no fucking clue, but admitting that to her wasn't about to solve anything.

'I saw her today. Cycling along St Giles.' Niamh felt Leo stiffen against her, heard him clear his throat before speaking.

'And?'

'Nothing. She didn't see me.' But she wished she had. She wished she could have been brave enough to chase after her, say sorry and somehow try to mend a little of what she was partly responsible for breaking.

'Have you spoken, you know, since?'

It was a strange question, given they had spent practically the whole summer together. Every moment of every day and every night for weeks on end, with nobody else for company; besides which, surely he knew she would have told him if she had decided to contact Erika?

'No. But maybe I should.'

Leo didn't reply, instead looking away and scratching at the back of his neck.

'What aren't you telling me?' Niamh said, tilting back her head so she could look at him properly.

'Nothing.' He let go of her and stepped back, shoving his hands in his pockets and rocking back and forth on his heels. 'I just don't think she's the sort of friend you need right now.'

'Then what do I need, Leo? Enlighten me, please, because I am terrified about what happens next.'

'There's still time,' he replied, drawing her back to him, kissing her hair and breathing in her familiar scent. There was no tobacco now, but the oranges were still there, hiding in her curls. 'Everything will be OK, I promise.'

'Say that again,' Niamh whispered.

'I promise to take care of you, Niamh,' he said as he kissed her gently. 'No matter what.'

ERIKA

SNOW GLOBE

London, 1999

It is Sunday, a day of rest or worship, or perhaps both, and I am holed up in the house Hector shares with his sister. Michelle has been on a yoga retreat in Thailand for over a week, so we have the place to ourselves and I can't remember the last time I felt quite this content.

It's two months since we first met in this very same house, on a crisp spring night when I nearly didn't make it to the party. Hector was sitting next to a firepit in the back garden, arguing with his little sister, but his head turned as soon as I stepped out from the kitchen and I found myself unable to look away.

He was dressed head-to-toe in black, the buttons of his shirt open low enough to reveal the edge of a tattoo creeping over his chest. Not quite the PhD geek Michelle had described to me, nor was I prepared for the stir of heat in my belly that slowly made its way up to my face.

I sat down next to him, took a hit of vodka from the bottle he offered, and found it difficult to concentrate on anything at all, due to how very close he was. Close enough to see he had one eye of blue, another of green, and a small scar hidden underneath the stubble on his chin. He kept looking at me, then looking away, and I wondered if it was the alcohol or the nearness of him that was making me so dizzy.

There was a conversation drifting around the fire, but I wasn't really concentrating on the words. I remember looking through the contents of my wardrobe only an hour before, trying to decide whether or not it was worth getting changed, just for a house party. Then I'd stood in front of the bathroom mirror, carefully applying a second coat of mascara, and thinking that perhaps the night held the promise of something more than just celebrating Michelle's birthday.

It was the same thought I had when, despite all my rules about not relinquishing control, I followed Hector upstairs instead of going home.

Fast-forward to today, and a discarded breakfast tray is on the floor next to the bed, along with the clothes I was wearing last night. He cooked me dinner, we shared a bottle of Riesling and then he undressed me slowly, leaving a trail of kisses all the way along my spine and whispering how I was more delicious than anything he'd tasted before.

I look over at him, at the mess of hair that always sticks out at odd angles in the morning. He is propped up in bed reading *Steppenwolf*, and every so often he reaches out a hand to touch me. It is ridiculously reassuring, the idea that even when focused on something else, he wants me to know that he's there.

'What's it about?' I ask, peering over his shoulder to see if I can understand a little of what he's reading.

'I think it's about man's journey of self-discovery,' he says with a yawn. 'About overcoming despair through love.'

'Bit different to Captain America,' I tease, looking over at the bookshelves where early editions of Marvel comics sit next to everything from Fitzgerald to Tolstoy, with some King thrown in for good measure.

'Don't diss Captain America,' he says, poking me in the ribs. 'He met the love of his life and then was frozen for seventy years. When he woke up she was gone but nobody else ever came close to the way he felt about Peggy.'

'You and Layla should get together,' I say as I slip from the bed, for they are both soppy and sweet and eternally optimistic when it comes to love.

I'm beginning to open up to him, only a little but enough to realise how vulnerable this could make me. I confessed something of the argument with my family back in Stockholm, and how I can no longer be the person they expect me to be. But he didn't push, he didn't try to force me into revealing anything more, which made me feel safe and, more than that, wanted. Sometimes, at odd moments like when he's making eggs for breakfast or unloading the dishwasher (we have become rather domesticated in a very short space of time, which is an unexpected but lovely surprise), I catch myself on the very tip of revealing everything. But then I change my mind or get scared, or perhaps just distracted by the sight of him coming out of the shower, and the secret gets pushed away.

I wander over to the record player standing on a cabinet in the corner and, like always, my fingers run across the rows of cardboard spines. It was something of a surprise to discover a vintage player in his room, along with stacks of books and a collection of snow globes from all over the world. There was a little bit of dread laced through that surprise, even though it was perfectly normal for someone to choose vinyl instead of CDs. But I soon discovered he is something of an old soul, preferring blues to hip-hop and books to film.

I listen to the soft crackle of anticipation as the stylus lowers on to the disc, then the sound of strings permeates the air as Etta James begins to sing.

It's the same song he played the night we met, when I held my breath for fear of what he might choose to play and whether it would take me back to Oxford, to the people who I still have to try not to think about too often.

'Good choice,' Hector says as he curls his arm around me and kisses the back of my neck, then trails his lips down and around the tattoo of a lotus flower that sits between my shoulder blades. It's a mark of rebellion as well as rebirth, something I did on a rainy afternoon with Duncan during our very first term. He dared me to go with him so that we could be branded together, purely because it was something our parents would disapprove of. It took him all of five seconds to chicken out, but the sound of that needle didn't scare me the way it did him. I didn't really understand pain back then.

I miss him. I miss the way he would tease me about being scared of fish and once believing that a satellite was in fact a shooting star.

I turn around, pushing all thoughts of my wonderful friend aside as I press myself against Hector and bring his mouth up to mine. Every single part of me feels alive, alert and on edge, because of him. I know that I'm falling hard and fast and the lack of control makes me feel giddy and reckless. It's a risk, a huge risk, but whichever part of my brain that for years has been telling me not to let go, not to show myself to anyone, has finally decided to shut up.

The song is interrupted by the sound of a ringtone and Hector leaves me wanting more as he steps away to answer it.

'It's Michelle,' he says, flipping open the phone and I can't help but roll my eyes in frustration as I go next door and turn on the shower.

So far, I have managed to resist the pull of technology. I have refused to buy a mobile or set up an email account. It's the one thing Hector and I have argued about, because I hate the idea that everything about my life would be available for someone to download. Hector claims the internet is going to change the world, making everyone and everything connected, which is precisely why I want to stay as far away from it as possible.

Internet cafés are opening up everywhere across London. Wherever you look there are adverts for ways you can use the web to search for everything from holidays to houses and anything else your heart might desire. I went into one on Oxford Street, paid my fee and sat in a wooden cubicle, waiting for the dial-up to work.

I even found the courage to type a name into a search engine, deleted it and replaced it with another. But I couldn't bring myself to click on that one little word – 'search'. Because just like Pandora and her box, if I did I would end up discovering all sorts of things I didn't want to know. Like how happy they are, living the life that I don't deserve to be a part of.

Hector comes into the bathroom and slides the shower door open a crack.

'Do you have any idea what a Furby is?'

'What?' I open my eyes then close them again and tip back my head to wash out the rest of the shampoo.

'A Furby,' he says, handing me a towel. 'Michelle cut out before she could tell me what it is.'

'It's a weird talking robot alien thing.' I wipe my face then wrap the towel around me.

'Any idea where I can get one?'

'Why?' Using my fingers, I tease out the knots in my hair, then pick up the toothbrush I now leave here and squeeze a white line of paste on to the bristles.

'It's my cousin's ninth birthday and apparently Michelle thinks a weird talking alien would be the perfect present.' Hector picks up his own toothbrush and together we stand, brushing our teeth. 'Although I think she'd like the new Harry Potter book more.'

'Buy the book,' I say, spitting into the sink. 'Unless you don't like her parents. In which case buy her the annoying robot.'

'Her dad's only ten years older than me. He used to take me out on the back of his motorbike when I was little and taught me how to blow smoke rings to impress the girls.'

'Except you don't smoke.' I look over at him, then bend forward to rinse my mouth out under the tap. As I do so, he slips his hand under my towel and I swat it away.

'No, but I still managed to impress you.' He dips his head to kiss my collarbone, pulling the towel apart and dropping it on the floor.

'We should really think about getting dressed and leaving the house.'

'Why?' His hands are on my waist, turning me around then tracing over the curve of my backside.

'I should go home at some point. Check on Uncle Alex.'

'Is he OK?'

'He's fine.' I haven't spoken to him all week, other than leaving a short message to say I was staying with a friend, and the knowledge makes a pebble of guilt appear in my stomach. He was there for me when no one else could help and is the only person alive who knows the truth, the whole truth and nothing but the truth.

I close my eyes, allowing myself to fall right back under Hector's spell. 'I'm also starting to forget what the real world looks like.'

'My whole world is right here with you.' Hector steers me back into the bedroom and together we fall on to the bed.

'That's so cheesy.'

He pushes himself up on to his forearms, staring down at me with an intensity that makes my heart tighten. 'And yet you love me nonetheless.'

'I guess I do.' The words are out before I've even considered them. Is it really that easy to fall for someone? Did I simply have to trust that something good could still happen to me?

'I want to take you home,' he says with a smile. 'Meet the parents and all that.'

'OK.' The idea should terrify me. I should be running as far away from him and his declarations as I can possibly get. But something is making me stay, making me dare to believe that this time I won't fuck it all up.

'And we can tell them how you're going to be the rich, successful one,' he says, interspersing his words with kisses all over my skin. 'Whilst I'll be the poor, impoverished writer stuck at home, waiting for his beautiful wife to come back for the dinner he's so lovingly prepared.'

I'm getting used to him talking about our future. It was tentative at first, him asking whether I'd ever consider moving back to Sweden. Subtle questions that hid the true depth of feeling. A bit like a dance, or bare-knuckle fighters squaring up to one another and looking for any signs of weakness. Only this time I've realised that he is just as vulnerable, just as fearful of getting hurt as I am.

'Bit of a role reversal.' I push him on to his back and climb on top.

'Until I've written my bestseller,' he sighs as we come together. 'Then we can concentrate on getting you fat and pregnant.'

NIAMH

Zemblanity (n.) – *the inevitable discovery of what we would rather not know*

Oxford, 1996

The sky was slick with rain, the promise of more to come hanging in gunmetal clouds. Thousands of droplets fell, striking the alabaster stone of Queen's College clock tower under which a girl, just shy of twenty-one, stood waiting.

He wasn't coming. It was obvious he wasn't coming and even though she had dared herself to believe that everything was going to be OK, a little voice inside her head kept laughing at her naivety. She had been across the road to the college lodge twice in the last hour, asking the porter if there had been any messages left, and he had smiled his apology both times.

Of course he wasn't going to marry her. Of course he wouldn't be so stupid as to throw away his future for somebody like her. If only she'd listened to her doubts and never told him about the baby, perhaps then everything could have been different.

If she went to his house, confronted him, would it make any difference? Would the pain that was seeping through every part of her body be lessened in any way? Or would the sight of him, pity and regret written all over his beautiful face, be more than she could possibly bear?

What now? Carry on as normal, pretend nothing was the matter? How could she try and focus on her studies and ignore the swelling at her centre? It could work; it wouldn't be hard to hide away with nothing more than books and music for company. She'd done it for years and she was used to being on her own, so why should now be any different?

But he was here. Leo was here and she could bump into him at any given moment. The hands of fate were unlikely to be kind and allow her to stay out of sight.

If not Oxford, where was she supposed to go?

Why, why, why had she been so stupid as to trust him, to believe him when he said he would look after her? Because she wanted to. Because she loved him, but clearly it had all been a lie.

I wish Erika was here. The idea popped into her head, making her heart swell, and she had to bite down on the back of her hand to stop herself from screaming. It was too late. There was no time to try to make amends because there was a new life growing inside her. A life that she had to protect, no matter what. And that meant swallowing all her pride, all her fear, and doing what was best for someone other than her.

It had only been two weeks since she'd found out. Fifteen days, to be precise, since she'd peed on that bloody stick and everything was turned into chaos. She'd barely seen Leo due to a combination of her being exhausted and him trying to get the wedding organised, but perhaps he had been keeping his distance on purpose? It was so hard to figure out what was real and what was a result of her over-thinking, of questioning every tiny gesture or word that came out of his mouth.

The last time she'd seen him he was holding something back, she was certain of it. It was two days ago, when they were watching

True Romance for what felt like the thousandth time up in his bedroom, accompanied by the sound of all his housemates watching the football filtering up from downstairs. The film had been a distraction, a way for them to avoid actually talking to one another about the enormity of what was happening, but she couldn't focus on the screen due to the raging hunger inside her so she had sent Leo out for strawberries and chocolate cake.

When he came back, hair wet with rain and carrying a box of raspberries, she had to stop herself from throwing them at him.

'What's the difference?' he'd said, running his hands through his hair and glancing back at the door as the sound of his housemates shouting at the TV when somebody scored wound itself up the stairs. It was like an angry reminder of what he should be doing, a harsh glimpse into the future when his life would still be dictated by the needs of a small child, instead of his own selfish desires.

'The difference is I'm not hungry, the baby is hungry and I have no control over what it wants.' She could tell he wanted to be downstairs, to be one of the gang, just a normal student. Before the baby that's exactly what he would have been doing and she wouldn't have minded, choosing instead to catch up on some work or spend the evening with her friends. Except that was life before Leo, not just before she fell pregnant.

'There's someone here to see you,' Leo said, glancing again at the door.

'Who?' But she already knew.

She'd spotted Erika again the other day, upstairs in the history section of Blackwell's. Niamh had heard her before she'd seen her, the boom of her laugh as it exploded from the other side of a bookshelf. Niamh had retreated into a corner, kneeling down and ducking her head so she didn't know if Erika had seen her as she passed by, but the scent of her perfume was enough to make her stomach ache worse than any morning sickness could.

A second later and Niamh had got up, followed Erika out of the bookstore and along Broad Street, watching as she went inside the entrance to Balliol College and hating the fact she had no idea who it was she had gone to meet. It wasn't that long ago they knew everything about one another. Well, clearly not everything; that was what had caused all the problems in the first place. But enough to not be terrified of bumping into one another, of being able to talk to your best friend about what the hell you were supposed to do about the baby that was growing inside you.

She missed her friends with such a keenness; she wanted to be able to talk to them more than ever before, but she knew it had been too long, too much time had passed and so much had changed.

'She asked me to give you this,' Leo said, holding out a small plastic troll with pink hair and a lopsided smile. Niamh stared at it, thinking all the way back to the night she and Leo had met, before which it had just been her and Erika, putting on make-up in her room and deciding what to wear to a stupid college bop.

'Did you tell her?'

'About the baby? I kind of figured it should come from you. It might help, you know, to tell her. Have someone to talk to.'

'I don't want her to know.'

'Why?'

'Because then she'll forgive me for all the wrong reasons.' Niamh wiped the back of her hand across her face, all too aware of how much it was shaking.

'She came all the way here,' Leo said, trying to decide whether or not Niamh would let him comfort her. 'Don't you at least want to hear what she has to say?'

'Tell her to go.'

Leo paused at the door, his fingers drumming against the frame and Niamh could tell he was deciding what he should do, whether or not to stay or hide downstairs inside a bubble of denial.

255

'What's really going on, Niamh?'

'Nothing. I'm just tired.' She was always tired. It was like having a teeny-tiny succubus growing inside her, drinking up all her energy and turning her into a walking, ravenous zombie. 'I don't know if I can do this, Leo.' The words were soft, barely more than a whisper, even though they'd been running around her mind for days.

'Do what?' He turned to her with a frown and part of her wanted to scream at him for not having a clue what she was thinking.

'Keep the baby.'

'But you said—'

'I know what I said.' The words were louder now, as if raising her voice would make the idea more convincing. 'I know it's wrong, that it's a mortal sin. But I'm scared, Leo. I'm so fucking scared that you'll change your mind. That this is already tearing us apart.'

'Hey,' he said, perching on the edge of the bed and taking her hand. 'I'm never going to leave you.'

'You say that now,' Niamh replied, wiping her eyes and wishing she could stop crying at the drop of a hat.

'I'll say it always,' he said, kissing her forehead, then her cheek and then a long, slow kiss on the mouth. 'Because I love you. Both of you.'

Niamh closed her eyes, gave in to his kiss as she wrapped her arms around his neck and tried to tell herself that he meant it. That he would always be there for her, no matter what.

'You should get some sleep,' he said, pulling away, and she tried to ignore the cold sense of dread that was left behind. 'The next few days are going to be a bit mad.'

He hovered in the doorway, watching as Niamh eased herself under the covers, one hand instinctively finding her swollen centre. She looked back at him, tried to read the expression on his face, wishing it was one of sympathy, of love and not regret. Then he pulled the door to, one thin line of light stretching across the carpet towards the bed, and she listened to the sound of him hurrying back downstairs, to where her best friend was waiting.

He wasn't coming. The realisation hit her fast and furious, right in the solar plexus and Niamh gasped at the sudden, sharp pain that wriggled through her ribcage and stuck itself inside her heart.

There's still time, she told herself, thinking that all she had to do was get as far away from there as possible. Because the more distance between them, the easier it would be to breathe.

The Oxford Tube stopped at the pedestrian crossing further up the High Street and she shouldered her bag. Stepping out to the kerbside, she held out her hand, waiting for the coach to pull up alongside her. Without a backward glance, she boarded the coach and found a seat by the window.

'Mum?'

There was a pause on the other end of the line. 'Niamh, is that you?'

'Yes.'

'Why are you calling so late?'

Niamh traced her finger in a circle on the glass pane of the phone box. It was still raining, and the streets were busy with traffic and pedestrians, all hurrying home at the end of their working week.

'I need your help.'

257

She heard her mother sigh and could picture her checking the clock that stood by the front door. 'Well, you better be quick about it. *EastEnders* is starting.'

'I . . .' How was she supposed to explain what had happened, when she couldn't bring herself to accept it?

'Spit it out, child.'

Niamh closed her eyes, because clearly that would make her confession so much easier. 'I'm pregnant.'

There was a horribly long pause, behind which Niamh could make out the tinny theme tune to her mother's favourite soap.

'I see.'

'Mum?'

'And the father?'

'He's . . . I don't know.' He was gone. He wasn't there, with her, as planned. There would be no wedding at Chelsea Town Hall. There was no need to carry around the ivory dress and shoes that she'd found in a charity shop on the Iffley Road. He had made his choice without her, and now she needed to figure out what came next. Even if that meant going back to Cork, to a house that had never been a home and two parents who had struggled to ever make her feel like she belonged.

'Just like your bloody mother.' The bitterness in her voice travelled oh-so easily across the sea and down the line into Niamh's brain. It wasn't unexpected, but that didn't make it any less painful to bear.

'Mum, please.' She was crying now. Long lines of wet that matched the falling rain outside.

'No, it won't do,' her mother shouted back. 'I won't have it.' Then came the sound of the phone's receiver being thrown down, followed by raised voices in the distance and the opening and slamming of doors.

Niamh waited, cradling her own receiver between cheek and shoulder as she rummaged in her bag for more coins. The timer on the phone was counting down, flashing the remaining seconds at her before she would be cut off. Pushing more coins into the slot, she saw the number climb back up just as another voice came on the line.

'Hello?'

'Dad?' Niamh exhaled her relief.

'Is it true?' His voice was measured and calm. But Niamh knew he would be rubbing at his temples as he struggled with the emotional depth of what he was having to ask.

If she didn't answer then it wouldn't be true. Because a truth is only a truth if somebody believes in it. Or was that a tree falling in the forest? Fuck. Nothing made sense any more. Her mind was so muddled and confused and filled with all kinds of feelings that it was proving impossible to latch on to any of them for more than a second at a time.

She heard him sigh, which told her his answer even before he spoke.

'I can't help you, I'm afraid.'

The apology was meaningless, because he wasn't really sorry. He just did whatever made his life easier, even if that meant abandoning his child.

'Can't or won't?' Her emotions had tipped from sad to angry in less time than it took for her father to betray her. They had taken her from the convent into their home with the unspoken promise to take care of her, to love her. Now she couldn't help but think that she would have been better off staying in the convent. At least with the nuns, you always knew where you stood.

'She won't let you back in the house. Not after what she's been through.'

The loss of a child wasn't something Niamh could empathise with, even now her own stomach was beginning to swell with new life. She understood, though, the powerful sense of unfairness that her mother believed belonged only to her. The idea that life can be so very different, depending on what you're born into, what genes you inherit. Just like Leo and his perfect family, a family that wasn't about to open up its doors and invite her in.

'But I've nowhere to go,' she whispered as she held out one hand to the doorframe, afraid that her knees were going to buckle and she'd end up sprawled on the filthy floor.

'And whose fault is that?'

'Dad, please?' The seconds ticked away on the screen in front of her, faster and faster until she heard three long beeps telling her she was out of time. Even before the line went dead, she knew her father had hung up, that she was completely and utterly alone.

What now? Niamh replaced the receiver and picked up her bag. Pushing wide the red metal door, she looked across the road to the station. Her purse held little more than a few coins and dust, but her fingers found the thin plastic rectangle that winked at her with possibility. It was only supposed to be for an emergency, not even to be considered unless all else had failed. But what other choice did she have, other than to go back to where it all began?

ERIKA

BUTTERFLY BROOCH

London, 1997

It's a Monday afternoon, too early even for the regular punters, but the pub will be full once the end-of-day commuters start to pour in. December means all the usual rules about no mid-week drinking are thrown out of the window, even by the most health-conscious of Londoners.

The pub looks like Christmas on steroids, with a giant tree in one corner, garlands strung from the ceiling and a dancing Santa at the end of the bar. Mariah Carey seems to be playing on repeat and the landlord has even mentioned the idea of all the staff dressing up as elves in order to 'get into the festive spirit'.

I have no desire to get into any kind of spirit, despite Alex's best efforts to bring a little cheer into the household. Term is over for the holidays and for weeks now I have been smiling and saying no, I'm not going back to Sweden this year. Instead I will be spending it with my uncle and his neighbour, who has already started work on the Christmas pudding and ordered enough turkey to feed a village.

'Sorry I'm late.'

I look up as the pub door opens, bringing with it a cold blast of winter and a girl who is half-hidden behind an enormous pink scarf. I watch as she begins to unwind it, walking towards the bar and smiling across at me before using her teeth to pull off her gloves.

'I'm Layla,' she says, dumping her accessories on the nearest table and shrugging off her oversized parka. Underneath she's wearing a tartan mini-skirt and black roll-neck, with over-the-knee socks and DM boots. 'Are you Erika?'

I nod, watching as Layla tips her head upside down and fashions all those tight curls into a bun.

'Hey,' Layla says as she comes around to this side of the bar and points at me. 'We're matching.'

'I guess.' I smile as I look down at my denim mini-skirt and red jumper that I've paired with Adidas trainers and ribbed tights.

'You a student?' Layla asks as she takes down a pint glass and fills it with Coke from the bar gun.

'LSE.' I take a sip of my water, thinking I should have gone for some caffeine as well.

'Ah, one of them.' Layla drags an empty beer crate across the floor, then uses it to reach up to the top shelf for a tin of festive sweets.

'One of what?' I'm pretty sure those sweets belong to the landlord and shouldn't, under any circumstances, be stolen. But I still help myself to one wrapped in orange foil, and then also a toffee when Layla rattles the tin at me in encouragement.

'Super nerd.' Layla twists open a nougat-filled chocolate, nibbling at one corner as she tosses the purple wrapper in a nearby bin.

'What about you?' I ask, looking at how the undersides of Layla's fingernails are a deep shade of blue, but not the kind that comes from hours of essay-writing.

'St Martin's,' she says, reaching into her handbag, which has a clasp made up of two golden Cs. She catches me looking as she takes out a sketchbook and places it on the bar. 'I know, it's a cliché. Poor little rich kid studying art because I have no idea what else to do.'

'If you're rich,' I say, aware that I'm lisping due to the toffee that's stuck to the top of my mouth, 'why are you working here?'

'Mum said I needed some grounding.' Layla puts the tin back on the top shelf, then opens the dishwasher and stands back to let out all that steam. 'To actually realise what it's like to earn my own money.'

'Sounds fair.' I hand Layla a tea towel and we work together, one drying, one restacking the shelves.

'Oh, she's annoyingly hip and totally au fait with weed and shit, because she used to smoke it back in the day.'

'Does it help?'

'With what?'

I nod towards her sketchbook. 'Your painting. I've heard cannabis creates psychotomimetic symptoms.'

Layla blinks back at me. 'I have no idea what you just said.'

'It's a way of making your brain break free from ordinary thinking. You know, tap into your subconscious.'

'You really are a nerd,' she says with a laugh, flicking the tea towel at my leg.

'Friend of mine studied psychology,' I say, trying to dodge away from another flick. 'He also smoked a lot of weed.'

'Is he single?'

'Gay.'

'All the best ones are.' Layla drapes the towel over one shoulder and leans on the bar, using her thumbnail to try to pick out some of the paint from under all the others. 'Do you live locally?'

I point out the window and across the street to where I know Alex will be at his desk with the radio on, marking papers and drinking endless cups of sweetened tea.

'Cool. I'm on the other side of the park.' She reaches back into her bag and takes out a packet of Marlboro Lights along with a Zippo. 'We should hang out some time, you know, apart from in here. Want one?'

I do, but I'm out of practice, so I shake my head as Layla flicks open the lighter and clicks her fingers over the wheel in order to create a flame. It's the same trick Duncan used to do, one that I never could master. I can picture his face so clearly, can hear the exact tone of his voice when he gets all animated about something – usually a boy, but also his beloved rats – and the intensity with which I miss him, all of them, is like being pierced by a very long, very sharp blade.

'I'm trying to quit.'

'Why?' Layla squints back at me as she takes a long drag. If she heard the tremor in my voice, she's decided not to say so.

'I need a break from my old life.' I pour out the contents of my glass, then refill it with full-fat Coke. I'm half tempted to add some vodka to the mix, but that would be pushing my luck too far.

'Is that what the hair's about?' Layla waves her hand in the direction of my face and I turn to peer at my reflection in the mirrored splashback.

'It's not that bad,' I say, tucking a few strands behind one ear and turning my head from side to side.

'Babe, it's a hack-job. Did you do it yourself?'

'Maybe.'

'There's a guy at Rush in Camden who does my hair, and believe me that's not an easy task. Mention my name and he'll do you a discount.'

264

Both of us look up as the door opens and a couple of tourists come in, armed with backpacks and a crumpled map. One of them is pushing a buggy, the face of a toddler with bright-blonde hair peeping out from above a pale-blue blanket. They go over to sit by the fire, which is spitting at best, and shrug off their anoraks.

I notice something on the floor and go over to retrieve a small, grey duck that must have fallen out of the buggy. Such a simple thing, of no real value at all, yet I know that one day it will mean so much to that boy not yet grown. I take it over to the table, tap the mother on the shoulder and hold out the toy.

'*Hyvänen aika*, thank you,' she says in what I think might be Finnish, but I couldn't say for sure. 'Nikolas would be so upset if he lost little Terence.'

'How old is he?' I dutifully ask with a glance at the buggy, seeing two dots of high colour on Nikolas's cheeks.

'He's just turned two.' The mother smiles at her son with unabashed pride. 'This is his first time to London.'

'You should take him to Harrods,' I say. Nikolas is watching me and I poke out my tongue, which makes him giggle. 'It's wonderful at Christmas time. If you need anything, just order at the bar.'

'Where are you from?' Layla asks as I go back to the bar. She's not even pretending to look busy. 'I can't figure out your accent.'

'My family are from Sweden,' I say, looking back to see Nikolas has managed to half escape from his buggy and is now banging a plastic cup on the table. 'But I've been in the UK so long that my accent's all over the place.'

'Not going home for the holidays?' Layla heaves herself on to the bar, drumming against the wood with the heels of her boots.

I stop watching the happy family and turn to face her. 'No.'

'Can I ask why?'

The question, the blatant curiosity, surprises me. Even more surprising is that it doesn't bother me, when usually it would.

'I have no desire to be told, once again, that I should be finding a husband instead of studying for another degree.'

'You already have one?' Layla flicks her cigarette in the vague direction of an ashtray and I reach out to brush all the tiny grey particles on to the floor.

'Sort of,' I say, watching the ash slowly drift to the ground, disappearing the instant it meets the sticky layer of old beer and melted ice. 'I was at Oxford before.'

'Super, super nerd.'

'I left.' Without a trace. No note, no forwarding address, because at the time I had no idea where I would end up. Certainly not here, serving pints to London's finest, whilst studying for a degree in economics. Just over a year ago I could barely force myself to get up in the morning, let alone believe that there was a way out for me. A chance to start again, to build something out of the wreckage that happened in Oxford.

'Why?'

'Lots of reasons.' Except there was only ever one. I look across at Layla, who is watching me with her head cocked to the side, waiting for more of an explanation. 'Including me waking up and realising that an arts degree was never going to land me a decent job.'

Which is true. At least, that's what I've been telling myself all term because I'm learning that just because you're good at something, doesn't necessarily mean you should do it. I mean, distribution theory and macroeconomics aren't exactly the most exciting subjects, especially when you compare them to Shakespeare, Alcott or even Dahl.

'Define "decent".' Layla stubs out her cigarette, this time managing to find the ashtray.

'Something that pays enough so I never have to be reliant on anyone else.'

266

'Sounds kinda dull.'

Dull is safe. Dull means independence, which is about the best I can hope for, given what I did. It hurts to think about it. But is it even possible to miss something that wasn't really yours, at least not for long enough to claim it as your own?

'What about you?' I ask, peering at a sticky mark on the bar and trying to figure out if it's ketchup or glue.

Layla goes to the other end of the bar to serve the male tourist, offering up a smile and a laugh at something he says. Two pints of Guinness and a packet of crisps later and she turns her attention to the rather pathetic collection of CDs stacked next to a dusty machine at one end of the bar. She holds one up in my direction, but I shake my head at her choice and Layla raises her brow in surprise. I have no desire to listen to Pulp, not now. I had more than my fill of them when *Different Class* was first released and it seemed to play on repeat during my first stint at university, along with Oasis and Blur and all the other bands I can no longer bring myself to listen to.

'The plan is,' she calls across to me, 'for Jude Law to walk in any second, fall madly in love with me and realise what a huge mistake it was to marry Sadie. Then we'll run off into the sunset together and make sweet, beautiful music. And children. Lots and lots of children.'

'Sounds kinda cheesy.'

'Cheese runs in the family,' she says, putting a CD into the player and turning the volume way up. 'My grandfather fell in love with a local Bahamian girl – quite the scandal back in the day. He flew her back to England, but bought her a house on the islands that we sometimes visit at Christmas. You should come one year, because I can already tell we're going to be friends. But stay away from my brother, he's a total sleaze.'

'You're not going this year?' I shout over the sound of Alanis Morissette singing about Mr Duplicity.

'Grandma Nelle's got the flu,' Layla shouts back, her head bobbing along to the music. 'She's holed up with us for the festive season.'

'Must be nice having her at home.' I look across as the tourists gather up their belongings and leave the pub, pointedly staring at Layla and shaking their heads.

Layla is completely oblivious to their disapproval, jumping about and singing at the top of her (not particularly tuneful) voice. At the end of the song she shimmies over to my end of the bar and rummages through her bag.

'It is,' she says, taking out a tatty paperback and easing the pages apart to where a corner is folded down. 'Apart from the fact she insists on playing eighties power ballads at full volume and eats all the chocolate biscuits.'

I fetch my own book from next to the till, thinking that there isn't much point even pretending to do any work now we've chased away our only customers.

'*The God of Small Things*?' Layla reads out the title as she peers over my shoulder.

'It's about a brother and sister whose lives are destroyed by the rules of love.' I hand the book over and watch as she reads the blurb on the back cover. 'It's beautiful, but tragic.'

'I prefer Stephen King,' Layla says as she gives the book back. 'Especially because he always writes whilst completely off his face and listening to heavy metal.'

'You like horror? And heavy metal?'

'So?' Layla opens her sketchbook to a clean page and I watch as she begins to add long, careful strokes of ink to the paper.

'But you're reading an ancient Buddhist text.' I point at the scruffy paperback she's clearly read through more than once. Several sentences are underlined and there are even notes scribbled in the margins.

'Don't judge a book, and all that,' Layla says without glancing up from her drawing. 'You have not lived until you've played "Welcome to the Jungle" at full blast. Drowns out all the demons and makes you feel incredibly alive.'

There is no right way for me to respond, and only partly because I'm now thinking about how much I could do with drowning out my own demons. The bastards keep waking me up at three a.m., proceeding to do a little dance around my brain with all their memories and accusations. The only issue is, I don't think Alex, or the rest of the street, would appreciate being woken in the middle of the night by the dulcet tones of Axl Rose.

'Is that Blake?' I ask, tilting my head to get a better look at the figure Layla is drawing.

'He's one of my favourites,' Layla says, adding some detail to the face that I recognise as being that of Virgil. 'I'm trying to figure out a way to use the Katha texts in a new way. Much like Blake did with *The Divine Comedy*.'

'And you accuse me of being a nerd,' I say with a chuckle and outstretched hand. 'Can I see?'

Layla slides the sketchbook along the bar and I go back to the beginning, studying each picture in turn and recognising different parts of the story on every page. There's more here than simply copying what Blake himself created. There are tiny fragments dotted all over that suggest another, hidden picture.

'I like the idea of making people look twice,' Layla says as I turn the sketchbook upside down. 'Show them something they think they already know, but from a different angle.'

'I guess we all have to face Death, at some point.' I peer at a tiny, cloaked figure in the top corner of the page, seemingly watching over the scene below.

'You've read the Katha?'

'I live with my uncle,' I say, handing the book back. 'Who's an ethics professor. Plus, I don't have much of a social life.' For months, all I have done is attend lectures, sit in the Shaw Library or go running with Michelle. My Friday nights mostly consist of listening to the sound of jazz filtering up through the floorboards from Alex's study, whilst I diligently make my way through his vast collection of books.

'A social life I can definitely help you with,' Layla says, reaching out to tuck a strand of hair behind my ear. She looks at me for a moment, almost as if she senses that I'm hiding something, and not just from her. 'Come out with me sometime. There are lots of pathetically beautiful men on my course who would love a slice of you.'

'I'm not really looking.' I glance at my watch as the clock on the mantelpiece chimes out the end of my shift. Slipping my arms into the sleeves of a faux fur coat and covering up my terrible haircut with a knitted cap, I can feel her watching me. Perhaps she heard the sigh behind my words. Maybe she also understands what it feels like for a heart to break.

'That coat makes you look like one of those seventies groupies.' Her eye falls on the filigree brooch that I've pinned to the collar and I really hope she doesn't ask where it's from. 'Or even Stevie Nicks,' she says as I shoulder my bag and head for the door. 'If you grew out your hair.'

NIAMH

Sisu (n.) – *extraordinary determination, courage and resoluteness*

London, 1997

Home for the past few months had been an end-of-terrace, four-storey house with a bright yellow door. Niamh's room was up in the eaves, but she had her own bathroom and a view over the park. She was staying with Sister Ingrid's cousin, a college professor who lived in Primrose Hill, which was like a mini village just outside the heart of the city. In exchange for some household duties (which seemed to mainly involve locating items her new landlord had lost), Niamh was living rent-free in one of the most expensive parts of town.

She had no need to venture more than a few streets away in order to find all she could possibly need. There was everything from a library, delicatessen, cafés and pubs aplenty, including one that was spitting distance from the house. Niamh had also befriended the neighbour, an elderly lady called Gladys who smoked like a chimney and swore like a trooper but sang opera as if it was what she had been born to do. Niamh would take Gladys's dog for walks up and down the park hills each morning, in exchange for a token wage, thick slices of home-made ginger cake and stories about the 'good old days' of London society.

Niamh had settled into a quiet routine, rising around six a.m., setting a pot of coffee on the stove, before heading next door to retrieve Frank the beagle. When she returned, the study door would already be shut, with a thermos of sweetened coffee and a plate full of biscuits to keep the professor going until lunchtime.

Niamh was usually tasked with running some errands or fetching lunch from the local deli, which could be anything from quiche to oysters. She would leave it on a tray outside the study door and then have the rest of the day free. At six on the dot, he would head down to the basement kitchen and announce it was time to start thinking about supper, which they always prepared together.

It had been a simple enough existence, made easier by the summer sunshine, but every time she saw a pram, or heard a baby's cry, Niamh would question all over again her decision to give up her child.

'Big day tomorrow,' the professor said whilst slicing some tomatoes for the pasta sauce. He handed the chopping board to Niamh, who slipped the vegetables into the pot on the stove and began to stir them through the spicy chilli oil.

'I guess,' she replied, reaching across to the salt pig and taking out a generous pinch.

'Are all your papers in order?' He wiped his hands on a tea towel, then sat at the back door and began to stuff his pipe with tobacco. The cat twirled through the legs of the chair, waiting for him to rub at its fur, then darted out to the small patio garden at the sight of a daredevil squirrel.

'I double-checked them earlier,' Niamh said as she put the kettle on to boil and added strands of spaghetti to another pan. She was so very grateful to him for taking her in and not asking too many questions. There had been several hushed telephone conversations back to Ireland over the summer, but not once did he pass judgement on the plan she and Sister Ingrid had concocted together whilst walking through the gardens where Niamh had liked to play as a child.

'And you're absolutely sure this is what you want?' He tapped the end of his pipe on the windowsill before looking around for a light.

'I'm sure.' Niamh passed him a box of matches, watching as he took three long puffs before the kitchen was bathed in fragrant smoke. She had to be sure, because what other choice did she have? Moving forward was her only option, and if that meant leaving behind everything she had ever known, then where better to do it than hidden within a city of millions?

'If you need anything, my office is in the adjacent building.'

'Thank you, but I'm sure I'll be fine.' She looked out the window to where the cat was sitting, cleaning its paws in a circle of sunshine. There had been a ginger tomcat back at the convent who was liable to scratch unless you placated him with a tin of sardines. Shaking her mind free of the memory, she opened the fridge and took out a block of parmesan, ready for grating. 'Do you still want me to make you coffee in the morning?'

'*Det vore underbart,*' he replied in Swedish as he took another puff of his pipe, watching Niamh move around the kitchen and trying to remember what life was like before she had arrived.

The first phone call from Ireland had come on a wet winter's evening, when the nights were still too long and the cat barely ever moved from in front of the fire. His cousin's explanation had been brief and to the point, as was Sister Ingrid's way, without any embellishment or emotional guilt thrown in. It was such an unexpected request, one that filled him with a mixture of trepidation and excitement, and he had said yes on a whim, without thinking through the multitude of logistics.

But Niamh had proven herself to be both reliable and personable. She somehow understood his routine, his desire for normalcy, better than he did himself and had soon slotted into his life and his home with barely a foot out of place.

Together, they had figured out a way to coexist that complemented the other and he found himself looking forward to their evening conversations about everything from politics to film, accompanied by the sound of Radio Four in the background. But even after all those weeks spent in such close proximity, he still couldn't understand the final piece of her plan, and why she felt it to be necessary.

Sitting on the 168 bus, Niamh felt like a nervous child on the first day of school. Twice already she had checked the contents of her bag, her fingers seeking out the leather notebook that contained not only her mother's letter, but also a photograph of her cradling Luke on the day he was born. She didn't need to take it out to know the exact way his tiny fist was clenched around a strand of her hair. Nor could she ever forget the torrent of pain that he had put her through, a whole day of labour that only ended when the sun was finally pushing past the horizon on the first morning of May.

It had made her think of Leo, as most things tended to. She had looked down at her newborn son and wondered whether his father was gathered outside Magdalen College, along with all the other students who were waiting for the choir to start singing from the clock tower. Perhaps he had spent the night before in celebration at a May Day ball in a muddy field on the outskirts of town. Or maybe he had been in New College bar, playing table football and not thinking about her at all.

There was a woman opposite her with a toddler on her lap and a briefcase at her feet. She was trying to read through some notes whilst simultaneously placating the child, who was clearly in no mood to be ignored. Niamh watched as the little girl wriggled and jiggled and then threw herself backwards, so that her mother had to drop her papers and wrap her arms around the child.

'Tabitha, please. Would you just stop,' the woman said as she attempted to put her daughter back in the buggy. Tabitha responded by arching her body and letting out a scream that seemed too loud to have come from such a small person.

Niamh bent down to retrieve the papers, casting her eye over their contents and deducing that the woman in question was on her way to the Royal Courts of Justice.

'A day in court is so much less stressful than staying with her.' The woman smiled as Niamh handed back the papers. Her cheeks were nearly as flushed as Tabitha's and there was a smear of something green on her blouse. 'If I'd known what it was going to be like, I would have put it off for a few more years.' The words were accompanied by a pained laugh and a glance in her daughter's direction.

Tabitha stared at Niamh with two unblinking eyes rimmed with tears. Niamh covered her own eyes with her hands, then popped them open and mouthed 'boo', which rewarded her with a shy giggle followed by a yawn.

'Do you have kids?' the woman asked as she wiped at her blouse with a tissue.

'No,' Niamh said as she glanced out of the window, mentally calculating how much longer the journey would take.

'Didn't think so. You look far too young.'

Except she wasn't too young, just stupid enough to believe that once she'd left the hospital and signed her son over to the social workers, she could carry on as if nothing had happened. But he was there with her always, buried deep inside her heart and refusing to ever let go. Sister Ingrid had called her the day before the process was due to be completed, sixteen long weeks after Luke had been born. She said that there was still time for Niamh to change her mind, to take him back and figure out a new plan. Niamh had given the same reply as she had every week when she called – that Luke had been with his adoptive parents for so long now that it would be cruel and selfish for her to pull his family apart.

Although that didn't mean she had stopped missing him, or his father.

As the bus made its way down Kingsway, heading for the Strand, Niamh shouldered her bag and pulled at the overhead rope, signalling to the driver that she wanted to get off at the next stop.

'Would you mind?' the woman asked as she stood, pointing at the buggy that held a now-sleeping Tabitha.

'Of course.' Niamh stepped off the back of the bus then turned around to help the woman carry the buggy on to the pavement.

'Is this yours?' The woman held something out to Niamh, then set off at a pace, not waiting for a response.

Niamh looked down at the brooch she had been given, wondering where it had come from and whether or not she should hand it to the bus driver. But the 168 had already left, and so there was nobody to ask about the art deco silver butterfly with two tiny pearls set on the end of its antennae.

Pinning it to the strap of her bag, she lifted her gaze to catch sight of herself in the window of a café. She was wearing faded Levi's, ballet flats, a white body and a cream leather jacket gifted to her by Gladys. Turned out the woman was something of a hoarder and hadn't thrown anything away since 1975. She was also rather generous when it came to Niamh, inviting her to help herself to anything she wanted from one of the enormous wardrobes in the back bedroom.

But it wasn't the clothes that were making Niamh feel a little unsettled, nor was it the way her hair was cropped short and dyed a rusty sort of blonde using a shop-bought kit. It was more what was waiting for her in a building around the corner that made her heart stammer and shake. The door to the café swung open, covering Niamh in the scent of burnt coffee and toast, along with a song that had seemingly been playing on repeat for weeks.

Elton John's tribute to Princess Diana was heart-wrenching and Niamh always found it difficult to listen to. Even more so since watching the funeral on television – she, like countless others, would never forget the sight of those two young boys following their mother's coffin. It was a single moment that affected so many, not just those boys but everyone who picked up a copy of the newspaper that fateful morning to discover that Lady Di had been killed. One turn of the wheel, or the decision to chase someone simply for the sake of a photograph, and look what had happened.

Niamh had been left with the overwhelming notion that everything you do has an impact – a ripple effect through time that never seems to end. Did Leo ever stop to think about how failing to turn up would change everything about her life? And not just hers, but their son's, along with the people who adopted him? There would be more subtle ripples too – so many people touched by a person they had never even met, but would nonetheless be affected by the consequences of his inaction.

Her fingers sought out the butterfly brooch, tracing over the delicate strands, and told herself that it was a sign, a symbol of regeneration that she could remember whenever it felt as if life was becoming too much.

'To new beginnings,' she whispered to herself as she spun on her heels and joined the parade of students heading towards the student services department of LSE.

Standing in line, awaiting her turn for registration, Niamh looked around at the plethora of different faces. A small part of her expected to spot a Swedish goddess either arguing with a Jarvis Cocker lookalike, or flirting with all the boys who were unable to take their eyes off her. Even though she knew it was ridiculous, that the likelihood of either them, or Leo, being here was pretty much zero, another part of her was afraid that she would spend her life catching her breath every time she spied a boy with dark, curly hair. Because he was still with her, the ghost of him forever lurking in her subconscious.

'Hey.' The girl behind her held out her hand with a smile. 'I'm Michelle. Has anyone told you that you look just like Stevie Nicks? Apart from the hair, obvs.'

'Actually, you're the first,' Niamh said in response. Michelle was about six foot tall, with platinum hair and the kind of beauty that made you stare. But her smile was genuine.

'What are you studying?' Michelle asked as the queue slowly moved forward.

'Economics,' Niamh replied.

'Me too. Perhaps we can sit together, at least for today?'

'That would be great.'

'I'll come find you later,' Michelle said with a wave as Niamh walked to the far end of the counter where a young man was sitting, ready and waiting.

'Welcome to LSE,' he said. 'Can I take your name?'

'Lindberg,' Niamh replied as she handed over her paperwork. 'Erika Lindberg.'

NIAMH

THIMBLE

London, 2012

If you listen carefully, you might hear the sound of the cat's purrs from where it is sleeping upstairs on the end of Layla's bed. Or the soft tap of a branch against the fence in our small courtyard garden. Or perhaps even the dull clunk of a car door and the click of a cigarette lighter as a man wearing polished brown brogues looks along the lane to where a pink mews house stands.

What you won't hear is the hiss and whir of Layla's mind as she tries to piece together the crazy puzzle of events that I have just walked her through in order to tell her that her best friend is, in fact, a fraud.

'Wait, what?' Layla is sitting at the kitchen table cradling a cup of coffee and I wonder if I should give her something stronger.

'It's a lot, I know,' I say with hands raised, as a lion tamer might do to a wary cub. 'But I promise there's a good reason.'

'There better bloody be.' Layla goes over to the fridge and peers inside, taking out a half-finished bottle of wine and pulling out the cork with her teeth. She takes several long swallows and uses the back of her hand to wipe her mouth. 'Your name isn't even Erika? It's, fuck, I don't know what it is.'

'Niamh.' I perch on the end of the sofa, a cold cup of tea at my feet. I am aware of my breathing, ragged and shallow, and I've got a trapped nerve somewhere in my leg that's making my knee jiggle up and down.

'Niamh. Right.' Layla takes another swallow of wine, then dumps the bottle on the countertop and goes back to the fridge in search of something even stronger. 'Changing your hair or your clothes after a break-up is one thing. Changing your entire identity is a bit extreme, don't you think?'

'I didn't want anyone to find me,' I say, watching her take out jars of sauce and packets of fresh pasta, piling them next to the wine bottle and not bothering to pick up a lone tomato that has rolled on to the floor. I didn't want anyone to come looking for me and try to convince me to give Leo a second chance. Nor did I want all those voices and opinions and judgements as to what I was supposed to do next with my baby – the person I have missed with every single molecule in my body from the moment I chose to give him away.

'There's vodka in the freezer,' I say and Layla shoots me a look. But she doesn't say anything because she doesn't even know my love of vodka started off as a lie. I guess it's one habit I acquired from Erika, the real Erika, that has become part of me.

She opens the freezer and takes out the ice-cold bottle and I watch as she pours out two generous measures then comes to sit on the sofa next to me.

'But why?' She hands me a glass and we clink the rims together before downing the contents in one.

My body shivers its objection to having quite so much alcohol dumped inside it in one go. But I need it, we both need it to cast a veil over the shock of what I have finally found the courage to reveal. I also need it to push me into filling in the last detail, the very last piece of the puzzle that makes everything else somehow less important.

In the pocket of my bag is a notebook that I have carried with me for as long as I can remember. In the back of that are two photographs and a letter worn thin with love. I hand one of the photographs to Layla, but not before I look at it one more time.

'Because of him,' I say, pointing to the baby boy I am cradling in the photograph. A picture that was taken on the same day he was taken away. 'Because of Luke.'

Layla stares at the photograph, tracing the tip of her finger over the tiny bundle wrapped in my arms. Then she looks over at me, at the clothes I'm wearing, down to my feet and back to the photograph of a woman wearing cowboy boots underneath a red gypsy skirt. The same skirt I am now wearing, which has been hidden in the back of my wardrobe since 1997.

'He's . . . I mean . . . you have a baby?'

'I did. Fifteen years ago.' I have to tilt my head back in an effort not to cry. Because it still seems so desperately unfair, even after all the time that has passed. I miss him every single part of every single day. Every time I see a baby I'm reminded of what I did, and each time I catch my breath in anticipation that it might be him. Even now, when Luke wouldn't be a baby any more and I have no idea what he looks like.

'I gave him away because I had no idea how to do it by myself.' My hands are shaking, so is my voice, and it feels like all the words of my confession are fighting with one another to be set free. 'I was so afraid that I'd hurt him.'

'What do you mean?'

'I was so broken.' I'm openly sobbing now, air catching in my throat, tears soaking my skin before falling onto my lap. 'I was terrified that I wouldn't know how to love him. That every time I looked at him I would be reminded all over again that I wasn't enough.'

'And the father?' Layla asks, although I'm pretty sure she knows the answer even before I give a contemptuous laugh in response.

'Fuck knows.' I go over and retrieve the bottle of vodka, pouring myself another shot and holding back the urge to throw it and my glass as hard as I can against the wall. 'He never showed up.' Even now, I can't get rid of the anger, of the feeling that it was my fault for ever believing that a boy like Leo would actually choose a girl like me.

After Leo betrayed me, after my mother turned her back on me, I started to think it was my fault, that there was something wrong with me because why else would nobody love me? Then I convinced myself that whatever it was that made me so unlovable would be passed on to my unborn child. That the pain, the mourning I carried in my heart would seep into the womb and taint his soul.

Giving him up is the hardest thing I have ever done, but I still believe it was the right thing to do. Because he deserved the very best, the absolute best chance of happiness and I knew it couldn't come from me.

'Did you ever ask him why?'

I swirl the vodka around the glass, staring at the clear liquid and thinking about how it could so easily have been different. If I hadn't gone to the bar or decided to go for a punt, or even applied to Oxford in the first place. At one point I was going to turn the offer down, but my history teacher threatened to scalp me if I even breathed such a ridiculous idea ever again. Because opportunities like that very rarely came knocking and I would be a fool not to at least try.

'I wrote him a letter every single day for a month. Countless more the entire time I was holed up in the convent in Liverpool where Luke was born.' I still remember making that reverse journey across the Irish Sea, six months pregnant and deliberately avoiding eye contact with all those people who so clearly disapproved of my condition. Sister Ingrid thought it might be a mistake, but I was determined to give birth in England so that my son would have the option I never did – to find his mother.

'But Leo never wrote back,' I say with a drawn-out sigh. 'And neither did Erika.'

'So why take her name?'

Technically I only took her first name; the other one came from Uncle Alex, who, along with Sister Ingrid, tried to get me to change my mind, but I refused to back down. I refused to even consider any other name but hers.

'Because she was right.' My words come out pitched and strained, riddled with anger and frustration. 'I never should have chosen Leo over her. She was the only one who understood what it meant to lose the person you love most of all. I pushed her away because I thought she was asking me to choose between her and Leo. But all she was asking was to be my friend. Every single day I think of her, of all of them, and am thankful that I knew them, if only for a little while.'

'And you have no idea where they are now?' Layla says, reaching for her phone and I know what it is she intends to do. Maybe it's time. Maybe, now that I have someone to help, I'm ready to face up to how much of their lives I chose not to be part of.

I used to imagine them living together in Oxford, in that blue-painted house where I wasn't welcome. They would no doubt have thrown momentous parties for all their friends and told themselves how stupid they were to have taken pity on an Irish reject. Then the fantasy would move on to their glittering careers, with Duncan a professor in Oxford and Erika running a global corporation, safe in the knowledge that she was always so much better and more deserving than everyone else.

Finally, the dream would turn into a nightmare, with Erika and Leo surrounded by their adoring children, him kissing his beautiful wife and telling her that I was nothing but a terrible mistake.

But I never went so far as to discover if any of what I feared might be true.

'Don't,' I say and Layla lifts her head from the screen.

'I could look,' she says, glancing back down at whatever it is she has clearly already found. 'Then just give you the bullet points?'

'They're here.'

'Who?'

'I saw someone this morning. In the café.' I can't help but laugh at the admission. Because saying it out loud means it's real; it's not a figment of my twisted imagination. 'At first I didn't realise because I'd stopped looking. It's ridiculous really, to have spent all those years scared of who might suddenly walk back into my life and then *bam*, right out of nowhere the past decides to turn up.'

'It was him, wasn't it?' Layla's voice comes out as a whisper. 'It was Luke's father.'

I shake my head. Why is it that even now, even after I've done everything I can to distance myself from that part of my life, Leo continues to have such a profound effect on me?

'I couldn't breathe, Layla. I couldn't think, I couldn't figure out what on earth I was supposed to do if he saw me.'

'So you ran.'

Just like always, I ran to forget. I run every morning, with the music turned up loud, trying to push away the demons and the doubts. Because I ran that night, all the way to Ireland and I have never dared to go back.

'I wish I hadn't. I wish I'd gone right up to him and punched him as hard as I possibly could. Because he broke me, completely and utterly broke me and took away my chance to be a mother.'

'Could you . . .?' Layla looks down at the photograph, the one of me when I was little more than a child, cradling the boy who I loved but lost.

'I agreed it would be up to Luke to come and find me. But that's assuming his parents even told him.' I wrote him letters too. Every year on his birthday and again to mark all the big occasions of childhood – starting school, learning to ride a bike, even his first kiss. I have no idea if I sent them at the right time, if he prefers football to music or if he ever learnt to swim in the sea.

But I never heard back. No pictures, no letters, no teasers of information, and I told myself it was for the best, that being shown what I could not have might be too much for me to bear. The not knowing meant I could imagine him happy and grown, surrounded by people who love him.

'He's got your hair.' Layla is crying now, and I know only part of it is to do with me. The other part is her own sorrow, her own regrets at not having a family. 'Your real hair, before you hacked it all off.'

'I always hated my hair.' I sit back down next to her and give her hand a gentle squeeze.

'It suits you.' She reaches out to finger the velvet waistcoat I'm wearing over a simple white vest and gypsy skirt. 'So does this. It's very . . .'

Stevie Nicks, I think to myself as I take back the photograph and smile down at my son.

'It was his birthday not long ago. He'll probably be taller than me now.'

'Right,' Layla says, jumping to her feet and beginning to pace up and down the room as she speaks. 'Let me get this all straight in my head. Alex isn't your uncle.'

'Nope. He's the cousin of the nun who raised me.' And kind and wonderful and an absolute gem of a man who I am so very thankful for.

'Back in Ireland.' Layla points at me, but the pacing doesn't stop and it feels like I'm watching a bizarre game of tennis, with neither balls nor opponents. A second later my head begins to spin, so I bend forward to rest my forehead on my knees.

'Yes,' I mutter, closing my eyes and clenching my jaw as a horrible high-pitched sound rings from somewhere deep inside my brain.

I can still remember that hateful journey, made in a state of heightened panic because not only had Leo rejected me, so too had the only parents I'd ever known. There was a sense of otherworldliness to it all, as if I was watching a film of somebody who looked exactly like me as they emptied their bank account and bought a ticket to Liverpool. All those lonely hours spent travelling across the country with no soundtrack, no story, nothing to keep me company other than the voices in my head saying I was not worthy. Then the Irish Sea, which brought with it the temptation to jump overboard, give myself to the creatures that lived in the darkness, become food for the fish that scare me so.

Luke saved me then. I knew it was a boy from the very first time I felt him kick, a reminder that I wasn't allowed to give up. He was the only reason I stepped off the ferry and on to a rusty old bus that bumped and rattled all the way back to the place I was born. I must have looked like some kind of creature from the deep, arriving at the convent in the middle of a thunderstorm, soaked right through and incoherent with exhaustion.

When Sister Ingrid came downstairs, she crossed herself then ordered one of the younger nuns to run a bath, hot as hell itself, and then fetch me some tea. It was so many years ago, and yet I can still taste that sweetened offering, still hear the sound of Sister Ingrid's voice as she helped me out of my sodden clothes and poured jug after jug of hot water over my back. I didn't need to tell her about the baby; my swollen middle was screaming it loud enough for all to hear. But she never judged, she never reprimanded and she walked with me through the gardens every morning for weeks until we came up with a plan.

'You're not Swedish?' Layla asks.

'Nope.'

'But your best friend at Oxford was.'

'Yep.'

'And you broke up with her because of a boy.'

'Leo.' I haven't spoken his name since. Not even to Sister Ingrid or Alex, because his name made him real, made the pain and the betrayal oh-so real and I had to pretend otherwise. I had to pretend he was nothing more than a character in a storybook with a very unhappy ending.

'And you got pregnant.'

I look up to find Layla in front of me, hands on hips like some kind of recalcitrant superhero. But there are tears in her eyes and sorrow stitched all over her beautiful face and I hate putting this on her, for not telling her the truth from the very beginning.

'And then he dumped me. Well, I guess that's what you call being stood up for a wedding?'

'Haven't you ever thought about finding him? Confronting him?' She is shouting, not directly at me, but it's actually quite terrifying because Layla never shouts. Swears, breaks things, cries at the soppiest of romantic comedies, but shouting isn't part of her usual repertoire. 'Not even after Luke was born?'

'What would be the point?' Now I'm shouting too.

Layla puffs her cheeks, then slowly blows out all the air. Which means she's trying to decide whether or not to voice what it is she's wanting to say and isn't quite sure how I'm going to take it.

'Did you never think he might be worth a second chance?'

There it is. The reason I never told anyone. Because a baby changes everything. Dump a girl and you're a bastard. Dump a pregnant girl and you're a double bastard, but every child deserves a father, so maybe he didn't really mean it and you should forgive him for being so cruel?

I lie my head on the back of the sofa and close my eyes. Leo's face swims into view, with its lopsided grin and eyes that were never afraid to hold my gaze. I can picture the curl of hair at the nape of his neck and still know each and every mole on his back, like a map only I was allowed to read. I can see the way his hand always curled around my waist when we slept, and I can still taste the exact feel of his lips on mine, the way he made me come alive like never before.

I can picture every single thing about him and hate the fact it's just as painful as ever.

'He was,' I whisper as the tears fall all over again. 'And I gave him that chance when I wrote to him. But he abandoned me, even after everything I'd told him about my childhood, about the fears I had for our unborn child. It hurt too much for me to keep trying, and I was so young. I was so stupidly young and naive.' I wish more than anything I could go back and tell myself to try harder, to fight harder, because even if Leo didn't want me, that doesn't mean I couldn't have loved our son.

'It explains a lot.' Layla crouches down and rests her chin on my knee.

'About Hector.' I look at her, thinking that she now looks like some kind of demented poodle, with downturned mouth and all that hair.

'About you,' she says, giving my leg a quick poke. 'But yes, also about Hector.'

'I never felt like I deserved him. Plus, I was terrified of what he would think of me if he ever discovered the truth. And you.'

'Me?' Layla says, falling back on her heels. 'Why me?'

'Because apart from Alex, you're the only family I've got.'

'Then you should know that family don't judge. And I will love you even when you're old and senile and have lost all your teeth.'

We're both crying now, staring at one another and not quite sure what to do next.

My heart is still beating ten to the dozen, but the knot of fear in my stomach is almost gone. Almost, but not quite, because I still can't shake off the idea that my confession and the spilling of secrets isn't yet done.

'Thank you,' I say, wiping away my tears and taking a couple of slow, deliberate breaths.

'What for?'

'Not hating me.'

'Oh I do. A big part of me hates you for not telling me. Another part hates Leo for being so fucking idiotic as to think he could ever find anyone better than you.'

I stand up and go to the sink, turning on the tap and bringing the cool water up to my face. As I turn to reach for the towel that always hangs from a hook on the wall, my eye lands on the first ever memento I decided to keep.

'He gave me this,' I say, picking up the silver and emerald thimble that Leo once told me was the exact same shade as my eyes. Around the base is engraved the words *Be true in love as a turtle dove*. I remember smiling because I knew that thimbles used to be given as a sign of intent, back when gentlemen had to court their women. I thought it meant he loved me. I thought it meant he would keep his promise to never let me go.

'It's all I've got. Everything else was left behind, in Oxford.'

'Do you think Leo was here, in Notting Hill, to find you?'

'I have no idea.' I put the thimble on the top shelf, because out of sight and all that. Problem is, he's never out of mind because I carry him, and Luke – all of them – with me always.

'No.'

'No, what?'

'I know that look.' Layla shoves me out of the way and reaches back up for the thimble. 'And you are not allowed to run away,' she says, brandishing it at me like a weapon. 'Not now. Not after fate or the universe or whatever it is has handed him back to you.'

'He could be anywhere.' And the idea of going out to look for him is making my heart stammer and shake.

'He could also have been right around the corner all this time. Come on.' Layla grabs my hand, pulling me in the direction of the hall.

'Where are we going?' Except I already know. I have known all along that I would have to be the one to close the gap of both distance and time.

'Back to the café.'

'Layla, wait.' I look in the mirror that hangs in the hall, fluffing my hair and wondering if he's even going to recognise me. As I do so, Layla opens the front door and nearly collides with someone standing on the other side. Someone who is taller than Layla, with huge brown eyes, long wavy hair and an elfin slant to her nose.

'Hello.' There's a tilt to her voice and even from here I can smell her perfume, which is exactly the same as the contents of the tiny bottle I bought in London and kept hidden in a box upstairs. 'I'm looking for Niamh,' she says. 'I don't suppose she's squirrelling away back there?'

Niamh.

It's a name I haven't heard for over fifteen years, suddenly spoken out loud by someone I convinced myself I would never see again. Part of me doesn't want to turn my head, to find out why today of all days was when the past decided to come knocking.

But I've known it would come eventually. And even though my heart is crippled with doubt, there is still a small part of it that is singing loud enough to make me run to the door and throw myself into the arms of someone I love with all my heart.

'It's you,' I say with a high-pitched laugh, all too aware of how my entire body is shaking. Staring up at the face of my long-lost friend, I smile at the tears that are rolling down her cheeks. 'Erika.' It's so strange to say her name, the name that I stole and kept for myself as a way of remembering.

She smells of patchouli and bergamot. And the gap in her front teeth hasn't been closed, which means her smile is just as intriguing as it was the very first day we met.

'Niamh,' Erika says in return. 'What did you do to your hair?'

Before I have a chance to say anything more, to ask the myriad of questions that are running through my mind, someone else comes into sight. His hair may be dappled with the first signs of grey and the cut of his cloth more refined than when we were students, but he has the same gait to his walk, the exact same crinkle of eyes when he smiles.

'I nearly didn't recognise you,' Duncan says as he touches one hand to my cheek then pulls me into a hug.

'What are you doing here?' I gasp, looking between them and still not quite believing what I'm seeing.

'We came to find you,' Erika says, draping one arm over my shoulder and whispering against my hair just like she did the night we first met.

The three of us stumble back to the kitchen and stand in a circle, laughing and crying and then laughing some more, but none of us able to put into words what it is we're feeling.

Then we step away from each other, not much, but enough that we can look and stare and marvel at how little has really changed.

Out of the corner of my eye, I watch as the hands of the kitchen clock slip round to another hour.

'Where's Leo?' I ask, wiping at my face and trying to ignore the enormous diamond that still sits on my finger. Hector will be here soon. But I need to see Leo, to speak to him before I can figure out what to do.

'Leo?' Duncan says and I see the look that passes between him and Erika. One split second and my entire world is flipped all over again. Another second more and my heart hammers out the answer I do not want to hear.

'Yes, Leo,' I say, although the words sound muffled and strange because of that high-pitched ringing in my ears that won't leave me alone. 'He was in the café. Isn't he with you?'

'We thought you knew,' Erika says, taking a step towards me but I back away because I know what her face is saying and I can't – I won't – listen. 'We thought that's why you left.'

LEO

Thantophobia (n.) – *phobia of losing someone you love*

Oxford, 1996

He was late. He was always late, but not today of all days. His mother had rung all the way from New York to ask him if he was OK. Thankfully she wasn't able to see down the line, to notice the slightly startled look on his face or that he kept fiddling with something in his pocket. He had promised her all was fine, listened to her talking about the Christmas lights at Bloomingdale's and how she was going to see a show that evening with his father, assuming he left the office on time.

Leo had hung up and stared at the phone, wondering whether he should call her back, tell her about Niamh, about the baby. But they'd agreed not to say anything until after the wedding. Besides, he wasn't sure if it was the sort of thing to announce to his mother when she was on the other side of the Atlantic. Better to wait. Do it in person. A family gathering back home at Christmas when they could share their happy news.

'Come on, Leo,' he said as he opened his rucksack and threw in a change of clothes. 'Focus.'

Looking around the bedroom, he grabbed his essay from the desk along with his camera. For weeks he had carried on as normal, pretending that he was just another third-year student, hiding in the library to try to avoid all the invitations to parties and college bops. But when they came back from London and their secret was shared, what then? Would Niamh move in? Would his housemates mind having a pregnant woman and then a baby living in their bachelor pad?

There was so much they hadn't talked about and he knew they were both avoiding the inevitable. Denial was so very alluring when you didn't have a clue what you were supposed to do.

But there was always something hanging over them, a great big swathe of responsibility that Leo didn't think he was ready for. Would he ever be ready? He'd pictured the two of them carving out a life together that at some point would include a family. He just hadn't expected it to happen before he'd even graduated. Nor did he expect the swell of emotions he had every time he thought of Niamh and the life that was growing inside her. A life – no, a person – they had created out of love; someone he was already fiercely protective of and couldn't wait to meet. It was terrifying, but he also couldn't wait for it all to begin.

Reaching into his pocket, he took out the small velvet pouch containing the wedding bands he'd picked up that morning. He slipped hers onto the tip of his finger, allowing himself to wonder what dress she'd chosen to wear.

He loved her more than he'd ever thought it was possible to love someone, and she had promised to be his, now and forever more. He may not have had the foggiest as to what would come next, but he knew that as long as he had her, it would all be OK.

'One day at a time,' Leo said to himself as he cast a gaze around the room before shouldering his bag and bounding down the stairs.

The threat of rain hung in gunmetal clouds overhead, the air already damp and chilled. The wheels of Leo's bike skidded as he had to stop suddenly in order to avoid a fox that shot out of someone's front garden. The creature looked back at him, then scrambled over a fence and was gone.

Leaning forward over the handlebars, he flicked on the front light. The beam was weak, he should have changed the battery, but it was better than nothing. He glanced up at the sky that was beginning to drip, turned up the collar of his jacket and pedalled off in the direction of town.

Cycling along St Giles, he passed a man carrying an enormous bunch of roses. Should he head for the Covered Market, get a bunch for Niamh? No time, he told himself, and they'd only get crushed in his bag. And did she even like roses, or was it lilies? There was still so much they didn't know about one another, and even though they were about to spend the rest of their lives together, it felt as if he was running out of time. The idea had been there ever since he woke that morning, churning his stomach and making him anxious for the day to be over, for him to be with her again.

Broad Street was busy with people and bikes, all heading in different directions, and he had to swerve to avoid a cyclist who turned without even looking.

Please still be there, he thought to himself as he cycled up to the crossroads. What would he do if she wasn't there? The idea of her not being there, or thinking that he wasn't coming was haunting in its enormity. Because he had to admit things had been somewhat strained between them of late. Not surprising really, given what they were trying to process. Add to that the looming pressure of finals and a heavy dose of morning sickness and it was no wonder they were both happy to ignore the elephant in the room.

The traffic lights flicked to red and the bike in front of him skidded to a halt. A split-second decision, to wait or carry on, and he swung out to the right of the cyclist and then freewheeled around the corner, at the very same moment as a man stepped off the pavement to cross the road.

There was no pause, no slowing of time as Leo was thrown from the saddle and across the asphalt. Nor did his life flash before his eyes as his head collided with the windscreen of the car coming the other way. There was no accompanying song as the contents of his bag were tossed through the sky and the lens of his camera shattered on impact with the ground.

But he did have a final thought, a final picture in his mind in the moment before he was taken from the world. As always, he thought of her, of Niamh.

NIAMH

Erlebnisse (n.) – *the experiences, positive or negative, that we feel most deeply*

London, 2012

I am sitting at my kitchen table drinking sugary tea and staring across at the people I never thought I'd see again. But someone is missing. Leo is missing, because he's gone and so I will most definitely not be seeing him again.

A boy who will never grow up, never grow old and grey and be given the chance to carve out a life with the girl he fell in love with. Nor will he be a father or a grandfather. His family has been torn apart in so many ways, like a ripple on a pond that stretches even further than the eye can see.

Do they even know, his parents? Do they even know about me, about Luke? What must they think of me, to simply disappear and never contact them again? But then there are the letters I sent. So many letters that I assumed he simply had no desire to respond to. Did his mother read them? No, because then she would have learnt about Luke and I cannot for one minute believe she would have abandoned him. Which means she probably threw them away, so consumed by her own grief that she had no desire to share it with me.

'Why didn't you write back to me?' I am gripping my cup so tight that my knuckles have turned white, but I have to stop my hands from doing something far, far worse. If only one of them had replied. If only one of them had realised that I had no idea about Leo, then perhaps, just perhaps, I could have kept my son.

'Who, me?' Erika is leaning against the countertop, dunking a biscuit into her sweetened cup of coffee and looking at me with a frown.

'Yes, you.' *Don't fall apart. You must not fall apart; not until you know absolutely every last detail, every excuse, every possible reason as to why they never came looking.* 'I wrote to you after Luke was born.'

'I never . . .' Erika looks to Duncan for reassurance, but he just lifts his hands in a gesture so familiar that we could have been back in our student days, and I have to blink twice to make myself focus on the here and now.

'I sent it to your parents' place in Sweden. Just to make sure it didn't get lost or ignored at college.'

'Oh, Niamh,' Erika says with a sigh and her whole face sags. 'We sold the house. After my mother got sick.'

What are the odds? What are the chances that because I decided not to send the letter back to Oxford, I would lose it all? I was afraid Erika might not read it if I sent it directly to her. I was afraid she could so easily claim never to receive it, and I don't know whether to laugh or scream at how utterly unfair all of this is.

'Is your mother OK?' I need her to be OK. I need something good to come out of all this crap.

'Yes, thankfully. But everything was boxed up and shipped to the summer house, so it probably got lost in amongst all the chaos when we moved.'

'We?'

'After the ball . . .' Erika's face stills, her eyes looking at something far away. 'After the ball,' she says again. 'Everything seemed to be unravelling. You were in Europe, Duncan was in Cambodia. Even when we were back in Oxford, it wasn't the same. Duncan and I seemed to forget how to be around one another.'

'Without you,' Duncan says with a shy smile, 'we sort of drifted apart.'

'Then my mother got sick and it felt like the universe was against me, that it was all my fault. I felt that somehow I was responsible for making her sick, for Leo dying, for losing you. Just like Astrid.' She darts a look at me and then turns her head away. It takes me a moment to realise that she's crying, really crying, the whole of her body shaking with great heaving sobs.

'Erika,' I say, but I can't move. I can't make myself go over there to comfort her and I don't know if it's because part of me is still angry or if it's simply because I've never seen her cry like this before.

'So I went home. And never came back,' she says with a laugh, wiping at her eyes, and even through the tears she is so very beautiful. 'Seems like I was running away from the wrong thing all along.'

'Wait, you didn't finish your degree?' As I say it out loud I can't help but consider the absolute irony – or is it coincidence, or another word that I don't seem to be able to think of right now? What are the odds that our lives could have been so very far apart, and yet also follow a similar path?

'No,' Erika says, sniffing loudly and giving her head a small shake. 'For months I wasn't capable of doing much more than getting out of bed each morning, and going for long walks around the lake with my mother. Given everything that happened, a degree just didn't seem so important.'

'What about you?' I ask Duncan, although I can guess what his answer will be.

'Oh, I stayed until the bitter end,' he says, crossing one long limb over the other and transporting me back to 1995. 'Never left, actually. Although I'm over the road at Magdalen College with all the deer now.'

'Did you . . .' I start to speak, then have to stop, take a breath, because even though I have imagined it so many times, pictured the life they shared without me, it still hurts to think that I broke them too. 'Are you still friends?'

'Yes,' Erika says, looking at Duncan and then back at me. 'But not in the way we were before.'

'I'm so sorry, Niamh,' Duncan says, and now he's crying, which to be honest doesn't surprise me in the slightest. It actually makes me smile to know he's still as hopelessly emotional as always. 'That stupid fight we had ruined everything.'

'It wasn't your fault.' I say the words without even thinking and he looks at me through uncertain eyes. 'It wasn't anybody's fault,' I say again, sinking back into the chair.

'I wish I'd done things differently,' Erika says and it makes me laugh, because it's the same thing that has plagued me over the years: the idea that if only I'd done or said or not said something, then life would have turned out just fine, thank you.

She's in front of me now, clasping my hands and forcing me to look at her. 'I thought you didn't want to see me. That you were too angry with me to share your pain. But I never saw a letter, Niamh. I wish I had, more than anything else in the world, I wish I had known.'

'He never read my letters.' I gasp as the whole stinking mess comes crashing down. All this time I thought he'd abandoned me, when in fact he'd died in the middle of a street less than five minutes away. It is so painfully, agonisingly wrong, because if I'd known . . .

'He loved you,' Duncan says as he reaches out to take the cup from my hands. 'He loved you so very, very deeply.'

'Then why does it hurt so much?'

'Because you loved him too.' Erika wraps her arms around my shoulder and pulls me close.

It's all a mistake. A misunderstanding, a miscomprehension. A mis-something because it shouldn't be this way. Everything that happened to me and everything that didn't happen to Leo, is false. All because of one stupid, irrevocable moment that spun my entire existence out of control.

Why? Why did it happen and who is to blame for what I've lost? Is it my fault, for deciding not to have an abortion? Plus there wouldn't have been such a need to get married, to 'make things right', if I'd never fallen pregnant in the first place.

Or should I have stuck to the original plan and gone travelling with Erika, accepted the internship? More than that, I shouldn't have allowed myself to fall so madly in love with a boy who deserved a chance at a perfect kind of life. A life that, because of me, he no longer has.

Pushing back my chair, I go over to the sofa and pick up the tapestry bag I bought with Erika on a daytrip to Blenheim. I open it and dump the contents on the cushions. All those memories of a given point in time were meant to keep me connected to Leo and, in turn, Luke. They were supposed to make me remember that I chose him over my friends, that I chose to give up my child because of not being worthy. It also made me careful, too careful, about falling in love again.

And now I see that it was all a lie.

'Niamh?' Erika moves closer to me, watching as I clench and unclench my fists. A split second later and I've picked up the bottle of perfume and thrown it as hard as I can against the wall. Fragments of glass are flung back towards me as the bottle shatters into tiny pieces.

He died alone. He died without me knowing that he was coming for me and I hate myself for not being there, for not being able to make it all OK.

Next, I pick up the moonstone necklace, swiftly followed by a golden monkey. Moments of happiness now forever stained with the guilt that I was even allowed to feel anything at all. I have lived, but I have wasted the life I chose. Would he have done the same? Wallowed in self-pity and loathing, believed himself unworthy of love? I doubt he would have done anything other than dive in deep, explore absolutely everything and anything that crossed his path. He might have even forgiven me, but he would never have given up the chance to be a father.

'Niamh, stop.' Layla grabs my arm but I shrug her off and turn my attention to the table, picking up Duncan's cup and lobbing it at the wall.

'Why?' I scream at nobody and everybody at once, watching the cup break cleanly in two. 'I've lost both of them now. I've fucked everything up – his life as well as my own.' All because I listened to the voices in my head that told me I wasn't deserving of Leo and the life we were supposed to have together.

'He stole my life.' I am roaring like a caged animal, desperately looking for a means of escape. 'I'm not the person I'm supposed to be because he never fucking showed up. I've been hiding in plain sight, afraid of getting close to someone. Afraid of showing Hector who I am for fear of getting hurt. And it's all Leo's fault.'

'He died, Niamh,' Erika says, reaching out a hand to me, then taking it back when I whip round to face her, not bothering to hide the grief I am now allowed to lay bare.

'I know that now. But I didn't know it then and everything' – I take a shuddering gasp, then smack my hand against the countertop, hard and fast – 'everything that has happened since. Every tiny decision I've made. Every person I've pushed away. Every time

302

I've thought it was all my fault for not being enough is because I thought he simply didn't turn up. God, if I'd known.'

'You would have been destroyed.' Erika places a tentative hand on my back and I hear her let out a small sigh of relief when I don't flinch or move away.

'But I would have chosen differently.' I am crying again, great vibrations of loss and remorse coursing through my soul and spilling all the contents of my heart into the room.

'You don't know that.' Layla is on my other side, and together she and Erika guide me back to the sofa.

'Except I do,' I say, brushing some pieces of glass on to the floor and sucking at a cut on my finger when it begins to bleed. The pain is real and so much more bearable than the one that's inside me. A pain that I'm terrified will never go away. 'Luke is the only thing left of Leo and I would never, never have given him up if I'd known.'

'About that,' Duncan says, clearing his throat and shifting in his seat.

'About what?' I ask, seeing once again a look that passes between Duncan and Erika. This time it's more excitement than fear, but there's definitely a little bit of nerves in the mix. I can tell because Duncan is rubbing the end of his nose, which means he's itching to tell me something but isn't sure whether or not he's supposed to.

'How do you think we found you?'

OK, so now he's grinning. And tapping a number into his phone as he nods across at Erika. Without telling me anything more, he walks out of the kitchen and I can hear him talking to someone as he leaves the house.

'Where is he going?' I ask, but I can picture it all so clearly in my head. He turns right, going along the street to where a car is parked. A car that doesn't belong and yet is most definitely supposed to be there.

Time slows, giving me a moment to take a breath, to try and grasp on to what I think is about to happen. I feel the world tilt in an altogether new direction, one that is pushing me towards something instead of allowing me to run away. It's a feeling that has been there ever since I woke this morning and went for a run. The dog that came up to say hello, that man in his brand-new trainers, the song that was playing on the car stereo. All of them were steering me to the café, and the person who was waiting inside. Waiting for me to notice him.

'Duncan got an email,' Erika says and I turn to look at her, but I am only half aware of her words. It's like I'm looking through a frosted pane of glass, or my head is underwater and there's someone standing over me, telling me things I cannot hear.

'Who from?' I ask, but my heart already knows the answer.

'He said he was looking for his mother, and wondered if Duncan might be able to help. Apparently, he only ever discovered the letters when his adoptive parents moved from Cornwall back to London. He opened a box without knowing what was inside.'

I feel her put something in my palm and I look down to see a silver angel hanging from a chain. My mother's necklace, the one she left behind in the convent and I in turn sent to my son.

'He read the letters?' I say, blinking through tears, so scared it hurts to breathe.

Erika nods and I think she's crying too, but it's hard to tell because I don't feel like I'm attached to this world any more. It's more like floating, or being at the end of a very long tunnel and unsure whether I'm supposed to walk towards the light or away from it.

'The adoption agency had no forwarding address for you, other than the convent.'

I never gave them any other address because I stopped believing Luke would one day write back. It didn't stop me from writing to him though. I don't know why, perhaps I just liked telling him a little bit about my life, as well as wanting to let him know that I thought of him, always.

'But Sister Ingrid died,' I say and I register the touch of Layla's hand on mine as I speak.

'The convent told him about Oxford,' Erika says. She's talking to Layla over my head and it should annoy me, but I am so very overwhelmed at having the two of them here, together. Let alone being able to focus on, to make sense of, the story that Erika is trying to tell.

'He emailed the college, who then forwarded it on to the one person still living in the city who might have a clue where his mother could be.'

'But that still doesn't explain . . .' I don't finish my sentence, because I'm trying to figure out how Duncan might have found me. I was so very careful not to leave any breadcrumbs behind.

'He hasn't changed,' Erika says with a smile that transports me straight back to the very first time we met. 'Duncan's still capable of charming the pants off anyone, even a nun.'

'But Sister Ingrid died.'

'You said that already,' she says, rolling her eyes and making me feel eighteen again. 'Everyone leaves something behind.'

'I wrote to her,' I whisper. I wrote to her every single week from the day I left the convent, all through school, university and then from an end-of-terrace house in Primrose Hill where I lived with a man who was willing to lend me his name. A man who was Sister Ingrid's next-of-kin and whose contact details would have been kept in a large, grey ledger in the office of the convent where I was born.

I can imagine the rest. Duncan would have tracked me down in less time than it once took him to roll a joint. Then he would have called Erika, demanded she be there when the universe brought us all together again. No doubt she was also somewhere in that café, humming along to 'Disco 2000' as it spilled from the radio on the shelf behind the counter. I suspect it was Duncan who called out to me as I ran, asking me to wait, because it wasn't him, it wasn't Leo who I saw.

I'm not really listening or paying attention to Erika any longer, because all my focus, all my energy, is being directed towards the hall, where I can hear a door being shut and two sets of footsteps heading my way.

Everything stops. Time really does stand still when he walks into the room. A boy at least a head taller than me, with dark curls, a tilt to the end of his nose and eyes as green as any emerald. He stands in front of me and we both offer up a tentative smile, pause a moment to drink in the sight of someone who should be a stranger and yet it feels like we've known each other our whole lives.

'Luke,' I whisper as I reach out a hand and trace the contours of his face.

'Hi, Mum,' he says in a voice so very like his father's, warm and rich and true.

Just like that, a little piece of my heart, one that I thought would be lost forever, gets stitched back into place.

NIAMH

Ikigai (n.) – *a reason for being, the thing that gets you up in the morning*

London, six weeks later

The scent of damp lingers in the early morning air. I can feel the soft splat of dew against my bare calves as we walk across the lawns of Kensington Gardens towards the statue of Peter Pan. It seems impossible to believe it was only six weeks ago I came here during my morning run, somehow aware that the day would turn out to be monumental.

'Mum?'

I turn my face up to Luke, smile at the openness of his gaze. It still surprises me every time I look at him, how much he resembles his father. There's a lot of me in there too and, I can't help but wonder, perhaps a little of my own mother. But that's the crazy thing about genetics: you never know what's going to be passed along to the next generation. Then there's the whole nature versus nurture debate, and I have to keep reminding myself that he is still the same boy I gave birth to all those years ago. That the soft Cornish burr to his voice doesn't matter, that his childhood was no better or worse for growing up by a different sea to the one where I once lived.

I have to keep reminding myself that he is alive, that he is here, with me.

'I'm fine,' I say, looping my arm through his and leaning in to him. He's already a head taller than me, broad in the shoulders but with a little ungainliness to his stride, as if he's still trying to figure out how he fits inside his own skin. 'It's a bit strange coming back here with you. That's all.'

'Is this where you came? You know, that morning?'

I nod my response, because I have slowly been filling him in on as much as I can possibly remember about that day. He arrived at the house last night, standing in the kitchen all shy and awkward, until I set down an enormous bowl of pasta on the table and he smacked his lips in appreciation.

The information I have learnt about him from our lengthy phone calls and endless emails over the past few weeks has felt a bit like reading from a textbook, or making a long list of things I need to remember. Having him in the house with me, sharing my space, seeing the way his body folds into a chair in the exact same way as Leo, feels like I'm getting a better and more accurate picture of what my son is really like.

I know that he likes football, old movies and art. I also now know that he sings in the shower, drinks endless cups of tea and his second toes are longer than his big ones, just like his father – Erika too, and I can't wait to tell her.

'There was a man,' I say, scrolling back through my memories to the morning when everything changed. 'And a dog who looked just like one that used to live next door when I was a kid.'

'Back in Ireland?'

'Back in Ireland.' I look along the river, think of the wildness of the Irish Sea, of the convent garden I first explored as a child, and then again with Sister Ingrid when I was trying to figure out what to do about my unborn child.

'Did you speak to them?'

I have barely thought about my adoptive parents in the intervening years, the pain of being so decisively cut off preventing me from doing so. But Luke asks all sorts of questions and is quite possibly the nosiest person I have ever met. Which is understandable, given the circumstances, but sometimes he throws me a curveball, just like when he suggested it might be time to reach out, to offer the veritable olive branch to the people I once called Mum and Dad.

'I left a voicemail. But it's been so long, I have no idea if they'll ever call me back.'

'They were still your parents.'

'Not in the way I wanted them to be. Or how I wanted to be, with you.' I wanted so many things, none of which I ever believed would be possible. Taking a long, slow breath, I tell myself that there's nothing I can do to change what's happened. There's nothing I could have done to stop Leo from taking the turn too fast, too soon.

Telling Luke about Leo was hands down the most painful, torturous thing I have ever had to endure. It breaks my heart; I can literally feel it quiver whenever I think about the look on his face when he asked me about his dad and I burst into tears. The fact they will never meet is quite possibly the worst concept that's ever swum through my mind. It's too difficult to process, too intangible to try and explain, but somehow I have to, for Luke.

'It's not your fault.' It's like he can see inside my head. It's a strange but welcome feeling, to be so completely open and willing to tell him anything he wants to know.

'I know. I just wish . . .' I don't really know what I wish any more. For so long, all I wanted was to hide from the past, to bury myself so deep in another life that it would be impossible for any-one to find me. But I would also wake in the middle of the night, breathless and pained from the dreams I kept having about the people I thought had abandoned me.

He tilts back his head, puffs out his cheeks and shoves his hands in his pockets, all of which tells me he's doing his best not to cry. We have spent a lot of time crying, together and apart, over these past weeks. Crying for what happened, what *didn't* happen and everything else in between. The pain he is feeling must be so very complex and tortured, and I desperately want to take it from him, carry that weight instead.

The knowledge, the understanding, that he is hurting makes me want to wrap my arms around him, hold him close and tell him everything will be OK. It also makes my heart ache for all the years I couldn't be there for him, simply be with him and watch him grow.

'I wish my parents had told me,' he says.

'They had their reasons.' His parents were a bit tricky to begin with, clearly unimpressed that Luke had tracked me down without either their knowledge or permission. But they at least had the decency to be ashamed at not passing on any of my letters, claiming that they thought it best to wait until he turned eighteen before flooring him with the announcement that he was adopted. Not that it's my place to judge (although clearly I can't help it, and Erika has made no secret of how she feels about it all), because from what Luke tells me, they have been nothing but kind and supportive and loving to him.

'But still,' he says with a loud sniff. 'Don't you wonder what would have happened if they'd told me from the very beginning? Given me the letters? Let you be a part of my life?'

It hurts, really hurts, whenever I think about this. But if there's one thing I have learnt from discovering what happened with Leo, it's that looking back, wishing you could change things, is nothing more than a complete waste of time.

'They were trying to protect you,' I say.

'Protect me from what?' he asks with a frown. 'From you?'

'In a way.' I tilt my head back to the sky, searching for the right words. 'My mum gave me away because she had to. And even though I understand why, it never stopped me from missing her, even after I was adopted.'

'I guess,' he says, looking down and away. He is still so young, there's still so much for him to try and comprehend, and I wonder if there will ever be enough time to make up for all the years that we've lost.

'No regrets, remember?' I still regret so much, but I am grateful for so much more. Not least the understanding that Leo, *my* Leo, wanted me, wanted us both.

'What was he like?'

'Your dad?' I ask and Luke gives a shy smile in response. 'He was sort of perfect, really. Brilliant and kind and filled with a sense of longing for something more. He was the first person who ever made me feel like I was worthy, that I was deserving of love.'

'What about Aunt Erika?'

I have to smile, because sometimes I forget that he knows every single part of the story. And not just from me, but from Erika, Duncan, even Layla. They've all given him their version of events, some of which were more painful to discover than others. Like Erika telling me about the night she bumped into Leo in the pub on St Giles and told him he had to promise to take care of me. I was always so nervous of her beauty, it blinded me to how incredibly protective she is over those she loves.

'Oh, she loved me, but in an altogether different kind of way. You'll find that out for yourself,' I say, bumping my hip against his. 'Won't be long before you'll have all the girls chasing after you.'

'Mum.'

'Sorry,' I say with a grin, because I can't get over the fact that he's here, with me, and calling me by a name I never thought I'd hear him or anyone else say.

'I wanted to show you something,' I say as we stop by a bench underneath the shade of an old oak tree. Sitting down next to one another, I reach into my bag and take out a Polaroid picture. It was taken the same night as the one of Erika, Duncan and me. The one I showed to Layla and she never thought to imagine that I might not have been who I claimed to be. This one is of Leo and me, kissing under a moonlit sky and thinking we had the rest of our lives to look forward to.

I hand it to Luke, watch his face for some kind of clue as to what he might be thinking about as he looks at a picture of the parents he never knew, one of whom he will never get to meet.

'Leo's mother, your grandmother, sent it to me.' It arrived one morning in a box filled with photographs taken that summer Leo and I spent together. Photographs of all the places we visited, as well as dozens more of the two of us, wrapped around one another and smiling back at the camera. I nearly fainted when I first realised what they were, then let out a cry of alarm loud enough to make Layla sprint down the stairs when I saw that all the letters I wrote to Leo were in there too.

I called Mrs Bonfiglio the day after Luke found me. She cried, I cried, then she cried some more because we were connected in the worst possible way. When I told her about Luke, she openly sobbed, the sound laced through with laughter and all manner of words I barely understood.

'You really loved him, didn't you?' Luke says as he turns to me, and there are tears in his eyes, one of which falls down his face and he makes no movement to wipe it away.

'I did,' I say, cupping his face in my hands, then leaning forward to place a kiss on his cheek. 'And he loved us too.' He doesn't flinch, doesn't shy away, as if it's the most natural thing in the world for me to be comforting him. And I guess it is. I guess there are some things that are far too strong to break.

'Luke,' I say, dropping my hands to my lap and willing my voice to stop shaking. 'I want you to know that I love you. That I've always loved you.'

It astounds me how much I love him and how instantaneous it was the second he stepped into my kitchen. A great wave of feeling, so different to anything I've ever had before. It made me realise it was there all along, even before he was born and I held him in my arms, crying into his hair because I was so afraid of getting it wrong.

Motherhood seems to be a strange mix of fear and elation, an idea – no, an understanding – that sits right in the very centre of you. I was so afraid I wouldn't love him, was incapable of it, didn't deserve to have that kind of relationship in my life. The relief I felt when I saw I was wrong is one of those turning points, those 'aha' moments that I will carry with me always.

'I love you too,' Luke says and I can't help but laugh and cry and laugh all over again as he pulls me in for a hug.

It is Luke who has saved me, all over again. He was the one to make me determined not to give up on those horrendous ferry journeys across the Irish Sea. The power he had over me before he was even born became magnified tenfold when he was there in my home, smiling that beautiful smile that is exactly like his father's used to be.

I remember so much about that day, but mostly I remember being overcome by a sense of calm. As if all the grief I'd been carrying around for sixteen years decided that it was time to leave me be. I also remember the look on Hector's face when he walked into the kitchen and came face to face with all the things I'd never been able to tell him.

The journey between then and now has been rocky, with tears and laughter and a whole lot of vodka to help wash away all my regret. Luke has proven to be the glue that holds us all together. He has given me a purpose, a reason to forgive and forget and decide to start again with a promise that there will be no more secrets, no matter what.

I look down at the ring that still sits on the third finger of my left hand. The wedding didn't happen; there was no way either of us could have stood up in front of a congregation when pretty much everyone there (including my husband-to-be), had no idea about who I really was. But he hasn't left. He hasn't abandoned me in the way I assumed he would if he ever found out the truth.

Hector has been close to saint-like when it comes to understanding why I did what I did. Not just about Luke, but him too. All those years when I pushed him away because I was so afraid, so convinced that I didn't deserve to be happy. But that doesn't mean it's been easy for him to realise that he wasn't the first person I truly loved.

'Can't be much fun competing with a dead person,' was how Layla described it, making me snort and choke on my drink, not least because it's the exact same thing Erika had said to me only hours before. I still feel afraid: for the future, for what may or may not happen between Hector and me.

'What if it was all for nothing?' The words slip out before I've had a chance to consider them, consider who I'm saying them to. 'Oh, no. Luke, I didn't mean . . .'

'It's OK,' he says with a nod at my ring. 'He'll come around.'

I laugh and shake my head, because for fifteen, Luke is remarkably astute. Or maybe it's because I'm starting to be more open, no longer hiding my feelings behind a fake smile. Or perhaps it's because Luke is simply so very good at reading me, just like Leo.

'I hope so,' I say, because after all this time, when I'm finally ready and willing to be completely honest about what has happened, who I am, and who it is that I love, I really want Hector to be willing to give me one more chance.

NIAMH

Anam Cara (n.) – *a person with whom you can share your deepest thoughts, feelings and dreams*

Oxford, one year later

The Queen's College clock chimes out the hour and I turn my head to look. There is no rain today, just warm summer sunshine and the most gentle of breezes. I didn't want to come back, not at first, but the combination of Erika and Duncan can be so very persuasive. Add Layla to the mix and I never really stood a chance.

Everything is the same, and yet it has changed, because whenever I have thought about this place, I have always thought of Leo. To be in this city without him isn't something I ever thought would be possible, but love – real heart-wrenching, painful love – has shown me that I am far stronger than I ever believed.

'Niamh?'

I turn at the sound of my name and watch Erika let go of a little girl's hand to come over to me.

'You OK?'

'Bit nervous,' I reply, looking over at her eldest daughter, whose middle name is the same as my own. I cried when Erika told me. Then I cried some more at the idea that there was so much I have missed, that we've all missed, because I was too afraid to tell my best friend the truth about a long-lost summer.

So many conversations have been spent trying to fill in all the gaps – discovering how Erika left Oxford right after me, returning to Stockholm because her mother was sick. She never came back, instead choosing to marry the boy next door (he really did live next door and they used to play together as children), and eventually taking over the family firm. They have a house up on the lakes that she took us to last summer. Those days spent swimming in the achingly cold water and swapping stories during nights that never seemed to get dark are some of the happiest I can think of.

When I say 'us', I don't just mean Erika, Duncan and me. We forgave each other the second they walked back into my life and now we are a team once more, texting or calling one another several times a day and visiting as often as our lives will allow. But the team has new members now, including the woman standing next to Erika, both of them wearing replicas of the dress once discovered in that antiques shop on the King's Road. Little and large, as I secretly call them, and I know that I am ridiculously blessed to have them both in my life.

'Don't cry,' Duncan says as he takes a pristine handkerchief out of his pocket and dabs at my cheek. 'You'll ruin your beautiful face.'

I laugh at his backhanded compliment and he gives my hand an encouraging squeeze before heading to the other side of the quad. Today he is dressed in a beautifully cut morning suit, but the first time I came back to visit, he bounded across the lawn in Magdalen College, his robes flapping behind him and startling a deer in the process.

Doctor D, as we all refer to him now. He lives out by the Trout (the pub with the albino peacock where Erika and I argued over *Little Women* whilst drinking far too much vodka, always vodka) in a nineteen-thirties semi, the interior of which would make any self-respecting designer weep with envy. Gone are the rats, replaced by a lazy French bulldog called Cyril who sits in the basket of his bike as they cycle to work every day. From what I gather, he is loved by peers and pupils alike and is soon to head off on a trek to Nepal – with Uncle Alex no less.

They are just friends, but I wonder if there hadn't been so much time and space between them, they might have become more.

'See you in there,' Layla says with a smile as she and Erika walk inside the chapel, accompanied by the sound of someone singing 'Ave Maria'.

There is one more member of our illustrious clan, someone I have been terrified of losing for over a decade. Someone who is standing at the end of the aisle, waiting for me. It's like something out of a storybook, the irony that it took Leo dying to make me realise I was worthy of love, deserving of it even.

I feel an arm curl around my waist and I look up into the face of the person who has made everything about this day both possible and perfect.

'Ready?' Luke asks, and I have to blink back the tears, because every time I catch sight of him my heart squeezes in response.

He loved us, I think to myself, smiling at the memory of Luke and me going for a walk one Sunday morning when we ended up in Kensington Gardens and I told him everything. I told him about the pain and the sorrow, but most of all about the love. Because I know now that if he had lived, Leo would have given us the most wonderful life.

At the entrance I pause, looking down at the bouquet of cabbage roses in my hands, inside of which is hidden an emerald thimble. I will carry you with me always, Leo. I will love you for the rest of my days, but that doesn't mean I can't give myself to another. To a man who has accepted me, warts and all, and is still willing to say 'I do'. At least I hope he bloody is.

Peering inside the chapel, I look along the rows of expectant faces. My eyes meet those of Leo's mother, a woman whose forgiveness I did not envisage, but who has been truly magnanimous and has pulled her grandson deep into the heart of her family, one that now belongs to my son.

Slowly, I have learnt to forgive myself, to understand that there is no going back or undoing what we each have done.

I allow my eyes to travel all the way to the altar and there he is, my Hector, fiddling with his cufflinks, glancing back in my direction but not really looking. I want to ask him what he's thinking, but there's plenty of time still to come.

There's a word for this, this overwhelming sense of being with the ones you care for most of all . . .? One that I read in a storybook about Celtic legends of old, on a wintry night when I dared to dream that there was something, someone, beyond the walls of the convent who might show me how to love.

Anam Cara, I think to myself as I glance at my son and he catches me looking, frowning at whatever it is he can see on my face.

'It's OK, Mum,' he says, bending down to whisper in my ear just as the organ pipes begin to play. 'I've got you.'

ACKNOWLEDGMENTS

Writing a book is a bit like having a baby – messy, painful and it literally takes a village to nurture, care for, and help it grow into something you can be proud of. This book was no different, and so I'd like to say thank you to the people who helped make it possible.

First and foremost, my incredible agent, Hayley Steed. She has been with me all the way and was instrumental in turning Erika and Niamh's story into something people would want to read.

Secondly, my heartfelt thanks go out to Sammia Hamer at Lake Union Publishing. As a writer, I couldn't have asked for a more passionate, welcoming editor and I feel honoured to be part of the Lake Union team. In addition, thanks go to Sophie Wilson for showing me how to polish the story, make it real, make me remember what it felt like to be caught in the middle of a best friend and true love.

To the team at Jelly London and Heike Schüssler, thank you for creating such a beautiful cover design that really captures the essence of the story. To Sophie Goodfellow and everyone at FMcM, I'm so grateful for all the work you have done in sending the book out into the world.

This book wouldn't exist at all if it weren't for the love and support of so many others, especially my writing buddies, without whom I would have given up long ago. In no particular order . . .

Tom Bromley, for his unwavering belief and support; Deborah Masson, who was there from the very beginning and who I cannot wait to drink whiskey by a fire with; Hannah Persaud, for listening to all my doubts and telling me to keep on writing no matter what; Sophie Wing for reading a chapter in the basement café of Waterstones on Piccadilly and telling me to go for it; Chloe Combi, Natasha Fricker, Noel Smaragdakis and Hynam Kendall, you are all brilliant people, as well as exceptional writers and I'm very grateful to have you in my life.

There is, of course, my family, all of whom have been so very understanding about my need to put down on paper the trials and tribulations of imaginary people. I've wanted to be an author ever since I wrote my first book aged twelve (which my mother accidentally deleted from the computer), and I never stopped dreaming that one day it would become more than a hobby. To my husband, Neil, thank you for allowing me the time and space to write. Last, but no means least, this and every story is for my children, Dylan and Scarlett. I love you more than even I could find the words to say.

ABOUT THE AUTHOR

Katherine Slee has a master's in Modern History from Oxford University, is a member of Mensa and used to work as an investment banker. She lives in Kent with her husband, two children and disobedient dog.

Did you enjoy this book and would like to get informed when Katherine Slee publishes her next work? Just follow the author on Amazon!

    1) Search for the book you were just reading on Amazon or in the Amazon App.

    2) Go to the Author Page by clicking on the author's name.

    3) Click the 'Follow' button.

    If you enjoyed this book on a Kindle eReader or in the Kindle App, you will be automatically offered to follow the author when arriving at the last page.

LAKE UNION
PUBLISHING